# POINTS OF DANGER

## By Edward Marston

### THE RAILWAY DETECTIVE SERIES

The Railway Detective • The Excursion Train • The Railway Viaduct
The Iron Horse • Murder on the Brighton Express
The Silver Locomotive Mystery • Railway to the Grave • Blood on the Line
The Stationmaster's Farewell • Peril on the Royal Train
A Ticket to Oblivion • Timetable of Death • Signal for Vengeance
The Circus Train Conspiracy • A Christmas Railway Mystery
Points of Danger • Fear on the Phantom Special
Inspector Colbeck's Casebook

### THE RESTORATION SERIES

The King's Evil • The Amorous Nightingale • The Repentant Rake
The Frost Fair • The Parliament House • The Painted Lady

### THE BRACEWELL MYSTERIES

The Queen's Head • The Merry Devils • The Trip to Jerusalem
The Nine Giants • The Mad Courtesan • The Silent Woman
The Roaring Boy • The Laughing Hangman • The Fair Maid of Bohemia
The Wanton Angel • The Devil's Apprentice • The Bawdy Basket
The Vagabond Clown • The Counterfeit Crank
The Malevolent Comedy • The Princess of Denmark

### THE HOME FRONT DETECTIVE SERIES

A Bespoke Murder • Instrument of Slaughter • Five Dead Canaries
Deeds of Darkness • Dance of Death • The Enemy Within
Under Attack • The Unseen Hand

### THE BOW STREET RIVALS SERIES

Shadow of the Hangman • Steps to the Gallows
Date with the Executioner • Fugitive from the Grave

### THE CAPTAIN RAWSON SERIES

Soldier of Fortune • Drums of War • Fire and Sword
Under Siege • A Very Murdering Battle

a&b

# POINTS OF DANGER

## EDWARD MARSTON

Allison & Busby Limited
11 Wardour Mews
London W1F 8AN
*allisonandbusby.com*

First published in Great Britain by Allison & Busby in 2018.
This paperback edition published by Allison & Busby in 2019.

A CIP catalogue record for this book is available from
the British Library.

10 9 8 7 6 5 4 3 2 1

ISBN 978-0-7490-2328-7

Typeset in 10.5/15.5 pt Adobe Garamond Pro by
Allison & Busby Ltd.

The paper used for this Allison & Busby publication
has been produced from trees that have been legally sourced
from well-managed and credibly certified forests.

Printed and bound by
CPI Group (UK) Ltd, Croydon, CR0 4YY

# CHAPTER ONE

## *1861*

Seated opposite each other, they were alone in a first class compartment. As the train slowed right down, the man took the gold watch from his waistcoat pocket, looked at it then heaved a sigh of frustration.

'Late again,' he said.

His wife made no reply. She was always slightly queasy when travelling by rail and had to sit facing the engine. Going backwards for any length of time made her want to vomit. She was a still handsome woman in her forties, short, slight, impeccably dressed and with almost elfin features. Both she and her husband exuded a sense of wealth and importance. He was a big man in his fifties with an air of distinction that offset his unprepossessing features. He looked as if he might have been born to wear his glistening top hat.

Irritable by nature, he soon had more cause for complaint. The train juddered unexpectedly and squealed as the brakes were applied. After a glance through the window, he struggled to his feet.

'What the devil is happening?' he demanded. 'Instead of going into the station, we've been diverted onto the branch line.'

'Sit down again, Jarvis,' she suggested.

'Somebody will suffer for this,' he warned. 'We're already late enough, as it is. And now, we're going in the wrong direction.' He flopped back down on his seat. 'This is unforgivable.'

He continued to fulminate but his protests were abruptly cut short. The train came to a sudden, jolting halt. Above the furious hissing of the locomotive, they heard the sound of hooves approaching. A rider with a hat pulled down over his face then appeared outside their window, extending a hand to fling open the door. He pointed a pistol at the man and yelled his command.

'Hand over your wallet and watch.'

The man was outraged. 'Do you know *who* I am and *what* I am?'

They were the last words he ever spoke. The robber knocked off the man's hat before shooting him between the eyes from close range. Blood spurted everywhere. The woman screamed in horror and drew back, her reticule falling from her lap. Steadying his mount, the robber reached in to divest the man of his wallet and watch before scooping up the reticule. He then galloped off with his booty.

In less than a minute, he had rewritten railway history.

# CHAPTER TWO

'He's changed,' said Leeming. 'He's changed for the better.'

Colbeck was unconvinced. 'I hadn't noticed.'

'You must've done, sir. The superintendent is a different man. Ever since the abduction, he's been much kinder to us.'

'That's hardly surprising, Victor. We did, after all, help to save his life. Anyone would be grateful to people who did that.'

'It's almost as if he's learnt to respect us – and not before time, if you ask me. I'm almost glad he went through that ordeal. It taught him a lot and turned him into a normal human being.'

'I'd never describe Superintendent Tallis as in any way normal,' said Colbeck with a wry smile, 'and I'd certainly never take pleasure from the fact that he came so close to being murdered in the most agonising way. I wouldn't wish that fate on my worst enemy.'

'But he *is* your worst enemy.'

Colbeck laughed. 'My enemies are on the other side of the law, Victor. With all his faults, the superintendent believes passionately in justice and has dedicated his life to law enforcement.'

The two of them were in his office, Leeming standing and Colbeck adjusting his cravat in the mirror. Though it was months since the event, the crime they were discussing was still at the forefront of their minds. Shortly before Christmas, the superintendent had been kidnapped in Canterbury, held captive and – when he was finally rescued – on the point of being flayed to death by a vengeful soldier from his old regiment. After such torment, most people would have needed a long rest before they returned to work but Tallis's resilience was legendary. Too proud to show the mental and physical pain he was suffering, he'd been back at his desk almost immediately.

'He's more subdued, I grant you,' conceded Colbeck, 'but, in essence, he remains the same person he always has been.'

'How can you say that, sir?' asked Leeming in surprise. 'In the old days, we were called to his office with a bellow. You stood up to him, somehow, but I always felt that I was in the dock awaiting sentence. Yet now,' he went on, 'he speaks softly to us as if we're friends as much as fellow detectives.'

'That may not last, Victor.'

'Yes, it will – he's seen the error of his ways.'

'He's been through a dreadful experience,' argued Colbeck, 'that shook him to the core and left him severely bruised. But those bruises are fading by the day. When they've disappeared, the same Edward Tallis will spring back to life.'

'For once, I disagree, sir.'

'Does that mean you'd risk a wager?'

Before Leeming could reply, there was a polite knock on the door, then it opened to reveal the very man about whom they'd been talking. Tallis was uncharacteristically subdued, his body sagging and the glint in his eye replaced by a hesitant glance.

'Can we help you, sir?' asked Colbeck.

'I'm not the one in need of help,' replied Tallis, 'but you can certainly help the Eastern Counties Railway. Its telegraph summons you by name.'

'That's very gratifying.'

'You and the sergeant must leave for Norwich at once.'

'But I have to visit someone, sir,' said Leeming.

'Cancel the arrangement.'

'Can't we go to Norwich tomorrow, instead?'

'You heard me.'

'It's a very special event.'

'This case takes precedence.'

'I promised my wife faithfully that . . .'

The words died on his lips as he saw Tallis undergoing a sudden transformation. It was extraordinary. Gone were the courteous manner and the gentle voice. They were instantly replaced by the old truculence and the familiar growl. In the space of a few seconds, the superintendent was bigger, louder and infinitely more hostile.

'You know my motto, Leeming. Work comes first.'

'Yes, sir,' said the other, cowering.

'Some paltry arrangement of yours shrinks to insignificance beside a gruesome murder on a train.'

'Yes, sir.'

'Then why do you dare to question my order?'

'It was a mistake, Superintendent.'

'That, alas, is not a novelty. Your whole career at Scotland Yard has been a compendium of mistakes.'

'That's unfair, sir,' said Colbeck, coming to the aid of his friend. 'Sergeant Leeming has been an exemplary detective. There's nobody in this building as reliable as him.'

'In one sense,' said Tallis, 'you are quite right. The sergeant can always be relied on to put family before duty and to ask inane questions at the most inappropriate time. In short, he is reliably *un*reliable.'

'That's a bit harsh, sir,' bleated Leeming.

'It's both harsh and unjust,' argued Colbeck. 'But let us turn our attention to the call for help. Who is the murder victim?'

'Come to my office and we'll give the matter our full attention.' Tallis glared at the hapless sergeant. 'We can discuss the crime more sensibly without the irritating presence of a man obsessed with his social life and poised to make his latest mistake.'

Storming out of the room, he left Leeming dazed as if from a blow. Colbeck raised a teasing eyebrow.

'Do you still think he's a new man, Victor?'

Now that she'd passed her first birthday, Helen Rose Colbeck was an even more definite presence in the family. Having taken her first halting footsteps, she'd quickly learnt how to totter boldly around the room and make light of any tumbles. Her personality had blossomed, her laugh was infectious and identifiable words were coming from her mouth. The child's face glowed with what her parents chose to believe was a blend of happiness and intelligence. Every day seemed to bring some small but exciting development. Whenever Colbeck returned home from work, his wife welcomed him with the latest bulletin.

Though Madeleine enjoyed spending more time with her daughter, it came at a price. She could no longer disappear into her studio for the best part of a day and devote herself to her latest painting. Helen's needs came first. Having played with her that morning, her mother was relieved when the nanny came to put the child down for her customary nap. It would allow Madeleine precious time in which to work. Before she could go upstairs, however, she was intercepted by the maid who handed her a letter that had just arrived. Since she didn't recognise the elegant handwriting, Madeleine's curiosity was aroused. She opened the missive at once and read it.

Her eyes widened with a mixture of surprise and delight.

In his own office, Tallis reverted to his former self, pulling himself up to his full height, glowering at Colbeck and rasping out his question.

'Well, what do you think?'

'I think that the Eastern Counties Railway company has done us a favour,' said Colbeck, handing the telegraph back to him. 'As a rule, any plea we get is terse to the point of rudeness. This one actually gives us some real information.'

'The victim is obviously held in high regard.'

'That's understandable, sir.'

'Why – is he a director of the company?'

'Jarvis Swarbrick is much more than that. He is – or, at least, he was until today – its appointed saviour. Not to put too fine a point on it, the ECR has a perfectly awful reputation. It was the first railway to be constructed in East Anglia and, from the very start, has been dogged by all manner of setbacks. Jarvis Swarbrick has ambitions for the company. The one thing the telegraph omitted to tell you is that he happens to be a Member of Parliament.'

'How on earth do you know that?'

'I always like to follow notable developments on the railway system,' explained Colbeck. 'That's how his name came to my attention. East Anglia is bedevilled by its profusion of railway companies and by the chaos they often generate. Mr Swarbrick has been trying to introduce a bill in Parliament to effect an amalgamation that will both simplify the system and make travel in the region more efficient. In my view, that gives us a possible suspect.'

'Does it?'

'Someone is set on preventing the merger.'

'This crime has nothing to do with it,' said Tallis. 'The telegraph makes that clear. Mr Swarbrick was shot by the man who robbed him.'

'There's a telling detail that you missed, Superintendent.'

Tallis looked at the telegraph again. 'Is there?'

'What does it say about the gentleman and his wife?'

'They were travelling alone in their compartment.'

'That's the crucial piece of information, sir. There were, no doubt, several other people in the first-class carriages. Other compartments may well have been filled to capacity.'

'I don't follow your argument.'

'That's because you don't think like a criminal, sir.'

Tallis reddened. 'I should hope not, damn you!'

'Consider this,' said Colbeck. 'If someone intended to rob passengers on a train, he'd surely wish to maximise his profits. Why settle for a compartment containing only two people when he could have found others with far richer pickings?'

'Ah,' said Tallis, fingering his moustache, 'I'm beginning to catch your drift. He deliberately chose Swarbrick's compartment.'

'The robber was there to kill as well as to take their valuables. There was no need to shoot Mr Swarbrick. When a pistol is pointed at someone, he or she is usually quick to comply with any demand. I may, of course, be wrong,' admitted Colbeck, 'but my first reaction is this. The robber was either stupid enough to ignore compartments that would have yielded a far bigger haul, or he was a hired assassin with only one person in mind. I prefer the second option,' he went on. 'The killer knew exactly where to find his victim and went straight for him.'

Tallis blinked. 'How ever did you deduce all that?'

'It's no more than an informed guess, sir.'

'And it's a persuasive one, at that.' He snapped his fingers. 'Well, don't hang about, man. Get on the next train to Norwich.'

'I will,' said Colbeck, moving to the door before turning on his heel to face the superintendent. 'Oh, by the way . . .'

'What is it now?' snarled Tallis.

'Welcome back, sir.'

# CHAPTER THREE

Madeleine never ceased to count her blessings. Chief among them was her husband. When they'd first met, it never occurred to her that their relationship would ever outlast the solving of the crime that had brought them together in the first place. While Colbeck was an eminent detective with a measure of private wealth, she spent most of her time looking after her father in their humble home. Caleb Andrews, an engine driver, had been shattered by the death of his wife. Without a daughter to offer him practical support, he might never have recovered. It was Colbeck who'd rescued her from that life and introduced her to a world where she lived in a fine house, occasionally took part in his investigations, albeit secretly, and, with his encouragement, developed her skills as an artist to the point where she actually enjoyed commercial success.

The arrival of a beautiful daughter meant that she no longer had the same time to indulge in dreamy reminiscences of her husband but there was one person who always brought him to mind. But for Colbeck, she would never have met the woman who'd now become her best friend. When Lydia Quayle arrived that afternoon, therefore, Madeleine was reminded instantly of the way they'd been drawn together during an investigation into the murder of her estranged father. As a result of meeting her, Lydia had been able to refashion her life completely, visiting the house on a regular basis as a friend of the family and honorary aunt to Helen.

As they sat opposite each other in the drawing room, Madeleine felt an upsurge of affection for the other woman.

'I'm so glad we met, Lydia,' she said. 'You're one of the best gifts Robert ever gave me.'

Lydia laughed. 'You make it sound as if he bought me in a shop and handed me over tied up with pink ribbon.'

'We both know the grim circumstances that brought us together and I suggest we draw a veil over them. The point is that we found each other, and it's been a constant source of pleasure to me.'

'The feeling is mutual.'

'I've got something to show you,' said Madeleine, picking up a letter beside her and passing it to her friend. 'Read that.'

'Who sent it?'

'It's from a gentleman who adores my paintings.'

'And so he should, Madeleine – they're wonderful.'

'He wants to offer me a commission.'

'So I see,' said Lydia, reading the letter.

'Isn't it exciting?'

'Yes, it is . . .'

But it was only a token agreement. It was clear that Lydia didn't share the thrill that Madeleine had felt when the letter first arrived. Instead of beaming at the flattering words, Lydia was more circumspect. When she gave the letter back to her friend, her tone was serious.

'Have you shown it to Robert?'

'I haven't had the chance,' said Madeleine. 'He's had to go off to Norwich to begin another investigation. A message came by hand from Scotland Yard earlier today. I've no idea when he'll be back.'

'That's a pity.'

'Why?'

'I think that he ought to be made aware of this putative admirer.'

Madeleine was disappointed. 'I thought you'd be pleased for me.'

'If this offer is genuine, I'm very pleased. On the other hand . . .'

'Why are you so sceptical?'

'I'm always wary of anonymous strangers.'

'But he's not anonymous. His name is Mr Fairbank and he lives in Windsor. He's listed the prints of mine that he's bought in the past and now wants an original painting.'

'How did he know your address?'

'He didn't, Lydia. He wrote to the art dealer who handles my work and the letter was forwarded here. I simply can't see why you should accuse him of sinister motives.'

'I'm not accusing him of anything,' said Lydia. 'I just think you should exercise great care. Hopefully, Mr Fairbank is exactly who and what he claims to be. If that's the case, I congratulate you. It's a real feather in your cap.'

'But you still have doubts.'

'It's very easy to invent a false identity, Madeleine.'

'Lionel Fairbank is his real name.'

'I thought that about Daniel Vance.'

The reminder silenced Madeleine. She'd forgotten that her friend, an attractive young woman, had been stalked by someone who called himself Daniel Vance. It had been a nerve-racking period in Lydia's life and had only been ended by police intervention. Her tormentor had concealed his own name behind that of the first ever headmaster of his public school. Madeleine felt thoroughly chastened.

'I'm so sorry, Lydia,' she said. 'I should have remembered the nightmare you went through. But there are differences in this case.'

'You can't be sure of that, Madeleine.'

'Yes, I can. To begin with, Mr Fairbank is much older than the man who stalked you. He mentions his grandchildren in the letter. They love my paintings as much as he does.'

'I sincerely hope that it's true and that my reservations are quite unfounded. Yet I do advise caution. Don't agree to see him alone.'

'He admires me as an artist,' said Madeleine, 'and he explains why at some length. Stop fretting unnecessarily. He's not trying to kidnap me.'

'No, of course not,' agreed Lydia. 'Ignore my pessimism. I always tend to fear the worst. That letter is a cause for celebration rather than suspicion. Mr Fairbank is clearly an art collector of taste. You must meet him as soon as possible.'


Victor Leeming was always disgruntled when forced to travel on a train, but he was even more annoyed this time. In a typical year, there were few days he held sacred. One of them had just been ruined by Edward Tallis.

'It was cruel of him,' he moaned.

'The superintendent didn't realise what was at stake.'

'Yes, he did. He *enjoyed* ruining our plans.'

'Wedding anniversaries are meaningless to a confirmed old bachelor like him.'

'It wasn't the wedding we wanted to celebrate, sir, it was . . .' He became almost sheepish and needed a few moments before he blurted out the truth. 'It was the day when I proposed to Estelle.'

'Then it was very worthy of celebration.'

'I hate having to let my wife down.'

'It wasn't *you* who did that,' Colbeck pointed out. 'It was the Eastern Counties Railway. Besides, you can simply postpone the event. A murder investigation, by contrast, can't be put off so easily.'

Leeming lapsed into a brooding silence. The train that was taking them to Norwich had favoured them with an empty carriage, enabling them to have the sort of conversation about their case impossible in the presence of other passengers. Colbeck had shown his companion the telegraph from the ECR and voiced his first thoughts about the crime, but the sergeant had shown scant interest. All he could think about was the deep disappointment his wife would have suffered when she read the letter he'd dashed off before they'd left Scotland Yard.

'Have you ever been to Norwich?' asked Colbeck.

'No,' said Leeming, sourly, 'and I wish I wasn't going there now.'

'It's a beautiful cathedral city. Hundreds of years ago, it was second only to London in size and importance. Unfortunately, our work will prevent us from seeing the sights.'

'The only sight I want to see is the train that takes us back home.'

'What did you think about my theory?'

Leeming was bewildered. 'Theory?'

'Yes – the one regarding the murder.'

'To be honest,' said the other, guiltily, 'I was only half-listening.'

'I said that the robber was there specifically to kill his target.'

'You're probably right, Inspector. You usually are.'

'Do you have no opinion at all to offer?'

Leeming made a visible effort to concentrate. He tried to remember the information he had actually heard.

'It sounds to me as if the man was a very good horseman. He struck like lightning and got away before most passengers realised what was happening.'

'What else do you have to offer?'

'I believe he was acting alone and nursed a grievance against the man he shot. They must have had a feud of some kind.'

'That's not impossible but I have to correct you on one point. This was no solo venture. He had an accomplice, possibly more than one.'

'Why do you think that?'

'Someone switched the points so that the train went off on the branch line. The rider didn't do that. He was hiding somewhere, ready to spur his horse into action. Now we come to the key question,' said Colbeck. 'How do we catch him?'

'I wish I knew, sir.'

'The answer is that we don't even try – not in the first instance, anyway. The man we search for is the accomplice. It has to be someone who works for the ECR and knows how to switch points. Railwaymen are not well paid, as my father-in-law never ceases to complain. All that was needed was a hefty bribe.'

'Then he might even be a railway policeman. Some of them are not as honest as they ought to be.'

'That, I'm afraid, is an all too accurate observation.'

'Villains sometimes use a uniform as a hiding place.'

'Quite so,' said Colbeck. 'But, in speculating too much, we're getting ahead of ourselves. We need more facts. At least we know where to start, however. We search for the person who sent that train to the exact place stipulated by the rider. Take heart, Victor. You may be home with Estelle sooner than you imagine,' promised Colbeck. 'All we have to do is to catch the accomplice and he'll lead us to his paymaster.'

Cecil Freed was a tall, thin, angular man in his sixties with gaunt features perpetually distorted by anxiety. Unable to keep still, he paced up and down a platform at Norwich Thorpe Station as he waited for a train to arrive from London. As chairman of the ECR, he was accustomed to coping with the many disasters that could befall a railway company, but he'd never had to deal with a murder before, especially one that robbed him of a dear friend and trusted advisor. The crisis had thrown him into a deep panic. It made his eyes dart wildly and raised his voice to a much higher pitch.

'Ah, there you are!' he said with relief as he spotted a uniformed figure coming towards him. 'Is there any news?'

'If you're asking if we've made an arrest,' replied the other, 'then the answer is we haven't. We're still gathering information.'

'Hand it over to Inspector Colbeck.'

'I will, Mr Freed.'

Sergeant Bartram Duff managed to disguise his resentment. He was a middle-aged man of medium height with broad shoulders and a craggy face. In charge of the railway police, he relished his power and was loath to relinquish any part of it. He was particularly annoyed at having to work on the murder investigation in the shadow of Colbeck.

'Did you ever come across him?' asked Freed.

'No, sir, our paths never crossed.'

'But you must have been aware of his presence.'

'I left the Metropolitan Police Force over ten years ago, Mr Freed. Inspector Colbeck wasn't quite so famous then.'

What he didn't say was that he'd been dismissed from his post and forced to return to the county of his birth. The uniform he now wore carried nothing like the status of the one he'd had in the nation's capital. Relegated to the railway police, he felt that he'd been unfairly treated. The arrival of two detectives from Scotland Yard would only intensify his bitterness because their presence would revive memories he'd been trying to forget.

'Inspector Jellings is not going to be happy about this, sir,' warned Duff. 'He thinks that the Norwich City Police should handle the case.'

'I did exactly what Mr Swarbrick would have advised – get the best possible man. That's why I sent a telegraph to Scotland Yard.'

'Well, don't expect Inspector Jellings to be pleased.'

'He can obviously take part in the investigation – as will you, of course – but there's only one person capable of leading it and that's Colbeck.' He glanced down the line. 'I just wish he'd actually turn up.'

'What's the latest news about Mrs Swarbrick?'

'I daresay she's still in a state of shock. My wife is with her now, offering what comfort she can. Mrs Swarbrick worshipped her husband. Seeing the man she loved shot dead in front of her must have been a hideous experience.'

'Mrs Swarbrick is not the strongest of women.'

'No, she's been a martyr to ill health these last few years.'

'She has my sympathy.' Duff took a step closer to him. 'I'm assuming that there'll be a reward on offer?'

'Yes, of course, and it will reflect the respect the ECR had for Mr Swarbrick. We'll pay almost anything to catch his killer.'

'Supposing that somebody other than Inspector Colbeck solves the crime?'

'Then he will be entitled to collect the money. All we need is evidence of individual initiative. From what I've heard about him, Colbeck has that in abundance.'

'But he lacks any knowledge of the ECR or, indeed, of East Anglia itself. There are several of us with far more understanding of the way that things are done in this part of the country.'

'That's undeniable, Duff. I'm sure the inspector will draw on your expertise and that of Jellings, of course. This crime took place in broad daylight. I'm sure that you found lots of witnesses who saw that horse galloping beside the train.'

'I did, sir,' said Duff. 'I've taken dozens of statements, though nobody told me anything about what actually happened in Mr Swarbrick's compartment. There's only one person who can do that.'

'Yes – it's his poor wife.'

'Inspector Jellings has gone to the house to speak to her.'

'He may have a long wait before he can get anything coherent out of her. I saw her when she was led from the train. She was in a state of abject terror. It was a heartbreaking sight. That's why I asked my own wife to go to her side,' said Freed. 'What she needs most in a calamity like this is the soothing presence of another woman.'

Anthea Freed was a bosomy woman of middle years with a face that radiated a sort of aggressive kindness. She stood in the hall of the Swarbrick residence and looked hopefully up the stairs. Inspector Mark Jellings had been irritated to find her there, fearing that she'd be an obstacle between him and the person he needed to interview. Though she looked benign, Anthea had a reputation for good works, which had been achieved by her tenacity at bullying money out of friends for the various charities in which she played an active part. Jellings could handle the most unruly criminals with ease. Gaining the upper hand over someone as potent as Anthea Freed was another matter. Since she was married to one of the richest and most influential men in the county, he had to tread carefully. The inspector was a well-built man in his forties with cheeks burnished by his fondness for alcohol and watery eyes that made him look like a woeful bloodhound.

'If it's at all possible,' he said, respectfully, 'I'd like a word alone with Mrs Swarbrick first.'

'That's out of the question, Inspector. I'm Grace's dearest friend. She'd want me beside her.'

'You might be a distraction, Mrs Freed.'

'Arrant nonsense!' she exclaimed. 'I'm as anxious as you are to catch the monster who killed her husband. Unless I hold Grace's hand, you'll hardly get a word out of her. You *need* me, Inspector.'

He stifled a sigh. 'Perhaps you're right.'

'While we have a moment,' she said, facing him for the first time, 'I'd like to take this opportunity to ask you to address us at one of our meetings. As you well know, I play a leading role in the Temperance Association here in Norwich.'

'Much as I'd like to accept the invitation,' he said, quickly, 'I'm afraid that I'm far too busy even to consider it.'

'But you'd be an ideal choice of speaker for us. Nobody has more experience of dealing with drunkenness than you. Most of the crimes that besmirch this city are committed by men – and women, alas – who are under the influence of drink.' She jabbed a finger at him. 'Your voice would carry weight.'

He squirmed at the prospect. 'I'm sorry but I'm not—'

'Don't you *want* to join in the fight against the evils of drink?'

'You have my tacit support, Mrs Freed.'

'I was expecting more than that.'

He quailed slightly. Far from condemning alcohol, he felt at that moment desperately in need of some to bolster his spirits.

She was about to press him on the subject when they heard a door open and shut upstairs. The pair of them moved at once to the bottom of the stairs. Moments later, the doctor appeared and looked down at them.

'You're waiting in vain, I fear,' he said. 'Mrs Swarbrick is in no condition to speak to either of you. I've had to give her a sedative.'

# CHAPTER FOUR

Knowing the reaction she'd get from her father, Madeleine didn't tell him what had happened until he'd played with his granddaughter. It was only when he came into the drawing room afterwards that she explained where her husband was. Caleb Andrews exploded.

'The Eastern Counties Railway!' he yelled, spitting the words out as if they were poisonous. 'It's the worst company in the entire country.'

'They sent for Robert because one of their senior directors was shot dead on a train.'

'The whole board deserves to be shot, Maddy. The ECR is a disgrace to the name of railways.'

'You say that about any company except the LNWR.'

'That's far and away the best,' he asserted, 'and not only because I happened to work for it for so long. It overshadows all the others and puts the ECR to shame.'

'Is it really that bad?'

'It's a laughing stock.'

'I hadn't realised that.'

'In your position, I'd be scared stiff. If Robert has gone to sort out their problems, it will take him weeks – even months. You may not see him again until next Christmas.'

'Don't exaggerate.'

'Ask any railwayman. They all know about the ECR.'

Though Madeleine was always pleased to see her father, she was upset by his warning that Colbeck might be away for a long time. To cheer herself up, she changed the subject and reached for the letter that had arrived that morning.

'Someone has written to me about my prints,' she said. 'He's very complimentary.'

'And so he should be. You have a gift, Maddy.'

'He wants to commission a painting from me.'

'Really?' Andrews was delighted. 'How much is he offering?'

'Mr Fairbank doesn't give an exact figure. He's leaving that to me. It's obvious that he's a wealthy man.'

'Then ask him for a thousand pounds.'

'Father!'

'All right, make it two thousand.'

'Don't be silly. That's a ridiculous amount.'

'Some paintings sell for much more than that.'

'Yes, but they're masterpieces by famous artists and they're hundreds of years old. I can't compete with people like that. My work sells for much lower prices because – let's be honest – that's what I'm worth.'

'You're as good as any of them,' he said, loyally.

'That's not true, Father, and we both know it. One of the reasons I've had some success is that I only paint locomotives or railway scenes. Very few artists do that. I may well be the only woman who does it.'

'You do have the assistance of a man. Be fair, Maddy, you never take anything to that art dealer of yours unless I've seen it first. I've had to correct you about details more than once.'

'I rely heavily on you, Father. All that I can do is to look at railways from the outside. You were part of the industry for your whole working life.'

He smiled nostalgically. 'I miss it every single day.'

'Do you miss the filth and the noise and physical strain?'

'You get used to that.'

'Then why did you never stop complaining about it?'

'I didn't complain,' he said, indignantly.

But his daughter knew the truth. She'd lost count of the number of times when he'd come home exhausted, bedraggled and covered in coal dust. Andrews was a wiry, spirited man in his sixties with a fringe beard. His short temper was about to be ignited once again.

'Let me see that letter,' he said.

'There's no need. I've told you what Mr Fairbank says.'

'I'd like to read it myself. When a strange man writes to you out of the blue, you can never be too careful. As your father, I've got your best interests at heart.' He extended a scrawny hand. 'Give it to me, Maddy.'

She was hesitant. 'Well . . . if you insist . . .'

Handing it over, she braced herself for his reaction. There was something she hadn't mentioned about the commission. When his eye fell on the missing detail, he roared with anger.

'Tell him you refuse,' he demanded.

'A moment ago, you were very pleased for me.'

'That was before I realised what he wished you to do. I'm not having a daughter of mine painting a locomotive from the Great Western Railway. That would be a betrayal.'

'I have to give a client what he pays for, Father.'

'Don't touch his money. It's tainted.'

'I can't pick and choose people who wish to commission my work. Since he lives in Windsor, Mr Fairbank probably travels on the GWR regularly. It's only natural that he'd choose one of its locomotives.'

'Refuse to have anything to do with him, Maddy.'

'I can't just turn him away. He's an admirer.'

'Yes,' said Andrews, scornfully, 'he's an admirer of Brunel and that godforsaken railway of his. You know how I feel about the GWR with its broad gauge and its dreadful trains. Refuse to have anything to do with this Mr Lionel Fairbank.' He passed the letter back to her. 'I feel as if I have to wash my hands after touching that.'

Madeleine was hurt. For the second time that day her hopes had been dashed. In showing the letter to Lydia Quayle, she'd expected to get warm congratulations but her friend had instead warned her to be circumspect. Knowing her father's hatred of the GWR, she'd expected some criticism but was relying on his pride in her achievement to override it. Friend and father had both let her down. She began to wish she'd never even heard of Lionel Fairbank.

'Well,' asked Andrews, 'what are you going to do, Maddy?'

* * *

As soon as they reached Norwich, Colbeck realised that he'd have to review some of his earlier assumptions. Being able to view the scene of the crime gave him a much clearer idea of what had actually happened. Cecil Freed had been waiting for the detectives on the platform, welcoming them as if they were members of a relief army that had just reached a stricken outpost. Duff was at Freed's elbow. Once introductions had been made, the newcomers were taken to the exact spot where the murder had occurred. Between them, Freed and Duff supplied a rough commentary. When he'd heard all the facts, Colbeck took over.

'What happened to the body?'

'It was removed to the police morgue,' said Freed. 'Mrs Swarbrick was distraught and had to be given medical assistance before she was taken home. We couldn't leave the train itself here because this track is in continuous use. It was moved back to the main line so that people could get off at the station. You can imagine the effect the murder had on the other passengers.'

'The effect on Mr Swarbrick was far worse,' observed Leeming.

'I'd like to see the compartment in which he was killed,' said Colbeck. 'I'm assuming you took the whole carriage out of service.'

Freed nodded. 'Where is it now?'

'It's in a siding beyond the station,' said Duff, pointing. 'I've put one of my men there to guard it and keep people away.'

'Were you on duty at the time of the incident?'

'Yes, I was, Inspector. I was waiting on the platform with the stationmaster. We couldn't believe it when the train veered off on the branch line.' He tapped his chest. 'I saw everything.'

'It's a pity you didn't see the points being switched,' said Leeming, drily, 'or you might have prevented the crime.'

'You can't blame this on me,' said Duff, defensively. 'Constable Pryor is in charge of those points and is supposed to make sure that nobody interfered with them. He may lose his job over this.'

'Let him keep it until we've had a chance to question him,' suggested Colbeck. He looked back at the station. 'If you were on that platform, you'd have had a good view of what went on here.'

'Yes, I did, Inspector.'

'You and Mr Freed have already given us the outline details. I'd like you to give a fuller account to Sergeant Leeming so that he can record it in his notebook. Since I'm sure you'll have taken statements from other witnesses, please pass those on to the sergeant as well.'

'I will, sir,' grunted the other.

'Lead the way,' said Leeming. 'I'll be right behind you.'

Duff set off towards the station with the sergeant at his heels. Once the two men were out of earshot, Colbeck turned to Freed.

'How efficient is Sergeant Duff?' he asked.

'I've heard no complaints about him,' replied the other.

'Is his manner always so surly?'

'He speaks to everyone like that. He means no disrespect.'

'I sensed bitterness. He objects to our presence.'

'Duff's opinion is immaterial, Inspector. I sent for you because I've followed your career with interest. Railway policemen are ill-equipped to do anything more than their allotted duties and the local constabulary has never handled a murder case before.'

'Who has been assigned to the investigation?'

'Inspector Jellings – a good man but parochial by your standards.'

'What's his view of the crime?'

'He believes that it was a robbery that went wrong.'

'Then I'll have to correct him. Having heard more detail, I'm even more convinced that the robbery was just a cloak for the real purpose of shooting Mr Swarbrick dead.'

Freed was alarmed. 'You think that it was *deliberate*?'

'I'm certain of it, sir. That raises the question of suspects. Can you think of anyone – anyone at all – who might have had cause to hate Mr Swarbrick enough to want him killed?'

'No, I can't. Jarvis was universally liked.'

'He was a politician. They always have enemies.'

'That's true, I suppose. It's unavoidable.'

'How many MPs does Norwich have?'

'Two – they represent a city of well over seventy thousand.'

'Mr Swarbrick was a Conservative, I believe. What about the other Member of Parliament?'

'David Repton is a Liberal.' He saw Colbeck's eyes light up with interest. 'You can eliminate him at once. I abhor almost everything that Repton stands for but he'd never hatch a murder plot. Strangely enough, he and Jarvis Swarbrick got on very well.'

'Give me some other names then, if you will.'

'Well,' said Freed, brow corrugated in thought, 'I suppose that I ought to mention Oliver Trant – though I do so reluctantly.'

'Who is he?'

'Oliver is an over-ambitious man who had to be edged off the board. It's rankled with him ever since. He blames Jarvis.'

'Is he a vindictive person by nature?'

'I suppose that he could be.'

'You don't sound very sure.'

'Where Oliver is concerned, it's difficult to be sure about anything. He's such an odd character. One can never fathom the man. I may be maligning him unfairly, but I fancy that there's a mean streak lurking somewhere inside him.'

'Let's move on from Mr Trant. Who else should we look at?'

'I wish I knew.' Freed twitched as if startled by a sudden thought. 'No,' he told himself, 'no, that's out of the question. He couldn't *possibly* be involved. It's cruel of me even to think it.'

'Whom did you have in mind, sir?'

'Andrew Swarbrick – he's Jarvis's son.'

'Go on,' urged Colbeck.

'It's a sad business, Inspector. Father and son were estranged because Andrew strongly disapproved of Jarvis's second marriage. Heaven knows why! Grace Swarbrick is a delightful woman, but her charm was lost on Andrew. He was antagonistic towards her from the very start. It was a cross that Jarvis had to bear,' said Freed. 'Andrew swore that he'd never set foot in the house again until his stepmother had left it.'

'Does Andrew Swarbrick live in Norwich?'

'No, he left in disgust when his father remarried.'

'Where is he now?'

'Somewhere in London – he works in a bank there.'

'How do you think he'll react to news of his father's murder?'

Freed sucked his teeth. 'I really don't know . . .'

Andrew Swarbrick was a tall, lean, striking man in his thirties who prided himself on his physical fitness. Since he had a sedentary occupation, he always found time after luncheon for a brisk walk. It had become his trademark. Other employees at the bank were amazed that he was undeterred by inclement weather and would happily stride out without an umbrella in heavy rain. Only a foot or more of snow would have stopped him from keeping to his daily routine. As a deputy manager of a major bank, he had a large and well-appointed office. When he returned there that afternoon, he found a telegraph awaiting him. He read its contents and gave a cold smile.

Victor Leeming did not enjoy being in a confined space with the railway policeman. In addition to a churlish manner, Duff had bad breath and smelt as if in desperate need of a bath. His defects were magnified in the pokey, airless room the two men shared. On the credit side, Duff had clearly been working hard to gather information from other witnesses. Leeming studied the man's notebook with interest and, after weeding out the inevitable repetition, copied a lot of useful information into his own notebook.

'Who was supposed to operate those points?' he asked.

'Constable Pryor.'

'I'd like to speak to him.'

'I've already done that,' said Duff.

'Nevertheless, I want to have a word with him myself.'

'Horace Pryor will be disciplined, I can promise you.'

'If you don't cooperate with us,' warned Leeming, 'you'll be disciplined alongside him. The last thing we need is someone who doesn't understand an order. The inspector and I belong to a *real* police force. Remember that.'

'I'm sorry,' muttered the other.

'Is he still here at the station?'

'Yes, he is.'

'Then I want you to fetch him.' As Duff rose to leave, Leeming put a hand on his shoulder to ease him back into his seat. 'Before you do that, I'd like to ask your opinion.'

'About what?'

'How long have you worked here?'

'Ten years or more – I was born and bred in Norwich.'

'So you know everything there is to know about this place.'

'I wouldn't say that.'

'What sort of man is Mr Freed?'

Duff was non-committal. 'He's doing his best for the ECR.'

'What about the murder victim?'

'Oh, he was the power behind the company. He never stopped fighting for it. Mr Swarbrick had big ambitions for us.'

'Do you think that someone wanted to thwart those ambitions?'

'Not really,' said Duff with a shrug. 'Mr Swarbrick was unlucky, that's all. Someone tried to rob him. Knowing Mr Swarbrick like I do, I'd say that he'd refuse to hand over anything and it cost him his life.'

'Why did the killer single him out in the first place?' asked Leeming. 'More to the point, how did he know which compartment Mr Swarbrick and his wife were in?'

'I never thought about that,' admitted Duff.

'Then it's time you did. There must have been lots of other passengers travelling in first class, yet he was picked out. That means the man knew exactly where to find him.'

'That's impossible.'

'Then how did he come to choose Mr Swarbrick?'

'It could just have been a coincidence.'

'How can you say that?' asked Leeming in disbelief. 'This murder is the result of careful planning. Did Mr Swarbrick just happen to be alone with his wife in that compartment? Did the points get switched entirely of their own accord? Did that man on the horse ride past completely by chance and seize his opportunity? Of course not,' he added, derisively. 'Of one thing you can be sure, Sergeant Duff. Coincidence had nothing to do with it.'

'I can see that now,' said Duff, uncomfortably.

'Do you get much crime here?'

'We would do if I didn't keep the place well protected. Thanks to the way I've drilled my men, we've caught thieves, pickpockets and those who simply want to cause damage to property.'

'What do you do with them?'

'We haul them up before a magistrate,' replied Duff. 'It's usually children who are responsible for vandalism or trespass. If it's a first offence, I give them the fright of their lives then let them go.'

'What if they repeat the offence?'

Duff gave a dark chuckle. 'I make them regret it.'

'So there have been no major crimes at this station?'

'Not since I was put in charge.'

'Nothing more serious than irate passengers complaining about the price of tickets – is that what you're telling me?'

'My men know how to do their jobs.'

'Constable Pryor doesn't.'

'That was a rare slip on his behalf.'

Troubled by the stink, Leeming turned away and coughed.

'I want you to put your thinking cap on,' he resumed. 'Is there anyone you know – or might have heard about – who is capable of committing the daring crime that took place here earlier today?'

'No,' said Duff with categorical certainty.

'You answered that question far too quickly for my liking,' said Leeming, 'so I'd like you to take a little time to think carefully before you speak. In your position, you must have come across all the local villains from time to time. Correct?' Duff nodded. 'Could you pick one of them out as a possible suspect?'

There was a long pause this time. The railway policeman did

actually seem to be giving the question due consideration. When it came, however, the answer was the same.

'No,' said Duff.

Leeming suspected that he was lying.

# CHAPTER FIVE

Colbeck couldn't help feeling sorry for Cecil Freed. Since he held such a crucial position in the ECR, the man was already under heavy pressure because of its poor performance as a railway company. At a time when he most needed the help of a strong, guiding hand, Freed had lost the one man who could have provided it. Swarbrick's death had cut him adrift and he was floundering. Freed was pathetically grateful that the Railway Detective had come to his aid so swiftly, allowing him to feel that the murder of his dear friend would soon be solved. It was the one thing that would bring him a degree of solace.

Having examined the murder scene, Colbeck was taken to the siding where the carriage in which the victim had been travelling had now been left. A railway policeman stood nearby, nodding deferentially when Freed appeared. Colbeck's gaze ran the length of the carriage.

'Which was their compartment?' he asked.

'It was the one at the far end.'

'In which direction was the train travelling?'

Freed raised a hand to indicate. 'It was coming this way,' he said. 'Whenever he travelled with his wife, Jarvis insisted on taking the first-class compartment furthest away from the engine.'

'Why was that, sir?'

'Grace – Mrs Swarbrick, that is – always felt a trifle unsettled in a train and liked to be as far away from the engine as possible.' He laughed nervously. 'It's a paradox, isn't it? A man whose whole life is bound up with a railway company was married to a woman who hated travelling by train.'

'That may turn out to be a vital piece of information.'

'I don't see why, Inspector.'

'Did many people know about Mrs Swarbrick's aversion?'

'Oh, yes, it was common knowledge. When they were together, they always had what amounted to a private compartment in the last of the first-class carriages.'

'You may just have explained how the killer knew where to strike.'

Freed gaped. 'Good Lord!'

'It could be a breakthrough of sorts.'

'Why is that?'

'We're dealing with a local man, sir. That narrows the field.'

Freed was shocked. 'Are you telling me that . . . it was one of us?'

'It was someone who was aware of Mr and Mrs Swarbrick's habitual arrangements when travelling by train. That's my feeling, anyway.'

40

'I trust it implicitly.'

'Then I must ask you a special favour, sir.'

'It's granted before you even put it into words.'

'Because of his position as a Member of Parliament,' said Colbeck, 'Mr Swarbrick's death is going to attract a lot of attention. Reporters from national newspapers will descend on Norwich in a swarm and try to hassle us for information. It's a point of principle with me that I never disclose details of my investigation or discuss any clues I may find.'

'In other words,' said Freed, 'I'm to keep my mouth shut.'

'Thank you, sir. In some ways, the gentlemen of the press perform a valuable service. In other ways,' he added, lowering his voice, 'they can be a confounded nuisance.'

'You don't need to tell me that, Inspector. The ECR has been the whipping boy for many a newspaper editor. Rely on my discretion.'

'Right,' said Colbeck, grateful for his help, 'let's take a closer look at that compartment, shall we?'

Horace Pryor, the railway policeman, was a moon-faced individual in his late twenties with stooping shoulders and an apologetic grin. When he caught sight of Leeming, he immediately began to plead his innocence. Duff gave him a firm nudge.

'Shut up, Horry,' he ordered.

'I'm entitled to say my piece.'

'The sergeant will hear it when he's good and ready.'

'That's right,' said Leeming. 'Before I do that, I must ask you to leave. There's hardly enough room for two of us in here. Three of us will just keeping bumping into each other.'

'But I ought to stay,' insisted Duff.

'Why?'

'I want to hear what Horry tells you to make sure it's the same excuse he told me.'

Pryor bristled. 'It's not an excuse, Bart. It was the truth.'

'I'll listen to it in private,' said Leeming, meaningfully.

Duff glowered at him for a second, then left the room reluctantly. After sizing up the newcomer, Leeming motioned for him to sit down, then he started to probe.

'How long have you worked here?'

'It must be nearly five years now,' said Pryor.

'So you should be able to discharge your duties blindfold.'

'I like the job and I always do it proper.'

'That's not what Sergeant Duff claims. He blames you for allowing the points to be switched.'

'That's unfair!' insisted Pryor.

'Explain.'

'Well, it's like this. I'm supposed to watch the track at all times to see that nobody tries to climb onto it or play about with the points. I patrol the platform, then walk up and down between the various tracks.'

'Isn't that dangerous?'

'Not if you know all the train times,' said Pryor, tapping his skull with a forefinger. 'They're locked up in here. I know exactly what train is coming on which line and where its final destination is.'

'So what went wrong today?'

'Someone switched the points.'

'Then why didn't you see them?'

'I was distracted. It's obvious, now I think of it. Not long before Mr Swarbrick's train came in, I was made to look the other way. Something hit me on the back of my neck and made me jump.

Children round here love playing with catapults. My first thought was that one of them had aimed a stone at me. I charged off to search for him.'

'Is that what you told Sergeant Duff?'

'Yes, sir, but Bart – the sergeant – didn't believe me.'

'Did you catch the boy who aimed a stone at you?'

'No, the little devil hopped it. But you can see the wound,' he went on, turning around to show Leeming the back of his neck. 'It drew blood.' He brought something out of his pocket. 'And here's the stone.'

'Yet Sergeant Duff didn't accept your explanation.'

'It's only because he wanted someone to blame. Bart reckons that I got that wound on my way to work because nobody would dare to use a catapult on this station.' He pocketed the stone. 'But I know the truth.'

'When was this?'

'Not long before Mr Swarbrick's train was due. Actually, that was late, which is fairly normal for the ECR.'

'So you think the points were switched when you were distracted.'

'It's as plain as the nose on your face.'

'Frankly, it's not. There must have been other people on the platform at the time. *You* might have been looking the wrong way but one of them would surely have spotted a figure walking towards the points.'

'I've been thinking about that,' said Pryor, seriously, 'and I may have the answer. Soon after I was hit on the neck, a goods train went slowly through the station. The long line of wagons would have blocked out any view of the points. *That's* when it must have happened.'

'It's a plausible theory,' conceded Leeming, 'but that's all it is. Have you been in trouble with Sergeant Duff before?'

'It happens from time to time, sir. He's like that.'

'What do you mean?'

'He gives us a roasting to keep us on our toes.'

'You don't like him, do you?' Pryor withdrew into a watchful silence. 'It's all right. I'm not going to report to Duff anything you tell me in confidence. You can speak freely. We need to know all we can about the people based at this station – especially those with protective duties. Tell me about Sergeant Duff.'

'He has too high an opinion of himself,' said Pryor. 'Everyone knows that. He thinks that he's too good to be a railway policeman and that this job is beneath him.'

'He struck me as a man who likes to swagger.'

'That's exactly what he does, Sergeant. He walks around as if he owns this station and boasts about the time when he worked in London.'

'Oh? What was he doing there?'

'He was in the Metropolitan Police Force.'

'Why did he leave?'

'Bart says it was because his wife could never settle so they came home to Norwich.'

Pryor started to ramble on inconsequentially about life as a railway policeman and Leeming had to interrupt him to stem the gushing torrent. He couldn't quite make up his mind about the man. He opened a palm.

'Could I see that stone again, please?'

'Yes,' replied Pryor, 'of course, you can.'

Taking it out again, he gave it to Leeming.

'That's odd,' said the detective, scrutinising it. 'Are you sure that this is what hit you on the back of the neck?'

'Yes, Sergeant, I found it on the platform.'

'Then why doesn't it have your blood on it?'

When she had time alone again, Madeleine withdrew to her studio and read the letter once more. It no longer gave her the same excitement. Between them, Lydia and Madeleine's father had robbed it of its magic. Someone had been so impressed by her artistic talent that he wanted to commission a painting from her. The fact that Lionel Fairbank already had prints of her work showed that he loved railways and the way that she depicted them on canvas. Madeleine had wanted to reply instantly to his offer and arrange a meeting to discuss the terms of the commission. She was no longer so keen to do so because Lydia had sown the seeds of doubt in her mind, raising the possibility – however remote – that her admirer might not be all that he claimed to be and might even turn out to be a threat to her.

Caleb Andrews had poured scorn on the invitation, saying that his daughter couldn't possibly produce a painting of a GWR locomotive because he would see it as an insult to him. His devotion to the LNWR was such that he couldn't bear her taking an interest in other railway companies. Her readiness to accept the commission had unleashed all his prejudices and left her wondering what she should do. If she declined the commission, she'd be turning away someone who clearly had a passion for railway art; if, on the other hand, she accepted it, she'd be alienating her father. Madeleine wrestled with the question of which was the more important – her work or her father's feelings.

After thinking it over, she decided that an instant reply to Fairbank would be a mistake. What she needed most was her husband's advice. Sooner or later, he'd write to her from Norwich and she would have an address where she could contact him. Colbeck would be wholeheartedly on her side and she felt the need for his support. Putting the letter aside, she picked up her brush and went over to her easel.

After examining the compartment in which Jarvis Swarbrick had been killed, Colbeck asked to speak to the stationmaster. Freed led him back towards the platform, assuring him as he did so that Ned Grigson, the stationmaster had, reportedly, been a tower of strength in the emergency. When word spread among the passengers that someone had been shot dead on their train, there was fear and commotion. All that most people wanted to do was to flee the station as quickly as possible. Grigson had somehow managed to instil calm on the agitated travellers, persuading them to leave in an orderly manner instead of scrambling for the exits. The moment he saw the stationmaster, Colbeck could believe the report of his actions. Smart, slim and upright in his uniform, Grigson was an unusually tall, middle-aged man with a firm handshake, a warm smile and a silver beard. He seemed to embody wisdom, competence and unforced authority. Taking him at face value, Colbeck dared to believe that he'd finally met someone working for the ECR who really seemed to know what he was doing.

'It's good to meet you, Inspector,' said Grigson in a voice both deep and reassuring. 'Your fame goes before you.'

'I hear good things of you as well, Mr Grigson.'

'Thank you.'

'As for fame, it's more of a burden than a blessing. One's actions are always being judged against past achievements and no human being can get everything right all the time.'

'You seem to manage it,' said Freed. He turned to Grigson. 'The inspector would like to ask you some questions, Ned.'

'I had a feeling he might,' said Grigson with a smile, 'so I took the precaution of writing a report of what happened while it was still fresh in my mind. If you'd care to step into my office, you can both read it.'

'I'm very grateful to you,' said Colbeck. 'You're obviously a man with foresight.'

'It saves time.'

Grigson ushered them into his office, a large, exceptionally tidy room with charts and timetables pinned neatly to the walls. When his guests sat down, he handed Colbeck his report. The stationmaster was in no way abashed by the presence of the chairman of the ECR.

'I won't apologise for our shortcomings,' he said, 'because there are too many of them. What I will do is to offer my sympathy that you had to travel from Bishopsgate, our London terminus. Mr Freed knows my low opinion of it.'

'I share it, Ned,' said Freed with embarrassment. 'It does the ECR no favours. In time we'll move to a better location in the capital.'

While the two of them had what was patently a regular discussion of the company's hopes and aims, Colbeck was reading the report. It was long, well written and comprehensive. All that it lacked was the name of the person who had switched the points.

'This is extremely helpful,' said Colbeck.

'Find him, Inspector,' urged Grigson. 'Catch the villain who killed Mr Swarbrick and caused such turmoil in my station. If there's anything at all I can do to help, just tell me what it is.'

'In providing this,' said Colbeck, holding up the report, 'you've done all I would have asked of you.'

'Who could possibly have done this?' said the other, his attention shifting to Freed. 'The whole city admired Mr Swarbrick. He did so much for us over the years. And now we've lost him.'

'Yes,' said Freed. 'The full horror of it hasn't sunk in yet. It's a crippling blow to suffer.'

'You seem to have a fairly large staff here,' said Colbeck.

'That's true,' replied the stationmaster, 'but this is a busy place. We have a probationary clerk, goods clerks, booking clerks, parcel clerks and a one-legged old soldier who comes two days a week to help me tend the garden. Oh,' he added, 'then there are the railway policemen.'

'I'm sure you know each and every one of them, Mr Grigson.'

'It's part of my job.'

'Then I'd like you to go through them one by one,' said Colbeck, taking out his notebook. 'Start with the names of those on duty when the train went off on the branch line.'

'I'll be happy to give you a full list. But first I need to ask Mr Freed a question I should have put to him earlier.'

'What's that?' asked Freed.

'I'm very worried about Mrs Swarbrick. She was more or less carried off the train. I can't stop wondering how she is.'

'My wife is with her and should bring news fairly soon.'

'There is someone else in the family, of course,' said Grigson, quietly, 'and that's the son. Young Mr Swarbrick was an only child. The murder of his father will come as a terrible shock to him.'

'There's no question about that.'

'How do you think he'll react, sir?'

When the ECR's permanent London terminus was first opened in 1840, it bore the name of Shoreditch. Seven years later, it was enlarged and renamed Bishopsgate after the major thoroughfare in the heart of the financial district. The intention had been to lure more employees from the City into using the station. Whatever its name, the terminus remained a rather grubby, unimpressive, badly located place that seemed to attract pickpockets as readily as passengers. Striding towards the appropriate platform, Andrew Swarbrick kept a wary eye out for any loitering thieves, though his physique and fast pace were enough in themselves to frighten off any criminals.

At the time when he'd turned his back on Norwich, he'd vowed never to return if his stepmother was still there. Circumstances had changed dramatically. As he settled into a first-class compartment, he actually began to look forward to the journey.

Colbeck and Freed were just leaving the stationmaster's office when Anthea Freed came bustling along the platform with a determined look in her eye. She was introduced to the inspector and, when she'd got her breath back, delivered her news.

'Grace is fast asleep,' she said. 'The doctor gave her a sleeping draught.'

'That may be the best thing for her,' said her husband.

'Inspector Jellings didn't think so. He was dying to speak to her and had the gall to ask to be allowed to be the first to do so. Didn't he realise how *close* Grace and I are? I'm her best friend.'

'That's whom she needs most at this point in time,' said Colbeck.

'I'm glad that someone else understands that.'

'Your husband has explained Mrs Swarbrick's domestic situation.'

'It's caused her endless worry,' she said, 'though she has an even bigger cause for concern now, of course. Her stepson rejected her and she's now been robbed of her dear husband. Oh, I do feel so sorry for her. But let's talk about the search for the killer,' she went on, briskly. 'Have you had time to form an opinion yet, Inspector?'

'Not really, Mrs Freed.'

'What do your instincts tell you?'

'At the moment,' he confessed, 'my attention is fixed elsewhere. Sergeant Leeming and I have to find some accommodation in the city.'

'No search is needed. We insist that you stay with us.'

'Yes, yes,' said Freed. 'That goes without saying.'

'It's a kind invitation, sir,' said Colbeck, 'but we'd prefer to . . . be on our own.'

'Of course you do and we're not expecting you to stay in the main house with my wife and I watching you like hawks. That would only impede you. We have a cottage in the grounds. You and the sergeant can have that as well as the services of a maid and, of course, our cook.'

'Well . . .'

'We won't hear any argument,' said Anthea. 'It's all settled.'

'The cottage will give you much more privacy,' argued Freed. 'If you stay at a hotel, you'll be plagued by reporters.'

'That is a consideration,' admitted Colbeck.

'My wife and I will be delighted to act as your hosts.'

'Yes,' she said. 'We have only one requirement, Inspector. No alcohol is allowed on the premises. Temperance is a virtue that's close to my heart. I'm counting on the fact that you and your companion will not bring intoxicating liquid on to our property. Is that understood?'

It was more of a command than a question.

# CHAPTER SIX

Without realising it, Victor Leeming had been right. The superintendent was a changed man. The outer shell of steel might be back and so might the caustic tongue, but they were hiding his pain and his deep insecurity. Edward Tallis had never feared danger in the past. His military career pitched him time and again into perilous situations and – especially in India – he'd always survived them. There had also been many occasions during his days in the Metropolitan Police when he'd faced desperate criminals without flinching. He'd been shot at, stabbed, belaboured with a cudgel and even had a rope put around his neck, yet had nevertheless won through in the end. Tallis had seemed invincible.

To the naked eye, he still was the looming figure he'd always been. Underneath the daunting carapace, however, there'd been a steady loss of self-belief. He'd been forced to accept that he was mortal, after all, and that – but for the intervention of others – he'd now be in his coffin. When he'd been kidnapped while staying with an old army friend, he was held prisoner by two brutal men who'd already scrawled their names on his death warrant. Try as he might, he couldn't possibly escape on his own. He was completely at the mercy of his captors and mercy was a concept entirely foreign to them.

Had his rescuers come an hour later, they'd have found the blood-covered corpse of Edward Tallis. That thought haunted him constantly and kept him awake at night. It was the reason he returned to Scotland Yard much earlier than he should have done, shunning the advice of his doctor. At home, he was in torment; in his office, smoking his customary cigar, surrounded by evidence of his status, he could pretend to be the heartless martinet he'd always been. Yet even there he was no longer safe. Memories of the abduction still disturbed him at a deep level. Though he was trying to read a report, his mind was miles away, focussed on the farm in Kent where he'd been kept a prisoner awaiting execution. He could feel the ropes biting into him, the pangs of hunger gnawing at his stomach, the sense of isolation making him shiver. He could hear the triumphant sneers of the two men as they mocked and threatened him.

The more he thought about it, the more intense became his agony. In his febrile reconstruction of events, there was no rescue at the hands of his three colleagues. Tallis was utterly helpless, unable to speak let alone to move. He was like a

'If they live on a big estate,' said Leeming, 'they must have a mansion, the kind of place where people usually brew their own beer.'

'This house is an exception to the rule, Victor.'

'Are you saying we might go for weeks without proper drink?'

'I don't think it will take that long to solve this crime.'

'I'll be *parched*, sir.'

'Your needs will not be neglected.'

Leeming brightened. 'Are we going to smuggle in a few flagons?'

'No,' said Colbeck, 'we're going to use the trap so thoughtfully provided for us by our hosts to drive out to a quiet hostelry now and then where you can slake your thirst with a pint of beer and I can have a dram of whisky.'

'That sounds better.'

They were in the stationmaster's office, kindly vacated by Grigson so that they could compare notes alone. Anticipating a protest, Colbeck had saved the news about their accommodation until the end. Since he'd now pacified the sergeant, he was able to return to a discussion of the crime. He felt they'd made some progress.

'Oliver Trant is obviously a man worth looking at,' he said. 'If he feels that he was forced off the ECR Board by Swarbrick, it will be a running sore. He lives locally, so will know this station and its staff well.'

'He'd have a choice of accomplices, sir.'

'Sergeant Duff or Constable Pryor – who would you pick?'

'I fancy that both could be bought for the right amount,' said Leeming. 'Duff would be my choice because he knows how to keep his mouth shut. Pryor is more likely to give the game away.'

'Did you believe his story about the catapult?'

'Strangely enough, I did.'

'Yet he couldn't find the child who used it – if there ever was one.'

'It's not only children who can use a catapult, sir. What if it was an adult? That would explain why Pryor didn't find the culprit. He'd never suspect that a grown man would aim something at him.'

'Fair point,' acknowledged Colbeck. 'We can eliminate Duff as the person with the catapult. At the time, he was talking to the stationmaster.'

'Why was there no blood on that stone?'

'What was *his* explanation?'

'Pryor reckoned that it must have been rubbed off when he thrust it into his pocket. He was lucky it didn't lodge in his neck instead of bouncing off. Catapults can be nasty things.'

Colbeck grinned. 'Yet I daresay you had one when you were a boy. I know that I did. They were part of growing up.'

'I can't believe that you ever played with a catapult,' said Leeming, almost shocked. 'They were for . . . boys like me.'

'I wanted some fun so I made one myself. Anyway,' he went on, 'that's enough about me and my juvenile follies. Let's go back to Sergeant Duff. Did he really used to be in the Metropolitan Police?'

'That's what Pryor told me.'

'Why did he leave?'

'His wife wanted to come back here to live.'

'Is that likely?'

'What do you mean, sir?'

'Well, I didn't spend as much time with Duff as you do but I'd say that he's the sort of husband who doesn't pay the slightest attention to his wife's wishes. He makes all the major decisions in the marriage.'

'I suppose that he does,' said Leeming, reflectively. 'According to Pryor, he loves throwing his weight around here. Why should he be any different when he's at home?'

'He's not, Victor. I'm certain of it. When I send my next report to the superintendent, I'll ask him to find out the real reason why Duff left his job in London.'

'That's a good idea, sir.'

'Right,' said Colbeck, 'we now have names of three people who need watching. Let's come to the fourth.'

'Mr Swarbrick's son?'

'Yes, Victor. I just can't see why he stalked out of the house. Was he really so shocked by his father's remarriage?'

'I haven't a clue.'

'There's something rather odd going on.'

Leeming grinned. 'I know that look on your face,' he said. 'You're suspicious.'

'I'd put it no higher than being very curious at this stage.'

'Why is that, sir?'

'Mr Freed and his wife both told me what a nice woman Mrs Swarbrick is – pleasant, mild-mannered and highly intelligent. How could her stepson possibly object to her?'

'I don't know.'

'The Freeds love the woman yet Andrew Swarbrick hates her.'

'Do you want me to find him, sir?'

'There's no need, Victor.'

'Isn't there?'

'As soon as he hears the news,' said Colbeck, 'he'll come to us.'

* * *

As a rule, Andrew Swarbrick was inclined to doze off during a train journey but it was different this time. There was too much to keep him wide awake. His mind was buzzing as he considered what his next move should be. He shed no tears for his father. Jarvis Swarbrick was dead. That raised an intriguing possibility. Norwich would need to replace one of its Members of Parliament. Who better than the son of the former holder of the seat? Andrew had started to nurse political ambitions for it and there had been a time when his father had encouraged them. It was only a question of persuading the members of the local Conservative Association to accept him as their candidate. In every way, his time had at last come.

Inspector Mark Jellings had no difficulty identifying the two men. When he saw them emerging from the stationmaster's office, he could see at a glance that the elegant figure in immaculate attire must be Colbeck and that the man with the ungainly walk and ugly face was the sergeant. Eyeing Colbeck warily, Jellings introduced himself and exchanged handshakes with both men, wincing as Leeming squeezed his hand hard. Since the platform was now covered with passengers, Colbeck invited Jellings into the office.

'Mr Grigson said that we could have use of this as long as we wish,' he explained.

'He's an obliging soul,' said Jellings.

Colbeck closed the door behind them. 'I gather that you drew a blank at Mr Swarbrick's house,' he said. 'Mrs Freed told me what happened.'

'Mrs Swarbrick is fast asleep' said Jellings. 'It's inconvenient for us but probably the best thing for the lady herself.'

'How do you get on with Mrs Freed?' asked Leeming.

'Why do you want to know that, Sergeant?'

'We're staying in a cottage on their estate.'

'Then I suggest that you try to keep well clear of her.'

'Why is that?'

'She has a tendency to . . . get in the way.'

'You obviously speak from experience,' said Colbeck.

'I do,' admitted Jellings, ruefully. 'Mrs Freed is a redoubtable lady and a true Christian. Her compassion for others is remarkable. She's involved in all kinds of charitable organisations and is tireless in promoting them. Mrs Freed is a trustee of everything from the Workhouse to the Jenny Lind Hospital for Children.'

'And she's in the Temperance Movement as well,' said Leeming, rolling his eyes. 'Strong drink is banned from their estate.'

'That's what I wanted to warn you about. Keep off the subject of alcohol or you'll have a long lecture on sobriety. Mrs Freed believes that drunkenness is an abomination.'

'A pint of good beer is every man's right, Inspector. There's nothing wrong with alcohol if taken in moderation.'

'I couldn't agree with you more, Sergeant.'

'I didn't know that Jenny Lind endowed a hospital here,' said Colbeck, interested. 'How did that come about?'

'Her concerts were always very popular here. Out of the kindness of her heart, Jenny Lind refused to take any of the ticket receipts. It was decided use the money to build an infirmary for sick children and to name it after her. The hospital admitted its first inpatients in 1854 – all thanks to the Swedish Nightingale.'

'We once had the privilege of hearing her sing in Birmingham. She really was a nightingale.'

'It was wonderful,' recalled Leeming. 'I'd never heard anything like it. We were acting as her bodyguards at the time. Mrs Freed might like to hear about that.'

'Not for a while,' warned Colbeck. 'It can wait. The murder takes precedence over everything else.' His gaze shifted to Jellings. 'We've gathered information from the railway policemen, Inspector, but your men will also have been busy.'

'Anything we've garnered is at your disposal,' said Jellings.

'Thank you.'

'I'm sure that you'd like to view the body. I'll take you to the police station and hand over whatever information we have. It's not far away. We can talk at leisure there.'

'There won't be much leisure during this investigation.'

'Don't say that,' protested Leeming. 'We can't be on duty twenty-four hours a day.'

'We might have to be. This is going to be a complex case.'

'Then we'll need plenty of what you call thinking time.'

'That sort of thing is best done with a pint of beer,' said Jellings with a smile. 'My brain seems to work so much better in a pub.'

Leeming nodded. 'You're a man after my own heart, Inspector.'

'Let's have something to celebrate before we raise our glasses,' said Colbeck, firmly. 'We're a long way from achieving anything yet. We need to settle in here and to carry out exhaustive research. Your help will be invaluable, Inspector.'

'It's yours to command,' said Jellings.

'I assume that Mr Swarbrick's son has been contacted?'

'Yes, he has. I sent off a telegraph immediately. Andrew Swarbrick will have received it hours ago.' He narrowed his eyelids. 'You won't have to teach us *everything*, Inspector.'

There was more than a hint of pique in his voice.

Sergeant Eric Burridge had been a policeman far too long to be surprised by anything. He knew all about man's inhumanity to man and was equally aware of the lengths that ruthless women would go to in order to achieve their ends. It fell to him that afternoon to conduct Andrew Swarbrick to the morgue to view the body of his father. Burridge found it best to say as little as possible on such occasions, standing close to relatives of the deceased in case they were overcome by grief. Over the years, he'd carried out a number of people unable to bear the sight of a loved one on a cold slab. Burridge never rushed anyone. If someone wanted to gaze at a corpse for a long time, he allowed them to do so, remaining invisible until he or she was ready to leave.

Andrew Swarbrick arrived at the police station and demanded to see the body of his father. Burridge escorted him down the dank steps to the morgue. He unlocked the door, invited Swarbrick in, then gently pulled back the edge of the shroud to reveal the face. The son looked down at his father long enough to see the ugly wound in the forehead and the distorted face.

'That's him,' he said, brusquely.

Without another word, he walked straight out of the room. From start to finish, the whole thing had taken less than fifteen seconds.

Detective Constable Alan Hinton was feeling cruelly underused. Having just helped to catch a burglar, he was now awaiting his next assignment. In the interim, he was given mundane tasks at Scotland Yard itself. It bordered on humiliation. Months earlier, he'd assisted Colbeck and Leeming in the capture of the two men who'd kidnapped and tortured the superintendent. Hinton thought he was entitled to be treated with a new respect and given more challenging crimes to solve. Instead of that, he was cooling his heels in an office. At the very least, he'd expected Tallis to be grateful to him and, whenever they met, to acknowledge the bravery shown by the constable in securing the older man's release. It had been signally lacking. Whenever he passed the superintendent in a corridor, Hinton didn't even get so much as a nod. It was as if he was not there. The eager, fresh-faced young constable was hurt by his treatment.

When he was asked to take a report to the commissioner's office, Hinton obeyed at once, concealing his annoyance at being given such a simple errand. Something did then lift his spirits slightly. As he handed over the report, the commissioner not only thanked him, he used Hinton's name. That simple act of recognition buoyed the detective up. His route back to the office took him down a flight of stairs and across a hall. He was halfway down the steps when he saw a figure sitting motionless on a chair and gazing fixedly in front of him. It was Edward Tallis. Here was Hinton's opportunity. Rather than wait until the superintendent actually remembered who he was and what initiative he'd shown, Hinton decided to remind Tallis of his existence. Standing in front of him, he cleared his throat noisily. Nothing happened. Hinton clapped his hands but there was still no response. It was as if he was confronted by a statue of Tallis.

In the end, he resorted to shaking the man by the shoulder. It brought the superintendent back to life with a vengeance. He leapt to his feet and subjected Hinton to his fiercest glare.

'What do you want?' he shouted.

'I just wondered if you were all right, sir.'

'Of course, I'm all right. Why shouldn't I be?'

'No reason at all, sir.'

'Who *are* you?'

'I'm Detective Constable Hinton. You may recall that I was . . .' His voice died as he looked into a pair of molten eyes. 'I'm sorry, sir. I'll get out of your way.'

'Good,' said Tallis, nastily. 'Stay there.'

# CHAPTER SEVEN

Colbeck, Leeming and Jellings arrived at the police station to find a reporter from a local newspaper awaiting them with his notebook open. He pressed them for details of the investigation. Colbeck gave him a short statement then the three of them went straight to the inspector's office. It was much smaller and far more cluttered than the one that Colbeck had at Scotland Yard. A stickler for order and tidiness, he recoiled from the mild chaos around him. It would hamper any work done there rather than facilitate it. They were soon joined by Eric Burridge who told them that the murder victim's son had turned up earlier and viewed his father's body. When he explained how quickly Andrew Swarbrick had come and gone, they were astounded.

'Was the visit really that perfunctory?' asked Colbeck.

'Yes, sir,' said Burridge.

'Did he express no emotion at all?'

'He didn't stay long enough, sir.'

'Where is he now?' asked Jellings.

'He told me that he was going home.'

'But he hasn't been inside that house for years.'

'Things are different now, Inspector,' said Burridge. 'Young Mr Swarbrick made that point to me. In effect, it's *his* property now. He's here to claim it.'

'That's going to cause friction,' said Jellings, worriedly. 'I don't want his stepmother waking up to find him standing there and threatening to evict her. If he's not moved by the fact that his father was shot dead, then he certainly won't show any pity towards *her.*'

'One moment,' advised Colbeck, 'let's not make assumptions. How do we know that his father has bequeathed the property to him?'

'He must have done, Inspector. It's been the family home for generations. To preserve tradition, he'll want to hand it on to his son.'

'Mr Swarbrick may have changed his mind.'

'There's no chance of that happening, I promise you. Once he made a decision, he stuck to it. To him, it was a matter of honour. I'm sure that he's made adequate provision for his second wife,' said Jellings, 'but his only child will be the main benefactor.'

'That doesn't give him the right to barge in there and upset his stepmother,' said Colbeck. 'Andrew Swarbrick will get nothing until the will is proved and that may take some time. Until then, he has no legal right to ownership.'

'It won't stop him trying to hassle his stepmother.'

'Is he that impatient?'

'He could be,' said Jellings. 'I'm sorry, Inspector, but I feel that I should get over to the house right now to tackle him. Mrs Swarbrick needs rest and sympathy, not someone barking at her heels.'

'I'll come with you,' decided Colbeck. 'The sooner I meet Andrew Swarbrick, the better.'

'Be warned – it won't be a pleasant experience.'

'I'm accustomed to dealing with awkward individuals.'

'We get plenty of practice at it,' said Leeming as an image of Tallis popped up in his mind. 'Do you want me to come with you, Inspector?'

'No,' replied Colbeck, 'you stay here and say nothing to that over-eager reporter lurking outside. Sergeant Burridge will no doubt be able to tell you what action the police have so far taken.'

'I'll be happy to do so,' said Burridge, obligingly.

There was a flurry of farewells, then the two inspectors went off together. Burridge spread his arms in a gesture that invited a question.

Leeming grinned. 'Where do we find the best pub in Norwich?'

Beth 'Binnie' Wymark had been housekeeper to the Swarbrick family for over fifteen years. During that time, she'd been thrilled by her employer's achievements in public life and had shared in his private woes. Chief among the latter had been the death of his first wife from tuberculosis, a tragedy he dealt with by throwing himself into his political work. Binnie was a plump, plain, motherly woman who'd spent most of her life in domestic service. Having lost her husband to a heart attack after a mere five years of marriage, she'd been able to understand more than most people Swarbrick's anguish at his bereavement. In the wake of his murder, it was her turn to feel the stabbing pain of loss once more.

'Where is my stepmother now?' demanded Andrew Swarbrick.

'She's asleep in bed, sir,' replied Beth. 'Mrs Swarbrick was so upset by what happened that the doctor gave her a sleeping draught.'

'How long will it last?'

'I was told not to disturb her until morning.'

Pulling a face, he clicked his tongue in irritation. He'd arrived at the house to find it in a state of disarray. The murder had shocked the entire domestic staff. Every member of it had had great respect for their former master. Coupled with their sorrow was the unease that came from wondering what their respective futures might hold for them. Looking at Swarbrick now, Binnie feared the worst. If he was to inherit the house, changes were inevitable and her position might well be in danger. They were in the hall and Swarbrick was looking around with a possessive glint in his eye. His unexpected arrival had unnerved the housekeeper slightly.

'Where will you be staying tonight, sir?' she ventured.

His tone was haughty. 'Where else would I stay but right here?'

'I'll have your old room prepared for you at once.'

'So I should hope, Mrs Wymark.'

'Do you have any instructions?'

'I have an abundance of them,' he said. 'Let me settle in first.' He gazed around the hall again. 'This place is even stuffier than I remember. Look at all these paintings – they're so dull and lifeless. They'll be the first to go.'

'You'll keep the portrait of your father, surely?' she said.

'I don't know about that, Mrs Wymark.' He marched off to the drawing room with the housekeeper trotting at his heels. Above the mantelpiece was the oil painting of Jarvis Swarbrick, striking a pose in the lobby of the House of Commons. His son looked up at it with disdain. 'To be honest, I never really cared for it.'

'We all think that it's a perfect likeness of him, sir.'

'The servants' opinions are an irrelevance. Whether or not the portrait remains is solely my decision.'

'Mrs Swarbrick will have a view.'

'Oh, I shan't take any notice of that,' he said, dismissively.

They heard the sound of a horse approaching and of wheels scrunching the gravel. Beth glanced through the window.

'It's Inspector Jellings,' she said, 'with another gentleman.'

Alan Hinton was alarmed by Tallis's strange behaviour. He was convinced that there was something seriously wrong with the superintendent, a man renowned for his alertness and ability to keep fatigue at bay. Those qualities seemed to have vanished. On two separate occasions when Hinton had met him, Tallis had been in a kind of trance, wholly unaware of the presence of someone else. Hinton had had occasional daydreams himself – most of them featuring Lydia Quayle – but he'd snapped out of them instantly as soon as anyone came near him. The superintendent hadn't done that. Even though Hinton was standing so close to him, Tallis hadn't seen or heard him. He seemed to be in a state of paralysis. It was very disturbing. While he never had what might be characterised as affection for the superintendent, Hinton had the highest regard. If the man was ill, he should be helped.

His problem lay in finding someone to take his concern seriously. When he'd confided in two of his colleagues, they simply laughed, assuring him that Tallis's behaviour had always been peculiar and that Hinton should learn to ignore it. But he simply couldn't allow himself to do that. Knowing the ordeal Tallis had been through at the hands of his captors, he felt profoundly sorry for him. There had to be someone to whom he could turn in what he believed was an emergency. He even toyed with the notion of reporting his disquiet to the commissioner but he soon rejected the idea, fearing that the comments by a lowly detective constable wouldn't be taken seriously. What he needed was someone as sensitive to Tallis's needs as he was, someone he could trust to offer sound advice. Only one person came to mind.

'Why did you spend so little time at the morgue?' asked Colbeck.

Swarbrick bridled. 'Don't be so damned impertinent!'

'We were told that you hardly looked at the body.'

'Would *you* enjoy looking at your dead father if someone had put an ugly hole in his head?'

'I might not enjoy it, Mr Swarbrick, but I'd certainly give him, or any other victim, more than a cursory glance. The nature of any injuries tells you something about the person who inflicted them. One shot was all it took to kill your father,' said Colbeck. 'In my time, I've had to examine murder victims with dozens of hideous wounds, not to mention missing limbs.'

'I went, I paid my respects and I left. What's wrong with that?'

'You were somewhat irreverent, sir.'

'Each of us grieves in his own way, Inspector.'

'That's true, I suppose,' said Jellings.

He and Colbeck were in the library, seated either side of Andrew Swarbrick. It was a room with generous proportions and well-stocked shelves. At the mahogany desk in the window, Colbeck surmised, the former MP had written speeches for delivery in Parliament or at board meetings of the Eastern Counties Railway. While the father had reputedly been an effective debater, the son had now shown that he could also give a good account of himself in any argument. Whatever questions they fired at him were swatted contemptuously away. It was time for Swarbrick to ask a question of his own.

'When will the body be released?'

'There will have to be an inquest first,' said Jellings, quietly.

'Why? Isn't it glaringly obvious what happened?'

'It's important to follow the legalities, sir.'

'I should have thought you'd be keen to attend the inquest,' said Colbeck, 'because it will provide detail about your father's murder. In your position, I'd want to know everything I could.'

'Yes,' retorted Swarbrick, 'but you're not *in* my position, are you? My main interest now is in the funeral arrangements.'

'They'll be left to Mrs Swarbrick, surely?'

'He was *my* father, not hers.'

'Your stepmother may still have prior claim, sir,' said Jellings. 'You and your father haven't spoken to each other for years.'

Swarbrick laughed. 'What on earth makes you think that?'

'I thought the two of you were estranged.'

'We never met under this roof, perhaps, but I did see Father from time to time. As a matter of fact, we dined at the House of Commons only last week. He was not the only member of the family with an interest in politics, you know.'

'Was Mrs Swarbrick aware of these occasional meetings?'

'Of course not,' said the other, curling a lip. 'It was no business of hers. Blood is thicker than water, Inspector. The ties between a father and son can never be entirely broken.'

'I accept that, sir.'

Mark Jellings was much more respectful towards him. Since the Swarbrick family had held such power in the city, his approach to any member of it was always tentative. Policemen who overstepped the mark with someone like Andrew Swarbrick would be swiftly put back in their place. Colbeck had no need for such deferential behaviour. As a member of the Detective Department of the Metropolitan Police Force, he was beyond Swarbrick's sphere of influence and thus able to ask more robust questions. He'd taken against Swarbrick on sight. The man was arrogant, pompous and – on the evidence of his brief visit to the morgue – almost indifferent to his father's fate. He showed no sign of being in mourning.

'Since you seem to have kept in touch with your father,' said Colbeck, 'you may be able to help us.'

'Don't bank on it,' said Swarbrick.

'During the times you spent together, did he ever tell you that he sensed danger?'

'No, he didn't. It would have been completely out of character for him to do so. My father was fearless, Inspector. Nothing worried him.'

'His death was no accident, sir. Someone wanted him killed. Do you have any idea at all who that person might be?'

'You're the detective. Get out there and find him.'

It was time to go.

Since her father rarely called at that time of the evening without a prior arrangement, Madeleine was surprised to see him. She was even more astonished when he told her his reason for returning to the house.

'I wanted to apologise, Maddy.'

'For what?'

'I shouldn't have lost my temper this morning.'

'Oh,' she said with a smile of resignation, 'I'm used to that.'

'I spoilt it for you,' he confessed. 'When you were excited about that commission you were offered, I poured cold water on the idea.'

'Actually, it was very hot water. Your comments scalded my ears.'

'I feel terrible about it,' he said, penitently. 'Do you forgive me?'

'I've been trying to forget all about it.'

'Well, I was wrong. I spoke out of turn. It's your decision to make and not mine. I'm still not happy about it but I can see that you should be allowed to paint whatever you choose and to ignore your cantankerous old father.' She gave him a kiss of gratitude. 'I don't deserve that.'

'No, you don't,' she agreed.

'Right,' said Andrews, 'I'm off now.'

'There's no need, Father.'

'I didn't mean to intrude. It's just that I've been brooding on it all day. I wanted to get it off my chest.'

'I'm glad that you did.'

She took him into the hall and paused at the front door. His visit had pleased her and it had certainly cleared the air where her commission was concerned. He'd promised not to interfere and that was heartening.

'I'll make it up to you, Maddy,' he promised. 'When you arrange to see this gentleman, I'll come with you.'

'Lydia has already agreed to do that.'

'She can come as well, if she likes, but I ought to be there.'

'Why?'

'It's my duty as a father to protect you. What if this Mr Fairbank is not the nice old man you think he is? You'll need me.'

'We'll be meeting at the art dealer's gallery, Father. I'm in no danger. There'll be other people there as witnesses. Nothing unpleasant will happen.'

He took umbrage immediately. 'Are you saying that you don't want me there?' he asked. 'Are you telling me that Lydia

Quayle knows more about steam locomotives than *I* do?'

'Don't be ridiculous.'

'Mr Fairbank obviously loves railways and so do I. We're bound to get on very well together.'

'But you won't,' she said, 'and that's the trouble. As soon as Mr Fairbank starts to sing the praises of GWR locomotives, it will be like waving a red rag at a bull.'

He was enraged. 'Oh, so I'm nothing but a bull now, am I?'

'Calm down, Father.'

'I didn't come here to be insulted.'

'I'm just being realistic. Given your passion for the LNWR, it's safer to keep you apart from someone who believes the GWR is better.'

'Nothing created by Brunel can ever be better!'

'You see. You're doing it again.'

'I'm merely stating a fact, Maddy.'

'And how do you think Mr Fairbank will react if you state that same fact in front of him? It could lose me my commission.'

'I'll never shrink from telling the truth.'

'My decision is made,' said Madeleine, firmly. 'Kind as your offer is, I won't be taking it up. I'm going to see someone who has taken an interest in my work. That means a great deal to me, Father. I will not have you – or anyone else – getting in the way.'

'If that's your attitude,' he said, angrily, 'I'm off.'

Flinging open the door, he stormed off along the pavement.

When they actually reached the cottage, most of Leeming's objections to it promptly disappeared. It was the most enchanting accommodation they'd ever had during an investigation. Standing in its own garden, it offered complete privacy, exceptional comfort and some pleasant views. Its rooms were comfortable and there was a pervading air of wealth. The detectives had three bedrooms from which to choose one each. Cecil Freed was as good as his word. Once he'd shown them around, he left them alone. Having given them both a cordial welcome, his wife had also withdrawn. Their hosts were soon replaced by a maid who asked what meal they wished to have cooked. When they'd made their choices, she hurried off to the kitchen in the main house.

'This place is amazing,' said Leeming. 'All it needs is a barrel of beer and it would be perfect.'

'Wait until you get upstairs, Victor.'

'What do you mean, sir?'

'I took a quick look at the bedrooms while you were bringing in the luggage. On the pillow in each one of them is a tract on the blessings of temperance.'

'It doesn't have any.'

'It does while we're guests here, especially when we're in Mrs Freed's company.' He lowered himself on to the sofa. 'What did you learn at the police station?'

'I found out where the best pub is,' said Leeming, happily.

'I was asking about their response to the murder.'

'Oh, they've done all the right things, sir, but not fast enough for my liking. Their problem is lack of numbers. If Norwich wants a good police force, it should pay a lot more for it.'

'Sergeant Burridge seemed an able man.'

'He does his job well and the important thing is that he's on our side. I'm not sure that I can say that about Inspector Jellings.'

'He's still weighing us in the balance, Victor. His fear is that we'll get all the credit. He desperately wants the murder solved but only if he's instrumental in arresting the culprits.'

'There's not much chance of him doing that,' said Leeming. 'What did you make of Andrew Swarbrick?'

'I think he should definitely be on our list of suspects.'

'Why?'

'He stands to gain so much from his father's death,' said Colbeck, 'and I don't just mean in financial terms. He hinted that he'd like to take over his father's seat in the House of Commons.'

'Is that a strong enough motive for murder?'

'We'll have to see. Swarbrick is something of an enigma. He walks out of the family home because of his father's choice of a second wife, yet he continues to see him in secret.'

'Did he say *why* he despises the second Mrs Swarbrick?'

'According to Jellings, it was because the marriage took place too soon after the death of the first wife. There was no decent interval.'

'Who decides how long that should be?'

'There are unspoken rules, Victor.'

'What else told you that Swarbrick needs to be watched?'

'It was the speed with which he reacted to the news and the composure he showed when he got here. Any other son would be distraught. It was almost as if he'd been waiting for the telegraph that brought him home. Mrs Swarbrick was lucky to be sedated. If it had been left to him, he'd have had his stepmother leave at once.'

'Does he have a right to do that, sir?'

'He's the kind of man who believes he has the right to do anything he chooses. His sense of entitlement is overwhelming.'

'I hate people like that.'

'Swarbrick is not an engaging man,' said Colbeck, 'but his bad manners don't of themselves mean that he plotted the murder. He must be on our list but not necessarily at the top.'

'Who is above him?'

'I fancy that it may be Mr Trant. From the very start my instinct was that this crime is rooted in the railway. Trant used to be an active member of the board of the ECR. Getting kicked unceremoniously off it would have hurt him deeply. Mistakenly,' Colbeck went on, 'he blamed Swarbrick for getting him ousted. By arranging to have him killed, he'd achieve two ends: he'd satisfy his lust for revenge and create a vacancy on the board which, I predict, he's determined to fill.'

'So our choice is between Andrew Swarbrick and Trant, is it?'

'They'd need help from men like Constable Pryor, for instance.'

'Sergeant Burridge warned me about him.'

'Oh?'

'He said that Pryor was sly, lazy and not very intelligent.'

'Anything else?'

'Pryor is always short of money. He'd do anything to get it. And there's something else to consider, sir.'

'Go on.'

'Well, since he's supposed to be dim-witted, how did he work out how the points were switched? He told me that it must have been when a goods train went through and acted as a screen. There's no platform on the other side,' said Leeming, 'so the person who switched the points was blocked from view. Pryor could only have come up with that explanation if he knew it in advance. He's too stupid to work it out for himself.'

'The stationmaster is far from stupid,' said Colbeck, 'and, in his report, he made exactly the same suggestion. Knowing the time when that goods train was due to come through, someone used it to hide behind.'

'I think Pryor could be involved somehow.'

'If he is, he'll give himself away before too long. Let's go back to Duff, shall we? What did Burridge tell you about him?'

'He doesn't like the man, sir, but I doubt if many people do. The sergeant said that he struts around the station as if he's cock of the walk. Duff is good at keeping the railway policemen in line and even better at making them do all the work while he just looks on.'

'I'd still like to know the reason he left the Metropolitan Police.'

'He dared to poke fun at Superintendent Tallis?'

Colbeck smiled. 'If that was a crime,' he said, 'we'd both have been hanged for it years ago. Well, Victor,' he continued, 'so far we have four names in the hat. Others will no doubt soon be added. Hopefully, one of them will be the name of the killer.'

'You did point out that we needed to find his accomplice first.'

'Is it Pryor, perhaps?'

'No,' said Leeming, thoughtfully. 'I'm wondering if Duff is our man. He's much more cunning.'

When he turned down the alley in the fading light, Bartram Duff first looked up and down to make sure that nobody could see him. He then knocked hard on a door. Almost immediately, it was opened.

'What kept you?' asked a gruff voice.

# CHAPTER EIGHT

Madeleine Colbeck had not long finished her breakfast when she was told that she had a visitor. Delighted to find that it was Alan Hinton, she took him into the drawing room.

'I can't stay, Mrs Colbeck,' he warned. 'I'm due at Scotland Yard very soon. I just wondered if I might ask a favour.'

'Yes, of course – what is it?'

'If at all possible, I need to get a message to your husband.'

When he explained why, Madeleine was touched by his concern for a man who'd treated him so badly. Evidently, there was something wrong with Edward Tallis and it was typical of Hinton that he wanted to do something about it, especially when his colleagues refused to believe that there was any problem. In seeking Colbeck's advice, Hinton had a secondary purpose. It gave him an opportunity to ask after Lydia Quayle.

'Have you heard from Miss Quayle recently?'

'She was here only yesterday,' said Madeleine, 'and she mentioned your name in passing. Since you were commended for your actions during the rescue of the superintendent, Lydia was wondering if you'd had a promotion.'

'The very opposite has happened,' he said with a hollow laugh.

She was taken aback. 'You've been *demoted*?'

'Not exactly – but it feels like it sometimes. I've not been employed in the way that I'd hoped.'

'Is my husband aware of that?'

'Oh,' he sighed, 'the inspector is always too busy on a new case to worry about me.'

'If he realised what was happening,' said Madeleine, 'I'm sure that he'd speak up for you. He'll be very upset to hear of the way that the superintendent has treated you.'

'Thank you, Mrs Colbeck.'

'Do you have a message for Lydia?'

The question caught him unawares and he came close to blushing. Having seen him and Lydia together, she knew how deep their feelings for each other were but neither of them seemed to know how to move the relationship on beyond a formal one. Hinton felt that the gulf between them was too wide to bridge. While he was a detective constable on a modest wage, Lydia had inherited a large amount of money from her mother. For her part, she felt that the differences in their background were meaningless, but she couldn't bring herself to make that first vital step towards him. She had befriended Hinton when he was assigned to protect her from the attentions of a stalker. He'd not only provided much-needed reassurance for her, he'd arrested the man and ensured his conviction. Lydia's gratitude had been mixed with a growing affection for him.

'Well,' repeated Madeleine, 'do you have a message for her?'

'Please give her my warmest regards,' he said.

Oliver Trant turned out to be a man of medium height and middle years whose bald head gleamed as if it had just been expertly polished. He was the owner of a factory that made boots and shoes. Well groomed and well dressed, he gave Colbeck a warm welcome when the inspector called there that morning. They met in Trant's office. Shelves along one wall had various pairs of gleaming shoes on display. A faint aroma of leather hung in the air. Offered refreshment, Colbeck declined it. He sat opposite Trant and appraised him carefully.

'You've heard the sad news, I take it, sir.'

'It's not merely sad, Inspector,' said the other man with apparent sincerity, 'it's nothing short of a disaster. Jarvis Swarbrick was a man of exceptional talents. In political and in commercial terms, he seemed to have a magic touch.'

'That could be the reason he was murdered, sir.'

'I thought he was killed during a robbery that went awry?'

'There was nothing awry about the crime, sir. Somebody was set on shooting him dead.'

Trant looked startled. 'What possible motive could anyone have to murder Jarvis?'

'The obvious one is envy.'

'Ah,' said the other, adjusting to the news. 'Now I understand why someone has whispered *my* name in your ears. But you've been fed false information, I fear. I was never really envious of Jarvis. I just disagreed with his plans for the ECR. That's why we fell out.'

'I was told a rather different story, sir.'

'Yes, yes, I'm sure you were. Don't believe what Cecil Freed had to say. I have not been waiting for the chance to wreak my revenge on Jarvis, nor have I been labouring under the misapprehension that he was directly responsible for getting me voted off the board. In reality,' said Trant with a disarming smile, 'that was Cecil's doing and I knew it from the start. He was the one who put down the poison. In his eyes, I was a disruptive influence. Don't ever trust what Cecil Freed tells you. He's a devious fellow. Given the choice,' he added with a twinkle in his eye, 'I'd have preferred it if the killer had shot *him* instead.'

'Are you saying that you *approve* of murder?' asked Colbeck.

'Nobody in his right mind would do that, Inspector. I just wanted to let you know the sort of person Cecil Freed is.'

'Why did you oppose Mr Swarbrick's plans for the ECR?'

'In principle, I supported them. There just happened to be some problematical clauses in the bill he was hoping to present in the House of Commons. I simply sought to have them removed. In the event,' he said, producing the disarming smile again, 'the only thing removed was me.'

'You don't seem rancorous about it, Mr Trant.'

'Why should I be? Setbacks are bound to happen.'

'Would you like to rejoin the board?'

'Of course, I would – but only on my terms.'

'You'd have to accept Mr Freed's authority again.'

'Oh, I know how to work around Cecil. He's not as wily as he imagines. With Jarvis no longer available, I'm needed more than ever. I have an eye for detail that nobody else on the board possesses.'

'That's an extravagant claim, Mr Trant.'

'Examine my record, if you wish. I can show you the minutes of board meetings where I voiced my concerns about Jarvis's bill. I picked out potential anomalies that nobody else had spotted.'

'Not even Mr Swarbrick himself?'

'He wasn't infallible, Inspector. Even the best horse stumbles.' He looked quizzically at his visitor. 'How much do you know about ECR?'

'I know that it's had a troubled history.'

'That's an understatement. It got off to a very bad start.'

'Yes,' said Colbeck, seizing the opportunity to show his credentials. 'The directors ignored the advice of their engineer and foolishly adopted a five-foot gauge. When they were forced to convert to the standard gauge, over eighty miles of track had to be adapted at an average cost of one thousand pounds per mile. Am I correct?'

Trant blinked in surprise. 'You're very well informed, Inspector.'

'I have a passion for railways, sir, so you don't need to give me a history lesson. I know that George Hudson, the notorious Railway King, was your chairman in earlier days before leaving you in an unholy mess. And there have been many other calamities since then. What concerns me, however,' said Colbeck, 'is not the ECR's past but its present. Mr Swarbrick's ambition was to unify the disparate companies into the Great Eastern Railway.'

'We all shared that ambition.'

'Yet it was not without its detractors, it seems. What better way to frustrate that ambition than to kill the man who might have brought the plan to its fruition?'

Trant sat back in his chair and looked at Colbeck in a new light. He could see that he was dealing with someone who clearly had insight into the workings of the ECR and its competitors. It made him more cautious. Trant's glib assertions would never be taken at face value. Colbeck was too astute to be easily misled.

'You look as if you wish to ask me something, Inspector.'

'I think you know what my question would be,' said Colbeck.

'Then the answer is that I have no connection whatsoever with any of the other companies operating in East Anglia. That's not to say I haven't been approached to join other boards of directors,' admitted Trant, 'but I've refused all entreaties. My heart remains with the ECR and I fervently hope to see it exert a controlling influence on the future Great Eastern Railway.'

'Who might wish to stifle that ambition?'

'Those who feel they might lose by it.'

'Could you supply me with any names?'

'Look at the directors of the smaller railway companies. Some of them fear being swallowed alive by the ECR then spat out like pips.'

'Amalgamation must come one day.'

'Agreed – but killing Jarvis will definitely delay it.'

'Did he really have a magic touch?'

'In some ways, he did. From our point of view, the vital thing was that he was well respected in Parliament. In debate, he was forceful and persuasive.'

'You and he must have had some interesting tussles at board meetings.'

Trant grinned. 'We certainly did.'

'Thank you, sir,' said Colbeck, rising to his feet. 'I may need to speak again before too long.'

'You're always welcome here, Inspector,' said Trant, getting up from his desk. 'This may not be the right moment to draw your attention to the shelf behind you but, since you are clearly a man of exquisite taste, you might care to look at some of our shoes. Their quality is unrivalled.'

'I'll take your word for it, Mr Trant.'

'Jarvis Swarbrick was a regular customer of ours. He'd never wear shoes made by anyone else. The same goes for his son. Andrew walks through life in our excellent footwear.'


Andrew Swarbrick was thwarted at every turn. Hoping to confront his stepmother that morning, he was delayed by the arrival of the doctor who examined her, found her still in a state of distress and advised that she remain in bed until she felt well enough to get up. As soon as the doctor departed, he was replaced by another barrier to Mrs Swarbrick. It was the last person Andrew wished to see. For her part, Mrs Freed was not at all pleased to see him.

'Inspector Colbeck told us that you were here. I must say that I was surprised. What are you doing here?'

'This is my home, Mrs Freed.'

'Yes, but you've chosen to turn your back on it for years.'

'In the wake of Father's death, everything has changed.'

'Have you spoken to your stepmother?'

'Chance would be a fine thing!' he complained.

'It's all for the best. As he left the house, the doctor told me what his advice was. In any case, I don't think that she'd be happy to see you at this moment. You'd only revive unhappy memories.'

'I need to discuss the future with her, Mrs Freed.'

'Heavens above!' she exclaimed. 'Show some pity. Your father's body is probably still warm and you want to start talking about what happens next! You'll have to be patient, Andrew. Can't you see how upsetting it will be for Grace to find you here?'

'I have every right.'

'Legally, that may be true, but you don't have the right to hector a woman in such a fragile state. It's cruel. Learn to wait.'

'You should have given that advice to my stepmother,' he said, pointedly. '*She* didn't show any patience, did she? No sooner had my mother died than she came sniffing around my father.'

'That's not what happened at all. It was months before she even met your father.'

'You might have swallowed that story, Mrs Freed, but I don't.'

'It was the truth. Grace told me how their paths crossed.'

'I'm not prepared to argue about that now,' he said, testily. 'The simple fact is that she and I have a lot to talk over.'

'What you mean is that you want to harry her while she's at her most vulnerable. That's despicable of you, Andrew. What do you think your father would say about your behaviour?'

'He's not in a position to tell me.'

'I find that remark in appalling taste.'

'Truth *is* sometimes distasteful.'

'You should be ashamed of yourself.'

'I'll take no lectures from you, Mrs Freed.'

'Do you have to be so unconscionably rude?'

'Father was a person who did what he felt was right,' he declared, 'and that's all that I'm doing. I'm standing up for myself.'

'Well, you're not going to harm Grace in the process,' she warned, eyes ablaze. 'I'm here to protect her. A tragedy like this should bring the two of you together, not license you to hound her. This is a time for mourning. Join the rest of us in our grief.'

But he was in no mood to do so. Turning on his heel, Swarbrick left the room angrily and slammed the door behind him.

Madeleine was, as always, pleased to see her friend. Lydia had timed her arrival to coincide with the hours when Helen would be alone with her mother. As the child tottered around the drawing room, the two women urged her on and applauded her. It was only when the nanny came for Helen that they were able to have a quiet conversation at last.

'I had an unexpected visitor earlier on,' said Madeleine.

'Who was it?'

'Alan Hinton.'

Lydia was curious. 'What did he want?'

'Ideally, he wanted *you* to be here.'

'Don't be silly!'

'It's the truth, Lydia. I could see it in his eyes.'

Madeleine told her about Hinton's request and how she admired him for trying to help someone who was so obviously unwell, even though he'd felt the lash of Tallis's tongue twice in a row.

'That's very considerate of him,' said Lydia.

'Would you expect anything less?'

'No, I wouldn't. Alan is such a thoughtful person.'

'And we both know whom he thinks about,' teased Madeleine. 'As it happens, a letter arrived from Robert not long before you did. Since I now have an address where I can reach him, I'll pass on the request and tell him how Alan Hinton feels overlooked at Scotland Yard.'

'Did he . . . mention me at all?'

'Of course, he did. When I told him that you'd been asking after him, he was delighted. He sends you his warmest regards.'

'Thank you, Madeleine.'

'I'm sure that he'd have preferred to pass them on in person.'

Lydia smiled. 'I would have liked that.'

When the summons from Edward Tallis came, Alan Hinton was at first apprehensive. It could only mean that he'd be the victim of another burst of vituperation. His uneasiness was, however, tempered by hope. Could it be that the superintendent actually wanted to apologise to him? On the previous day, Tallis had spoken unkindly to him yet he was now inviting Hinton to his office. Instead of frightening him, it might be seen as a good sign. Bitter experience suggested that it was not. Obeying the call, Hinton stood outside the superintendent's door for a full minute before he built up the courage to knock.

'Come in!' shouted Tallis.

Hinton entered the room. 'You wanted me, sir?'

'That's why I sent for you. I require your assistance.'

'What must I do, sir?'

'You're about to take part in a murder investigation.'

'Am I?' said Hinton, heart pumping instantly.

'Let's see if you're up to the task.'

'I'm sure that I will be, Superintendent. Where am I to go?'

'The record office,' said Tallis, brandishing a telegraph, 'and you can take this with you. Colbeck sent it from Norwich. One of the men on his list of suspects claims to have worked as a policeman in London.'

'How long ago was that, sir?'

'Read the telegraph and it will tell you.'

'Thank you,' said Hinton, taking it from him.

'Colbeck wishes to know if this man, Bartram Duff, left of his own account or was discharged. Do you think you could find out for him?'

'I'm sure that I can, sir.'

Mastering his disappointment, Hinton was about to leave when he noticed that Tallis was no longer looking *at* him but right through him. It was quite eerie. The glassy look he'd seen twice before in the older man's eyes had returned once again. Tallis didn't even know that Hinton was still in the room. The constable took no risks this time and refrained from any attempt to establish contact again. Anxious not to rouse him, he crept silently away.

Out in the corridor, he glanced at the telegraph. Finding the information Colbeck needed would be a straightforward task but it was not Hinton's idea of being involved in a murder investigation. And what he discovered in the record office might well have no bearing on the case at all. He consoled himself with the thought that he'd spoken to Tallis and come away without being unfairly berated. It was progress of a kind and he settled for that.

The moment he saw the goods train coming, Victor Leeming took the watch from his waistcoat pocket. Waiting until it reached the station, he timed it as wagon after wagon rumbled past. There was a symphony of banging, rattling and squeaking from rolling stock that had clearly seen better days. When the train had gone past, he memorised the time it had taken. Horace Pryor suddenly appeared at his shoulder.

'What are you doing, Sergeant?' he asked.

'I'm putting your theory to the test.'

Pryor was confused. 'What theory is that, then?'

'You told me you thought the points were switched when a goods train went through the station. That might well be what happened. Anyone standing on this platform wouldn't have been able to see what was happening.'

'Yes, and the goods train that went through yesterday was much slower because it had far more wagons to pull.'

'Thank you – that's worth knowing.'

'I could be wrong,' said Pryor. 'It was only a guess.'

'It was a policeman's guess and they're usually worth listening to.'

Leeming looked up and down the platform. Several passengers were waiting for the next train and they all seemed ill at ease. The murder on the previous day had left everyone feeling nervous.

'Have you been disciplined yet?' asked Leeming.

'I get told off regular.'

'Sergeant Duff thinks you might even lose your job.'

'I hope not,' said the other with sudden alarm. 'I've got four mouths to feed apart from mine. If I told my wife that I'd been sacked, there'd be ructions. You married, Sergeant?'

'Yes, I am.'

'Have you got any children?'

'We have two sons,' said Leeming, proudly.

'Me and Sally have three daughters who eat like gannets. I must take home a wage.' He squinted at Leeming. 'What would happen if *you* lost your job?'

'I'll make sure that I don't.'

'How do you do that?'

'By working very hard.'

'Do you and the inspector *always* solve a murder?'

'To be honest, we don't.'

'What about this one?'

'Oh, we'll certainly find the killer this time,' promised Leeming. 'I can feel it in my bones.'

Breaking away from Pryor, he walked off down the platform. Pryor was not left alone for long. Someone soon sidled up to him.

'What did *he* want?' asked Duff.

Anthea Freed's arrival made an immediate difference. Admitted to the bedroom, she persuaded Grace Swarbrick that, to aid her recovery, she needed to have a light breakfast and it was duly sent up. While her friend picked at her food, Anthea watched her carefully, noting the pale cheeks and the haunted eyes. Though Grace occasionally managed a grateful smile, it seemed an effort for her. When she'd finished the meal, and the tray had been removed by a maid, the two women were able to talk properly. Anthea sat beside the bed and held her friend's hand.

'How do you feel now?' she asked.

'All the better for something to eat – I haven't touched a thing since . . . it happened. Thank you, Anthea.'

'You looked as if you were famished.'

'I was,' said Grace. 'I need a favour from you.'

'Whatever it is, you shall have it.'

'The doctor told me that my stepson is back in the house. I begged him to keep Andrew at bay until I feel better. At the moment, I feel so dispirited that I couldn't possibly face him.'

'You won't have to,' said Anthea, decisively. 'I've already made that clear to him.'

'What did he say?'

'Let's ignore him and think about you instead. You're the one in need of sympathy and support. You've been through a horrid experience, Grace. Getting over it will take time.'

'I don't think I'll get over it. Jarvis was shot dead when he was as close to me as you are. He slumped across my feet. In fact . . .' Unable to find the words, she lowered her head.

'You don't have to suffer it again for my benefit, Grace. It would be far too taxing for you. I just hope that you'll find the strength to speak to Inspector Colbeck.'

'Is he from the Norwich Constabulary?'

'No,' replied Anthea, 'he's from Scotland Yard. Cecil sent him a telegraph and he came at once. He and Sergeant Leeming are staying at our cottage.'

'I see.'

'They've already been busy.'

Grace was circumspect. 'What sort of person is the inspector?'

'He's a real gentleman and utterly charming. Oh, and I should add that he's a very intelligent man. He doesn't look a bit like a detective.'

'That's a relief.'

'I know that policemen can be uncouth at times – the sergeant looks as if he might be like that – but the inspector is quite different. He's kind, sympathetic and very patient. At the same time,' she went on, 'he has asked me to point out that's it's vital for him to interview you as soon as possible.'

Grace tensed. 'I'd rather not speak to him.'

'You must. There's nothing to fear. I'll be there.'

'Is that a promise?'

'Of course,' said Anthea, squeezing her hand gently.

'I'm not sure that I can be much use,' said the other. 'It all happened in a flash. I never got to see the man's face and I couldn't even hazard a guess at his age. When I saw that gun of his, I was in a panic.'

'Just tell the full story to the inspector.'

'That *is* the full story. There's nothing else that I can add, really. Oh, I feel so useless, Anthea. I'm desperate for that man to be caught yet I can't really help the police to catch him.'

'Will you at least agree to see Inspector Colbeck?'

'Of course,' said the other, making an effort to compose herself. 'My husband would expect it of me.'

# CHAPTER NINE

When he'd been given what sounded like a chore, Alan Hinton had felt once again that he was being treated without respect for his proven abilities. At the same time, he'd been allotted a task and wanted to perform it quickly, drawing some comfort from the fact that he might actually be assisting Colbeck in his latest investigation and not just dredging up information that would prove wholly irrelevant.

The record office was a small, dusty, featureless room with ledgers stored on a series of shelves. He'd had to sign for the key to open the door and took a moment to get his bearings. The telegraph instructed him to go back at least ten years but, out of curiosity, he first looked at statistics relating to the formation of the Metropolitan Police Force in 1829.

It was a chastening experience. Of the first 2,800 men enlisted, over three-quarters had been dismissed in due course, the vast majority being found guilty of drunkenness on duty. Hinton knew that uniformed policemen were still leaving in appreciable numbers but none that compared with what had happened in the early stages of its existence. He eventually found the ledger relating to 1851 and began to leaf through the names. After a thorough search, he accepted that Bartram Duff was not among them and reached for the ledger dealing with the previous year. That, too, contained no reference to the man who was now a sergeant in the railway police in Norwich.

Hinton's third search was more successful. In the list of dismissals for December, 1849, he came across the name Bartram Walter Duff from the Marylebone Division. It had to be the same man. When he saw what Duff had actually done to merit dismissal, his eyes lit up with interest.

'There's no hurry, Mrs Swarbrick,' said Colbeck, soothingly. 'Don't say a word until you feel ready to do so.'

'Thank you, Inspector.'

'And if, at any time, you feel that talking about the incident is too uncomfortable for you, we can always have a rest.'

'That's very considerate of you,' said Grace.

'I told you what a kind man the inspector is,' said Anthea, seated beside the bed and holding her friend's hand. 'He promised that he'd put you under no pressure.'

'I have great reserves of patience,' said Colbeck with a smile. 'Don't be afraid to keep me waiting.'

It had taken him over ten minutes to calm Grace Swarbrick down. When he'd first been invited into the bedroom, he could see how fearful she was, having to talk to a complete stranger about an event that had changed her life irrevocably. She was, by turns, nervous, distracted, uncertain, disturbed, embarrassed and helpless, looking as if she was unequal to the challenge now offered. While Anthea offered her friend unconditional sympathy, Colbeck concentrated on trying to win the confidence of the murder victim's wife. He eventually succeeded.

'I think that I'm ready now, Inspector,' whispered Grace.

'Go at your own pace, Mrs Swarbrick.'

'Where do I start?'

'Well,' he suggested, 'you might begin by telling me why you and your husband were travelling on that particular train.'

'When we've spent the weekend in London, we always return on Monday morning on the same train. Indeed, we invariably occupy the same first-class compartment. We have exclusive use of it.'

'Is that because of Mr Swarbrick's status?'

'It's partly that but it's also because I'm a poor traveller. Though I've never actually been sick, I always feel as if I'm on the point of doing so. I'd hate to disgrace myself in the company of strangers.'

'If it's such a problem,' asked Colbeck, 'why travel by rail at all?'

'There are social obligations in London,' Anthea interjected. 'As a devoted wife, Grace hates to let her husband down.'

'I accepted it as a necessary sacrifice,' said the other woman. 'My husband expected it of me.'

'Tell me about the journey itself,' invited Colbeck.

'It was much the same as any other.'

'You didn't feel watched in any way when you left London?'

'No, we simply did what we always did.'

'Can you remember anyone peering into your compartment?'

'I was too busy bracing myself for the journey, Inspector.'

'What was your husband doing?'

'His head was deep in *The Times*.'

'Let's move on to your destination,' he said. 'Describe what happened when the train was approaching the station.'

'Well,' she replied, 'everything seemed exactly as it should be at first. The train was late as usual and my husband, as usual, complained. And then it happened . . .'

Inspector Jellings was irked. Having surrendered leadership of the investigation to detectives from Scotland Yard, he felt duty-bound to pass on every scrap of information gathered before they had reached Norwich. When a new witness came forward, therefore, he summoned Leeming to the police station so that the sergeant could take part in the interview. Claude Ryle was a burly man in his fifties with weathered features and missing front teeth. He'd come into the city with his wife the previous day to sell their produce in the market. Ryle was slow of speech but had a kind of earthy honesty about him. When he shook his hand, Leeming noticed the dirt under the man's fingernails. They were in the inspector's office. Instead of being able to take the lead in the interview, Jellings had to defer to someone who held a lower rank than him. It was galling.

After finding out something of the witness's background and getting some idea of his reliability, Leeming took out his notebook and encouraged him to tell his tale. Ryle cleared his throat as if about to spit then looked from one man to the other before beginning.

'Well,' he said, 'I thought nothin' of it at the time. I mean, it does 'appen a lot. When you drives a cart like I do, you'll always get riders gallopin' past. This one was goin' faster than most. Then this mornin' I spoke to Archie Broadmead, a farmer I knows. I'm not a readin' man, you see, but Archie is and 'e told me about the notice in the paper.'

'That's right,' said Jellings. 'I was responsible for putting it there.'

'So 'ere I am.'

'And we're very grateful that you came,' said Leeming. 'Tell us more about the horseman who rode past you.'

'Well, sir,' resumed Ryle, ''e was goin' 'ell for leather as if 'e was in a race. It was only when Archie told me what it said in the paper that I begins to wonder, if you sees what I mean.'

'What time would this be?' asked Leeming.

'Oh, it'd be near eleven o'clock, sir. That's the time my wife and me is usually going 'ome after the market. We'd been there since six o'clock and, luckily, sold all we'd brought. Yes, I'd say eleven or near it'd be a good guess.'

'That would chime in with the time of the murder,' Jellings pointed out. 'Where exactly were you?'

'We'd be a little way outside the city, sir.'

'On which road would that be?'

'Our small'olding's near Acle.'

'Can you describe the man?' asked Leeming.

'Well, 'e's a good rider, I'll say that for 'im.'

'Do you have any idea of his age?'

'All we saw were the man's back, sir.'

'What was he wearing?'

'Dark clothes and a black 'at.'

'What about the horse?'

'It were a bay mare. I remembers that cos it went past so close to my old nag that it frightened 'im. "Why is that man in such an 'urry?" my wife asks me. Then we both forgets all about it cos we 'ad more important things to talk about. I'd never've remembered it if I 'adn't spoke to Archie Broadmead an' learnt about that murder. Was I right to come in?'

'You were, Mr Ryle,' said Leeming, 'and we're very grateful that you did. What you've told us could be extremely helpful.'

'Yes,' added Jellings, more or less hustling the man to the door. 'I endorse what Sergeant Leeming has said. It was so good of you to come.' Opening the door, he let him out. After closing the door, his tone changed. 'You can cross out what you wrote in your notebook.'

'Why is that?' asked Leeming.

'The rider that Ryle saw was definitely not the killer.'

'How can you be so sure of that?'

'Immediately after the murder, several people saw him gallop away and they all agree on one thing. He was riding a black horse. If Ryle saw a man on a bay mare, it was somebody else altogether.'

'I disagree,' said Leeming.

'Horses don't change their colour, Sergeant.'

'In effect, this one might have done just that.'

Jellings was perplexed. 'That doesn't make sense.'

'Put yourself in the killer's place,' advised Leeming. 'After you've committed the murder, you need to get away quickly so, while you're on railway property, you'll ride as fast as you can.'

'That's obvious.'

'Once you're clear, however, you have a choice to make. Do you continue to ride through the city at full pelt and attract the attention of everyone you pass, or do you choose a safer option?'

'You've lost me,' said Jellings, irritably.

'Apart from those in and around the railway station, how many witnesses have come forward to say that they saw a man on a black horse riding as if he had the hounds of hell on his tail?'

Jellings shrugged. 'To be honest, there haven't been any.'

'Doesn't that surprise you?'

'I never really thought about it, to be honest.'

'The killer must have changed his mount,' argued Leeming. 'That's why nobody saw him at full gallop on a black horse. He had a bay mare waiting somewhere and rode it at a moderate pace through the streets so that he wouldn't draw attention to himself. The moment he was out of the city – and that's where Ryle was, remember – he kicked the horse into action and off they sped. So you see, Inspector,' he went on, 'I don't need to cross out anything in my notebook. Thanks to Ryle, we know which direction the killer took.'

Jellings was impressed. 'You could be right,' he said.

'I believe that I am.'

'What should we do next?'

'Your men need to start asking questions along the road to Acle and beyond it. Other people will have noticed a horse racing past at that speed. If we talk to enough of them, we might discover which way he went and even work out his likely destination.' Leeming smiled. 'It's worth a try, isn't it?'

'Yes . . . I believe it is.'

Jellings looked at him with reluctant admiration.

When he entered the office, Hinton did so with a degree of trepidation, not knowing if he'd be the victim of another outburst of anger or find that the superintendent had drifted off into a reverie once more. As it was, neither possibility materialised. Tallis was civil rather than pleasant as he took the sheet of paper from his visitor.

'Thank you, Hinton,' he said. 'I'll get the information sent off to Colbeck immediately.'

'The inspector will find it interesting.'

'Then your time in the record office was not wasted.'

'It was eye-opening, sir. I hadn't realised how many policemen were dismissed on a regular basis.'

'If they don't reach the necessary standards,' said Tallis, 'out they must go. Colonel Rowan, one of the two original commissioners, insisted that the Metropolitan Police Force had a military structure and ethos. Men were arranged in companies at first, rather than the divisions we now have. Far too many officers fell by the wayside because of drunkenness. Those who came from civilian occupations found it hard to adapt to the more rigorous routine of a policeman's life.'

'I know, sir. I had great trouble at first.'

'Well, you seem to have adapted very well, Hinton. In some ways, you're an example to others.' He looked down at the details on the paper. 'Thank you again for providing this. Off you go.'

Hinton got out quickly before the superintendent's mood changed. Emerging into the corridor unscathed, he wondered how Colbeck would react to the information he'd just provided from the record office and whether or not it would have a bearing on the case.

Coaxing the full story out of Grace Swarbrick took time and forbearance. Colbeck said nothing, leaving any comments to Anthea Freed, who, as a friend of the other woman, was better placed to comfort, probe and urge her on. It took almost half an hour to describe an event that took less than a minute. Grace seemed hugely relieved when it was over.

'Thank you, Mrs Swarbrick,' said Colbeck.

'Don't rely too much on what I've told you, Inspector. My memory is still very hazy.'

'I believe that you gave me the salient facts.'

'The truth is that I've tried to block it out of my mind.'

'That's what any woman in your position would do,' said Anthea. 'It's a natural response. Don't you agree, Inspector?'

'Yes, I do,' said Colbeck. 'Some people find that the only way they can cope with disagreeable memories is to suppress them completely. It's as if the brain has its own safety mechanism, filtering out things that threaten to cause intense pain. Inevitably, however,' he continued, 'there are people or situations that set off that pain again. My fear is that one such trigger is pacing the carpet downstairs.'

'You're referring to my stepson,' said Grace with concern. 'The idea of seeing him when I'm in this condition is unsettling. Andrew has a right to be here, of course. I concede that.'

'But he doesn't have the right to upset you,' said Anthea, 'and I'm sure that he'd do that. Consideration of other people's feelings was never a strongpoint with Andrew.'

'Does he have a family of his own?' asked Colbeck.

'Oh, yes – a wife and two children. They live in London. Poor, dear Caroline is a timid little creature who should never have married someone as selfish and overpowering as Andrew.'

'Caroline is a lovely woman,' said Grace, 'Unfortunately, she's completely in her husband's shadow.'

'A wife should have some standing in a marriage.'

Anthea's abrupt declaration made Colbeck smile inwardly. In her marriage, he'd observed, she had certainly asserted herself. Few men would have chosen such a forceful bride, yet Cecil Freed had done so. What need it had satisfied in his life was anybody's guess.

'Thank you for being so understanding, Inspector,' said Grace.

'It's I who owe you gratitude, Mrs Swarbrick. In helping me the way you have done, you've shown true courage.'

'To tell you the truth, the effort has rather exhausted me.'

'Then I'll get out of your way,' he said, slipping his notebook back into his pocket. 'I won't need to trouble you again.'

'I'll step outside with you,' volunteered Anthea, opening the door. 'I'd value a moment of your time.'

'Have as much of it as you wish, Mrs Freed.'

They went out to the landing and closed the door behind them.

Anthea stretched up to her full height so that she looked into his face.

'There's only one thing that will put Grace's demons to flight.'

'I know.'

'You must catch that vile killer, Inspector.'

'We'll endeavour to do so.'

'Are you confident of success?'

'It never pays to be too confident, Mrs Freed,' he told her. 'What I will say is this, however. On the basis of what we've so far discovered, I see no reason why all the parties involved in this heinous crime will not be caught and punished accordingly.'

'Is that your professional opinion?'

'No – it's my promise.'


Horace Pryor was watching a passenger train pull out of the station when Victor Leeming came up behind him.

'Where's that heading?' he asked.

'It's the 12.15 to Great Yarmouth.'

'Then it's late.'

'That's nothing unusual, Sergeant,' said Pryor.

'You told me that you hold the entire timetable in your head.'

'I do. It's part of my job.'

'When is the next train due that will take the branch line?'

'Oh, it's not for an hour or more.'

'Then I want you to take me to the spot where Mr Swarbrick was killed and on down the line.'

Pryor's mouth was agog. 'Why?'

'As far as possible, I want to follow the route that the killer took. If he galloped off in that direction, when did he leave railway property and go into the city itself?'

'I've been wondering that myself.'

'Then let's find out together, shall we?'

When they were down on the track, Sergeant Duff suddenly turned up and asked where they were going. Leeming told him.

'Do you want *me* to come with you?' asked Duff.

'I prefer Constable Pryor's company,' said Leeming, blithely.

And they left Duff fuming in silence on the platform.

In addition to enjoying private wealth, Cecil Freed had a substantial salary as managing director of an engineering firm. He was in his office when his secretary brought in the news of his visitor. Though far from pleased, he decided, after consideration, to meet the man. Oliver Trant was soon shown into the room. There was a purposeful air about him. Offering him a limp handshake, Freed was unwelcoming.

'What's brought you here, Oliver?' he asked.

'Well, I didn't come to sell you a pair of shoes, you'll be relieved to know. As a matter of fact, I came to lodge a complaint.'

'Against whom, may I ask?'

'It's against you, Cecil.'

'Why? What am I supposed to have done wrong?'

'There are quite a few things you've done wrong, as it happens, but it would take too long to enumerate them. More specifically,' said Trant, tone hardening, 'I'm here to ask why you set that confounded detective on to me.'

'Inspector Colbeck is the man retained to solve the murder.'

'I gathered that. Why did he waste time coming to me? Did you tell him that, as well as manufacturing boots and shoes of superior quality, I was a trained assassin?'

'Don't be absurd!'

'Are *you* on his list of suspects?'

'Of course I'm not.'

'Then you've no idea how unnerving it is when he turns up out of the blue and starts to cross-examine you. Frankly, I was insulted. There was no need at all for him to speak to me,' said Trant, vehemently. 'Do you *really* think that I was the man who shot Jarvis Swarbrick dead?'

There was a long pause during which Freed searched for the right words to appease the other man. He pointed to a chair.

'Why don't you sit down, Oliver?'

'I'm not staying.'

'Then let me be honest. I did not set anyone on to you. When the inspector asked me about problems we'd had with the board of directors, your name came up as someone who'd clashed from time to time with Jarvis.'

'We had a candid exchange of views, that's all.'

'I heard the threats you made, Oliver.'

'I simply warned him that the bill would never be passed in its present state until he accepted my emendations.'

'Your language was inflammatory.'

'It was born out of my love for the ECR. And don't forget that

Jarvis had a wounding turn of phrase. I still have the scars. In any argument, he gave as good as he got and because he and I didn't see eye to eye,' Trant went on, 'you told Colbeck that I was behind the murder.'

'I merely said that . . . he should speak to you.'

'The day will come when you're actually forced to tell the truth for once, Cecil. Your tongue will probably burn to a frazzle with the effort.'

'There's no need to be offensive.'

'What's more offensive than being accused of murder?'

'You *weren't* accused.'

'Well, it damn well felt like it.'

'Look,' said Freed with an emollient smile, 'you mustn't take it personally. Colbeck is known for his thoroughness. He wants to speak to *everyone* who has a major link to the ECR, you included.'

'Because of you, I no longer have any link at all.'

'You were voted off the board by a majority decision.'

'Yes, and we all know who engineered that decision, don't we? It isn't just wire netting and associated products that you manufacture here,' said Trant with a gesture that took in the whole works. 'Betrayal and back-stabbing are also available at a price.'

'You're imagining things, Oliver.'

'Am I?'

There was a taut silence as the two of them glared at each other. Trant was throbbing with anger and Freed was wishing he'd never agreed to see the man. He suddenly felt invaded. There'd been a long, fraught history between them. Ironically, it had been Freed who'd invited Trant to join the board, a decision he soon regretted bitterly because the latter immediately set about trying to undermine his position as chairman. In a bid to get rid of him,

Freed strode to the door and opened it wide to indicate he should leave. Trant held his ground.

'Why don't I speak to Inspector Colbeck again?' he asked with a meaningful smile. 'Why don't I tell him what really happened behind the scenes – the things that never got into the minutes? What would happen then, Cecil?'

After simmering, Freed capitulated and closed the door.

'We must talk,' he said.

After his interview with Swarbrick's widow, Colbeck returned to the railway station so that he could take a second look at the scene of the crime. The moment he appeared, he was surrounded by reporters from national and local newspapers. He gave them a lengthy statement and repeated his conviction that the murder would soon be solved. As he was talking, he noticed that Sergeant Duff was lurking nearby and used him as a convenient means of escape.

'I'm still gathering information,' he said, 'and finding my way around Norwich, so I'm not the best person to talk to. Sergeant Duff was standing on this platform when the murder actually occurred and can tell you all you wish to know about the immediate consequences.'

'That's true,' said Duff, stepping forward importantly.

'At this stage, he's better informed than I am.'

The reporters shifted their attention to the railway policeman at once, firing questions at him from all angles. Duff was in his element, given a fleeting celebrity at last and blossoming at the thought of seeing his name in the newspapers. Colbeck, meanwhile, slipped away to the stationmaster's office for safety. He found Grigson seated at his desk.

'Ah,' said the other, rising to his feet and picking something up, 'you've come at just the right time, Inspector.'

'I'm in flight from the gentlemen of the press.'

'This telegraph arrived for you.'

'Thank you,' said Colbeck, taking the envelope from him.

'I'll leave you to read it in private. If the reporters ask where you are,' said Grigson with a chuckle, 'I'll tell them you went off to the police station.'

'I'm most grateful.'

The stationmaster left the office and Colbeck was able to read the telegraph sent by Tallis. The news did not surprise him.

# CHAPTER TEN

Since her husband was frequently away from home, Madeleine
Colbeck accepted that her relationship with him had to be an
epistolary one from time to time. It had its consolations. His
letters were so wonderfully characteristic of him that he seemed
to be there in person. Written in a neat hand and couched
in cultured prose, they deserved to be read again and again.
Colbeck always told her enough about an individual case to
give her some idea of the problems he and Leeming were facing,
but he also spent time telling her how much he missed her and
their lovely daughter. Madeleine had kept every single piece of
correspondence from him – even if it was merely a short note
– to remind her of the way that they'd met, become friends and

drifted gently into a romance that eventually ended in marriage.

Ordinarily, his latest missive would have joined the others but, once she'd written her reply and had it posted, she kept his letter by her so that she could study the passages relating to the murder. While she was profoundly sorry for the victim, she reserved her deepest sympathy for his wife. Grace Swarbrick had been dangerously close to her husband when he was shot dead. She must have been both horrified by what happened to him and in fear for her own life. Imagining herself to be in the same position, Madeleine knew that she'd have fought a losing battle against panic and despair.

She felt so sympathetic towards the woman that she wished she could do something to help. Until their child was born, she'd been able to work in secret on some of Colbeck's investigations, exploiting the fact that women could win the confidence of other women more easily than men. Madeleine found herself disappointed that she couldn't go and comfort Grace Swarbrick, learning things in the process that her husband would never be able to draw out of the woman. It would bring Madeleine that keen sense of satisfaction in being able to assist her husband that had disappeared since the birth of Helen Rose Colbeck. As she read his letter once more, she tried to picture the grieving widow and wondered how she was coping in such an appalling situation.

'Would you like me to go?' asked Anthea Freed.

'No, no, please stay.'

'But you keep dozing off.'

'I don't mean to, Anthea.'

'Did the doctor leave any of those tablets?'

'Forget about them,' said Grace Swarbrick, making the effort to sit up in bed. 'They sent me to sleep but they also gave me nightmares. I'd rather stay awake. It's no good trying to hide from the future. I've got to face it somehow.'

'We'll face it together.'

'Thank you.'

'It's a time when you must rely on your friends.'

'*You're* the only real friend I have.'

Anthea knew that it was, to some extent, true. After almost three years of marriage, Grace had still not been completely accepted in some circles. Her stepson was not the only person who looked askance when his father found himself a new bride before he'd gone through a full period of mourning. It shocked most people and alienated a few altogether. Because of the close alliance between Jarvis Swarbrick and her husband, Anthea had felt duty-bound to welcome, befriend and look after the new wife. Grace had turned out to be charming, dignified and possessed of far more intelligence than most of the women in Anthea's circle. She had another endearing quality. Unlike them, Grace had taken a serious interest in Anthea's charitable activities.

'You've been so kind to people less fortunate than ourselves,' said Anthea, 'that you deserve kindness to be shown towards you now. Not that I'm trying to turn you into one of my good causes,' she added, hastily, 'but you take my point.'

'I'm going to need a lot of support,' said Grace, wearily.

'You'll get it.'

'Andrew will be my main problem.'

'I've done my best to scare him off.'

'It's strange, isn't it? I worked hard to build bridges between Jarvis and his son but all to no avail. Andrew simply refused to countenance me. I managed to win over Caroline but, unfortunately, she has no influence over her husband. Now,' said Grace, 'I've actually got what I wanted in the sense that Andrew is back in the family home again, yet . . . I'm frightened of him.'

'He won't hurt you.'

'Why else is he here? It's certainly not to offer his condolences or to settle his differences with me. He still blames me for marrying his father. As long as he's under this roof, I'll be afraid to venture out of this room.'

Cecil Freed was slumped in his chair, sipping a glass of brandy. After his blistering interview with Oliver Trant, he wished to be left alone. Then his secretary told him who'd called to see him and his resolve melted at once. The one person he could not send away was Andrew Swarbrick. He went out to greet his visitor and bring him into the office.

'I was hoping you'd come, Andrew,' he said, solemnly. 'I don't have the words to say how desperately sorry I am about what happened to your father. It's a tragedy for the whole family and a catastrophe for us.'

'The family will survive somehow. I'm really here to talk about the amalgamation. Is it quite dead?'

'Without someone to pilot it through the House, it could well be.'

'Then we must find a way to resuscitate it.'

'If only we could!' wailed Freed. He flapped his hands in apology. 'Oh, do excuse my poor hospitality. Please sit down. I felt the need of a glass of brandy. Can I offer you one as well?'

'No, thank you. I like to keep a clear head.'

'I'm not allowed to drink at home so I keep a bottle hidden in my desk. If she knew, my wife would tear me to pieces.'

'Your secret is safe with me, Mr Freed.' Both of them sat down. 'I'll come straight to the point. I believe that there is one certain way to rescue the bill, but it depends very much on you.'

'I'm mystified.'

'Father's death will cause a bye-election.'

'I hadn't thought that far ahead.'

'Well, I have. I'd like to put myself forward to become the Conservative candidate and to continue his work in Parliament.'

Freed gasped. 'I didn't realise you had political ambitions.'

'You do now, and I hope I can count on your help.'

'Well . . .'

'You have great influence on the people who'll make the choice.'

'That's true,' said Freed, 'but I can't just wave a magic wand to guarantee your selection. There'll be other hats in the ring.'

'My father's record will surely give me an advantage?'

'Yes, but only up to a point. You'll be competing with people who've dedicated themselves to this constituency for years and who feel that they deserve a reward for their service.'

Swarbrick frowned. 'Are you saying that you wouldn't support me?'

'Not at all – I just need to adjust my brain to the idea. To be candid, you've caught me off balance.'

'I need hardly remind you of the relationship between my bank and the ECR. Over the years, we've provided vital finance for the company as well as expert advice.'

'Nobody denies that, Andrew.'

'Then why are you hesitating?'

'I can see that it could be a popular decision in some quarters,' said Freed. 'Your father had a loyal following. He increased his majority at every election. There isn't the slightest doubt that we will have another Conservative Member of Parliament.'

'And his name will be Andrew Swarbrick.'

'It could be . . .'

'I was expecting more enthusiasm from you, Mr Freed.'

'The more I think about it,' said Freed, trying to hide his misgivings, 'the more it grows on me. You wouldn't be the first person to inherit a seat from his father and I'm sure you have his ability to marshal an argument and speak well in public. Yes,' he went on, injecting a little passion into his voice, 'I'd certainly put my weight behind you, Andrew.'

The Ribs of Beef was a pub near the centre of the city. Built in the previous century, it stood beside the river and was renowned for the quality of its beer, the taste of its food and the warmth of its atmosphere. When they met there as arranged that afternoon, Colbeck and Leeming were able to find a table in a quiet corner where they could enjoy a light meal and discuss the case without interruption. Having wet his whistle, the sergeant first explained how Claude Ryle had seen a horse and rider fleeing the city at speed not long after the murder. Colbeck was impressed by his argument that the killer must have changed horses somewhere after leaving the railway.

'That must be the explanation,' he said.

'I think we found the exact spot,' said Leeming. 'I walked along the track with Pryor, following the hoof prints. They ended near a gap in a fence. I suspect that that's when he slowed down and slipped quietly into the streets before making his way to the place where he'd stabled the bay mare seen haring along the road to Acle.'

'Well done, Victor. You've done well and your advice to Inspector Jellings was sound. By dint of enquiries along that road, he may be able to find out where the man was heading.'

'What about you, sir?' asked Leeming, downing the last of his pint. 'How did you get on with Mrs Swarbrick?'

'She's still very confused.'

'Who can blame her?'

'I had to chisel the words slowly out of her. Recounting what happened when the robber appeared reduced her to tears. She was incoherent for minutes.'

'What about her stepson?'

'She doesn't feel strong enough to see him,' said Colbeck, 'and fears that he'll blame her, somehow.'

'That's ridiculous. Mrs Swarbrick might have been killed herself.'

'The stepson can only see things from his point of view, Victor. He seems to think that she brought bad luck into the family. One interesting fact emerged. It transpires that his stepmother was born and brought up in Jersey. She and her first husband were living in St Helier when he died of consumption. They had no children.'

'How did she meet her second husband?'

'She came to stay with a friend in London,' said Colbeck, 'and was introduced to Swarbrick at a social gathering. The fact that they'd both recently lost their spouses gave them something in common. I'd like to have learnt more about their early relationship, but my questions had already caused her enough distress. She's very vulnerable.'

'No wonder she wants to keep clear of her stepson.'

'Fortunately, Mrs Freed stands between them like a fence.'

'She was standing between me and my drinking habits until I found out about this place. What do you think she'd say if she caught us here?'

'We'll have to make sure that she doesn't.'

'She'd stand over us and make us sign the pledge.'

'The only pledge I'm making is that we'll find the killer.'

'What's our next move, sir?'

'I think we need to examine the other railway companies who'll be involved in the projected merger.'

'How many of them are there, sir?'

'Four,' replied Colbeck. 'The Norfolk, the Eastern Union, the East Anglian and East Suffolk Railway Companies have been squabbling with each other – and with the ECR – for years. Some of them run lines over identical routes. In practical terms, amalgamation is essential.'

'Then why hasn't it happened before?'

'That's what we need to find out. We'll take two each, Victor.'

'Which ones do I look into?'

'I'll handle the Norfolk and the Eastern Union, leaving the others to you.' He took a slip of paper from his pocket and passed it to Leeming. 'These are the people you need to question. Find out what their reaction is to the murder of Jarvis Swarbrick.'

'Do we meet up here again?'

'No, we've been invited to dine with Mr and Mrs Freed.'

'But there'll be no alcohol at the table,' protested Leeming.

'Denial is good for the soul.'

'It will be like slow torture to me. I thought that Freed said he'd leave us entirely alone.'

'He's the chairman of the ECR,' Colbeck reminded him. 'In short, 'he's a mine of information about his and the other railway companies. Talking to him in a relaxed atmosphere could yield information we may not get elsewhere.'

'*You* dine with them, sir. I prefer to sneak off and eat here.'

'We have to present a united front, Victor.'

'Is that an order?'

'It's a request that you can't ignore.' Leeming groaned. 'I'm sorry to be the bearer of bad news,' Colbeck went on. 'By way of extenuation, I'll tell you something that will lift your spirits.'

'Only a decision to take rooms here at the pub will do that.'

'I had a telegraph from the superintendent earlier.'

Leeming shuddered. 'Don't tell me he's coming to join us.'

'He was replying to my enquiry about Sergeant Duff.'

'Do you know why he left the Metropolitan Police?'

'I do, indeed,' said Colbeck, taking the telegraph from his pocket and reading from it. 'Bartram Walter Duff was dismissed for being drunk in a public house with a female when on duty at one o'clock in the morning.' He handed the paper to Leeming. 'What do you think about that?'


Cecil Freed was put under what amounted to a constant bombardment of demands from his visitor. It was clear that Andrew Swarbrick had set his heart on succeeding his father in the constituency. Freed had to raise both hands to stop the torrent of words.

'That's enough, Andrew!' he said.

'I just want you to understand my position.'

'You've made it abundantly clear.'

'It will be an honour to represent this city in Parliament and I'll do so with the same vigour and commitment shown by my father.'

'Stop!' yelled Freed, slapping his desk for emphasis.

Swarbrick fell silent at last. Annoyed by the interruption, he crossed his legs and folded his arms. Freed quivered under his sullen glare.

'Let me remind you of something,' he said, reasonably.

'What is it?'

'When your father remarried in what most people considered to be almost indecent haste, you were outraged. You felt that he should have mourned your mother properly first.'

'I did. I still do.'

'Well, aren't we in the same situation now? Within a day of your father's murder, you come here and start making demands regarding the bye-election.'

'I just wanted you to know where I stand.'

'Couldn't you at least have waited until after the funeral?' asked Freed. 'Your behaviour is, at best, inconsiderate; at worst, it's downright offensive. Is this the way to mourn the man who was your father?'

'No,' said Andrew, looking slightly shamefaced, 'it isn't and you're right to take me to task. I should have waited.'

'You should, indeed.'

'It's just that I have this urge inside me.'

'Try to control it, Andrew.'

'I will but it's going to damage my hopes.'

'I don't understand.'

'While I'm tied up with the funeral arrangements and providing information for reporters wishing to write an obituary of my father, the others will steal a march on me.'

'What others?'

'I'm referring to rivals for the right to stand in the bye-election,' said Andrew, petulantly. 'They'll be at it already, I daresay, building support, applying pressure, calling in favours. Father told me that when he first went in search of the nomination, one rival was shamelessly offering bribes.'

'It will be a small field,' promised Freed, 'and no bribery will be allowed. A shortlist will be drawn up. You need to be one of the three potential candidates to be grilled in turn by the members.'

'If I'm given the chance, I can beat *anybody*.'

'Confidence is a key factor and you clearly have that.'

'I also have a detailed knowledge of the proposed merger. I had to convince my colleagues at the bank that it deserved our utmost support. Who else could possibly compete with me?'

'There is someone, alas.'

'And who is that?'

'It's a man who called on me earlier. Like you, he was quick to see that a vacancy had occurred in Parliament. He hinted that he'd be doing all he could to fill that vacancy.'

'What's his name?'

'Oliver Trant!'

'Damn the fellow!' exclaimed Andrew.

'I had a feeling you'd react like that,' said Freed with a smile. 'Be warned, Andrew. This is not going to be easy. Trant will fight with all the weapons he can lay his hands on. Being the heir-apparent may not be enough to secure nomination for you.'


Horace Pryor was increasingly jumpy. Having been told by Leeming that he might lose his job, he worked harder than ever, hoping that he was seen doing so by Duff and by the stationmaster, two men with power over him. Dismissal would leave him in a very difficult position. Pryor was clambering up on to the platform when Duff pounced on him.

'Where did you go?' he demanded.

'I was just doing what I normally do, Bart.'

'That's not true. You went off with Sergeant Leeming.'

'Oh, yes,' said Pryor, 'I wasn't counting that.'

'Where did he take you?'

'We followed the hoof prints of the killer's horse.'

'How do you know that's what they were?'

'It was obvious. We started at the spot on the branch line where Mr Swarbrick was shot. You could see the marks where the horse had skidded to a halt beside the train. All we had to do was follow the prints he left when he galloped off.'

'And then what?'

'We think we found the place where the killer had left railway property and sneaked off to change his horse.'

'Why should he change his horse?' asked Duff, sternly.

'It's what the sergeant worked out he must have done.'

Pryor went on to explain that Leeming had made deductions on the basis of what a witness had told him at the police station. Duff listened intently, jaw tight and cheek muscles oscillating. When his recitation came to an end, Pryor struck a note of supplication.

'Bart . . .'

'What do you want?'

'Is it true that I might lose my job?'

'Yes, it is,' said the other, 'but there's one certain way to keep it.'

'Tell me what it is and I'll do it.'

'Report to me every single word that Inspector Colbeck and Sergeant Leeming say to you. Do you understand? I need to know exactly what they're thinking.'

'Why don't you ask them yourself?'

'They're more interested in you than in me,' said Duff. 'At least, the sergeant is. He's already told you things that never reached my ears. Whenever he's here at the station, stay close and pick up what you can. Do you think you can manage that?'

'It's a promise.'

'I want results. Get them for me.'

Caleb Andrews called at the house that afternoon and had the supreme pleasure of playing with his granddaughter and trying to teach her new words to add to her tiny vocabulary. Since her infant tongue was still not able to pronounce anything clearly, he settled for some enthusiastic burbles from her. Though he revelled in his role as a grandfather, Madeleine could see that he'd really come to see her. When they were alone together later on, he walked gingerly around the subject before finally plunging in.

'Maddy . . .'

'If you're here to talk about that commission,' she warned, 'I'd rather that we kept off the subject altogether.'

'But you don't know what I was going to say.'

'Whatever it is, Father, I'd prefer not to hear it.'

He was affronted. 'You can't just shut me up like that, Maddy.'

'I'm trying to stave off an argument.'

'There'll *be* no argument.'

Madeleine sighed. 'How many times have I heard that?'

'This time, it's different.'

'The subject is closed,' she declared. 'I've written to Robert and I'm certain that he'll encourage me to meet Mr Fairbank and listen to his proposal. Lydia will be there with me because you'd be unable to keep your prejuduces against the GWR to yourself.'

'I just want to make things right between us, Maddy. So I came up with an idea. You'll be so pleased with it.'

'What was it?' she asked, fear already lapping at her.

'I went to the gallery and spoke to Mr Sinclair.'

'You did *what*?'

'I spoke to the man who appreciates your work so much that he sells it in his gallery. I told him who I was.'

'You had no right to go there behind my back,' she said, angrily. 'Mr Sinclair and I have a business arrangement. It took me a long time to find someone who'd support me like that. What's he going to think of me if you go barging in there without my permission?'

'All I did was to ask a simple question.'

'You should never have been there in the first place.'

'Mr Fairbank is a regular customer of his, so I asked if the man was trustworthy.'

'I don't want to hear another word,' said Madeleine, putting her hands over the ears.

'Mr Sinclair told me that he was, and he's known the man for years. So, you see,' he announced as if he'd just given her an expensive gift, 'you can meet Mr Fairbank without the slightest worry because someone has vouched for him. Doesn't that make you feel better?'

'No, it doesn't,' she said, reining in her temper. 'It's made me feel very angry.'

'Why? I thought I was helping.'

'It's not help, Father, it's *interference*. It's hard enough being both a mother and an artist. I struggle to find a balance between the two. Out of the blue, someone says that he'd like to commission a painting from me and you raise objections immediately.'

'I tried to make amends, Maddy.'

'Well, you didn't. You only made things worse.'

'How?'

'If Mr Fairbank finds out we're checking up on him as if he's some kind of threat, he'll feel insulted. I might have to wave goodbye to that commission.'

'I'll speak to him in person and explain,' he volunteered.

'Oh, no, you've done enough damage as it is.'

'Mr Fairbank is a family man. He'll understand a father's concern.'

'You mustn't go anywhere near him,' she said, stamping her foot in exasperation. 'Being recognised as an artist means a lot to me, Father. I can't have you meddling like this. Instead of helping me, you're more likely to endanger my career. From now on,' she concluded, 'I'll never discuss my work with you again.'

Andrews bowed his head in shame. Her threat was like a knife between the ribs.

# CHAPTER ELEVEN

In quantity and quality, their breakfast was excellent and the maid was attentive. Because of his discomfort at receiving such a treat, Victor Leeming was only able to enjoy the meal when the woman had left. He helped himself to more bacon and began to relax.

'I feel so out of place here,' he admitted. 'I'm just not used to being waited on like this. Last night's dinner in the main house was even worse. I just didn't belong. I was afraid to speak at first.'

'Yes,' said Colbeck, 'I noticed. That's why I brought the name of Jenny Lind into the conversation and let you explain that we'd once escorted her from London to Birmingham where she was due to give a recital at the Town Hall. Mrs Freed was very impressed by that.'

'I had no idea that Jenny Lind had a connection with Norwich or how good she'd been to the city.'

'She's always been an exceptionally generous person, Victor. The Jenny Lind Children's Hospital only exists because of her. But the real advantage of dinner with our hosts,' Colbeck pointed out, 'was that it saved us so much time. We learnt an enormous amount from Mr Freed about the rivals of the ECR. In essence, not one of the four companies looks set to gain anything from the murder, though Mr Freed did mention that the chairman of the Norfolk Railway Company had crossed swords with Jarvis Swarbrick.'

'Yes, sir,' recalled Leeming after swallowing a mouthful of food. 'He also told us that the ECR had leased the Norfolk Railway some years ago. How could that be? I thought they were enemies.'

'It might well have been a case of financial necessity. Leasing arrangements like that happen all the time. What Mr Freed didn't mention was that there was no Parliamentary sanction for this particular one.'

'Do you mean that it was illegal?'

'Technically, it was, and it's not the only example of malpractice on the railway system. You just need someone who knows how to bend the rules and George Hudson – chairman of the ECR at the time – was a master at doing that.'

Colbeck addressed himself to his cup of coffee and they sat there in companionable silence for a couple of minutes. Sitting back contentedly, Leeming eventually spoke.

'That was a breakfast for a king,' he said, rubbing his stomach, 'but I'd still prefer to stay at the Ribs of Beef.'

'Mrs Freed called that pub a den of iniquity.'

'That's why I felt at home there.'

Colbeck laughed. 'It certainly had its attractions,' he said. 'Going back to last night, what do you think was the most valuable thing we learnt?'

'Don't invest your money in railways. They all struggle.'

'Yet back in the 1840s, they seemed like the ideal way to make a fortune. Money came pouring in during the Railway Mania, especially in East Anglia. Then the bubble finally burst.'

'It serves them right.'

'That might be what *you* remember best but I feel we heard something far more important from Mr Freed.'

'What was it, sir?'

'Andrew Swarbrick is hoping to replace his father in Parliament.'

'Is that reason enough to have him killed?'

'In this case, I doubt it.'

'Mr Freed wasn't certain that the son would be selected.'

'That's because Oliver Trant may also seek the nomination. Trant has the advantage of living here and having built up a lot of support while doing so. Swarbrick's son has been unable to do that because he's been in London for years now. It will be a bitter contest between them.'

'They're both still on our list of suspects.'

'And they'll stay there.'

'Do you think that Mr Trant has blood on his hands?'

'If we watch him close enough,' said Colbeck, 'we'll find out. The first thing I noticed about Oliver Trant was that he's very ambitious. He's the kind of man who'd go to any lengths to get what he wants.'

'*Any* lengths?' echoed Leeming.

'That was my impression,' said Colbeck.

He looked up as he heard someone unlocking the door of the

cottage. When the maid appeared, Leeming sat bolt upright as if on his best behaviour. She handed a letter to Colbeck.

'This has just been delivered, sir,' she said.

'Thank you,' he replied. 'If you've come to clear the table, the sergeant and I will get out of your way. Come on, Victor.'

He led the way into the adjoining room and immediately opened the letter to read it. Leeming watched him smile with pleasure before furrowing his brow.

'Is it bad news, sir?'

'It's good *and* bad,' said Colbeck. 'The good news is very good. My dear wife has been offered a commission from a private buyer for a painting of a locomotive.'

'That's wonderful, sir – what's the bad news?'

'It's a cry for help from Constable Hinton. He asked Madeleine to pass it on to me and I find it very distressing.'

'Why is that?'

'It concerns the superintendent. Apparently, his behaviour has become even more bizarre. To his dismay, Hinton can't get anyone else to believe that there's anything seriously wrong with Tallis.'

'Alan Hinton is an intelligent young man, sir. He wouldn't raise the alarm unless there was a good reason to do so.'

'That's my feeling,' said Colbeck.

'What are you going to do about it?'

'First of all, I'll sit down and reply to my wife's letter. Then I'll write a full report for the superintendent. You can then take the next train to London. I want you to hand over the report so that you can make your own assessment of Tallis. When you've done that . . .'

'I'm to deliver the letter to Mrs Colbeck.'

'That can wait its turn, Victor. While you're at Scotland Yard, try to make contact with Hinton to get the full story. Only when you've done that can you hand my letter over.'

'Do I wait for a reply?'

'No,' said Colbeck, 'you give my wife time to write it first. That means you'll be able to slip home to surprise Estelle and the boys. When you've done that, call at my house to pick up Madeleine's letter then get to Bishopsgate to catch a train back here. Can you remember all that?'

'Every word,' said Leeming, delighted with his orders.

'When I've consulted my copy of Bradshaw, I can tell you which trains to catch.'

'Where will we meet up, sir?' He looked around with dread. 'We're not dining *here* again, are we?'

'No, Victor, you'll find me at the Ribs of Beef with a glass of whisky in my hand. Now, get yourself ready,' urged Colbeck, 'and don't forget to track down Constable Hinton. The superintendent is essential to the operation of the Metropolitan Police. I want to know exactly what's happening to him.'

Alan Hinton was on his way to Scotland Yard that morning when he glanced down a side road and saw something that brought him to a halt. A man was walking uncertainly along the pavement, placing his hand on a wall from time to time to steady himself. It was moments before he recognised Edward Tallis. The superintendent looked old, tired and hesitant. All of his colleagues knew that he habitually walked to work but it was with a confident step and a straight back. Those telltale features were notably absent now. This time he was patently struggling. Hinton went straight to his aid.

'Good morning, sir,' he said.

'I wonder if you could help me, young man?'

'Yes, of course, I can.'

'Tell me how to get to Scotland Yard.'

'It's only three blocks away, sir.'

'I knew it was close. This road seems familiar.'

'As it happens,' said Hinton, 'I'm going there myself, so I can lead the way. Do you need a hand, sir?'

'No, no, I can manage quite well.'

But it was quite clear that Tallis could not. He lurched along beside Hinton with a supportive hand outstretched in readiness. When they reached the main road, he paused for a rest. Hinton looked into his blank face. Evidently, Tallis had no idea who his guide might be.

'I'm Constable Hinton, sir,' he explained.

'Then why aren't you in uniform?'

'I'm in the Detective Department. We wear plain clothes.'

'Ah, I see.'

'You help to run it, sir.'

Tallis was astonished. 'Do I?'

'That's why you're going to Scotland Yard this morning. It's your place of work, Superintendent.'

'Now that's a title I *do* remember somehow.'

'It's your rank, sir. You are Superintendent Edward Tallis.'

The older man's brows met to form a chevron of doubt. He shook his head dismissively at first, then slowly reconsidered what he'd heard. Tallis took a long, hard look at Hinton then nodded as if he'd recognised him at last. He looked around anxiously.

'I forgot, that's all,' he said with a strained laugh. 'I know perfectly well who I am and why I'm here. You didn't need to remind me, Hinton. My mind was elsewhere for a while. It's concentrated on my job now.'

He thrust out his jaw. 'I'm Superintendent Tallis and I'm a dedicated upholder of law enforcement.'

'That's right, sir,' said Hinton.

'Promise me one thing,' said the other, grabbing him by the wrist. 'Don't say a word about this to *anyone*. Do you hear? I'm fine now. In fact, I've never felt better in my life.'

Sergeant Duff's day began with a series of chores and a long chat with the stationmaster. It was some time before he had the chance to take Horace Pryor aside.

'Where was he going?' he demanded.

'Who?'

'Sergeant Leeming, of course – I saw you talking to him earlier.'

'He was catching a train to London.'

'Why?'

'He told me he was going to Scotland Yard.'

'Does that mean there's been a development?'

'Who knows?'

'You should,' said Duff, giving him a sharp push. 'I told you I wanted every scrap of information you could find out. It's no good asking the inspector but Leeming is not so guarded. You could have winkled *something* out of him.'

'I only spoke to him for a minute, Bart.'

'Work on him. Win his confidence. Get him to talk.'

'I'll try harder next time.'

'How long will he be away?'

'Ah,' said Pryor, glad of the chance to earn some approval at last,

'I can help you there. The sergeant is due back early this evening. I even know which train he'll be on.'

'Meet it.'

'But I'll have gone off duty by then.'

'Meet it,' repeated the other, reinforcing the order with a jab. 'I don't care if it doesn't arrive until midnight. You'll be here to greet him, Horry. And you must squeeze every piece of information out of him as if you're wringing out a wet cloth.'

'Why are you so keen to know what's happening?'

'That's *my* business. Your business is to do as you're told.'

'Yes, Bart.'

'Otherwise . . .'

'You don't need to threaten me again,' said Pryor, wincing. 'I know that my job is at stake. I'll do anything you tell me.'


Knowing that Mrs Freed intended to visit her friend again, Colbeck offered to drive her to the Swarbrick residence in the trap. From his point of view, it was an instructive journey because he learnt a great deal more about the second wife of the murder victim. Mrs Freed provided details that she hadn't mentioned at the dinner table on the previous evening. Once started, she talked at length and all that he had to do was to react politely to what he heard.

'It's a pity you haven't seen Grace at her best,' she said. 'She was a real beauty when she first arrived here. That was part of the reason so many people took against her, of course. They thought her too young for Jarvis and altogether too spirited. Then there was the other thing.'

'What other thing?' Colbeck prompted.

'Grace has French blood. It's highly diluted by now, I daresay, but you can see hints of it in her at times. It was another reason why

136

she was distrusted by everybody at first. People are so prejudiced, Inspector. They have this underlying suspicion of foreigners.'

'It's a mark of our insularity, Mrs Freed.'

'That's what I always say. Living on an island has its advantages but it does limit our horizons. I mean, when all is said and done, Jersey is much closer to France than it is to us. Grace has been able to imbibe a lot of French culture alongside our own. I see that as something to admire, whereas others take it as an additional reason to shy away from her. I once overheard someone say with condescension, "She's a foreigner, you know", as if it were the mark of the Devil.'

'Jenny Lind was much more of a foreigner yet, from what you've told me, the city welcomed her with open arms.'

'That's true, Inspector.'

'Mrs Swarbrick is fortunate to have you at her side.'

'I've tried hard to make up for the deficiencies of others.'

'That's admirable.'

When they reached the house, a servant came out to hold the horse's bridle while they got out of the trap. Waiting for them in the hall was Beth Wymark. She was openly relieved by their arrival.

'Mrs Swarbrick is still in her bedroom,' she told them.

'Has the doctor been?' asked Anthea.

'He left about ten minutes ago, Mrs Freed.'

'What were his instructions?'

'Mrs Swarbrick should remain in bed and have no distractions.'

'That's the first time I've been called a distraction,' said Anthea, amused. 'I'll go on up.' She glanced at Colbeck. 'Thank you for acting as my coachman, Inspector.'

'It was a pleasure, Mrs Freed.' He waved her off, then turned to the housekeeper. 'I've come to see young Mr Swarbrick.'

'He's in his father's study,' said the other. 'Perhaps you'd like to wait in the drawing room while I tell him that you're here.'

'Thank you, Mrs Wymark.'

Colbeck went off to the drawing room, which was aglow as morning sunshine flooded in. The bright light also seemed to animate the portrait of Jarvis Swarbrick that hung over the mantelpiece. Since he was kept waiting for over five minutes, Colbeck had plenty of time to study the painting. The artist had been kind to his sitter, making him slimmer and younger than he'd been in reality. It was, however, possible to read something of his character in his face. Colbeck could discern pride, determination, intelligence and fierce confidence. There was also more than a hint of pomposity. He was still staring up at the portrait when Andrew Swarbrick entered the room.

'It doesn't do my father justice,' he insisted.

'Good morning, sir,' said Colbeck, turning to face him. 'What are the defects in your view?'

'The portrait is too reductive. It's reduced his physical presence and his sense of power. Anyone who stood close to him was very much aware of both aspects. As for the setting, of course,' he went on, 'Father was not actually in the House of Commons lobby at the time. The artist did a sketch of that first, then used it as appropriate background.'

'It defines the sitter immediately. I can't comment on whether or not it's a true reflection of your father, but the artist has clear talent.'

'Do you know anything about painting?' asked the other, loftily.

'Yes, I do. My wife is a portrait artist, as it happens.'

Colbeck didn't tell him that Madeleine's work consisted largely of studies of locomotives. As was his intention, he'd

138

silenced the man for a few seconds and that pleased him. He indicated the portrait.

'I understand that you'd like to become a habitué of that lobby.'

'Cecil Freed will have told you that.'

'He feels that you have legitimate aspirations.'

'They're far more than aspirations, Inspector. My ambition is to continue the work that my father started, both with regard to the merger and to the constituency. I'll do my best to establish seamless continuity.'

'That's only possible if you win the nomination, sir.'

'I intend to do so with flying colours.'

'There'll be other contenders.'

'None of them have my credentials. The Swarbrick name opens lots of doors in this part of the country. I have no qualms.'

'Yet I hear that Mr Trant may be one of your rivals.'

'That doesn't worry me.'

'Don't underestimate him.'

'I thought you were here to solve a murder, not to discuss a bye-election.'

'The two are interlinked, sir. I can't ignore that fact.'

'If it's not a rude question, why are you bothering me again?'

'I thought you'd be interested to hear what we've so far uncovered, sir,' said Colbeck, 'and besides, I have a few questions to put to you.'

'This is getting very tedious.'

'If I was in mourning over the murder of *my* father, I wouldn't care how many questions I had to answer. I'd do everything I could to help the police catch the culprit.'

Swarbrick was peevish. 'Oh, very well, ask away if you must.'

'First let me tell you about the progress we've made.'

'What – in so short a period of time?'

'Thanks to the assistance of the local constabulary, we've been able to work out exactly how and where the killer left the city. It may even be possible to identify his eventual destination,' said Colbeck, meeting his gaze. 'We've not been idle.'

'I see.'

Andrew Swarbrick smiled uneasily.

When Mark Jellings got back to the police station, he invited Burridge into his office. Over a cup of tea, they discussed the latest discoveries. Certain that the man on the galloping horse had been the killer, the inspector had sent his men along the road to Acle and beyond in search of anyone who'd caught sight of the bay mare streaking past. Little by little, they'd built up a picture of the route.

'He was heading for the coast,' concluded Jellings.

'That's bad news, sir. He might have escaped by boat.'

'Then we find out where he embarked and pass on the details to Sergeant Leeming. He was adamant that nobody was ever allowed to get away with murder. They'll track him down somehow. He told me that he and the inspector once chased a killer all the way to America.'

'That's what I call dedication,' said Burridge.

'The sergeant is cleverer than he looks,' admitted Jellings. 'I thought that face of his belonged on the wrong side of the law, but I was mistaken. Now I've seen him in action, I'd say he was quite astute.'

'He can't compete with the inspector. The stationmaster reckons that Colbeck has got an amazing brain and Ned Grigson is a good judge.' He sipped his tea noisily. 'Do you think they *will* solve the murder?'

'I hope so, Eric, because one thing is certain. If they don't, nobody else will. I thought that we could handle this case on our own but it's turning out to be far too complicated for us. We don't have the experience or enough men.'

'All our hopes rest with Colbeck and Leeming.'

Victor Leeming tapped on the door and was invited to enter the room with a voice that sounded eerily hospitable. Tallis was seated behind the desk, pulling on a cigar before sending fresh wreaths of smoke up into the air. His visitor had difficulty at first making him out in the fug.

'Who are you?' asked Tallis.

'It's Sergeant Leeming, sir.'

'What, in heaven's name, are you doing here, man? You should be in Norwich with Colbeck.'

'The inspector wanted you to see his latest report, sir, so I brought it in person.' He placed it on the desk. 'It's very detailed. He told me to wait until you'd read it and given your reaction.'

'How reliable is it?'

'The inspector's reports are always strictly factual, sir.'

'But he has a cunning way of juggling the facts to obscure his lack of progress in an investigation. I hope that's not the case here.'

'He'd never think of doing such a thing,' asserted Leeming.

'Let me see.'

Placing his cigar in the ashtray, Tallis picked up the report and held it close to his face. He seemed to be reading it at first then it became clear to Leeming that the superintendent's eyes were trained on the same line. They never moved. Holding five pages in his hand, he only looked at the first one. There was a long, embarrassing pause. Leeming waited until his patience eventually ran out. He leant forward to touch the other man's shoulder with a gentle hand.

'Is anything wrong, sir?' he asked. There was no reply. 'Would you like me to read it to you?'

Tallis looked up. 'Who are you and why are you here?'

'I'm Sergeant Leeming and I've just brought that report.'

'Then stop staring at me as if you've seen a ghost.'

But that was exactly what Leeming was doing, looking sadly at the spectre of Edward Tallis. This was not the irascible man who'd terrorised him throughout his career as a detective. It was nothing but a sad, pale, lifeless substitute. Instead of scouring each line of the report, he couldn't read a single word. It was painful to watch. Uncertain what he should do, Leeming backed slowly away and made for the door. He was about to leave when he was stopped by an urgent plea.

'Don't mention this to anyone, will you?' said Tallis, hoarsely. 'I get a little dizzy now and then, that's all. I'm fully recovered now. You can tell Colbeck that I found his report crisp, concise and informative.'

'I will, sir.'

'Give him my regards.'

'Goodbye, sir.'

Leeming left the office with tears in his eyes.

Andrew Swarbrick was too well prepared. It was as if he'd sat down and made a list of all the questions likely to be put to him and worked out his answers. Colbeck was irritated by his smugness. In the end, he abandoned his line of questioning and became more personal.

'Why did you come here?' he asked.

'I'm the man of the house now.'

'But you turned your back on this place in disgust.'

'I had good cause.'

'That's a matter of opinion, sir. I would have thought that your duty to your father would have made you show more tolerance.'

'I am not tolerating that interloper up there,' snapped the other, pointing to the ceiling. 'She inveigled herself into my father's life and came close to destroying our family.'

'I really can't believe that,' said Colbeck. 'Having met her, I'd never describe her as the wicked stepmother you seem to think she is.'

'That's because you don't know how manipulative she can be.'

'Mrs Freed told me how gentle and undemanding she is.'

'That woman always thinks the best of people but even she was surprised by the speed with which my father remarried.'

'I hear that it was not exactly a lavish wedding.'

'It was a disgraceful affair, Inspector.'

'But I understood that you refused to attend it.'

'I spoke to some of the few people who did,' said Swarbrick, scornfully. 'It was a hurried, uneventful, hole-in-the-corner marriage ceremony because, I believe, my father was secretly ashamed of it.'

'Is that what he told you?'

'Not in so many words.'

'Mrs Freed said that they were extremely happy together.'

'She didn't know my father as well as I did.'

'But she saw him and his second wife together on many occasions,' said Colbeck, 'and so did Mr Freed. He is also very fond of your stepmother.'

'That's because she knows how to deceive men like him.'

'We're talking about two different people here, Mr Swarbrick.

You're telling me about someone who is cold, scheming and evil, whereas the person I've met is weak, defenceless and devastated by the murder of her husband. One of us is misled,' said Colbeck. 'At the very least, I'd have thought you could understand how terrible it must have been for her to be so dangerously close to your father when he was shot.'

'My sympathy is in short supply,' said Andrew, bluntly.

'Why do you detest your stepmother so much?'

'She tricked my father into marriage.'

'Come now,' said Colbeck, glancing up at the portrait. 'Mr Swarbrick doesn't look to me as if he'd allow anyone to trick him into something against his will. Look at him. The artist has confirmed what everyone has told me about Mr Swarbrick. He was strong, single-minded and decisive. Do you deny that, sir?'

'No, he was all of those things – until he met her.'

Colbeck changed tack. 'Mr Freed told me about the visit you made to him yesterday.'

'Why bother about *me*?' said Swarbrick, petulantly. '*I* didn't kill my father. You should be out there hunting for the heartless villain who did.'

'Apparently, he achieved the small miracle of wresting an apology from you. I've spent several years dealing with bereaved families, sir, and I've never met anyone less inclined to grieve over a murder victim.'

'I'm far too angry to grieve, Inspector.'

'When will that anger finally disappear?'

'It will only happen when I've attained my twin objectives.'

'And what are they, sir?'

'The first is to harry you into solving this crime so that my father's death can be avenged on the scaffold.'

'What about the second objective?'

'It will be equally satisfying, Inspector,' said Swarbrick with a malevolent grin. 'I'm going to throw my stepmother out of our house and family for good.'

# CHAPTER TWELVE

Detective Constable Alan Hinton was difficult to find at first. Leeming had to pick his way through a series of corridors at Scotland Yard before he ran him to earth. The two men adjourned to Colbeck's office, confident that they wouldn't be interrupted. Hinton was touched that his plea for help had produced such an immediate effect.

'I never expected you to come in person,' he said.

'It was either me or the inspector and he's needed in Norwich to lead the investigation.'

'Have you made any headway?'

'We're inching forward,' said Leeming. 'It's always slow going in the early stages. I brought a report for the superintendent so that I had an excuse to see for myself what state he was in.'

'How did you find him?'

'It was very upsetting.'

Leeming told him about his brief visit to Tallis and admitted that he'd been moved to tears by the experience. In return, Hinton recalled what had happened earlier when he met the superintendent on his way to Scotland Yard.

'He didn't even know who he was, Sergeant.'

'I don't know who *I* am sometimes,' said Leeming with a grin, 'but that's usually because I've had too much to drink. That's one thing we can't accuse the superintendent of,' he added, 'because he's always stone-cold sober when he's here.'

'What are we going to do?'

'I wish I knew.'

'There's nobody else I can confide in here. People are either too busy to pay any attention or, if they do listen, they tell me to forget all about it. They say that the superintendent will soon snap out of it.'

'I don't believe that,' said Leeming, gloomily.

'What was Inspector Colbeck's view?'

'He thinks that the superintendent needs a complete break.'

'We'd never get him to leave Scotland Yard.'

'If he can't do his job properly, he'll have to leave it.'

'What are we supposed to do?'

'Well,' said Leeming, 'if it gets any worse, it will have to be brought to the attention of the commissioner. In the meantime, the inspector has a suggestion.'

'What is it?'

'Tallis must be persuaded to take a holiday.'

'But where could he go?' asked Hinton. 'He doesn't have a family and there's nobody here who'd take him in. The superintendent has made a virtue of living alone.'

'I know. It's very sad.'

'Scotland Yard means everything to him. That's why he's devoted his life to it. He spends more time here than anywhere else.'

'It was pathetic,' recalled Leeming. 'When he realised that he'd given himself away in front of me, he begged me not to tell anyone.'

'He did the same to me. The truth is that he needs medical help.'

'If his mind is crumbling, we know what that means. He'd have to go into a mental hospital and I wouldn't wish that on anybody. We saw inside one of those places during an investigation in Devon.' He pursed his lips. 'It was grim.'

'What's the alternative?' asked Hinton.

'Inspector Colbeck may have the answer. Do you remember that friend of the superintendent's?'

'Captain Wardlow?'

'Yes, that's him. They were in the same regiment. The captain is the one person that he actually seems to like. What happened during the abduction in Kent brought them closer together. If the captain knew the state that his friend is in, I'm sure he'd come to his aid.'

'That's an excellent idea,' declared Hinton, smiling for the first time that morning. 'As soon as I come off duty, I'll take the next train to Canterbury.'

'Captain Wardlow will know what to do,' said Leeming, 'and he has a big advantage over you and me. The superintendent would actually *listen* to him.'

Seated in his office, Cecil Freed felt beleaguered. Since Colbeck was proving elusive, reporters turned their attention to the chairman of the ECR, popping up when least expected and demanding a statement about the investigation. The company had an unhappy relationship with the press because it had reported its multiple imperfections over the years, mocking its failures with glee. When one of the ECR's goods trains left the line and scattered vast quantities of coal over the countryside, Freed had even endured the misery of being caricatured in *Punch*, a magazine that allowed its readers to shake with laughter at the company's expense. While his distrust of reporters was absolute, the chairman still felt obliged to feed them with some information. Otherwise, he claimed, they would make it up.

Hearing his secretary enter, he feared that yet another newspaper was trying to corner him. In fact, his visitor turned out to be Colbeck. The overwhelming sense of relief made Freed leap up from his seat and pump the inspector's hand in gratitude.

'Thank goodness it's only you,' he said.

'I'm not sure that I'm flattered by the use of the word "only", Mr Freed,' teased the newcomer. 'It robs me of what little importance I actually have.'

'In my view, you're the most important person in East Anglia.'

'Let's not resort to hyperbole, sir.'

'I mean it, Inspector. I'm relying on you to solve the murder and take the ECR off the front pages of every newspaper.'

'You can satisfy the second desire on your own account. When you and the other companies merge to form the Great Eastern Railway, the ECR will vanish instantly. It will simply become a footnote in history.'

'Take a seat, Inspector. May I offer you refreshment?'

'No, thank you,' said Colbeck, sitting down.

'Is there any news to report?'

'I've just had a long chat with Andrew Swarbrick.'

'In that case, *he'll* have done most of the talking.'

'Quite right – was his father quite so assertive?'

'Jarvis liked to hear the sound of his own voice but, since I agreed with almost everything he said, it was a very sweet sound.'

'The son's voice is singularly lacking in sweetness,' said Colbeck. 'In fact, sweetness of any kind is an alien concept to him. He puzzles me. On the face of it, he's exactly what I'd expect of a banker, but there's a streak of fury in him that would never be tolerated at a board meeting.'

'Andrew keeps it well concealed at work.'

'He can't control it here. As soon as he's close to his stepmother, the bile starts to gush from him. Why should that be, Mr Freed? You and your wife assured me that Mrs Swarbrick is a charming lady in every way, yet her stepson abhors her.'

'Snobbery comes into it, I fear. He looks down on her. Andrew believes her family is too inferior to be linked to his own.'

'You must have met members of it at the wedding?'

'We met the few who were invited. I've never known such a deliberately muted occasion. Jarvis didn't want any fuss.'

'That seems at variance with his character.'

'It was,' said Freed. 'As a rule, he relished major events if he was to be at the centre of them. Hundreds of guests attended his first wedding. We were among them. At the second one, there was far less sense of occasion.'

'Was that Mr Swarbrick's decision?'

'Oh, yes. There's no question about that, Inspector.'

'What happened when his son stayed away in protest?'

'There was bad blood between Andrew and his father for a while.'

'It still exists between him and his stepmother. You'd expect the murder to bring them closer together, strengthening the bond.'

'It's driven them further apart than ever,' said Freed. 'That's why my wife feels that she needs to be there on sentry duty. How long she has to do that is anybody's guess. However,' he continued, 'that's not your concern. All your energies are directed at the investigation.'

'That's true, sir. My next port of call will be the station. I have to speak to Mr Grigson, the stationmaster. He's providing me with a list of staff and anyone else familiar with the operation of the station. We've been through the names of those currently employed there but I'd like to know more about those who left the ECR in the recent past. This crime was made possible by the switching of some points,' said Colbeck. 'The person responsible either works there or has done so.'

'Grigson is very thorough.'

'I've already found that out.'

'Have you had much help from the railway police?'

'Yes, sir – Sergeant Duff is cracking the whip over them.'

The London train was due very shortly and the platform was crowded. Bartram Duff bided his time until he saw the figure of a short, lean, middle-aged man join the other passengers. Taking something from his pocket, Duff stepped forward to mingle with the crowd. When the newcomer brushed past him, Duff slipped something into his hand. It happened so quickly and deftly that nobody saw a thing. While the railway policeman went back on duty, the man headed back to the exit and disappeared from the station altogether.

* * *

Lydia Quayle arrived at the house to find Madeleine in high spirits. Her friend had not only received an unexpected letter from her husband, she had encouragement from him to accept the commission she was offered. Lydia was pleased for her.

'How could he reply so quickly to your letter when he could only have seen it this morning?'

'Victor Leeming delivered it by hand.'

Lydia was surprised. 'He's back in London?'

'Indirectly,' said Madeleine, 'that was Constable Hinton's doing. His worries about the superintendent prompted Robert to act. He sent the sergeant to Scotland Yard with a report and orders that he should seek out Constable Hinton as a matter of urgency. The two of them discussed the superintendent's condition.'

'What did they decide?'

Madeleine told her what she herself had been told. While she felt sorry for the superintendent, Lydia was more interested in what Hinton had said and done. She pressed her friend for every detail. When she heard about the plan to go to Kent, she was very much in favour of it.

'How clever it was of Alan to think of Captain Wardlow.'

'Actually, it was Robert's idea.'

'But he's not here to do anything about it, is he? Constable Hinton is and was quick to volunteer. I admire him for that, Madeleine.'

Her friend smiled. 'Oh, I think you have many other reasons to admire him, Lydia,' she said. 'This is one more to add to the list.'

'I'll be interested to hear how he gets on in Canterbury.'

'If he brings any news, I'll ask him to pass it on to you.'

'I don't want to put him to any trouble.'

'He'll be thrilled to have an excuse to see you again.'

Lydia felt excited at the thought of meeting him again but

did her best not to show it. She asked if Madeleine was going to tell her father about Colbeck's advice and her friend produced an unbecoming grimace.

'Why did you pull a face like that?'

'I'm sorry, Lydia, it was uncalled for. The truth is that I wish I hadn't even mentioned the commission to my father. One way or another, it's caused a lot of trouble.'

'Why – what has he done now?'

'I'm sure he acted with the best of intentions.'

'There's an ominous note in your voice.'

'It's there with good reason,' said Madeleine. 'Without even telling me, he went to the gallery to ask what sort of person Mr Fairbank was. As a regular customer, Mr Fairbank is well known there. When my father told me what he'd done, I was mortified.'

'Mr Fairbank wouldn't be altogether pleased, either.'

'He wouldn't, Lydia. I keep praying that he'll never find out. It's as if we're treating him as a criminal. You saw his letter. There's nothing remotely suspicious about it.'

'Mr Andrews was too impulsive.'

'I share that fault with him at times,' said Madeleine, 'so I can't complain too much. But I was so *angry* when I heard. In future I'm simply not going to discuss my work with him.'

'He'll be very hurt at being excluded.'

'I know – but at least I'll have peace of mind.'

Caleb Andrews walked almost furtively along the street until he came to the Red Gallery, an art shop whose door, window frame and brickwork were painted in an attractive shade of red that made it stand out. The first time he'd ever gone there, he'd been able to put his nose against the window and gloat over his daughter's debut as a professional artist. Her painting of a locomotive steaming along had been displayed on an easel in the window. Prints of her other work had appeared regularly until childbirth had given her an enforced rest from her studio. Now, however, Andrews didn't feel that he was entitled to enjoy the sight of her work. He could no longer stand there and feel proud of Madeleine. She'd deprived him of that pleasure.

He was honest enough to realise that it was his own fault. In telling her to reject the offer of the commission because of Fairbank's likely preference for GWR locomotives, he'd overstepped the mark. When he went to apologise, however, he'd only distressed Madeleine even more. In a bid to win back her approval, he did something he thought would please his daughter, but it had only enraged her. Andrews could still hear the pain in her voice. She'd been deeply wounded by what he'd done. As a result, he'd been banished from an important part of her life and made to feel like an outcast. It was dispiriting.

When he glanced across the street again, he saw the owner in the window, rearranging some of the items on display. Sinclair looked up and recognised him. Overcome with embarrassment, Andrews pulled down his hat and scuttled away from what was now forbidden territory.

True to his promise, Ned Grigson had found all the information requested by Colbeck. As they sat side by side in the stationmaster's office, he worked his way down the list, providing details of each person. Colbeck's eye alighted on a familiar name.

'I didn't know that Sergeant Burridge once worked here.'

'Oh, yes,' said Grigson. 'Eric was a railway policeman in his younger days and a very competent one.'

'Why did he leave?'

'The Constabulary paid him a better wage and offered the promise of a promotion.'

'So, he'd know this station well.'

'He'd know it as intimately as I do, Inspector.'

As they continued to go through the names one by one, Colbeck was struck by how many employees had come and gone in such a relatively short time. Some had been dismissed for drunkenness or unpunctuality, but others had simply resigned.

'Can't the ECR hold on to its staff?' asked Colbeck.

'Long hours and low pay are not the best way to create loyalty, sir.'

'That's true of any place of employment, not least the Metropolitan Police Force. Those in uniform in London contend with the additional problem of continual danger. Policemen, alas, make tempting targets.' He spotted another name. 'Bernard Pryor – is he any relation to Horace Pryor?'

'Bernard's his cousin, sir.'

'He was dismissed for fighting, I see.'

'He was only here for three weeks. The wonder is that he lasted that long,' said Grigson. 'Horace has given us no real trouble but his cousin was a menace. He picked a fight with one of the clerks. I had to pull him off by the scruff of his neck.'

'Is he still in the city?'

Grigson chuckled. 'He's not in a position to leave it.'

'Why is that?'

'Bernard Pryor is serving a sentence in Norwich Prison.'

'Then I think we can safely eliminate him from our enquiries,' said Colbeck with a smile. 'Is there anyone else on this list who dabbled in criminal activities?'

'As it happens, there are one or two people . . .'

As the stationmaster picked out the names, Colbeck jotted them down in his notebook and resolved to check up on the individuals concerned when he was next in the police station. The chat with Grigson was productive, even if the stationmaster had to pop out from time to time to despatch another train. When they'd been through the list, Colbeck thanked him for his assistance.

'Before you go, Inspector,' said the other, 'could I make an observation?'

'Please do, Mr Grigson.'

'Well, you may already have worked this out for yourself but, in case you haven't, I believe that it wasn't the first time it happened.'

Colbeck was nonplussed. 'I beg your pardon.'

'I was on the platform when it occurred. It was some distance away, but I saw it all. The rider galloped alongside the train, reined in his horse then flung open the door of the compartment he wanted.'

'Go on.'

'It happened quickly but also precisely. In other words,' said Grigson, 'I don't think it was the first time the killer had done that. He'd have practised beforehand.'

'That's an interesting idea,' said Colbeck, 'and it had never entered my head. I'm grateful to you, Mr Grigson. If the killer wanted to make sure there were no mistakes, he'd have rehearsed the crime a number of times, probably.'

'But he wouldn't have done it on that particular section of the branch line because it was always in view, even at night. He'd have found somewhere more private.'

'And he'd have needed railway carriages to practise on. Are there any sidings where old rolling stock has been shunted?'

'There are a number of them, Inspector. I took the liberty of drawing up a list.' He took a sheet of paper from the drawer. 'Here you are, sir.'

'Thank you,' said Colbeck, taking it from him and looking at it. 'This is extremely useful. I'm ashamed to say that neither Sergeant Leeming nor I even thought about the speed with which the killer arrived. Luckily, you did. That's the value of having an intelligent witness like you, Mr Grigson. You've opened my eyes.'

Elated as he'd been by making a surprise visit home, Victor Leeming knew that he couldn't enjoy the company of his wife and children for long. He had a timetable to follow. After packing some clean shirts and underwear, he hailed a cab and set off for Westminster. Madeleine had the letter for her husband all ready, but she'd also written to Lionel Fairbank to say how pleased she was to accept his invitation. Leeming offered to post the letter for her.

'Lydia Quayle called here earlier,' she said.

'Oh, I'm sorry I missed her.'

'She thought that it was wonderful that you're all showing such compassion towards the superintendent, especially as he's been a hard taskmaster for you all.'

'He's in desperate need of help,' said Leeming. 'We have to forget our old battles with him and provide it.'

'I think that Colonel Wardlow may be the solution. He's an old and trusted army friend. He talks the same language as the superintendent.'

'That's true.'

'Well, I won't hold you up. I know you have to catch a train.'

'Is there any message for the inspector?'

'It's in my letter but you can tell him that his daughter sends her love. She keeps asking where Daddy is but, then, I suppose that your children ask where *you* are all the time.'

'According to Estelle, they never stop.'

She became serious. 'Is the superintendent really as unwell as you say he is?' she asked, face puckered.

'It's almost as if his mind is starting to crumble.'

'That's a terrible fate for a man of such keen intelligence.'

'I can only hope that he's not beyond recovery.'

'What are the chances of that, Victor?'

'I'm not a doctor.'

'Did you sense that it might be . . . too late?'

'It's in the lap of the gods, Mrs Colbeck. All I can tell you is this. I've despised that man for some of the things he's done to us and, when being yelled at by him, I've even wished him dead. But when I saw the superintendent earlier on,' confessed Leeming, 'I felt as if I was looking at his corpse.'

When he heard that Andrew Swarbrick had come to see him, Oliver Trant asked for him to be admitted immediately. Neither man actually liked the other but Trant was curious to see how Swarbrick had reacted to the murder of his father. Offering his condolences, Trant extended a hand to his visitor but there was no warmth in the handshake. Once they were seated, they exchanged meaningless pleasantries for a few minutes then Trant glanced down at the other's shoes.

'I see that you remain faithful to Trant footwear,' he said. 'Did you call in to buy a new pair?'

'No, I didn't.'

'That's a pity. We have some wonderful new designs.'

'I came because of something Mr Freed said to me.'

'And what was that, I pray?'

'He told me that you had political ambitions.'

'I've always had them and made no secret of the fact.'

'Yes,' said Swarbrick, 'but they were not linked to Norwich before. As long as my father was the sitting tenant, so to speak, your chances of taking over his seat were negligible.'

'I never entirely lost hope.'

'Freed reckoned that you'd been looking further afield.'

'It's true. Whenever I sniffed an ailing Tory MP, I did some research on his constituency. Until a couple of days ago, my best bet seemed to be in Nottinghamshire. One of the two members for Newark is reportedly on his last legs,' he went on, 'and will soon be forced to retire. My spies tell me that they have just over a thousand registered voters there. With my manufacturing background, I'm sure that I'd have a great appeal to them.'

'You'd be up against local candidates.'

'I have a habit of winning most battles I take part in.'

'Then I wish you well in your enterprise.'

'But my focus has shifted dramatically now, Andrew,' warned the other. 'Why go all the way to Nottinghamshire when there's a vacancy on my doorstep?'

'It's a vacancy I intend to fill myself.'

Trant rubbed his hands. 'Then I look forward to the contest.'

'There doesn't have to be one, Trant.'

'Why? Are you prepared to withdraw?'

'No,' said Swarbrick, fixing him with a stare, 'but I suggest that you should. It would spare you a lot of embarrassment.'

'Why should I be embarrassed?'

'You won't secure the nomination. I'll see to that.'

'Do you have enough of the right people behind you?'

'I will have in due course.'

'Then I've stolen a march on you,' said Trant, smirking. 'While you're still touting for support, I already have it because I've attended meetings of the Conservative Association on a regular basis. Also, of course, you've lived in London for years. That will count against you.'

'The Swarbrick name will count against *you*, Trant,' argued the other. 'It's not simply because my father represented this constituency with honour. The manner of his death will have a wide effect on the emotions of electors.'

'It's a shame it didn't have an emotional effect on *you*, Andrew.'

Swarbrick was stung. 'Why do you say that?'

'Look in any mirror. You won't see a man mourning his father.'

'I prefer to keep my feelings hidden.'

'Well, I don't. I wear my heart on my sleeve so that people know what to expect from me. It's another factor in my favour. You have to use your father as a stepping stone,' said Trant, 'because it's the only weapon you have, but everyone remembers that you and he were estranged. The stepping stone will wobble dangerously under your feet.'

Swarbrick was silenced. There was some truth in the taunt. Even when he lived in Norwich, he hadn't been as active in local politics as Trant had been, and there was a nagging fear that Cecil Freed would not give him the unqualified support that he needed. A different approach was required. Though it took a real effort, he conjured up a smile.

'Why on earth are we arguing?' he said, easily. 'There's so much common ground between us that we ought to be friends.'

'Do I sense a peace offering?'

'Let's be realistic. You have a thriving business to run. It would undoubtedly suffer without you at the helm. In pursuing your political ambitions, you'd be causing problems here.'

'Being an MP and running a company are not mutually exclusive. Lots of people do it very successfully. Take your father, for instance. He managed to balance his parliamentary and business interests without the slightest difficulty. However,' he added with a grin, 'I'm touched that you have such concern for the future of Trant Footwear.'

'Let me get to the point. One of us must stand aside.'

'Thank you for volunteering to do so.'

Swarbrick bristled. '*You* are the one who must give way.'

'On what possible grounds must I do that?'

'You'll be deferring to a superior candidate.' Oliver Trant laughed mirthlessly. 'It's true, damn you. That seat was bequeathed to me by my father.'

'What an intriguing notion,' said Trant. 'Are you telling me that there's a clause in his will to the effect that – when he gets shot dead in a first-class compartment – *you* will replace him in Parliament?'

'Don't be so crass.'

'Then don't be so insulting. You came here to frighten me off. When you couldn't do that, you shifted your position. I can smell an offer coming. Let's hear it, Andrew.'

'If you stand aside, I'll make it worth your while.'

Trant was shocked. 'You're surely not daring to offer me money?'

'Of course not,' said Swarbrick. 'What I can guarantee is that you'll be my second in command, as it were. You'll have the chance to influence every word I say in Parliament. That's a firm promise on my part.' Seeing the derisive look on the other's face, he raised his voice. 'And there's something else, Oliver. I'll ensure that you're restored at once to the board of directors so that you have a voice in the merger negotiations. That's my offer. Stand against me and you'll suffer a humiliating defeat. Support me and we'll represent this city together.'

'I'll think it over,' said Trant, masking his contempt behind a smile. 'Thank you for your kind offer and thank you for not bursting into my office to accuse me of being party to your father's murder.'

'Why should I do that?'

'In effect, it's what Inspector Colbeck did. Because of a perceived feud with your father, I was singled out as one of the main suspects.'

'That's a ridiculous idea.'

'I'm glad that somebody else thinks so.'

'If it's any consolation, Colbeck has even been suspicious of me.'

'Well, you do stand to gain from your father's death,' said Trant. 'You'll inherit his estate even if you don't replace him in Parliament.'

Swarbrick glowered. 'Is that your answer to my offer?'

'I saw it more as a last desperate gamble, Andrew. You pretend to discount my chances, but you know only too well that I can defeat you.'

'Balderdash!'

'You sound almost as pompous as your father.'

'Good day to you!' snarled the other, getting to his feet.

'It was generous of you to offer me a seat on the board,' said Trant, 'but Cecil Freed has already done so. When you turn up at the next meeting, you'll see me smiling at you across the table.'

Unable to find a cutting response, Swarbrick left the office abruptly and made his way to the stables. He was soon riding away from the factory with his teeth gritted and his blood racing. Confident that he could win Trant over, he'd been both outsmarted and rebuffed. As he cantered away, he felt the urge to take his anger out on somebody and the ideal person was waiting at the house for him. He resolved that he would not be baulked any further. When he got back, therefore, he handed the horse over to a servant, went in through the main door and charged up the stairs to his stepmother's bedroom. Still pulsing with fury, he flung open the door to confront her, only to find that she was not there.

The housekeeper appeared at his elbow.

'Mrs Swarbrick is not here, sir,' she explained. 'Mrs Freed thought it best to have her as a guest in her own house so that she could look after her properly.'

# CHAPTER THIRTEEN

Back in the police station, Colbeck pored over the map of Norfolk. It was on the desk in Inspector Jellings' office and had a number of pins stuck in it like so many tiny metallic trees.

'What do they designate?' asked Colbeck.

'They show the route that the rider took. At each point where you see a pin, we found a witness who remembered a horseman galloping past on the day in question.'

'I congratulate you, Inspector.'

'Save the praise for Sergeant Leeming. We were acting on his recommendation.'

'I'm glad that his advice was sound.'

'He told me that he tries to pattern himself on you.'

'I don't think the world is ready for *two* Inspector Colbecks,' said the other with a laugh, 'but I take it as a compliment.' He studied the map again. 'What happened in Yarmouth?'

'He disappeared, I fear. That's to say, he must have reached his destination and didn't need to ride quite as fast. He's either got somewhere to hide or . . .'

'He's escaped by boat.'

'Let's hope he's still there, Inspector. I've got some men still searching but they don't really have a proper description of the man. They're chasing a phantom.'

'I can tell you something about him. He's very agile and an expert horseman.'

'How do you know that?'

'I found out where he held his rehearsals.'

Colbeck went on to explain that the stationmaster had suggested that the killer would have needed to practise the murder. Armed with directions from Grigson, the inspector had managed to find a siding into which four carriages had been shunted.

'It *had* to be the place,' he insisted. 'He rode up to the same compartment time and again. You could see where his horse had skidded to a halt over and over again, churning up the earth. He must then have learnt how to bend over in the saddle to open the door. That was no mean feat, believe me.'

'What makes you say that?'

'I put myself to the test,' said Colbeck. 'I mounted the horse that pulled my trap and leant over to the compartment. I almost fell off the first time. It took me several attempts before I actually opened the door.'

'If rehearsals were needed, the murder must have been planned well in advance.'

'Yes, Inspector, and once again it points to assistance from a railway employee. It had to be someone who knew where to find a quiet siding with redundant rolling stock in it.'

'Most of the people at the station would have that information.'

'And so would a railway policeman.'

After another glance at the map, Colbeck turned away and was lost in thought for a while. Becoming aware that he was keeping the other man waiting, he gave Jellings an apology. It was waved away.

'What sort of a town is Yarmouth?' asked Colbeck.

'It's a bustling seaport,' replied Jellings, 'and the smell of fish will soon hit your nostrils. Yarmouth – or Great Yarmouth as some people prefer to call it – is built on a slip of land between the sea and the River Yare. There's a drawbridge connecting it with Little Yarmouth or South Town.'

'How big would it be?'

'Oh, the population must be at least thirty thousand, I'd say, and that number is increased in warm weather by people who go there on holiday. It's a very popular resort.'

'I don't think the killer went there to sit in the sun.'

'Nor do I, sir.'

'It's quite an ancient town, isn't it?'

'Yes, it used to be surrounded by a moat and fortified by embattled walls. There are four main streets, running parallel with each other. They're intersected by alleys or rows, so narrow that most carts are too wide to go down them. I'm told there are over and hundred and fifty of them in all.'

'In short,' said Colbeck, 'it's a rabbit warren. There'll be hiding places galore. I feel sorry for your men, Inspector. In a place like that, they won't know where to start looking.'

\* \* \*

Now that she was well clear of her stepson, Grace Swarbrick felt much better. She no longer had a sense of oppression. Dressed in black, she sat in a chair in the drawing room of the Freed residence, sipping tea and thanking her friend from what was tantamount to a rescue.

'Sooner or later, Andrew would have tired of waiting,' she said.

'That's why you needed to get out of there, Grace. All we had to do was to give instructions to one of the servants and we were driven here. I meant what I said,' emphasised Anthea Freed. 'Stay just as long as you wish. Your stepson will be kept well away from you.'

'Thank you, Anthea.'

'Treat the place as your own.'

'What will Cecil say when he finds me here?'

'He'll give you as cordial a welcome as I have,' said her friend, 'and, like me, he'll know when to leave you alone. Neither of us wishes to intrude on your grief.'

'It's more like despair,' murmured Grace. 'Before my first husband died, I had a warning well in advance. The doctor told me exactly what to expect. I was able to sit with Roland, watch him fade slowly away in front of me and then mourn him accordingly. There was nothing like the agony I suffered this time.'

'I can imagine.'

'My mind has been in turmoil ever since.'

'That's understandable. I know your time together was cut cruelly short, but you and Jarvis were so patently made for each other. He'd become morose after the death of his first wife. You turned him back into the person he'd been before.'

'He did the same for me, Anthea. It was incredible.' She muffled a yawn. 'Would it be rude of me to ask you to leave me alone for a while? I feel the need for a brief nap.'

'Then I'll slip away at once and give orders that you're not to be disturbed. When you wake up,' said Anthea, indicating the little bell on the side table, 'just ring that and somebody will come.'

'Dare I hope that it might be Inspector Colbeck with good news?'

'We may have to wait a little while for that, Grace.'

'He seems such a conscientious man,' said the other, drowsily.

Anthea was on her feet at once. 'It's time for your nap,' she said. 'You obviously need it. My thoughts will be with you.'

After depositing a gentle kiss on her friend's head, she went out.

Horace Pryor was too frightened to disobey orders. When he saw Leeming alighting from a London train, he made sure that he intercepted him and talked to him at length. As soon as the sergeant departed, Pryor went in search of Duff. He found him behind the waiting room, lounging against a wall and stuffing tobacco into a clay pipe.

'What do you want?' asked Duff.

'Sergeant Leeming has just come back.'

'Did you speak to him?'

'We had a long talk, Bart.'

'Well, don't just stand there. What did he tell you?'

After clearing his throat, Pryor repeated all that he could remember of the conversation. Though he got the sequence of events confused, he passed on the relevant facts. Lighting his pipe, Duff listened impatiently. When he'd heard everything, he wanted the details confirmed.

'So, he reported to his superintendent, did he?'

'Yes, Bart.'

'What's this about a letter to Colbeck's wife?'

'It saved her having to wait another day for it.'

'So instead of trying to track down a killer,' said Duff, curling his lip, 'the inspector is writing a billy-do for his wife. Then, when he'd handed the letter over, the sergeant went home to see Mrs Leeming.'

'That's right.'

'I come to work to *escape* my wife. I'd never dream of sneaking home to see her. We've got nothing to say to each other.'

Pryor smiled hopefully. 'Did I do well?'

'You did as you were told, Horry, that's the main thing.' He stopped to pull on his pipe before exhaling a cloud of aromatic smoke. 'So where has the sergeant gone now?'

'He's gone to meet Inspector Colbeck.'

'Yes, but *where*?'

Pryor bit his lip. 'I forgot to ask, Bart.'

As he'd promised, Colbeck was sitting at a table in the Ribs of Beef with a glass of whisky in his hand. The moment he saw Leeming enter, he ordered a pint of beer, giving him plenty of time to take the first reviving gulps of it before pressing him for a report. Colbeck was upset to hear of the way that Tallis had behaved both with Leeming and, earlier on in the day, with Alan Hinton. He was glad to hear that Captain Wardlow would be contacted that very evening. In a situation seemingly approaching a crisis, the superintendent was in need of a close friend.

'Do you have a letter from Madeleine?' he asked.

'Oh, yes,' said Leeming, retrieving it from his pocket and handing it over. 'Your wife and daughter send their love and want you home very soon, please.'

'We've a crime to solve first, Victor, so "very soon" could mean weeks, even longer.'

'Are we going to be in Norwich indefinitely?'

'Let me read my letter, then I'll tell you.'

After handing him the menu to look at, Colbeck opened his letter and skimmed through it. He was pleased to hear that Madeleine had written to Lionel Fairbank but irritated that his father-in-law had taken it upon himself to call at the art gallery in order to find out what he could about the man. When they'd ordered their meals, Colbeck told his companion how he'd spent his day. Leeming sat up in surprise at the stationmaster's shrewd observation.

'Why didn't we think of that, sir?' he asked.

'Our minds were fixed elsewhere, Victor.'

'And are you sure you found the right place?'

'No doubt about it,' said Colbeck. 'I went to all three locations and only one of them had such distinctive hoof prints. Also, it was the most isolated of the three sidings. He could have practised there unseen.'

'The stationmaster deserves a pat on the back.'

'And so do you, Victor.'

'*Me?*'

'Inspector Jellings was singing your praises. It was you who told him to deploy his men along the road to Acle in search of witnesses. He did just that and it paid off.'

'Did they pick up a trail?'

'They did, indeed,' said Colbeck. 'As a result, I can now answer your earlier question. Are we going to be in Norwich indefinitely? No, we're not. Tomorrow morning we're going to Great Yarmouth.'

\* \* \*

While she was relieved that her husband had welcomed the idea of her accepting a commission, Madeleine Colbeck was still worried that her father's visit to the Red Gallery might have imperilled it. Late that afternoon, therefore, she took a cab to the art shop so that she could speak to Francis Sinclair, the owner. He was a slim, elegant, ginger-haired man in his fifties with expressive features and a high voice. Since there were no customers on the premises, they were able to talk in private.

'Good day to you, Mrs Colbeck,' he said, smiling warmly. 'It's always a pleasure to see you here.'

'Thank you, Mr Sinclair.'

'Have you come to look at your latest prints?'

'No,' said Madeleine, clearly embarrassed. 'I'm here to apologise.'

'I see no reason for you to do that.'

'My father called here yesterday.'

'That's right. Mr Andrews was asking after one of our clients, a Mr Fairbank. He said something about a commission. Ordinarily, of course, I'd never reveal personal details about anyone who comes through that door, but your father was rather insistent. I told him what he must have passed on to you.'

'He had no business coming here, Mr Sinclair.'

'I assumed that you'd sanctioned his visit.'

'I'd never have done that,' said Madeleine. 'It put you in the awkward position and was, in any case, quite unnecessary. The letter from Mr Fairbank spoke for itself. He has a genuine interest in my work.' She lowered her voice. 'I'm here to ask two favours of you. The first is that I'd be very grateful if you made no mention to Mr Fairbank of my father's ill-considered attempt to find out more about him.'

'I wasn't intending to say a word on the subject, Mrs Colbeck,' he assured her. 'What's the second favour?'

'I've written to Mr Fairbank to suggest that he and I meet here in the first instance. I hope that you have no objection?'

Sinclair laughed. 'Why should I object to the arrival of one of my artists and one of my most respected clients? The pair of you can come and go as you, please.'

'Thank you so much. That's a great relief.'

They chatted for a few minutes then Madeleine was ready to leave. As he opened the door to let her out, he remembered something.

'Did you know that your father was here again?'

Madeleine started. 'When?'

'It was earlier today.'

'I do hope he wasn't pestering you again, Mr Sinclair.'

'Oh, no, he didn't come anywhere near me. As a matter of fact, he made a point of staying on the other side of the street. I was rearranging something in the window when I saw him.'

'Did he acknowledge you in any way?'

'On the contrary,' he said. 'Mr Andrews was looking wistfully in this direction until he realised that I'd seen him. He hurried away with his head down as if trying to hide from me.'

Madeleine's stomach lurched.


It was evening when Colbeck drove the trap to the relevant siding. Some distance from the station, it was shielded by thick bushes. When the vehicle came to a halt, Leeming looked carefully at the four carriages.

'They're all third class,' he pointed out.

'We can't expect the ECR to have left a first-class carriage here for the benefit of the killer. He pretended that the one at the far end was the carriage that Mr and Mrs Swarbrick used and knew they'd be travelling in the last compartment.'

Getting out of the trap, Colbeck beckoned to Leeming to follow him. As they walked alongside the four carriages, they could see dozens of hoof prints gouged into the turf, showing that someone had ridden up and down many times. Colbeck paused at the last compartment of the fourth carriage and explained how difficult it had been to open the door from the back of a horse.

'Try it for yourself, Victor. Sit on our horse.'

'No, thank you,' said Leeming, holding up both hands. 'You know the trouble I always have with horses. They don't like me. I'll take your word for it that opening that door takes skill.'

'It takes skill, balance and dexterity. After practising here, the killer was well prepared. What do you deduce from that?'

'He knew that he'd have to get it right first time, sir.'

'Exactly – speed was essential.'

'Explain one thing to me,' said Leeming. 'If his aim was simply to kill Mr Swarbrick, why did he pretend to rob him first?'

'He wanted to provoke resistance because that's what he'd be told he'd get. Mrs Swarbrick said that her husband refused to hand over any valuables. The killer had his excuse to shoot.'

'Who told him that he'd meet with refusal?'

'The person who hired him,' said Colbeck. 'He knew the victim well enough to be certain that Swarbrick would confront the man.'

'Then it must have been someone very close to him.'

'Andrew Swarbrick was closer than anyone.'

'What about that Oliver Trant?'

'Oh, I think that he could foresee how Swarbrick would react. They've tussled with each other for many years. You learn a lot about a man's character if you're in a constant battle with him.'

'You *do*,' said Leeming, thinking of his relationship with Tallis.

'From what his wife could remember of the incident, it seems that Swarbrick was indignant that anyone should demand his wallet and watch. He was a man of substance in this part of the country. He didn't think that anyone would *dare* to give him an order in that way.'

'That mistake led to his death.'

'Let's recapitulate,' said Colbeck. 'So far we have a trained killer who did what he was told. He was hired by someone wealthy enough to pay a high price and well acquainted with Swarbrick's character. Then there's the third person, a railway employee who told the killer about this siding and who contrived a diversion for him.'

'Horace Pryor?'

'It's possible but I'd have reservations about accusing him.'

'He's changed since we got here, sir. At the start, he tried to dodge questions and keep out of our way. When he sees me now, he pounces on me and asks where I'm going and who I'm off to see.'

'Perhaps he wants to know if we've stumbled on any significant evidence. That could mean he's anxious about his safety.'

'Should we question him more closely?'

'There's no need for that at this stage' said Colbeck. 'Give him the impression that he's not under any suspicion. Make him lower his guard.'

'What about Sergeant Duff?'

'We'll *both* keep him in mind.'

'Is he our man?'

'It's too early to say, Victor.'

'I don't trust him.'

'Let him stew in his juice until we've gathered more facts. Duff and Pryor are not going anywhere. If they were involved, we'll find out in due course.'

After another glance at the door of the last compartment, Colbeck headed back to the trap with Leeming beside it. When they drove away, neither of them looked over his shoulder to see a man emerging slowly from the bushes. Bartram Duff had heard every word.

Returning home from a day in his office, Cecil Freed was greeted by the news that Grace Swarbrick was now living with them. He was pleased that she'd been taken out of reach of her stepson and hoped that being in a much friendlier environment would aid her recovery.

'We seem to be acting as a sanctuary, my dear,' he said.

'Grace couldn't possible stay where she was,' argued his wife.

'You brought her here to hide from Andrew and I invited the detectives so that they weren't dogged by the press. I wonder who else is in need of somewhere to hide?'

'Don't be so facetious, Cecil.'

'It was a serious question.'

'Come and meet Grace,' she told him. 'She looks a trifle better but is still very frail. Be kind to her.'

'I always am.'

'She needs a very special brand of kindness now.'

'Nobody can provide that better than you,' he said, fondly.

They went into the drawing room to join Grace Swarbrick who looked pale and distracted. When she became aware of them sitting opposite her, she apologised for not seeing them at once.

'I'm never quite sure if I'm awake or asleep,' she said.

'You're wide awake now,' said Anthea, 'and we're delighted to see a hint of colour returning to your cheeks.'

It was a polite lie and Freed was happy to confirm it with a smile.

'Did Anthea tell you that your stepson came to see me?'

'Yes, she did,' said Grace. 'What sort of a mood was he in?'

'He was as forceful as ever. At one point, he came close to outright aggression but he veered away in time.'

'Did he want to discuss . . . arrangements?'

'No,' replied Freed, 'what he really wanted to talk about was replacing his father as Member of Parliament for Norwich.'

Grace blinked. 'You *have* surprised me.'

'Didn't you realise he nurtured political ambitions?'

'No, I didn't.'

'Jarvis never discussed such things at home,' said Anthea. 'When he was there, he liked to put politics to one side. That suited Grace.'

'It did,' agreed the other. 'It's a closed world to me.'

'Your husband was born into it, Grace,' said Freed. 'He was a natural politician with all the gifts that implies. I'm not convinced that his son has quite the same qualities.'

'How keen is he?'

'It's become a burning desire.'

'Well, there you are,' said Grace, sadly. 'He's ready to make a vital decision in his life and I have to hear about it from somebody else.'

'He came to Cecil in search of support,' explained Anthea. 'My husband's blessing would increase his chances of success.'

'I know nothing about elections.'

'You would do if women had the vote.'

'There you go again, Anthea,' said Freed, amused. 'The moment politics is mentioned, you start waving the flag for female emancipation.'

'It's a worthy cause.'

'Unfortunately, it's doomed to failure.'

'Tell me more about Andrew,' said Grace, diplomatically. 'Were you able to give him encouragement?'

'I was and I wasn't. Naturally, I offered him my support, but I felt obliged to tell him that he'd face a battle for the nomination. Oliver Trant is going to put his name forward.'

'He's a rather sinister man, I always think.'

'Oliver may be sinister but he's also very capable. He's had far more experience of public speaking than Andrew and is very popular in some quarters.'

'So who *will* be our next Member of Parliament?' asked Anthea.

'I honestly don't know, my dear.'

'Can't you pull a few strings?'

'I'll pull as many as I can lay my hands on. What I can't do, I'm afraid, is to give you any guarantees.'

'Well, I think it's all rather indecent. Andrew should be mourning his father and not getting obsessed about his own career.'

'I made that point to him.'

'How did he respond?' asked Grace.

'He did manage to mumble an apology.'

'He hasn't done much mumbling back at the house. Even from my bedroom, I could hear him shouting at the servants. Whenever he's there, Andrew always wants to create an atmosphere.'

'You'll have to sit down and talk to him at some point.'

'I accept that.'

'But the dust has to settle first,' said Anthea, firmly. 'Grace needs to be much stronger before she even thinks of meeting her stepson. And when she does, I'll be at her side.'

'Thank you,' said Grace, reaching over to squeeze her hand. 'You've been a rock, Anthea. Without you at my side, I'd have gone to pieces completely.'

Alan Hinton managed to catch an express train to Canterbury, thereby eliminating many of the intermediate stations on the way. He then took a cab to the village where Terence Wardlow lived. During the hectic search for Tallis after his kidnap, Hinton had got to know Wardlow very well and knew what a reliable friend he'd been to the superintendent. He had no qualms about calling on the former soldier but was sad that he'd have to pass on such disturbing news. Arriving at the house, he was shown into the drawing room. Wardlow came in using his walking stick. He was a tall, rangy man with an air of distinction.

'It's good to see you, Constable,' he said, offering a handshake, 'though I can't say I was ever expecting to find you here in Kent again.'

'It's a surprise to me as well, sir. Might I suggest that you sit down before I tell you what brought me here?'

'Oh dear, that sounds rather alarming.' He lowered himself slowly into his chair and put his stick aside. 'What's happened?'

'Superintendent Tallis needs your help, sir.'

'I can't believe he's been abducted again.'

'No,' said Hinton, 'it's nothing like that – though, in a sense, I suppose that it is.'

'You're not making much sense.'

'I'm sorry, sir.'

Hinton went on to explain the sequence of events that

179

led him to believe that Tallis was seriously ill, and suggested that his condition might be related to the ordeal he suffered at the hands of his kidnappers. He also mentioned that Victor Leeming had been distressed by the superintendent's strange behaviour. After plying him with a few questions, Wardlow sat back worriedly in his chair.

'This situation is not unknown to me,' he said, sombrely.

'Do you mean that you've seen him like this before?'

'No, no, I'm not referring to Edward. I'm talking about the extreme dangers that soldiers face in battle. Even if their bodies come through unscarred, their minds often bear hidden wounds. It makes them brood on the horrors of war, sometimes to the point where they're virtually disabled. In the worst cases, there are suicides.'

'I don't think the superintendent is in danger of taking his life,' said Hinton. 'What worries us is that he might be sacrificing his career in the police without even realising it.'

'He's fortunate to have such perceptive friends as you, Constable.'

'I wouldn't claim to be a friend in that sense, sir, and nor would Sergeant Leeming. But we can both recognise a man who is plainly ill and wish to do something about it.'

'I'm grateful that you thought of me.'

'It was Inspector Colbeck's idea.'

'Then he deserves my thanks as well.'

'What's the best way to tackle the problem, Captain?'

'Well,' said Wardlow, stroking his chin, 'the first thing I'd like to do is to see Edward and make my own estimate of his condition. To do that, I'll travel back to London with you and call on him this evening. I can spend the night at my club.'

'I regret having to impose on you like this.'

'Not at all, young man. You did the right thing. There may still be time for me to intercede before my old friend gets into serious trouble.'

'If he goes on like this, it's unavoidable.'

'It's strange, isn't it?' mused the older man.

'I don't follow.'

'Major Tallis, as I knew him in the army, was indestructible. He seemed to be made of iron. It wasn't simply that he was brave and fearless. It was his ability to carry responsibility lightly and to shrug off the appalling horrors one is bound to see in action. Yet here he is,' said Wardlow, 'apparently at the mercy of what happened to him during a few days in Kent just before last Christmas.'

'It's left him with a haunted look.'

'He never had that when he was in the army.'

'You know him better than we do, sir.'

'I just hope I'm in time to be of any real use.' He struggled to his feet. 'Forgive me while I break the news to my wife and pack some things to take with me. Since you're the person who actually came in search of me, I'm deeply grateful, but I hope to be able to thank Inspector Colbeck in person for calling on me.'

'That may not be possible, sir.'

'Why not?'

'The inspector is in Norwich, leading a murder investigation.'

After her visit to the Red Gallery, Madeleine Colbeck had arrived home with mixed feelings. While she'd been pleased that nothing would be said to Lionel Fairbank about her father's enquiries about him, she was upset to hear that Caleb Andrews had been back to the art gallery. The news that he was forced to sneak

181

past it in embarrassment was disconcerting. In telling him not to interfere in her work as an artist, she'd unintentionally deprived him of the pleasure he took in it. It made her feel cruel. Madeleine worried about it so much that she took a cab to his house that evening to apologise.

Andrews was reading a newspaper when she arrived. As a rule, he was always delighted to see her but this time he was cowed and wary.

'What are you doing here?' he asked.

'I went to see Mr Sinclair earlier.'

'You don't need to say any more, Maddy. I know I'm not allowed to take an interest in your work again. I poked my nose in where it wasn't wanted, and I upset you.'

'I was even more upset when I heard you'd been there again.'

'But I didn't,' he said, earnestly. 'I just happened to pass on the other side of the street. Mr Sinclair must have told you I didn't go anywhere near the gallery itself.'

'He told me how you behaved when you realised he'd seen you.'

'I was in a hurry to go somewhere.'

'You shouldn't have been there in the first place, Father,' she said, softly, 'because it must have been very painful for you. We both know that you went there deliberately. It's off the beaten track. You'd never just happen to be passing.' He lowered his head. 'I feel so guilty.'

'*I'm* the guilty one,' he said, looking up again. 'I barged in where I wasn't wanted. It's not the first time, Maddy. We live in different worlds now. Every so often, I'm reminded that I'm an outsider.'

'That's a silly thing to say!' she scolded.

'It's the truth.'

'You're an important part of our family and always will be. Helen doesn't have any other grandparents. That's why she loves you so much.'

'I don't feel loved at the moment.'

'Well, you are,' she said, putting her arms around him, 'even though you don't really deserve it.'

'I never meant to hurt you.'

'You were too hasty, Father. You didn't stop to think.'

'I can see that now.'

'And will you promise to take more care next time?'

'There won't *be* a next time,' he said, morosely. 'I'm banished.'

'Not any more,' she said. 'You're entitled to take pleasure from my paintings. All I ask is that you don't . . . act on impulse.'

'I won't, Maddy, I promise.'

'Then let's forget we ever had this row.'

He brightened visibly. 'Yes, let's do that. It never really happened.'

'We can carry on as before. Is that agreed?' He nodded gratefully. After kissing him on the cheek, she stepped back. 'And let's hear no more nonsense about being an outsider.'

'Does that mean you want me to meet Mr Fairbank?'

'No, it doesn't!'

He laughed. 'I was only teasing you, Maddy.'

'Well, don't do it again. Painting is not a hobby with me. It's a business. I need to be able to conduct that business without you being involved. Is that understood?'

'I'll be on my best behaviour from now on, I promise.'

'I'll hold you to that,' she said.


Edward Tallis lived in a set of rooms that afforded him peace, privacy and comfort. When he heard the doorbell ring, he ignored it at first. Nobody ever called on him. It rang again with more force. Hauling himself out of his chair, he put his cigar aside and went to open the door. He was amazed when he saw that he had a visitor.

'What are *you* doing here, Terence?' he asked.

Wardlow smiled. 'Hello, Edward . . .'

# CHAPTER FOURTEEN

Shortly after arriving back at the cottage that evening, Colbeck and Leeming had a visit from Cecil Freed, who apologised for disturbing them but thought they should know that Grace Swarbrick had been spirited out of the reach of her stepson.

'That was a sensible move,' said Colbeck.

'Did he protest very strongly?' asked Leeming.

'No,' replied Freed. 'They made their escape while he was out of the way. One of the servants drove them here by stealth. But for the circumstances, Grace said, she'd have found it quite exciting.'

'What if he turns up here?'

'He won't, Sergeant. He'll know that he wouldn't be allowed in. I daresay he'll take out his spite on the housekeeper, Mrs

185

Wymark, and accuse her of being part of the conspiracy.'

'That's unfair.'

'Men like that don't bother with fairness when there are high stakes,' said Colbeck. 'Ruthlessness is second nature to them.'

'Jarvis had a streak of that,' admitted Freed.

'Parliament is no place for the tender-hearted, sir.'

Since he hadn't seen Freed since much earlier that day, Colbeck gave him a brief account of their movements. Their host was pleased that the police had tracked the killer to Yarmouth and he praised Leeming for instigating the search along the road there. When he realised that one the ECR's sidings had been used to rehearse the crime beforehand, he was stunned.

'I didn't know that criminals *practised*.'

'The clever ones do,' said Leeming. 'The others take a chance and usually end up behind bars. The killer planned everything carefully.'

'That's worrying.'

'They all make mistakes in the end, sir.'

'Who was his paymaster?'

'That's what we've been asking ourselves,' said Colbeck. 'Initially, I thought that someone from another railway company wanted to block the merger by getting rid of the man most likely to achieve it, but I fancy that we must cast our net more widely now.'

'That's an apt metaphor, Inspector. Fishing is one of our major industries. If it ever comes into being,' said Freed, 'the Great Eastern Railway will service five ports – Harwich, Felixtowe, Lowestoft, Yarmouth and King's Lynn. We'll be able to convey huge quantities of fish from Lowestoft and Yarmouth to London and to the Midlands.'

'A great deal rests on the amalgamation, then.'

'That's why it must be salvaged.'

'Do you think Andrew Swarbrick is the person to do that?'

'He has the right credentials,' said Freed. 'He has a good working knowledge of the details of the merger because his bank has a financial stake in the venture. Whether or not he could get it safely through Parliament is another matter. I trusted his father. I don't trust Andrew.'

'Would you prefer Oliver Trant?'

'Neither of them can hold a candle to Jarvis Swarbrick.'

Conscious that he was interrupting them, Freed apologised once again for intruding and went off to the main house. Leeming closed the door behind him, then came back to the drawing room.

'How much would it cost?' he wondered. 'If you wanted to have someone shot dead – what sort of price would you have to pay?'

'It would be a very high one, Victor.'

'Swarbrick could afford it. He's a rich man.'

'So is Trant,' said Colbeck. 'He's also wealthy. He'd not only hand over whatever the killer demanded, he'd probably offer him a free pair of shoes as well.'

Oliver Trant arrived at the bank just after it opened. He was shown immediately into the manager's office and was pleased to see the wads of money sitting on the table.

'It's a substantial withdrawal,' said the manager. 'I assumed that you'd bring a bodyguard with you.'

'I have someone waiting outside to drive me back to the factory,' explained Trant. 'Besides, you and I are the only people who know that I'm carrying quite so much money. There's no danger.' He opened the leather bag he'd brought with him. 'Let's put it all in, shall we?'

The moment they arrived at the station, the detectives were approached by Horace Pryor who asked where they were going. Colbeck was happy to say that they were on their way to Yarmouth but he was careful not to disclose their reason for going there. No sooner had Pryor walked away than the stationmaster came hurrying across the platform to them. He was waving a telegraph in his hand. Colbeck thanked him and took it from him. When he read the telegraph, his face clouded.

'Is there trouble, sir?' asked Leeming.

'There might be, Victor.'

'Did the superintendent send it?'

'No, it's from Inspector Vallence, the *acting* superintendent.'

Leeming was agog. 'What happened to Tallis?'

'He's on indefinite leave.'

'Why?'

'He doesn't say, Victor. He simply tells me to report to him from now on. Vallence is a wise choice to replace Tallis.'

'Will he take over for good?'

'We can only speculate.'

Slipping the telegraph into his coat pocket, Colbeck was worried. So much was left unsaid in the message. He wondered why.

Expecting Lydia Quayle to call that morning, Madeleine was pleased when she heard the doorbell. The maid went to the door to see who it was then invited someone into the hall. She then went into the drawing room to speak to Madeleine.

'If that's Miss Quayle,' said Madeleine, 'show her in.'

'A gentleman has called to see you, Mrs Colbeck. He said that you'd know who he was.'

'What's his name?'

'Mr Lionel Fairbank.'

Madeleine was shaken. Getting to her feet, she went out into the hall where an elderly man in a smart suit was holding his top hat. Fairbank had a luxuriant silver moustache to match his curling locks.

'Do excuse me, Mrs Colbeck,' he said in a deep, educated voice, 'but your letter reached me this morning just before I caught the train to London. I was so grateful to know your address. It seemed to be heaven-sent. Instead of meeting you at the Red Gallery, I took the liberty of coming here. I thought that we'd enjoy more privacy.'

'Yes, that's true,' she said, slightly unnerved.

'This, after all, is where you have your studio, I presume.'

'It is, Mr Fairbank.'

'Then what better place is there to meet my favourite artist?'

'You're . . . very welcome.'

'I knew that I would be.'

After beaming at her for a few moments, he gave a gracious bow.


Andrew Swarbrick didn't even wait for the secretary to announce his arrival. He simply pushed past the man and went straight into Cecil Freed's office. The chairman of the ECR was working his way through a pile of daily newspapers, cringing at headlines that were openly critical of the company. When his visitor burst in, Freed got to his feet.

'Andrew!' he exclaimed. 'What are you doing here?'

'What do you think?' said the other, sarcastically.

'You've come at an awkward time, I'm afraid. I've got an important meeting with senior members of my staff in five minutes.'

'They can wait.'

'I'm known for my punctuality. It sets a good example.'

'You're going nowhere until I've spoken to you first,' warned Swarbrick, squaring up to him. 'Why did you smuggle my stepmother out of the house?'

'I did nothing of the kind. It was my dear wife's idea.'

'You obviously gave it your approval.'

'I was very glad to do so retrospectively,' said Freed. 'The doctor prescribed rest in a calm atmosphere. There was no chance of her getting that while you were rampaging around the house.'

'Your wife had no right to interfere.'

'When someone is in great distress, everyone has a right to offer help. We are only doing what we felt to be our duty.'

'I need to see her.'

'Not when you're in this mood, Andrew. Your father would turn in his grave if he knew you were behaving so boorishly.'

'He's not *in* his grave yet,' said Swarbrick, pointedly. 'It's one of the reasons I need to speak to my stepmother. I've made an appointment to see Father's solicitor. She ought to be there as well.'

'Stop issuing orders.'

'You can't hide her away for ever.'

'Mrs Swarbrick needs to be protected.'

'My father's death has consequences.'

'One of them is all too apparent,' said Freed, tartly. 'I've always thought of you as an intelligent and conscientious gentleman. At a stroke, you've turned into a rude, hectoring bully.'

'I was referring to *legal* consequences.'

'The only legal consequence that interests me is the arrest of the killer and the person or persons in league with him. Now stop being so truculent and sit down. If you want a sensible discussion, it's best done in a degree of comfort.'

Freed sat down behind his desk and ignored the other's glare. For his part, Swarbrick was annoyed that he hadn't intimidated the other man into making concessions. Though Freed looked nervous and ineffectual, he had a strong inner core that had now asserted itself. Swarbrick saw that he would get nowhere by trying to dominate him. After some tense moments, he eventually lowered himself into a chair.

'That's better,' said Freed with a cold smile. 'Now, what is it that you really want?'

'I need to ask my stepmother some questions,' said Swarbrick with an attempt at composure. 'Chief among them is the location of my father's last will and testament.'

'It will be somewhere in his study.'

'I've searched that. It's not there.'

'Then you'll have to wait until you see his solicitor.'

'My stepmother will know where it's hidden. In fact, I wouldn't put it past her to have taken it away with her just to annoy me.'

'That's an absurd accusation,' said Freed, 'and you know it only too well. When she agreed to come to us, Grace had to leave quickly before you came back. She barely had time to pack a few things with her. As for the will, I think it highly unlikely that she even knows where it is.'

'Oh, she *knows*,' said the other, bitterly. 'Believe me.'

'This attitude of yours is highly improper, Andrew. I have spent the last couple of days fighting off reporters and their sly innuendoes about the ECR. I've done everything in my power to defend the reputation of Jarvis Swarbrick. What do you think the newspapers would do if they knew about this incessant bickering behind the scenes?'

'It's none of their business.'

'They'll *make* it their business. The ECR has always had a bad press. We're the favourite whipping boy of some newspapers. If they interviewed you in this state, they'd sense the undercurrents at once. Is that what you want?'

'No, it isn't,' conceded Swarbrick. 'It's the reason I've refused to give them anything more than a few comments.'

Freed sighed with relief. 'Thank goodness for that!'

'There was one question I kept being asked but, if you've read this morning's newspapers, you'll have seen my answer.'

'I've only glanced at them, Andrew. There's been no mention of you, so far. What did you tell them?'

'I told them the truth. It seemed like a good opportunity to get some publicity for myself.'

'Publicity?'

'Yes,' said the other. 'I'm not one to hide my light under a bushel. When reporters asked me if I had any intention of following my father into politics, I told them that I did.'

'It was far too soon to do that,' complained Freed.

'I disagree. I want the voters of Norwich to know that there'll be continuity. Another member of the Swarbrick family is getting ready to represent them in Parliament.'

'Don't raise your hopes too high.'

'I wanted to show him that the fight starts right now.'

'Who are you talking about?'

'Oliver Trant, of course,' said Swarbrick. 'He was boasting

that the whole thing is a foregone conclusion and that he's certain to win.'

'I don't know about that.'

'Well, I've just fired a shot across his bows and, when he reads any of the papers this morning, he'll realise he's in for the battle of his life.'

After counting out his money, Trant put it away in the safe and locked the door. It was the money he'd set aside to secure his election as Member of Parliament for the city. Though bribery was illegal, wining and dining influential people could smooth his path considerably and that was viewed in a different light. It was also the way he planned to win the nomination for the seat. Persuading men to vote for him was done much more easily when they were in their cups. He then went back to his desk and picked up the first from a pile of newspapers. After flipping through the pages, he came to one which had quoted Andrew Swarbrick extensively. When he saw what his rival had said, he scrunched up the newspaper and hurled it angrily into the wastepaper basket. His day had suddenly soured.

The train journey to Yarmouth gave the detectives another chance to experience the shortcomings of the ECR. The train was late, the seats were uncomfortable and the compartment smelt of fish. Since it was only twenty miles or so from Norwich, they got there fairly quickly. What awaited them was a picturesque coastal town with a sense of verve and jollity about it. Leeming's first reaction was that he'd love to bring his wife and children there to sit on the sand in the sunshine and inhale the ozone. After their success in an earlier investigation, they'd been given free train tickets to

Brighton and the day the sergeant had spent there with his family still vibrated in his memory. He wanted to replicate the pleasure in Yarmouth.

The purpose of their visit was to find out if anyone had hired a bay mare from any of the stables there. Colbeck had already told Inspector Jellings to see if he could find the source from which the killer had hired the black horse on which he'd committed the murder. Having exchanged one horse for another, he might well have got rid of the second one in Yarmouth. They'd been loaned a map of the town by Sergeant Burridge and took time to study it before splitting up to begin the search. While Colbeck was concentrating on the matter in hand, Leeming's mind was preoccupied with something else.

'Do you think the commissioner just got rid of him, sir?'

'I hope not, Victor.'

'If he'd seen what I saw, he'd realise that the superintendent was not fit to be in such a responsible position.'

'Tallis does seem to have had moments of lucidity.'

'Yes,' said Leeming, 'he was quite normal at first – except that he wasn't trying to bite my head off. Whatever is wrong with him just comes and goes.'

'Alan Hinton said the same thing.'

'Do you think he managed to get down to Canterbury?'

'I'm sure he did,' said Colbeck. 'He saw the superintendent at his worst. Hinton is desperate to help him.'

'So am I, sir. I never thought I'd hear myself saying this but, I'd miss him. Superintendent Tallis was an important part of my life.'

It took Madeleine some time to adapt to the situation. When she'd written to Lionel Fairbank to say how delighted she was

194

to accept his invitation, the last thing she expected was that he'd turn up unannounced on her doorstep the following day. She'd have preferred their initial meeting to have taken place on neutral ground. However, Madeleine could hardly turn him away. Taking him into the drawing room, she'd offered him refreshment and he accepted. Seated on opposite sides of the room, they began to make an early appraisal of each other.

'You're so much younger than I imagined,' he said.

'Am I?'

'Your paintings have such maturity about them. I thought that I'd be talking to someone fifteen or twenty years older. Why do you have such a passion for railways?'

'My father spent his entire working life as a railwayman.'

'Ah, I see.'

'Also,' she confessed, 'I have no talent for portraiture.'

'I can't believe that. You're a born artist.'

'I know my limitations, Mr Fairbank. If you asked me to paint a portrait of you, I'd have to refuse the commission.'

'What I require is a railway scene – a very specific one.'

'I'll do my best to meet your wishes.'

'That's what I was hoping you'd say, Mrs Colbeck.'

'What appeals to you about railways, Mr Fairbank?'

'I have a vested interest in them,' he replied. 'That's to say I'm a major shareholder in the GWR. Most people hate the idea of having trains puffing across their land all day long. I'm the odd one out, a role that fate has always selected me to play. From the rear of the house, I have an excellent view of the railway lines snaking their way across land I sold to the Great Western Railway. I love watching trains steaming to and fro.'

Madeleine made a mental note to suppress any mention of his

link with the GWR in her father's presence. It would incense him once again.

'You're an unusual man, Mr Fairbank,' she told him. 'Many landowners have fought tooth and nail to keep railway companies at bay.'

'My late wife – God bless her – said that the thing that first attracted her to me was the fact that I was so eccentric.'

As she gradually relaxed, Madeleine came to like him. Fairbank was urbane, courteous and utterly benign. She'd soon forgiven him for giving her such a surprise.

'I don't suppose that I could prevail upon you to let me see your studio?' he said. 'I'd love to see the place where your paintings are brought so vividly to life.'

'It's far too cluttered for any visitors, I fear,' she said.

'A case of amiable chaos, is it? I suppose that's artistic licence.'

'It's sheer untidiness.'

'Yet your work is so scrupulously exact and detailed.'

'It takes a long time to achieve that effect, Mr Fairbank.'

He studied her quizzically for a long time before speaking.

'What were you expecting?' he asked.

'I beg your pardon?'

'When you first read my letter, what sort of a person did you think I might be?'

'I thought that you'd be exactly as you'd described yourself, and so it's turned out to be. When you spoke of your grandchildren, I had some idea of your age, and your graceful handwriting told its own story.'

He laughed. 'You're quite the detective, Mrs Colbeck.'

Madeleine heard the doorbell ring. Glancing at the clock on the mantelpiece, she saw that it was the precise time when Lydia had promised to call. Moments later, she heard the familiar voice echoing around the hall.

Fairbank was congenial company but Madeleine wondered why she nevertheless felt relieved by her friend's arrival.

It had taken Terence Wardlow a long time to persuade his old friend that he needed a holiday. When Tallis argued that he had to go to work in Scotland Yard, he was told that it was all arranged and that he simply had to be ready to leave on the following morning. Before he went to pick him up, Wardlow had gone to see the commissioner to explain that he needed to appoint someone else as acting superintendent because Tallis was too unwell to carry on. The commissioner had been very understanding and wondered why nobody inside Scotland Yard had alerted him to the fact that a senior officer was incapacitated.

On the journey to Canterbury, Tallis had hardly said a word to his friend, drifting off to sleep from time to time then coming awake with a start. There was a nasty moment when they actually left the station and got their first glimpse of the famous cathedral. Tallis recoiled in horror. It was in the cathedral cloisters that he'd been abducted by two men and hustled out of the city. The memory of it had ignited his fears. Wardlow had quickly hailed a cab and it had taken them out to the village where he lived. Mrs Wardlow was there to give Tallis a welcome before he was taken upstairs to his room. It was light, airy, spacious and comfortable. When he looked out of the window, all that the visitor could see was rolling farmland and a distant oast house. There was a wonderful feeling of serenity. It was a far cry from the frantic activity of Tallis's usual world.

'What am I doing here?' he asked, dreamily.

'You've come to stay with friends, Edward.'

'But they need me in London.'

'Someone else will take over your job for a while.'

'Will they?'

'Forget about work. You're here for a long, much-needed rest.'

'How can I keep in touch with Colbeck if I'm down here in Kent?'

'From what I remember of Inspector Colbeck,' said Wardlow with a smile, 'he'll manage perfectly well without you.'

They met as arranged at a pub they'd noticed near the beach. Over a refreshing drink, they were able to rest their aching feet and to compare notes. Their searches had so far been fruitless. Leeming was pessimistic.

'We'll never find him, sir.'

'I remain hopeful.'

'Have you seen those rows?'

'Yes, Victor.'

'There are hundreds and hundreds of places to hide down those alleys. We'd need an army to scour them properly.'

'Why should the killer go to ground there?'

'It's because he could disappear from the face of the earth.'

'Have you seen what's down those alleys?'

'Yes – lots and lots of dens.'

'He'd spurn the whole lot of them,' reasoned Colbeck. 'Why go to ground in a hovel when he could afford to stay at the best hotel here? We know that he'll be very well paid for what he did. Don't you think that he'd want to enjoy his sudden wealth? I would, in his position.'

'You'd never *be* in his position, sir. You've got moral standards.'

'I can still *think* myself into his situation.'

'And do you really believe he might be in a hotel?'

'If he's here, it's more than possible.'

'Then why don't we simply call on every hotel?'

'It's because I don't want us to be embarrassed, Victor.'

'Why should that happen?'

'Beyond the fact that he's a cold-blooded killer, we know nothing whatsoever about the man. We don't have any firm details about his appearance, his voice, his manner or even his age. Most embarrassing of all,' said Colbeck, 'we don't know his name. Imagine the look on the face of a hotel manager if we asked him if a nameless guest whose features we can't describe is staying there. He'd think we were mad.'

'I see your point, sir.'

'That's why we have to press on and find the stable where he hired the bay mare.'

'What if he didn't hire it, sir? It could actually be his horse.'

'I doubt it, somehow. That would mean he lived in this part of the world and could've been recognised by one of the many people who saw him galloping up to that branch line. No, Victor, whoever hired him brought him from somewhere else.'

'In that case, he may not even be in Yarmouth.'

'Let's at least establish what he looked like first,' said Colbeck. 'Once we know that, we have something to work with. It's unlikely that he'll have given anyone his real name, but we might discover where he was going from here.'

'I've already started to wear out the soles of my shoes.'

'Don't worry, Victor. We're in the right part of the country. Norwich is renowned for its shoe factories. If you speak nicely to him, Mr Trant might even give you a discount.'

\* \* \*

199

Having her friend there meant that she could have a second opinion of Lionel Fairbank. She felt much more comfortable now that there were three of them. He did not stay long. When he rose to leave, he took an envelope from his pocket and held it out.

'Haggling over money has always seemed to me to be a rather uncivilised way to behave,' he said, 'and that's why I've avoided it. What I have here, Mrs Colbeck, is my offer. You can peruse it at your leisure. If it's acceptable, please get in touch very soon. I'm staying in London for a couple of days with my son and his family. The address is also in the envelope.'

'Thank you, Mr Fairbank,' said Madeleine, getting up to take it from him. 'To be honest, the fact that you want to commission me is far more important than the amount of money involved.'

'Artists must eat.' He looked around with approval. 'Though, in your case, I can see that that is never going to be a problem.' He turned to Lydia. 'Goodbye, Miss Quayle. It was a delight to meet you.'

'Thank you, Mr Fairbank,' said the other.

After a flurry of farewells, Madeleine led him into the hall where he retrieved his top hat. While a servant let him out, she returned to her friend.

'Well?' she asked.

'I think he's a charming old gentleman,' said Lydia, 'though he must have given you a fright by turning up unexpectedly like that.'

'Yes, I was quite rattled at first.'

'You seemed very calm while I was here.'

'I was so glad it was you, Lydia. When I heard the doorbell ring, I prayed that it wasn't my father. Given the arguments we've had about him, I really don't want Father to meet Mr Fairbank, especially since I've learnt that he's a shareholder in the GWR.'

'Have the two of you been reconciled yet?'

'I hope so.'

'Good,' said Lydia. 'I'm glad for both of you.' She sat forward. 'There's something I couldn't ask you while we had company.'

'You want to know about the superintendent.'

'Yes, Madeleine.'

'As he promised, Constable Hinton went down to Canterbury yesterday and called on Captain Wardlow, the superintendent's old army friend. I'm sure he'll have responded to the appeal for help. Robert told me that he idolises the former Major Tallis.'

'What if it means the end of his career at Scotland Yard?'

'He'd be lost without it, Lydia.'

'But suppose that he *is* forced to retire. Would Robert be chosen to replace him?'

'He might be chosen but he'd reject the offer. Robert has been acting superintendent before and found it very irritating to be stuck behind a desk all day.'

'It would suit you to have him working in London all the time.'

'I'd never dream of saying that to him. He's always followed his own inclinations and he always will.' Lydia grinned. 'What's so funny?'

'You are, Madeleine.'

'What have I said?'

'It's nothing you've said, it's something you haven't done. If I was holding an envelope with an offer of money in it, I'd have torn it open at once. Don't you want to see how much he's prepared to offer you?'

'Yes, I do,' said Madeleine, opening the letter and reading the message inside. Her jaw dropped. 'I don't believe it!'

'What has he said?'

'See for yourself, Lydia.'

And she passed it to her friend with a trembling hand.

Having gone their separate ways, Colbeck and Leeming continued their respective searches. It was tiring work but they forced themselves on. Leeming looked with envy at all the people who were patently there on holiday, basking in the sun or enjoying the many delights of Yarmouth. As he passed the market, he loved the pervading aroma of fish. When he found another livery stable, he went through the questions he now knew by heart. Every time he stopped, he came away disappointed and decided that the killer had not stopped in the town, after all. Yells of joy took him down to the sand where a crowd of children had formed a semicircle around a booth in which Punch and Judy were giving a hilarious puppet show. Leeming couldn't resist sidling up to the edge of the crowd.

Colbeck, meanwhile, had dodged a pile of manure and gone into the pungent yard of yet another stable. The owner was a big, slovenly man dressed in rough attire and exuding a powerful smell of horses. Sizing Colbeck up, he ambled across to him.

'Are you looking to hire a horse, sir?'

'No,' replied Colbeck. 'I'm trying to trace a man who might have done so. The horse was a bay mare and it would have been returned here three days ago by someone who'd hired it perhaps a week ahead.'

'What was his name?'

'I don't know.'

'Can you tell me what he looked like?'

'I'd say he was in his twenties or thirties.'

'That's not much help.'

'I need to find him as a matter of urgency.'

The man smirked. 'But you know nothing about him.'

'I know the most important thing about him,' said Colbeck, crisply. 'He committed a murder in Norwich and may – just may – have ridden here on one of your horses. I'm a detective from the Metropolitan Police Force and I've come in search of him.' He was pleased to see the smirk vanish. 'Since he'd been riding at a gallop in warm weather, he'd probably have arrived here in a sweat.'

'Ah,' said the other, 'now that's interesting.'

'Why?'

'I did hire a bay mare to a man in his twenties and he was dripping with sweat when he brought it back three days ago.'

'Can you describe him?'

'He was about as tall as you, sir, but much sturdier. He had dark hair and beard and he wasn't short of money. He left a large deposit to be reclaimed when he came back.'

'Did he give you a name?'

'John Gorey.'

'Were you shown any proof of his identity?'

'I took him at his word, sir. In my line of work, you have to rely on your instincts. John Gorey struck me as honest and down to earth.'

'Did he say where he was going when he left here?'

'He was about to set sail.'

'When?'

'That very day,' said the man. 'You're wasting your time looking for him here, sir. He could be a long way from Yarmouth by now.'

Colbeck's hopes crumbled.

# CHAPTER FIFTEEN

Moving out of the family house had lifted a huge burden from Grace Swarbrick. While she was still trying to cope with the enormity of what had happened, she no longer feared a bruising argument with her stepson. There was faint colour in her cheeks again and she was less likely to reach for her handkerchief so frequently. Anthea Freed had given the servants strict instructions to treat their guest with tact and forbearance. In place of a tense encounter with her stepson, Grace was met with love, kindness and unconditional sympathy. Alone in the drawing room with Anthea, she took the opportunity to thank her.

'What you've done for me is truly remarkable,' she said. 'You've brought me back from the edge of despair.'

'That's what friends should do, Grace. They are the people to whom you can turn in times of stress and pain.'

'I've suffered both and, though I fought hard, I felt that I was being ground down by them. Miraculously, you rescued me.'

'You needed to be in a place where you felt loved and cared for.'

'I've even regained some of my appetite since I've been here.'

There was a tap on the door then the maid entered with a tray. She went through the ritual of pouring the tea and giving each of the women her cup and saucer. After she'd gone, they resumed their conversation.

'It was so different with my first husband,' confided Grace. 'Because he worked largely from home, Roland and I saw each other more or less every day of the year. Jarvis was the opposite, always on the move, attending meetings, going to the House of Commons, making speeches here, there and everywhere. He never stopped.'

'Yet I remember you telling me that you felt you somehow knew Jarvis more intimately than your first husband.'

'That's right, but I can't explain why.'

'You and he had a marriage of true minds.'

'We had something I cherished,' said Grace, dolefully, 'and it disappeared in a flash.'

'You still have warm memories of him.'

'It's not the same, Anthea.'

They drank their tea in silence. Grace seemed to have drifted off into a trance. Her friend waited patiently until her visitor came out of it again. Realising what she'd done, Grace was apologetic.

'It's so *selfish* of me to do that.'

'You're entitled to be selfish, Grace.'

'It's unfair on you.'

'I don't feel that,' said Anthea. 'It's such a pity you're so far away from your family. I've written to your brother at that address in Jersey you gave me, but there's no telling when my letter will reach him.'

'Mail deliveries to the island are rather irregular, alas.'

'When he hears what's happened, I'm sure he'll come.'

'I do feel the need of my nearest and dearest.'

Anthea smiled gently. 'I hope you include me in that number.'

'Yes, of course. Because my family members live so far away, you've certainly been the nearest and one of the very dearest.'

'That's all I wanted to hear.'

There was another pause. Grace finished her tea then praised the quality of the porcelain. She appeared to be gathering her strength to touch on a more sensitive subject. In the end, she blurted out her request.

'Have there been many obituaries?'

'Yes, I've kept every one of them for you.'

'Were they kind to Jarvis?'

'They applauded him for the work he'd done for the ECR and for his contribution to parliamentary affairs. Would you like me to read them to you?'

'No, no,' said Grace, holding up both hands as if fending something off. 'I'm not ready for that yet. And I'm certainly not able to face the prospect of the inquest.'

'That's been deferred until you've recovered,' said Anthea. 'You are the key witness, so your testimony is crucial. I know it will be harrowing for you, but I'll be there to lend support.'

'You're a saint, Anthea.'

'Cecil used to say that about me when we first married. Then I started to collect good causes to support and he complained that I was spreading my saintliness too thinly.'

'Does he *mind* my being here?'

'He's as pleased as I am to be able to look after you. No matter what happens, you can always count on us.'

Grace smiled weakly, her eyes filling with tears of gratitude.

Madeleine Colbeck still refused to believe it. She kept looking at the letter time and again to see if she'd misread the amount being offered. Lydia Quayle was equally astonished. Though she admired her friend's talent, she didn't think that it would ever bring in a commission as generous as that. Yet both women had met Lionel Fairbank and judged him to be a man of integrity and honesty. His offer was a serious one.

'Two hundred pounds!' said Madeleine. 'I've never earned anywhere near that amount for one of my paintings before.'

'You deserve every penny of it.'

'I wasn't expecting as much as that.'

'Perhaps you ought to,' said Lydia, mischievously. 'From now on, refuse to take anything less for your work.'

'I'm in no position to make demands.'

'Perhaps you need me to act as your agent. I'll tell Mr Fairbank that he needs to increase his offer to a thousand pounds.'

They burst out laughing. Madeleine felt wonderful at the thought of being rated so highly by her admirer. Famous artists could command vast sums for their work, but she was realistic enough to know that she could never attain such heights. She was essentially an outsider, a young artist who had managed to find a market and who'd received a steady, if rather modest, income from it.

'I'd go on painting even if I didn't get paid for doing it,' she said.

'If you take that attitude,' warned Lydia, 'you'll be exploited.'

'Yes, there is that danger, I suppose.'

'What exactly did Mr Fairbank ask you to do?'

'There's a particular GWR locomotive that caught his eye. He wants me to paint it pulling a train at speed across the landscape. According to him, I manage to get more sense of movement into a painting than anyone he knows.'

'Yes,' said Lydia, happily 'you'll have two hundred pounds worth of movement this time.' She got up to embrace her friend. 'Oh, I'm so happy for you, Madeleine. It's wonderful news.'

'Thank you.'

'You must share it with your father.'

'Oh, no, that would be a big mistake.'

'Why?'

'I'll be painting a locomotive from the Great Western Railway. Father wouldn't approve of that if I was offered ten thousand pounds.'

'What do you think he would have made of Mr Fairbank?'

'They'll never meet, Lydia. I'll make certain of that. The two of them live in different worlds. I'd rather it stayed that way.'


They met at the appointed place and time. It was now the hottest part of the day and Leeming was uncomfortable. It grieved him that Colbeck looked calm, relaxed and untroubled by the weather.

'Before you ask me,' said Leeming, 'I had no luck at all until I strayed on to the beach and watched a puppet show. Punch and Judy always make me laugh. My boys would have loved the performance.'

'You were searching for a flesh-and-blood person, Victor, not for a pair of puppets with a stormy marriage.'

'I scoured the livery stables and learnt nothing of note. What about you, sir?'

'I had success fringed with failure.'

'I'm too tired for riddles,' moaned Leeming.

'I'm fairly confident that I found the stable where the killer had hired one of the horses he used. There was only one problem.'

'What was it?'

'Once he'd returned the animal, he sailed off.'

'Where was he going?'

'That's what we have to find out.'

'Don't tell me that the rogue has sailed away out of our reach.'

'Nowhere is out of our reach,' insisted Colbeck. 'If we can find out what his destination was, we can go after him.'

'How can we get that information?'

'We must talk to everyone in the harbour who owns a vessel. I have a rough description of the man we're after. He's operating under the name of John Gorey. Let's make a start.'

'It could take us ages,' said Leeming, mopping his brow with a handkerchief. 'The harbour is full of vessels.'

'Then it's time to start asking questions on the quayside. Only this time,' he said, meaningfully, 'there'll be no slipping off to watch Punch and Judy. We have a killer to catch. Think of the man you saw lying on a slab in the police morgue. Mr Swarbrick needs us.'

For someone as addicted to work as Edward Tallis, the enforced rest soon felt like an imposition. Being in Canterbury again made him feel restless. He complained to Wardlow that he couldn't stay there because Scotland Yard would never run efficiently without him. Even when he was repeatedly told that the commissioner had sanctioned his holiday, he remained agitated. Wardlow found to his dismay that he was having the same conversation with his friend time and again.

'Don't you understand?' said Tallis. 'They'll *miss* me.'

'They appointed an acting superintendent, Edward.'

'Who is it?'

'Inspector Vallence.'

'I'm not sure that he'd be able to cope with the complexity of the role. It's not something one can master easily.'

'He'll follow your example.'

'Colbeck would have been my choice.'

'The inspector is dealing with a murder in Norwich. You talked about it when we chatted over a brandy last night.'

Tallis was surprised. 'Did I?'

'Yes, someone was shot dead on a train, one of the local Members of Parliament. You said that it was the kind of challenging case that only Colbeck could solve.'

'But he can only solve it with me harrying him remorselessly.'

'Inspector Vallence will have to do that now.'

'What about me?'

'You'll stay here until you start to feel better.'

'I *am* better, Terence. There's nothing wrong with me.'

'No, of course, there isn't,' said Wardlow with a reassuring pat on his companion's knee. 'But we all need a rest from time to time.'

They were ensconced in leather-backed chairs in the drawing room, two distinguished old soldiers who'd served together in India and survived all manner of dangers. Wardlow tried to guide the conversation around to an exchange of military reminiscences but he was soon interrupted by a visitor. The maid brought in a tall, skinny, sharp-featured man in his sixties. His gaunt face was ignited by his smile. Wardlow struggled to his feet to exchange a handshake, then he turned to Tallis.

'Edward, this is a friend of mine – Donald Kitson.'

211

'How do you do?' said Tallis, shaking hands with the newcomer.

'I'm very glad to meet you, Superintendent,' said Kitson. 'Terence has told me a lot about you.'

'Don't believe him. He always exaggerates.'

Kitson grinned then took the seat indicated by Wardlow.

'I'm sure that you'll enjoy your stay here,' he said. 'Canterbury is a delightful place to live – though I gather that your last visit here was rather gruelling. Is that true?'

Returning to his office after his meeting with senior colleagues, Cecil Freed found someone waiting impatiently. Oliver Trant jumped up from his seat to confront him.

'Have you seen this morning's newspapers?' he asked.

'Yes, I have.'

'Swarbrick is quoted in nearly all of them.'

'He told me that he'd given them a brief interview.'

'Now we know what that interview was about,' said Trant, acidly. 'Instead of praising his dead father, he bragged about his determination to replace him as an MP.'

'I can't muzzle him, Oliver. He's free to speak.'

'You promised me that you'd try to dissuade him from standing, yet here he is, telling the whole world about his future in politics.'

'I'd still back you to win,' said Freed, 'and I'll use my influence for you behind the scenes.'

'I need you to do it more openly, Cecil.'

'That could cause difficulties.'

'For whom?'

'Principally, for me. Jarvis Swarbrick and I were close friends. Our respective wives are equally close. If I'm seen supporting you to the hilt, it could get very embarrassing for me.'

'You *promised* me.'

'All I said was that I'd help you to a degree.'

'Meanwhile, you'll be letting Swarbrick trade on the relationship between you and his father.'

'I can't help that, Oliver. I've tried to head him off by arguing that you have a lot of support here, but he's resolved to make a bid for his father's old seat. Whatever I can do to further your cause, I'll do, but it won't be visible.'

'In that case, it won't be effective.'

'Oh, yes it will,' said Freed, forcefully. 'You'll be surprised how much can be achieved by whispering in the right ears.'

Trant was partially mollified. 'I'll hold you to that.'

'If you'd come earlier, you could have met Andrew himself.'

'What was *he* doing here?'

'He was seething with anger because my wife had rescued his stepmother and brought her to our house for safety. Andrew has been dying to unload some of the resentment he's built up against her over the years. Thankfully, Grace Swarbrick has been spared that.'

'Your wife was wise to step in.'

'Andrew didn't see it that way,' said Freed. 'He believes that we've betrayed him. As for Grace, he claims that she's hidden his father's will somewhere so that he can't get his hands on it.'

'The solicitor will have a copy.'

'He'll be seeing him very soon. Andrew thinks that his stepmother should be forced to go with him.'

'Is she capable of doing that?'

'No, Oliver, she's far too weak. I doubt if she'll ever be the same happy and active woman ever again.'

'What is she going to do?'

'I don't believe she dares to look into the future.'

'Might she go back to Jersey?'

'She'd be there right now, if Andrew had his way.'

'He has no right to turn her out of the house.'

'He's hoping that the solicitor might give him that right.'

'Well, I'm glad there'll be a bitter family wrangle. It will help me.'

'Are you sure?'

'If Andrew Swarbrick gets involved in a long and acrimonious battle with his stepmother, he won't win any friends in the constituency. People will be appalled by the way he treats a defenceless widow.'

'Let me correct you straight away,' said Freed. 'Grace is by no means defenceless. She has my wife as her bodyguard and Anthea is a match for anyone.'

To counter the feeling that she was locked away with no freedom of movement, Grace Swarbrick was taken for a walk through the estate by her hostess. She admired the scenic beauty on every side. Strolling through the parkland in bright sunshine was a tonic for her. When the two of them sat on a bench beside the lake, they watched the swans glide effortlessly across the water, oblivious to the crisis that had brought Grace to the property.

'How do you feel now?' asked her friend.

'I feel safe. I'm so glad that you brought me here, Anthea.'

'You had to get away from Andrew.'

'There's something I haven't asked you – largely because I haven't dared to think about it.'

'You want to know what progress the detectives have made.'

'I feel strong enough to ask now.'

'Well, I can only go on what Cecil told me, which means that I've been feeding on scraps.'

'I want my husband's killer hanged,' said Grace with a sudden burst of anger. 'They will catch him, won't they?'

'It may take time,' admitted the other. 'According to Cecil, they've found some evidence but still haven't been able to identify the man. Inspector Colbeck, however, is tenacious.'

'He was also very considerate.'

'That's rare among policemen. In the course of my work, I've dealt with quite a few of them. They're not the most sensitive creatures.'

'What is the inspector doing now?'

'I daresay he'll be looking for more clues.'

'Well, I hope they lead him to the black-hearted devil who shot Jarvis dead right in front of me.'

'Try not to dwell on it, Grace.'

'I can't help it.'

'We must simply watch and pray.'

'I'm in such constant agony,' said Grace, wincing. 'Until they arrest that fiend, I'll have no relief from it.'


The harbour was bustling. Bobbing up and down, vessels of all sizes were moored there. As they walked along, Colbeck and Leeming had to step over ropes and take care to avoid being soaked by the water slapping the thick timbers and sending up spray. A stiff breeze cooled their faces. Above the babble of voices, they could hear the cry of the gulls as they wheeled, swooped and floated on the wind. There was a bewildering frenzy of activity. As one boat arrived, a fishing smack departed. As passengers boarded one vessel, people were disembarking from another. Cargo was being unloaded everywhere. Somebody was playing a concertina and singing. Watching it all, the detectives couldn't help admiring the bravery of sailors about to take relatively small craft across the unforgiving North Sea.

'I'd be too scared to do that, sir,' said Leeming.

'Yet you once crossed the Atlantic.'

'That was in a big steamship. It felt quite solid under our feet until we were caught in a squall, that is. I've never prayed so hard in my life.'

Their search was futile at first. Nobody remembered a passenger by the name of John Gorey embarking days earlier. Colbeck's description of the man was too general to be of any real use. In the course of their tour, they saw three or four young men who fitted it. Their only real hope lay with the name. They eventually came upon a couple of old salts, playing cards on an upturned basket. Both had weather-beaten faces, bronzed by the sun, and bare arms with thick veins entwined around them like small snakes. Leeming was fascinated by the tattoos they wore.

'I wonder if one of you gentlemen could help us,' Colbeck began.

The men cackled. 'We ain't no gen'lemen, sir,' said one.

'What are ye after?' asked the other.

'We're searching for a young man by the name of John Gorey.'

'Why?'

'He's wanted for a brutal murder in Norwich.'

'Ah, is this the one that happened on the railway?'

'Yes.'

'We read about that.' He peered at them. 'Who're you, then?'

'We're the detectives sent to arrest him.'

'D'you hear that, Sam?' he asked his friend.

'Be quiet,' said the other, a brawny man with a tattoo of a mermaid on his arms. 'It's that name as sounds a bit familiar.' He took a small ledger from his pocket and flipped through the pages. 'Did you call him John Gorey?'

'Yes,' said Colbeck. 'Do you know where he went?'

'Oh, yes, I got a list of passengers on our boat right here. You're out of luck, sirs,' he went on. 'John Gorey – if it is the man you're after – sailed on the *Flying Fish* three days ago.'

'Where was the vessel going?'

'Cherbourg.'

It was a chance visit that couldn't have been better timed. Having been sent to collect details of a burglary in Westminster, Alan Hinton couldn't resist calling on Madeleine Colbeck who lived only four blocks away. To his delight, he found that Lydia Quayle was still there. She was as thrilled by the encounter as he was. Seeing a rare opportunity for them to be together, Madeleine made a polite excuse and moved away. He stepped forward to intercept her.

'But I've come to tell you about the superintendent, Mrs Colbeck.'

'You can tell Lydia instead,' said Madeleine. 'She'll pass on the details to me later on.'

'Oh, I see.'

'I won't be long.'

When Madeleine disappeared, there was a slight awkwardness between the others. They sat down, gazed at each other and managed a few niceties. Lydia then asked about the superintendent. Hinton told her exactly what had happened the previous evening and how Wardlow had responded to the emergency in spite of his arthritis. When Hinton had arrived at work that morning, he recalled, he'd been told that Tallis was not there and that his orders would now come from Inspector Vallence.

Lydia was enthralled. Though she had great sympathy for Tallis, what she'd gleaned from his report was that Constable Hinton had behaved promptly and with compassion. She'd heard many accounts of the superintendent's fiery temper. Some detectives would have been loath to help a man with such tyrannical leanings, yet Hinton had put his dislike aside to go in search of the one man who might rescue Tallis before his peculiar behaviour got him into serious trouble.

'It was so kind of you, Alan,' she said, effusively.

'I tried my best.'

'You made such an effort on the superintendent's behalf.'

'I felt that it was the least I could do, Lydia.'

Since they'd now progressed to the stage of using first names, he let hers roll around his mouth like a chocolate. It tasted delicious.

'What happens now?'

'Captain Wardlow told me that he'd introduce the superintendent to a friend of his, a Dr Kitson. He wanted a professional opinion of his condition.'

'That was thoughtful of him,' said Lydia. 'They can't treat him properly until they know how poorly he really is.'

'The most important thing is to conceal Dr Kitson's medical background. If the superintendent knew the truth, it would upset him.'

'But he's a detective, Alan. Won't he work it out for himself?'

'It's unlikely. His mind wanders everywhere. He couldn't even find his way to Scotland Yard the other day. That's how serious it is, Lydia. I think he works far too hard. He drives himself on relentlessly. At long last, he's been taken off the treadmill.'

'You talk about him with such affection.'

Hinton laughed. 'Most of the time, I think he's a real ogre.'

'Then it's all the more credit to you that you can overlook any past slights and offer your help.'

'He won't thank me for it.'

'*I* will, Alan. What you've done is admirable.'

'Thank you,' he said, beaming. 'Thank you, Lydia.'


On the train back to Norwich, they were able to review their search. Leeming's reaction differed sharply from that of Colbeck. The sergeant believed that the exercise had not only been a waste of time, it had signalled an end to the possibility that they might ever catch the killer. He sagged despondently.

'We might as well give up and go home,' he said.

'Don't be so defeatist.'

'He's escaped from us, sir.'

'What about the person or persons who hired him in the first place? Have they escaped from us as well?'

'I was forgetting them.'

'You're also forgetting what those men told us,' said Colbeck. 'They're hoping that the *Flying Fish* will arrive back in Yarmouth some time in the next couple of days.'

'What use is that to us?' asked Leeming. 'It's not as if John Gorey is going to sail back to England for our benefit.'

'Perhaps not, but he may have told the captain what his destination was. After landing at Cherbourg, where would he go next? Once he was aboard that boat,' argued Colbeck, 'Gorey would have felt that he was safe. He'd have relaxed completely and chatted to the crew to pass the time. Someone was bound to have asked him where he was going.'

'I never thought of that, sir.'

'Losing him has been a setback,' conceded Colbeck, 'but we haven't lost those who'll know where he is.'

'I'm sorry, sir,' said Leeming, resignedly, 'but I still feel that he may have got away scot-free.'

'Would *you* like to be the one to say that to his widow?'

'No, I wouldn't.'

'We must remain positive, Victor.'

'I'll try my best, sir.'

They arrived at Norwich Station to find the platform filled with waiting passengers. While Colbeck went off to speak to the stationmaster, Horace Pryor fought his way through the melee. He grabbed Leeming by the sleeve and took him aside.

'How did you get on in Yarmouth?'

'I watched a Punch and Judy show.'

Pryor gaped. 'Are you serious?'

'It was very funny.'

'I thought you might have picked up a scent.'

'All we picked up was the smell of fish,' said Leeming. 'We could have got that in Norwich market. You'll have to excuse me. We have to go off to the police station.'

'Do you have anything to report there?'

'Oh, yes – I can recommend the Punch and Judy show.'

Leeming went off. Because he didn't look over his shoulder, he didn't see Sergeant Duff closing in quickly on Pryor.

Feeling the need for one of his cigars, Tallis went out into the garden to smoke it so that he didn't create a fug in the house. Wardlow and Kitson were left alone to talk about him.

'I had the impression that my plan worked,' said Wardlow. 'He didn't realise that you were a doctor.'

'That's because I didn't question him in the searching way I would have done had he come to my surgery.'

'You should have been an actor, Donald.'

'It's a precarious profession. I prefer to have a regular income.'

'What's your initial response to Edward?'

'He has a problem, and a serious one at that.'

'Is he beyond hope?'

'Oh, no, I wouldn't say that. All I've had so far is a brief chat with him, supplemented by those reports you gave me from two of his colleagues. I'll need to see more of him, Terence.'

'We mustn't make it too obvious.'

'In getting him away from his work, you've already taken the most important step. His convalescence has now started.'

'What I'm hoping for is a cure.'

'That might be asking too much.'

Looking through the window, they could see Tallis strolling around the garden and leaving a cloud of smoke in his wake. Wardlow pointed out that he'd done the same thing during his visit in the previous December. He'd had his cigars in the garden even though it was very cold out there.

'What was your wife's opinion of him?'

'Oh,' said Wardlow, 'Margery found him rather stiff and uncommunicative. Edward has never been at ease in female company. Though he's always polite, he tends to be shy.'

'And yet he's so forceful in the company of men.'

'He has the habit of command, Donald. At least he *did* have it,' he added, sadly. 'It seems to have deserted him now.'

'Who was that man he kept talking about?'

'Inspector Colbeck?'

'It's a name that rings a bell.'

'And so it should. Colbeck was instrumental in finding Edward and rescuing him from what would have been an excruciating death. It was in the national as well as the local newspapers.'

'That's how I must have come across the inspector.'

'I've been trying to steer him away from talking about any of his colleagues. The less he thinks about Scotland Yard, the better.'

'I agree.'

'It's just that Colbeck happens to be engaged in a particularly difficult case of murder at the moment. Edward feels that he should be urging him on to make an arrest.'

'It's strange that he didn't mention the inspector when I got him talking about his abduction. In fact, he hardly touched on the actual rescue. His obsession was with the brutal treatment he received.'

'Do you find that significant?'

'Yes, I do.'

Good news awaited the detectives when they got to the police station. As a result of their search, the police had found the stable from which the killer had hired the black horse he rode at the actual murder. The man had given the name of John Gorey and left a bay mare at livery. Leeming's theory about the exchange of horses had been proved correct and he enjoyed the praise that Inspector Jellings heaped on him.

'I thought at first it was a wild guess,' he said.

Leeming grinned. 'Yes, I could see that in your eyes, sir.'

'But I came to appreciate that it was a clever piece of deduction.'

'Victor has a talent for it,' said Colbeck.

They were in the inspector's office. Colbeck went on to give him an attenuated account of their visit to Yarmouth, admitting his irritation when he first heard that Gorey had sailed away from the town, yet still clinging to the possibility that someone in the crew of the returning *Flying Fish* might have some idea of the killer's ultimate destination. Jellings was disappointed.

'I'd hoped for better news,' he admitted.

'It will come in time,' said Colbeck, cheerily.

'Your optimism is reassuring.'

'No, it isn't,' said Leeming. 'I'm still worried that we've lost him.'

'He's followed a plan of escape,' said Colbeck. 'That confirms our earlier belief that the crime was not an opportunist one. There's clear evidence of preparation and collusion.'

'All we have to go on is the name – the false name, probably – of a man who's now gone to France or even further afield.'

'His confederates are still here, though,' Colbeck reminded him. 'Take heart, Sergeant. I have the feeling that we're getting closer to solving this crime than we think.'

The old man walked his dog through the streets until they came to a small park. Letting it off the leash, he smiled as it went bounding off across the grass. It disappeared into a thicket and its excited barking stopped. A moment later, it came running towards its owner with something between its teeth. The old man squinted.

'What've you got there, then?'

# CHAPTER SIXTEEN

Everyone in the city had seen the posters advertising a reward for anyone who could provide information that led to the arrest and conviction of the man who had killed Jarvis Swarbrick. Local newspapers also carried the relevant details. The tempting size of the reward encouraged a number of people to come forward with concocted stories. They were soon exposed as falsehoods and their authors were issued with a stern warning and sent on their way or – in two cases – given a night in a police cell to reflect on the stupidity of trying to get money by means of fraud. As the days passed, the fevered speculation didn't ease off in the slightest. It remained the main topic of conversation in Norwich and beyond. The killer was still at large. He'd left the whole region in a state of apprehension.

Bartram Duff didn't succumb to the general hysteria. Whenever he walked past the reward posters at the station, he simply smiled at them. Pryor passed on everything that Leeming had said to him and Duff found an even better source of information in Eric Burridge, who happened to drink in the same pub as the railway policeman. On the previous evening, Duff had learnt a great deal about the state of the investigation and it had only cost him the price of a pint. Leeming's comments on his return from Yarmouth confirmed that the detectives had failed to find what they had been after. Duff savoured the good news.

During a break that afternoon, he left the station to go in search of the friend who lived down the alley. When he banged on the door of the house, it was opened cautiously by the owner.

'What have you found out?' he asked.

'It's good news.'

'Tell me.'

'The police have got nowhere. We're in the clear.'

The other man grinned. 'You'd better come in, Bart.'

Though she had stopped weeping so pathetically all the time, Grace Swarbrick had not adjusted fully to her grief. Her face was still a study in anguish and her eyes were red-rimmed. When her friend entered the room, Grace was hunched on the sofa, hands tightly clasped.

'I'm not intruding, am I?' asked Anthea.

'No, no, do come in.'

'Thank you.'

'There's no need for thanks. This is your house.'

'It's also yours while you still have need for it.'

'I'll have to go back to face Andrew sooner or later.'

'I think you should wait until his temper cools,' said the other. 'If he behaves like this at home, then my sympathy goes out to his poor wife. Caroline must have a lot to put up with.'

'That's partly my fault.'

'I don't see how it could be, Grace.'

'If my stepson had behaved as his wife did, there'd be no problem. She was ready to accept me into the family but was shouted down by Andrew. Indirectly, Caroline suffered because of me.'

'How do you know?'

'I found her card among all the other condolences. She told me how upset she was that Jarvis had died before we could be united as a family. Needless to say,' she went on, 'Andrew doesn't know that his wife has been in touch with me.'

Before Anthea could comment, there was a tap on the door and it was opened, after a summons, by a maid. She bobbed politely.

'Excuse me, Mrs Freed, but Inspector Colbeck is here.'

'I'll come immediately.'

'I wasn't sent to find you,' said the other. 'He wants to speak to Mrs Swarbrick. He said that it was important.'

Grace rose from her chair at once.

Now that the air had been cleared between them, Madeleine was pleased to see her father that afternoon. Once he'd tired himself out by playing in the garden with his granddaughter, they were able to talk properly again. Andrews used a handkerchief to dab at the perspiration on his brow.

'I wish we'd had a big garden like that when you were born, Maddy.'

'We managed quite happily without.'

'Living here, Helen has so many advantages. I just hope that she grows up to appreciate them.'

'I had the advantage of a loving family,' said Madeleine, 'so I have no regrets about living in a small house with only a tiny garden.'

'That's good to hear.'

'Lydia called in earlier.'

'That was nice for you. There can't be many people who meet for the first time because one of their fathers is murdered, but that was the case with you and Lydia. You've become really good friends.'

'I'm not her only friend, Father.'

'No, she's got me as well.'

Madeleine smiled. 'I wasn't thinking of you, actually. While she was here, Constable Hinton called. I left them alone.'

'Why?'

'It was so that they could talk in private, of course. Lydia likes him and he obviously dotes on her. When he turned up, it was too good a chance to miss.'

'Are you plotting something, Maddy?' he said, warningly.

'No, I'm trying to help, that's all.'

'It sounds to me as if you're interfering.'

'When Alan had gone, Lydia thanked me for leaving them alone together.'

'What was he doing here in the first place?'

'Since he was in the area, he thought I'd like to know about what happened to Superintendent Tallis.'

'And what *did* happen?'

'He's on leave from Scotland Yard.'

'I don't believe it!' exclaimed Andrews. 'He hates the very idea of having time off.'

'I think it shows you how unwell he must be.'

'Will he ever come back?'

'I don't know, Father.'

'Well, I hope that he retires for good,' said Andrews. 'That way, Robert can take over as superintendent. Instead of gallivanting around the country on the railway system, he'd be able to work from home and have the pleasure of watching his daughter grow up.'

'That would suit me and Helen, but it wouldn't suit Robert.'

'How do you know?'

'He loves his work in the same way that you did, Father. He enjoys shooting off to different parts of the country to deal with major crimes. I accepted that when I agreed to marry him. Besides,' she said, 'nothing will stop Edward Tallis from taking over once he's better.'


Grace Swarbrick stared at the reticule with mingled horror and gratitude. Though it was a startling reminder of the murder, it was something that she valued very much. She had to struggle to hold back tears. Colbeck held it out to her.

'It had some grass stains on it,' he said, 'but I cleaned them off.'

'Where did you find it?' asked Anthea.

'A man was walking his dog in a park. When he let the animal loose, it came back with this between its teeth.'

'Take it, Grace. It's yours.'

'I could see that at a glance,' said the other. 'Jarvis bought it for me years ago.'

'Please look inside and tell me what's missing,' said Colbeck.

He handed the reticule to her and watched. She held it very gently as if it was fragile then she ran her fingers over it. They could see that memories were flooding back into her mind. Grace opened it very slowly and looked inside, taking out the items one by one. When she'd examined each one, she put them back in turn.

'Everything is here,' she said, 'except the purse.'

'I'm afraid that he kept that, Mrs Swarbrick,' explained Colbeck. 'With luck, he may still have it when we finally catch up with him.'

'And when will that be, Inspector?' asked Anthea.

'It may take time.'

'Do you have any idea where he might be?'

'Oh, yes, we know that he fled to Yarmouth. The sergeant and I spent the whole morning there. We tracked him to the stables where he'd hired a horse, using the name of John Gorey.'

I don't know anyone by that name,' said Grace, a perplexed frown appearing. 'Was my husband killed by a complete stranger?'

'I think he was hiding his true identity.'

'And where is he now?'

'That's the problem,' admitted Colbeck with a sigh. 'He sailed from Yarmouth on the day of the murder.'

'Do you mean that he's not even in this country?'

'I'm afraid not, Mrs Swarbrick. He boarded a vessel that was heading for Cherbourg.'

'Cherbourg!' she cried in alarm. 'You'll *never* catch him.'

She collapsed into convulsive sobs.


Acting on medical advice, Wardlow took his guest for a long walk that afternoon. Dr Kitson had told him that healthy exercise was a vital part of the patient's convalescence. They'd both agreed how important it was to keep Tallis unaware of the fact that he *was* being treated as a patient. To that end, Wardlow had suggested a stroll in as casual a manner as he could manage, saying that the pain from his arthritis had abated for once. Tallis was glad to accept the invitation. It was a fine day and he liked the feeling of the sun on his back as they strode along. By following the winding country lane outside Wardlow's house, they eventually came to the parish church of St Peter and St Paul in Upper Hardres. It was set in the middle of a sheep farm and they could see the flock grazing happily in the fields around them. Stopping beside the churchyard, Tallis let his eye roam across the gravestones, damaged over the years by the vagaries of the climate and rearranged in some cases by subsidence.

'Those are the fortunate ones,' said Tallis, quietly.

'I don't regard dying as in any way fortunate, Edward.'

'I was thinking of all the comrades of ours who fell in battle and who, in many cases, were buried in unmarked graves. No families would ever come with flowers or say prayers for the salvation of their souls. In a country churchyard like this,' Tallis went on, 'everyone has been laid to rest after a proper funeral, then mourned by their families and friends.'

'That's a rather morbid observation,' said Wardlow.

'It was one of the risks we took as soldiers. To die in a far-off land meant that we'd simply become anonymous casualties. I lost count of the number of letters I wrote from India to the parents of men who'd fallen in action. It was always a chastening exercise for me.'

'The families were very grateful to be told what had happened.'

'But that wasn't always the case, Terence.'

'Are you saying that some objected?'

'No,' replied Tallis. 'I'm saying that I often manipulated the truth to spare their feelings. Instead of telling them their son had been blown to pieces by an exploding shell or hacked to death so viciously that he was completely unrecognisable, I simply pretended that he was killed while fighting valiantly.'

'I think we should walk on,' suggested Wardlow. 'Standing beside a churchyard has prompted some unhappy memories for you.'

'It wasn't the gravestones,' said the other, falling in beside him as they moved on. 'I don't need those to induce thoughts of death. They come to me unbidden.'

'It's unhealthy to brood on such things, Edward.'

'I can't help it. The last time I was in Canterbury I was taught a salutary lesson. I am not – as I foolishly imagined – immortal. Death is only around the corner for me. It's already starting to crook its finger and beckon.' He touched his friend's shoulder apologetically. 'Forgive me, Terence. You've made such an effort to keep up with me on your stick and I reward you by lapsing into macabre introspection.'

'I'd hoped the fresh air would revive the both of us.'

'And it's done so in my case.'

'No, it hasn't. It's brought on this avalanche of dark thoughts.'

'They're gone now, I promise you.'

'Thank heaven for that.'

'By the way,' said Tallis, 'I meant to say how much I enjoyed meeting your friend, Kitson. He's good company and has a rich supply of anecdotes. What's his background?'

'He's a retired stockbroker.'

'Then he's a wise man.'

'Why do you think that?'

'There are not many stockbrokers who go to India in order to get slaughtered in a fierce battle fought in blistering heat. They leave that to reckless, misguided men with a patriotic urge to fight our enemies. Look at your friend. Living in comfortable retirement, Kitson is hail and hearty with no old wounds to plague him and no bad memories to torment him.'

'Would *you* rather have been a stockbroker?'

'No, thank you,' said Tallis, smiling. 'I'd have died of boredom.'

Madeleine went back to her studio with the intention of spending a couple of precious hours on her latest painting. The moment she picked up her brush, however, she felt her hand tremble with excitement. Instead of dealing with the canvas in front of her, she was preoccupied with thoughts of the commission from Lionel Fairbank. It had not merely boosted her confidence, she felt that it had somehow validated her as an artist. While still worried about the amount of money involved, she was keen to accept the commission. Colbeck had approved in principle and Lydia, who'd actually met and liked Fairbank, had urged her to give his offer priority.

Yet something still held her back. There was the lingering doubt that she might be unequal to the task, the fear that it would mean more time away from her daughter, the worry that her father might somehow find out what she was actually painting and, in spite of his promises, accuse her of betrayal, and, most important of all, the fact that her husband didn't know the full implications of the commission. Madeleine had written a letter of explanation, but it wouldn't arrive until the following day and she couldn't expect him to suspend his investigation and return home to discuss her situation. Critically, her husband couldn't meet and appraise Lionel Fairbank. That troubled her.

While not applying any pressure, Fairbank had asked for a decision to be made very soon. Ideally, he wanted her response during the two days when he was staying in London with his son. The address he'd left with her was in Belgravia and Madeleine was tempted to hire a cab to take her there so that she could give him her decision in person. She soon rejected that impulse, feeling that she should control her enthusiasm and appear more dignified. A polite letter was required. Ideally, she'd have liked Colbeck to have seen it first, but he'd always encouraged her to make all the decisions regarding her work by herself. Here was a case in point. Madeleine decided to follow her instincts.

When she'd written the letter, she asked one of the servants to take a cab to Belgravia to deliver it, ensuring that Fairbank got an early reply to his offer. During his visit to the house, he'd talked about Madeleine going to Berkshire to make sketches of the view and the locomotive from the vantage point of his house. Somehow she had to find the time to do that and was pleased when Lydia had volunteered to go with her. Now that the decision had actually been made, Madeleine shook off her nervousness. When she picked up her brush again, there were neither tremors nor hesitation this time. Madeleine was able to paint freely again.

The firm of Gilby, Tate and Regan Solicitors was located in a large, solid building near the centre of the city that gave it a view of the two defining edifices of Norwich. From one side, they could see the castle looming above them while, from the other side, the spire of the beautiful medieval cathedral was clearly visible above the intervening premises. As he approached the offices on foot, Andrew Swarbrick was irked by the fact that he'd had to wait for an appointment with Neville Gilby, their family solicitor. When he was admitted to Gilby's office, irritation showed clearly in his face.

'I'm sorry for the delay,' said Gilby, shaking his hand. 'You've caught us at an extremely busy time, Mr Swarbrick.'

'I would have thought that my father's murder gave me some sort of priority in your appointments diary.'

'Perhaps you're right.'

'I *am* right, Mr Gilby.'

'Then I apologise once more.'

As soon as they'd sat down, the solicitor started to offer his condolences, but he was silenced by a wave of Swarbrick's hand.

'We can dispense with the niceties,' he said.

'If that's what you wish, sir.'

'It is.'

Gilby was an obese man of middle years with greying hair bisected by a centre parting. When he spoke, his jowls wobbled.

'I must say that I found your request rather strange, Mr Swarbrick.'

'Why is that?'

'You didn't need to come here to ask about your father's will when he kept a copy of it at the house.'

'It's no longer there, Mr Gilby.'

'Really?'

'I've instituted a thorough search.'

'It would be kept in the safe, surely?'

'That was the first place I looked.'

'How odd!' said Gilby, frowning. 'Has it disappeared?'

'It's disappeared or been deliberately removed.'

'Could your stepmother shed no light on the mystery?'

'I've been unable even to see her, let alone have a conversation.'

'The shock of what happened must have dealt Mrs Swarbrick a fearsome blow. I can understand why she's still stunned.'

'Let's leave her out of this,' said Swarbrick, tetchily. 'I came here to see the terms of my father's will.'

'You must already know the general outline of it, surely?'

'I want the specific details.'

'Strictly speaking—'

'Don't shilly-shally, man. I have a legal right to know what my father's wishes were and I'd be obliged if you'd stop prevaricating. You've kept me waiting long enough already.'

'There's no need to take that tone with me,' said Gilby, retreating into pomposity. 'Your father and I enjoyed an excellent relationship for many years. It was built on trust and mutual respect.'

'I accept that,' said Swarbrick, tone softening. 'He spoke well of you, Mr Gilby. I hope that you and I can achieve the same level of understanding.'

'That will depend on you. What helped us was the fact that your father had read jurisprudence at Oxford, as I later did. Indeed, we went to the same college. Jarvis Swarbrick,' he continued, 'had an appreciation of how the law works. That's indispensable when it comes to framing legislation in Parliament. Your own background, I believe, is in finance.'

'That's immaterial,' said the other, smarting at what he saw was a deliberate jibe. 'The House of Commons needs people who have a grasp of the monetary system just as much as it needs lawyers. In any case, I learnt a great deal from my father. I watched him draft his bill for the amalgamation of five railway companies, and we went through it together line by line.'

'He was very punctilious.'

'So am I, Mr Gilby. That's why I deserve to replace him.'

The solicitor was startled. 'You wish to replace him as an MP?'

'Is that such an absurd ambition?' said Swarbrick, peevishly.

'No, no, in one sense, you'd be the obvious person. I wish you well. You follow someone who set a very high standard.'

'I promise to maintain – if not to surpass – that standard.'

'The people of Norwich will be pleased to hear that,' said Gilby. 'First, however, you have to gain the nomination. That will entail a contest with other potential candidates. One man, in particular, has coveted a seat in Parliament for many years.'

'I've already spoken to Oliver Trant.'

'He'll be your most dangerous rival.'

'I have qualities that he signally lacks.'

'But he lives and runs a business in Norwich. Mr Trant is very visible and highly esteemed.'

'I, too, will have my base in this city. When I acquire ownership of the family home, I'll move here at once with my wife and children. I think it's vital for a Member of Parliament to reside in the constituency that he represents.' He saw the look on the solicitor's face. 'Have I said something wrong?'

'Your plans are built on a supposition, sir.'

'There's no supposition involved,' asserted Swarbrick. 'I give you my word. I'm certain to win that nomination.'

'I'm not thinking about that, sir.'

'Then what's the problem?'

Gilby didn't need to put it into words. He simply looked at his client with a kind of reluctant sympathy. When he realised what must have happened, Swarbrick was rendered speechless. His jaw muscles tightened, his eyes bulged and his body went slack. All that he could do was to sit there like a rag doll. It was a full minute before Gilby broke the silence.

'I assumed that you knew, Mr Swarbrick,' he said.

'There must be a grotesque mistake.'

'Your father didn't make mistakes, sir. He had a lawyer's penchant for exactitude. When he changed the will in favour of his wife . . .' He paused as Swarbrick twitched angrily. 'Naturally, he left you a generous share of his capital and part of his property, but the house and the bulk of the estate will go to his spouse.'

'When did this happen?' demanded Swarbrick, now on his feet.

'It was well over six months ago, sir.'

'That can't be true. Father and I had started to see each other in London occasionally. We were mending fences. We were closer than we have been for years.'

'It's not reflected in his will, I fear.'

'Let me see it!'

'I don't think you should in that mood, Mr Swarbrick.'

'You can't keep it from me. It's a legal right.'

'When you calm down, I'll be happy to let you peruse it.'

'I *am* calm,' insisted the other. 'Where is it?'

Gilby stood up. 'I'll not be badgered, sir.'

'This is *her* doing, isn't it? When my father came to alter his will, my stepmother was at his elbow, wasn't she? It's disgraceful. I'm not having my inheritance stolen by that harpy!'

'I'd rather you stopped shouting, Mr Swarbrick.'

'Don't tell me what to do!' yelled the other. 'You're part of the conspiracy to rob me of what I was promised. I'll contest the will. That's what I'll do. I'll hire the best solicitor in London and fight you tooth and nail.'

'You're at liberty to do so, sir, but it will be a shameful waste of time, money and effort. When your father made those changes,' he stressed, 'he was in full possession of his faculties. You will just have to accept the decisions that he reached.'

'Never!' howled Swarbrick, banging on the desk with a fist. 'I want my rights and I'm determined to get them.'

Turning on his heel, he charged out in a towering rage.

Colbeck and Leeming had adjourned to the Rib of Beef to review the day's events while consuming their much-needed drinks. After quaffing more of his beer, Leeming smacked his lips with satisfaction.

'This is good stuff, sir,' he said, holding up his tankard.

'Don't let Mrs Freed see you with it, Victor. She'd evict us.'

'I'd like that. We could take rooms here instead.'

'We're better off in that cottage. Now that Mrs Swarbrick has moved into the house, we can see her any time we like without having to dodge her stepson, the young Hamlet.'

'Who?'

'He's the main character in Shakespeare's play of that name,' said Colbeck. 'When his father is murdered, he's horrified to hear that his mother has married again without mourning the death of her husband properly. In Swarbrick's case, it's his father who married with indecent haste after his first wife died, so you can see the similarity. I won't continue the analogy because it goes no further than that basic situation. Besides,' he added, 'Hamlet is young, highly sensitive and has the best soliloquies ever written by Shakespeare. We can't really put Swarbrick in that league.'

'According to you, he's an arrogant bully.'

'That's the kindest thing I'd say about him.'

'What about the father? Was he the same?'

'Common report has it that he was an exceptional man – a brilliant speaker, a tireless MP, a passionate believer in the future of the railway system and a thoroughly decent human being.'

'Who could want to kill such a man?'

'We go back to our earlier conclusion, Victor. It must be either someone with a grudge against him or a person wishing to replace him.'

'There is another possibility, sir.'

'I'd be glad to hear it.'

'Instead of looking at the murder victim,' suggested Leeming, 'perhaps we should look closer at his wife. Suppose that someone was very attracted to her and saw Swarbrick as an obstacle that had to be removed.'

'That's an interesting idea,' said Colbeck, pensively.

'Thank you, sir.'

'It wouldn't be the first time that thwarted love was a motive for murder. I can't believe that Mrs Swarbrick would ever encourage another man, but she must have been a beautiful woman in her younger days. You can still see vestiges of it.'

'Who would know if she had any other admirers?'

'Mrs Freed might.'

'How much older was Swarbrick than his wife?'

'Oh, it was several years.'

'Do you think that this other man – if there is one – will be younger than her husband?'

'Oh, no,' said Colbeck without hesitation, 'I'm inclined to think that he might actually be older than Swarbrick. Since she's already married one man from another generation, he could be hoping that it gives him a realistic chance of success.'

Feeling a need for some fresh air, Madeleine joined the nanny when she took Helen out in the pram for a stroll. The two women chatted away and the child contributed a regular salvo of burbles and giggles. It was pleasant to be out in the late afternoon sunshine and Madeleine felt the surge of maternal pride that always came whenever she was in public with her daughter. After following their established route, they turned back into John Islip Street. A cab rolled past them and stopped outside the house. Madeleine was astonished to see Lionel Fairbank alighting from the vehicle. After paying the driver, he caught sight of them approaching, instantly raising his hat.

'What a delightful picture you make!' he exclaimed.

'Good afternoon,' said Madeleine. 'I wasn't expecting to see you again today.'

'Is that a complaint?'

'No, it isn't.'

'I'm relieved to hear it.' He bent solicitously over the pram. 'And who is this divine little child?'

'It's my daughter, Helen.'

'How on earth do you manage to produce such wonderful paintings when you have to fulfil all the duties of a mother?'

'It's very difficult sometimes,' she admitted. 'But let's not stand out here in the street. Please, step into the house.'

'Thank you,' he said. 'I won't stay. That's a promise.'

The nanny wheeled the pram down the side entrance while Madeleine opened the front door with her key. She and Fairbank went into the drawing room, but he refused her invitation to sit down.

'This won't take long, Mrs Colbeck.' He beamed at her. 'I received your letter and I can't tell you how pleased I was that you accepted my offer. As for the fee, I suggest that I pay half in advance and the rest when the painting is finished.'

'I won't need any payment beforehand,' she insisted. 'Until you're completely satisfied with what I've done, I won't accept a penny.'

'That's very noble of you.'

'It's the way I prefer to work.'

'I'll be very satisfied with anything that you paint, be assured of that. However, let's not haggle over the money. What brought me back here was an idea I had. I do hope you'll forgive my boldness.'

'What idea was it?'

'Well, I'm returning home in a couple of days. I just wondered if there was any chance that you might come with me to make some early sketches of the landscape?'

'Oh, I'm not sure about that,' she said, uncertainly.

'It's not a long journey and, of course, you'd have first-class travel both ways. If we left in the morning, you could be safely back home by this time of day.'

'It's a rather sudden request, Mr Fairbank.'

'Yes, it is, and I apologise profusely for giving you such short notice. But I know you're anxious to start on the commission as soon as possible and the locomotive I have in mind will steam past the house close to midday. You'd have the opportunity to make a first sketch.' He shrugged his shoulders. 'I can see that the notion has no appeal to you. I'm sorry to have suggested it.'

'It did rather come out of the blue, Mr Fairbank.'

'Say no more, dear lady. I'll bid you farewell.' He led the way into the hall then turned to her. 'If you change your mind, please send word to my son's house.'

'I'll . . . think it over,' she said.

He smiled. 'That's all I ask, Mrs Colbeck.'

Terence Wardlow paid the penalty for the country walk with Tallis. His arthritis flared up and he could barely hobble around the house. Having got ready for dinner, he felt a greater need than usual for a prandial drink. Tallis had gone into the garden for another cigar. When his friend went out to join him, he had to grit his teeth against the stabbing pain. Tallis was seated on a bench but there was no sign of a cigar or of its aroma. He was staring fixedly into the distance. Wardlow called out to him but elicited no response. Getting within a couple of yards of him, his host tried again.

'Edward!' he called, raising his voice. 'It's time to come in.'

Once again, he got no reply and no indication that he'd been heard. Wardlow went slowly around the bench so that he was standing directly in front of Tallis, yet his friend remained wholly unaware of his presence. It was unsettling. Tallis was locked in a private world. Wardlow had to tap him on the shoulder for a reaction and it was not what he'd expected.

'What the devil are you doing?' roared Tallis, getting to his feet. 'And who *are* you, anyway?'

# CHAPTER SEVENTEEN

When they'd paid another visit to the police station to discuss the deployment of officers on the following day, Colbeck drove off in the direction of their cottage. Leeming was beside him in the trap.

'Mr Freed promised us he wouldn't get under our feet,' he said, 'and he kept that promise.'

'Having such leeway has been a bonus,' said Colbeck. 'There's only one thing that I regret.'

'What's that, sir?'

'Because of the demands of this case, we've had no time to explore Norwich. It has a fascinating history. Back in medieval times, it was a major city.'

'It's been dwarfed by big industrial towns now.'

'Look around you, Victor. It's still a flourishing community. Its weaving trade may have declined as a result of stiff competition from the mills of Yorkshire and Lancashire, but other trades are booming here. I remember what Mr Trant told me,' he went on. 'Boot and shoe manufacture is on the rise. Then there's engineering.'

'What about brewing?'

'That, too, is thriving.'

'It's a pity we can't take advantage of it,' said Leeming, soulfully.

'You'll have to survive on surreptitious visits to the Rib of Beef.'

'I like a drink at the end of the day.'

'The water here is excellent.'

Leeming pulled a face in disgust. When they reached the estate, the gatekeeper unlocked the iron gates and swung them open. The ride to the cottage took them past the main house but the sound of raised voices made them stop beside it. An angry altercation was taking place on the doorstep. Supported by a manservant, Cecil Freed was trying to send Andrew Swarbrick on his way. The visitor was refusing to leave.

'I gave orders to the gatekeeper that you weren't to be allowed in,' yelled Freed.

'That's why I found another way of getting on to your property. And having got this far,' warned Swarbrick, 'I'm not leaving until I'm allowed to see my stepmother.'

'She's not well, Andrew.'

'I don't believe that.'

'Go away and stop bothering us.'

'I'm coming in.'

Lurching forward, he pushed Freed aside and tried to get into the house. The servant grappled with him. Swarbrick threw him so violently against the side of the porch that the man released his

246

hold. Before he could dart into the house, however, Swarbrick felt himself being grabbed from behind by strong arms. Leeming had jumped from the trap to intervene. During his years in uniform, breaking up fights had been a regular exercise for him and he'd become expert at it. Though Swarbrick shouted, struggled and made vile threats, Leeming held him in a grip of iron. Freed stepped forward.

'Thank heaven you came, Inspector!' he exclaimed. 'Andrew turned up drunk and demanded to see his stepmother.'

'Let go of me, you thug!' cried Swarbrick.

'You'll have to calm down first, sir,' said Colbeck, 'or Sergeant Leeming will arrest you for assault.'

'Don't be ridiculous! I was simply exercising my rights.'

'You attacked Mr Freed and fought with his servant. Had we not arrived in time to stop you storming into the house, you'd have caused your stepmother great alarm.'

'It's no more than she deserves!'

'Go home, Andrew,' said Freed. 'We'll discuss this tomorrow.'

'I want to discuss it now. Do you know what that scheming bitch has done?' Mustering his strength, he tried to shake Leeming off but was held firmly. 'Get this idiot off me!'

'You are the one exhibiting signs of idiocy, sir,' said Colbeck, coolly. 'We overheard you boasting that you broke into the estate. That means we can add a charge of trespass to your list of offences.'

'That won't be necessary,' said Freed, displaying both palms. 'I just want him kept off my property. We promised to protect Grace from him and that's what we'll continue to do.'

'It's so *unfair*!' howled Swarbrick, giving up.

Colbeck took over. 'You can let him go, Sergeant,' he said.

'Very well, sir,' replied Leeming, adjusting his clothing.

'We'll look after him now, Mr Freed.'

'I'm so grateful,' said Freed. 'He behaved like a madman.'

'You should have let me in,' murmured Swarbrick, swaying.

'Come with us, sir,' said Colbeck. 'You've caused enough of a disturbance. I want to get to the bottom of this.'

Wardlow was mystified. When he'd brought Tallis out of his reverie with a tap on the shoulder, he'd been roared at and insulted. Two minutes later, however, his friend was apologising for his behaviour and assuring him that it wouldn't happen again. When they had a drink together, Tallis became once again the man that Wardlow knew and respected, pleasant, civilised and lapsing back easily into the indomitable soldier he'd once been. Because of the presence of Mrs Wardlow, he was more subdued during dinner but Tallis came back to life when he and his host were left alone. He tried to explain away his outburst in the garden and said that such a thing had never happened before. As a result of Alan Hinton's visit, however, Wardlow knew only too well that his friend's erratic behaviour fitted into a pattern. It was deeply worrying. While pouring two glasses of brandy, Wardlow pretended to enjoy the conversation, at the same time wondering how long this period of normality would last.

Now that Swarbrick's anger had spent itself, he cut such a sad figure that they were almost tempted to feel sorry for him. The impulse was short-lived. Having rambled on drunkenly, he sat with his head between his legs then straightened his back without warning and looked around the room with disdain.

'Where am I?' he demanded.

'You're in a cottage on Mr Freed's estate, sir,' said Colbeck. 'He's been good enough to give us free use of it.'

'I wish he'd been good enough to let me into his house.'

'He was right to refuse you entry. You came to cause trouble.'

'Aren't I allowed to see a member of my own family?'

'We've been told that you refuse to recognise Mrs Swarbrick as a legitimate member of the family. You even stayed away from the wedding.'

'I was making a gesture,' said Swarbrick.

'You were making another gesture when we arrived at the house,' said Leeming, 'and it was a violent one. What would your stepmother have made of you in that state?'

'I needed to speak to her.'

'I fancy that you were there to hurl abuse at her,' said Colbeck.

'She deserved it.'

'Why?'

Swarbrick looked sourly from one to the other, annoyed at their intervention yet sobered enough by it to realise that he'd behaved impetuously. With his self-control restored, he decided to confide in them and talked about his ill-starred visit to his father's solicitor. Moving between outrage and humiliation, he explained that his father had always given him the impression that he, as the only child, would inherit the family house and grounds. To learn that it was instead going to a woman he hated had been a shattering blow. Swarbrick claimed that his father hadn't been acting of his own volition. He'd been tricked into changing his will in her favour by his second wife.

'It's exactly the sort of thing that she'd do,' he said.

'Was your father a weak-willed person, sir?' asked Colbeck.

'On the contrary, he was very decisive.'

'Did your mother ever "trick" him into anything?'

Swarbrick tensed. 'That's a slanderous suggestion, Inspector,' he retorted. 'My mother was an absolute angel. She supported my father in every possible way.'

'The second Mrs Swarbrick vowed to do the same. We have Mrs Freed's word for that. Unlike you, she and her husband attended the wedding. They speak of your stepmother as loyal and undemanding.'

'That's how she may appear to them. I know better.'

'Then perhaps you can give us instances of her deceit, trickery, manipulation or whatever you wish to call it.'

There was a lengthy silence. Swarbrick looked hunted.

'We're waiting, sir,' said Leeming. When there was still no sound from him, the sergeant continued. 'Your stepmother hates to travel by train, yet she did so whenever required because she felt it was her duty. That shows what a caring wife she'd been.'

'My father didn't always think so,' sneered Swarbrick.

'What do you mean?'

'He didn't put it into words, but I could tell that something was amiss between them. Father was . . . disappointed.'

'Leaving the bulk of his estate to his wife is not exactly evidence of disappointment, sir,' observed Colbeck. 'I'd say that it reflected his love and gratitude.'

'She persuaded him to oust me.'

'There was no need. By shunning his second wife, you'd already ousted yourself.'

'Father and I were drifting back together again.'

'Were you getting on better with him?'

'Yes, I was.'

'Then why wasn't that improved relationship mirrored in his will?'

'It was because of *her*, of course.'

'You've no proof of that, sir.'

'She stabbed me in the back.'

'With respect,' said Colbeck, 'your stepmother isn't capable of stabbing anyone in the back. You seem to forget the ordeal that she went through when your father was shot dead. As for the will, I put it to you that she may have no idea at all what its contents are. Why should she? Until a few days ago, Mrs Swarbrick was expecting her husband to live for years. Any discussion between them of inheritance would have seemed premature.'

'I disagree.'

'What puzzles me,' said Leeming, 'is why you got so upset about it. Mr Freed told us that you're a very wealthy man. You don't need the house. You already have one. Why make such a fuss?'

'Mind your own business,' said Swarbrick, haughtily.

'I can answer your question, Sergeant,' said Colbeck. 'There are two reasons why ownership of the property is so important to him. First of all, it will allow him to evict a stepmother whom he has always seen as an interloper. Secondly, it will give him a base from which to operate if and when he takes over from his father as a Member of Parliament.'

'I wanted there to be a simple transition from my father to me,' explained Swarbrick. 'What's wrong with that?'

'On the face of it, I see nothing whatsoever.'

'Leaving the house to her was a grotesque mistake.'

'He's not in a position to rectify it, sir,' said Colbeck, smoothly. 'But let me give you some advice, if I may. I've never been an MP, though I did once have the pleasure of arresting someone who was. As you well know, appearance is all-important in public life.'

'What are you getting at?'

'This city is crawling with reporters at the moment. The sergeant and I spend most of our time dodging them. If any of

251

them had seen you yelling at Mr Freed earlier on, then grappling with his servant, you'd have been waking up tomorrow to some damning headlines.'

'Who wants to vote for someone like that?' asked Leeming.

'You were drunk, violent and abusive,' added Colbeck. 'My advice is that you should calm down and steer well clear of your stepmother. Or you'll be handing the seat to Oliver Trant.'

Swarbrick had the grace to look ashamed. Bad publicity would damage his chances of a political career and had to be avoided at all costs. Knowing that he had to rely on their discretion, he expressed his gratitude in a few, stumbling words. Then he left.

Inspector Jellings arrived at the police station next morning to learn that Oliver Trant was waiting for him in the office. After a token handshake, they sat down.

'What brings you here so early, Mr Trant?' he asked.

'It's more of a social call, really.'

'I don't have any leisure time to spare, sir. There's the small matter of a murder to solve.'

'How is the investigation proceeding?'

'The best person to ask is Inspector Colbeck.'

'He's not always available,' said Trant, 'and, in any case, he has a maddening habit of holding back information from me. Let's forget the inspector. When the crime is solved, he'll go back to London and we'll never hear a word from him again. You and I, on the other hand,' he went on with a meaningful glint, 'will still be here.'

'That's true.'

'We belong in this part of the country. Colbeck is no more than a passing acquaintance with a love of stylish waistcoats. He and I could never be kindred spirits. I'm speaking to you as a friend – at least, I hope that I can do so.'

'Yes, of course,' said Jellings, warmly. 'We've known each other for years and, if I earned a proper wage, I'd buy far more of your shoes than I can presently afford.' Screwing up one eye, he peered at his visitor. 'I sense that you want something from me.'

'I'd like some honest answers. Is that too much to ask?'

'It depends on the questions.'

Trant grinned. 'Oh, they'll be very simple.'

Jellings saw no reason why he shouldn't divulge some of the details of the investigation. Trant was a major businessman in the city and had considerable influence. It wouldn't be advisable for Jellings to fall out with him. Though he held some details back, he gave Trant a clear and straightforward account of the investigation so far. The other man seemed pleased by what he heard.

'Thank you,' he said. 'What is Colbeck up to now?'

'I can't speak for him, I'm afraid, but I can tell you what Sergeant Leeming is going to do.'

'What's that?'

'He's off to Yarmouth.'

'Yarmouth?' said Pryor. 'I thought you went there yesterday.'

'I liked it so much, I'm going back again.'

'What are you hoping to find?'

'Well, I wouldn't mind watching Punch and Judy again.'

'Do you think the killer is hiding there somewhere?'

'No,' said Leeming. 'The one thing we do know is that he's no longer in the country. I'm hoping to find out where he's gone.'

'You can sail almost anywhere from Yarmouth.'

'No, thanks – I prefer to stay on land.'

'Where do you think the killer *might* have gone?'

'That's a secret,' said Leeming. 'You'll find out when we eventually catch him – and the person or persons helping him.'

Pryor took a pace backward. 'Don't look at me like that.'

'Like what?'

'Well, as if you think I was involved somehow.'

'You *were* involved, albeit against your will. Because you took your eyes off the track, someone was able to switch the points. One of the people working at this station aided and abetted a murder.'

'Are you accusing *me*?' said Pryor, hotly.

'Why – do you think I ought to?'

'No, it was nothing at all to do with me.'

'Unfortunately, it was.' He heard the train approaching. 'Here it is at last. That's a relief.'

'How long will you be in Yarmouth?'

'I'll be there as long as it takes,' said Leeming.

Madeleine Colbeck had endured an uncomfortable night, waking at intervals and brooding at length until fatigue plucked her back into unconsciousness. When she got up the next day, she was confronted by the same dilemma. Since her husband wasn't there to discuss it with her, she had to pin her hopes on Lydia Quayle. Though she tried to work in her studio, her mind refused to allow her. In the end, she gave up and went back downstairs. While eager to see her friend, she hoped that her father wouldn't take it into his head to call in. He was the one person with whom she wouldn't dare to share her problem.

Lydia eventually arrived. Seeing her through the window of the drawing room, Madeleine ran into the hall to open the door wide.

'Well,' said Lydia, laughing, 'I wasn't expecting a welcome like that. What have I done to deserve it?'

'I need to talk to you.'

'Why – has something happened?'

'That's the trouble, Lydia. I don't really know.'

Taking her by the arm, she led her visitor into the drawing room, then sat beside her on the sofa. Lydia was surprised to see that someone who had remarkable self-possession as a rule was now trembling.

'Whatever is the trouble, Madeleine?' she asked.

'I think I may have made a horrible mistake.'

'How?'

'It's Mr Fairbank,' said Madeleine. 'He came back again.'

'Why did he do that?'

'I sent him a letter by hand to say that I accepted his commission. Hours later, when I was returning from a walk with Helen and her nanny, I saw him getting out of a cab.'

'What did he want?'

'He came with a proposition. I'd accepted that I'd have to go to his home at some stage in order to make sketches, but he wanted us to travel there together by train very soon.'

'That's rather sudden.'

'I felt as if I was being rushed into it, Lydia.'

'What did you decide?'

'I was so flustered that I played for time. I told him that I'd think it over. From the way I said it, he could see my reluctance.'

'How did he react?'

'Oh,' said Madeleine, 'he was as polite and charming as he had been before, but I thought I detected a subtle change in his attitude towards me. Thinking about it kept me awake half the night.'

'I can see why you're so perturbed.'

'It was not so much what he said, more the way that he said it.'

'Well, I think it quite wrong of him to turn up here without warning,' said Lydia. 'It was inconsiderate. He should have sent a message, asking when it would be convenient for him to call.'

'I was prepared to forgive him for that, Lydia. When someone is that enthusiastic about my work, I'm ready to make allowances. Then, of course, there was that amazing offer of two hundred pounds.'

'What was he expecting to buy with it?'

'When he pressed me to go to Windsor with him, that worrying thought flashed across my mind. Did he want more from me than a painting? What is he really interested in – my work or me?'

'You were right to be suspicious, Madeleine.'

'I wish that I'd never encouraged his interest.'

'You did nothing of the kind,' said Lydia. 'When he made a second visit here, Mr Fairbank crossed an invisible line. You should be glad that you sensed something was wrong.'

'But I don't know for certain that I did. It's what I wrestled with all night, Lydia. Is he really not the person he seems or am I being grossly unfair to him?' She chewed her lip. 'I can't make up my mind.'

'There are two things you can do, Madeleine.'

'What are they?'

'Well, the first one is to mention the fact that your husband is a detective inspector. If he does have designs on you, that would frighten him away at once. In fact,' said Lydia, 'I'm surprised you haven't done that already.'

'Robert and I agreed that I must stand on my own feet as an artist. That's why I never mention him. Robert says that, as far as my work goes, he's quite irrelevant.'

'I take his point.'

'What's the second thing I could do?'

'Well, you could find out more about Mr Fairbank. I don't mean that you should question the art dealer, as your father did. All you'd get was what you already know.'

'Where do I go, then?'

'You have his London address, don't you? Why not institute some discreet enquiries among the neighbours?'

Madeleine was shocked. 'I can't do that, Lydia.'

'I wasn't suggesting that you did. With Robert away, you may have lost one detective, but you still have another one to call on.'

'Constable Hinton?'

'Why don't you get in touch with him?' said Lydia. 'If you have qualms about doing that, I'll speak to him on your behalf.'


Terence Wardlow drove himself into Canterbury and pulled the dog cart to a halt outside his friend's house. He'd left Tallis back at the house and given him free use of his study where his guest could browse through the many books on military history. Admitted to Dr Kitson's house, he recounted the episode in the garden before dinner the previous evening.

'You say that he was staring ahead of him.'

'That's right, Donald.'

'In which direction was he looking?'

'Well, I suppose it would be in *this* direction.'

'Doesn't that tell you something?' asked Kitson. 'When you and Tallis first arrived in Canterbury, you told me that he'd recoiled from the sight of the cathedral. It obviously aroused searing memories that caused him both pain and a sense of shame.'

'Shame?' echoed Wardlow. 'He has nothing to be ashamed of.'

'He thinks that he does. It only took a few minutes in his company for me to see the sort of man he was. Edward Tallis is accustomed to being in control. He's always had people beneath him whom he can order about. Last December,' said Kitson, 'he lost that control completely and it must have been a terrifying experience for him.'

'It was. I remember seeing him when he was finally rescued from that farm. He was silent and subdued. That's highly uncharacteristic.'

'His behaviour at Scotland Yard was also unusual, you say.'

'Only in recent times,' said Wardlow. 'The kidnap was days before Christmas. He was back at work by the New Year and functioning as well as ever. And that was the story for several months. All of a sudden, his concentration started to falter. Why *now*?'

'I wish I knew the answer to that.'


Victor Leeming arrived in Yarmouth to be met by a strong wind that threatened to dislodge his top hat. Holidaymakers seemed unconcerned with the discomfort because they were there to enjoy themselves and made light of any adverse changes in the weather. Leeming was there with a specific purpose and found the gusts a nuisance. Making his way to the harbour, he sought out the two old sailors who worked for the owner of the *Flying Fish*. When he asked them why it hadn't arrived yet, they laughed.

'What's the joke?' said Leeming.

'I can see you're no sailor, sir,' said the older of the two. 'Ships and boats are not like trains. They don't stick to timetables because you can never tell what the sea will be like.'

'You told us the *Flying Fish* would be back here this morning.'

'I said that it *might* be. I gave no promises.'

'It's a long voyage for a small vessel,' said the other man. 'All sorts of things might happen to it on the way. It could get caught in a squall and blown off course or forced to pull into port somewhere if the weather really turned nasty.'

'When *is* it likely to come back, then?' asked Leeming.

'It may be later today, or it may be tomorrow.'

'*Tomorrow*?'

'The *Flying Fish* is at sea to make money, sir, not to fit in with your demands. Come back every few hours. That's the best thing.'

Though he was disgruntled, Leeming accepted that the delay was not their fault. He apologised for being so impatient and took their advice, electing to return at regular intervals. Resigned to a longer stay in the town than anticipated, he headed for the pub where he and Colbeck had enjoyed refreshment on their visit. Meanwhile, even in the searching wind, he could breathe in the clear air of a coastal resort.

After the perpetual grime and stink of London, it was a real tonic for him. The sound of children's laughter and the sight of people bathing joyfully in the sea made him wish that he could bring his family to somewhere like Yarmouth instead of keeping them within the bounds of the biggest and dirtiest city in Europe. It was, however, a doomed hope. Holidays of that kind only existed for him in the mind. They were for other people. His life was mortgaged to the Metropolitan Police Force. He was so busy thinking about the sacrifices he was compelled to make that he failed to notice he was being followed.

As he was about to leave the house, Cecil Freed was intercepted by Colbeck, who asked if he'd reported the scuffle outside the front door to Grace Swarbrick.

'It was impossible to keep it from her, Inspector,' said Freed. 'Andrew has a very carrying voice. Grace heard every word.'

'That's unfortunate.'

'As for Andrew, he was like a man possessed.'

'Actually, it was more a case of being *dis*possessed.'

Freed laughed grimly. 'That's horribly true.'

'Did you explain what the argument had been about?'

'I had to, Inspector. Grace asked me, and I could hardly tell her a lie. When she heard that she was the chief benefactor of her husband's will, she was struck dumb. It was clearly unexpected.'

'Her stepson thinks that his father was duped by her.'

'How typical of him!' said Freed. 'Andrew has many admirable qualities, but he has no insight into the way that women behave. He can't accept that Grace was exactly the person his father needed when his first wife died. In her own quiet, undemonstrative way, she transformed him.'

'That's what your wife told me and she's in the best position to know. According to Mrs Freed,' said Colbeck, 'Grace was a lively, handsome woman when she met Mr Swarbrick. Someone that buoyant and attractive must have had other suitors.'

'I'm sure that she did but Grace ignored them. She, too, was mourning the death of a spouse, remember. Anyone else trying to pay court to her was disregarded.'

'How would they have reacted to that?'

'Naturally, they'd have been disappointed.'

'Disappointment can often fester and become a cause for revenge.'

'Nothing like that happened,' said Freed, confidently.

'How do you know?'

'Had it done so, Grace would surely have confided in my

wife. Anthea and she have become like sisters. There are no secrets between them. If there'd been another man pursuing Grace, then my wife would certainly have known about it.'

'How much time did Swarbrick and his wife spend together?'

Freed gave a wan smile. 'How much time do you and *your* wife spend together?'

'Not enough,' said Colbeck, regretfully. 'The demands of my work push us apart far too often.'

'It's the same with me, Inspector. I'm often away from home on business. Anthea misses me but accepts that it's necessary. Yet I will wager this,' he went on. 'Jarvis Swarbrick saw far less of the woman he loved than we see of our respective wives. Members of Parliament work all the hours God sends.'

'Some of them do, perhaps. Many treat their job as a sinecure.'

'Jarvis didn't. He was indefatigable. I believe that's why he chose Grace as his wife.'

'She never complained?'

'She faded dutifully into the background, Inspector. Yet the moment Grace was needed, she was at his side to offer the love and unconditional support he needed.'

Much of the time, they sat in silence. Anthea Freed would read a book or make notes about the next meeting she had to attend. Grace always had a book to hand but she barely glanced at it. She liked to drift in and out of conversations, often breaking off in mid-sentence if she was caught on the raw by a painful memory. The two of them were now sitting opposite each other in the drawing room. After a prolonged silence, Grace finally spoke.

'I think I'm ready now,' she said, quietly. 'I can't keep hiding.'

'You're under great strain, Grace. Nobody will blame you for retreating from the world for a while.'

'I'm ready to face the inquest and . . . to discuss the funeral with Andrew.'

'You and he are best kept apart,' said Anthea. 'Have you forgotten what happened on our doorstep last night?'

'How can I forget something for which I was responsible?'

'The responsibility lies wholly with Andrew.'

'Indirectly, I'm to blame,' said Grace, sadly. 'I'm to blame for failing to achieve some sort of reconciliation with my stepson. I'm to blame for not being good enough for his father.'

'That's nonsense – Jarvis worshipped you.'

'In spite of everything, he still loved his son. I came between the two of them, Anthea. I caused both of them suffering.'

'You're the one who suffered, and it's Andrew's fault.'

'The house should have been bequeathed to him, not to me.'

'Jarvis's wishes must be respected, Grace.'

'But I don't deserve it. Having been his wife for such a relatively short time, I can't inherit things he spent a lifetime building up. I feel so uncomfortable about it.'

'You've earned every single thing he's left you.'

'I wish I could believe that.'

'Listen to me,' said Anthea. 'Death can sometimes bring out the worst in families. Underlying tensions suddenly come to the fore. Look at the way Andrew behaved last night. It was unforgivable. You, however,' said Anthea, 'have conducted yourself with dignity. It puts your stepson to shame.'

'I can see why he feels so cheated.'

'Let me just say this, Grace. Don't make any rash decisions or you'll come to regret them one day. It will be months – even

262

longer, perhaps – before you start to recover. Only then can you look at the situation in a clear light.'

'Thank you, Anthea,' said the other, squeezing her friend's hand. 'That's good advice.'

# CHAPTER EIGHTEEN

The discussion with Donald Kitson had been illuminating. On his way back home, Wardlow was able to reflect on it at length. Keeping the horse at a steady trot, he rattled along in the dog cart. When his friend had asked about Edward Tallis's symptoms, Wardlow had mentioned his lapse into a kind of trance, followed by a savage outburst and terminating in an abject apology. Kitson had suggested there might be a symptom that had escaped Wardlow's notice. To cope with his problem, Tallis was very likely to be drinking heavily to block out the torment he was so clearly experiencing. Since army life had given both of them a taste for generous amounts of alcohol, Wardlow saw nothing unusual in the way that Tallis had behaved when, after dinner the previous evening, they'd talked into the small hours with a decanter of brandy between them.

Now that he thought about it, however, he recalled his wife telling him that the maid who'd gone to turn down Tallis's bed had seen a bottle of whisky tucked under it. Having dismissed the news at the time, he now came to take it more seriously. Was his friend actually dependent on alcohol now? In turning to drink as a form of anaesthetic, could it be that Tallis was actually making his condition worse? Wardlow resolved to watch his guest more closely from now.

Of all the things Kitson had told him, however, the most interesting were two cases he'd cited. In both instances, there'd been a long delay before the impact of a traumatic event had been properly felt. One man had been rowing his wife in a boat when it struck a concealed rock and was overturned. Since she couldn't swim, the woman immediately began to panic, flailing around before going under. The man did his best to rescue her but they were too far from the shore and the tide was against them. By the time they were washed up on to the sand, he was exhausted and she was dead. Wardlow was surprised to hear that the man seemed to recover completely from the tragedy until – three years later – it came back to haunt him. He turned to drink, behaved irrationally, was forced to give up his job and ended up in an asylum.

The second case described by Kitson followed a similar pattern, except that the trauma at the root of it had occurred over ten years earlier. Having lain dormant for a decade, it had suddenly sprung to life again and reduced the man concerned to a gibbering wreck. Was that the fate that Edward Tallis was heading towards? Wardlow hoped and prayed that there was some way to rescue him. Persuading him to take a rest from work had been one important step but his friend was not quite sure what the next one should be. Kitson had advised that he should try to create the best conditions for recovery since Wardlow was now, in effect, in a parental position. If Tallis's behaviour worsened dramatically, it would be time to refer him to an asylum for treatment. The very idea of doing that was anathema to Wardlow. He couldn't bear to think of his friend being treated as a mental patient. It would be a failure on his part. When his house came into sight, he vowed to make a greater effort to offer comfort to Tallis and to be more tolerant of his aberrations.

He entered the house and found his friend waiting for him.

'What did Dr Kitson say about me?' asked Tallis.

'Kitson is a retired stockbroker,' said Wardlow, limply.

'You always were a poor liar, Terence. Now tell me the truth.'

Alan Hinton arrived back at Scotland Yard to find a letter waiting for him. He recognised the handwriting and tore open Lydia's missive eagerly. Without providing any details, she simply requested his help. After reading it a few times, he slipped it into his pocket and resolved to call on her the moment he finished work. With something so pleasurable to look forward to, he knew that time would race by.

After three hours away from it, Leeming returned to the harbour only to be told that there was no sign of the *Flying Fish* and that he should wait longer before coming back for the second time. Since he was facing the prospect of spending the whole day in Yarmouth, he decided to explore the town itself. There were shops in abundance and plenty of people milling around. Though he was not fond of reading, he was attracted to a little bookshop with trays of books set up on trestles. Leeming joined the few people who were browsing there. Searching for something that might be suitable for his children, he instead spotted an old atlas with frayed edges and discoloured front. He picked it up and began to leaf through it, pausing at a map of south-east England that also included a large segment of northern France. As he studied it, he realised why it was taking such a long time for the *Flying Fish* to sail to and fro.

Something then galvanised Leeming and sent him rushing into the shop. He waved the atlas at the old woman behind the counter.

'How much is this?' he asked.

'How much is it worth to you, sir?'

'It might be worth a great deal but I can't see a price on it.'

'Pay what you think is fair,' she said. 'That's our policy. It may look rather down-at-heel but it's still serviceable. We never argue about price. You make your own estimate. I'll be happy with that.'

'Then so will I.'

Thrusting a hand into his pocket he took out some coins and put them on the counter. She smiled in gratitude. For his part, he felt that he'd made a good purchase. With the atlas in his hand, he rushed back to the harbour. As soon as Leeming had disappeared around a corner, the man who'd been following him went into the bookshop.

'What did he buy?' he asked.

'It was a tattered atlas, sir,' replied the old woman.

'Did he say *why* he wanted it?'

'No, he didn't. He paid too much for it. It's falling to pieces.'

'Thank you.'

Leaving the shop, the man broke into a trot until he caught sight of Leeming in the distance, heading once more for the harbour.

* * *

Colbeck went to the railway station in order to send a telegraph only to find that one awaited him. It was from Acting Superintendent Vallence, asking him for the latest news about the investigation. More worrying for Colbeck was the information that Superintendent Tallis was likely to be away for some considerable time. The loss of someone as dedicated as Tallis at the helm would be nothing less than a minor catastrophe. It would mark the end of an era.

After sending his telegraph to Scotland Yard, Colbeck saw the stationmaster walking along the platform. Grigson waved cheerily.

'Good day to you,' he said, joining Colbeck. 'You've spent so much time here that I'll have to count you as part of the staff.'

'Watching trains all day would be a source of joy to me.'

'I suspect that catching criminals brings more satisfaction.'

'Infinitely more,' said Colbeck. 'The problem is that it's vastly more difficult. That's why I'm so grateful for any help I'm offered. We can't thank you enough for your suggestion that the killer practised his attack beforehand. Instead of my becoming part of *your* staff, you should be co-opted on to mine.'

Grigson laughed. 'Oh, I don't think I'd make a good detective.'

'You've already shown that you would.'

'It's kind of you to say so, Inspector, but I know my limitations. The truth is this,' he went on, seriously, 'I love this city and I love the job I do here. The murder has sullied us. It's made people feel unsafe. That's why I'll do everything in my power to help you clean up the mess left behind by the killer. Please catch him for us so that we can breathe easily once again.'

After checking his watch, Grigson put it back in his waistcoat pocket and walked off down the platform. Colbeck was not left alone for long. Bartram Duff suddenly materialised beside him.

'I hear that the sergeant has gone off to Yarmouth again,' he said.

'That's right.'

'Was there any need for him to go back a second time?'

'We'll have to wait and see.'

'What exactly is he hoping to find there?'

'You're being very inquisitive this morning. Why is that?'

'I'd hoped to be more involved in the investigation,' said Duff.

'I have all the manpower required.'

'Yet it doesn't seem to have produced any results.'

'Is that a criticism?' asked Colbeck, giving him a challenging glare. 'The only reason that Sergeant Leeming and I have come here is that a railway policeman was not vigilant enough to see someone switching the points and making a heinous crime possible. As the person in charge of security here, you must accept some of the responsibility for that.'

'It wasn't *my* job to watch the tracks,' said Duff, indignantly.

'It *is* your job to keep the other policemen alert. Since you clearly failed to do that, you can't be surprised that we've chosen to conduct this investigation without your direct involvement.'

'That could be a mistake.'

'Why?' asked Colbeck. 'Do you think that you could do far better than we seem to be doing?'

'What I think is that you should show us some respect.'

'You need to earn it first.'

'I've had years of experience in uniform, Inspector. When I served in the Metropolitan Police Force, I was commended for the number of arrests I made. I was in line for a promotion.'

'Then why did you leave London?'

'I wanted to return to my roots.'

'Was that the only reason?'

270

'Yes, it was.'

'So it was nothing whatsoever to do with the incident that led to your dismissal, was it?' said Colbeck, pointedly. 'According to your record, you were caught on duty in a public house with a female at one o'clock in the morning. I take it that the female was not your wife.'

Duff's face turned crimson. He tried to stammer an excuse but soon gave up and fled. Colbeck had the feeling that the man wouldn't bother him again.

While he expected some sort of apology, Cecil Freed didn't think that Swarbrick would be quite so penitent. It was a side of the younger man that he'd never seen before. Admitted to Freed's office, Swarbrick was racked with contrition and couldn't stop saying how ashamed he was of his behaviour. It was several minutes before he could be persuaded to calm down and take a seat. Even then, the apology continued.

'I *never* lose my control like that,' he insisted.

'You were inebriated, Andrew.'

'That's what appalled me the most. I am, habitually, a moderate drinker. I suppose that fact led to my downfall. Because I'm not used to excessive amounts of alcohol, it had a much stronger effect on me.'

'That's possible,' said Freed. 'Count yourself fortunate that my wife didn't come to the door when we heard you caterwauling outside. As well as receiving a lecture on the virtues of temperance, you'd have had a bucket of cold water poured over you.'

'I'd have deserved it.'

'Anthea was quite disgusted by what she could hear.'

'I've written a letter of apology to her,' said Swarbrick, 'and I've

271

sent a similar one to my stepmother. I've given a firm undertaking that I won't come anywhere near your house again.'

'You won't be allowed to, believe me. The gateman and the household staff are now on the alert. One of the servants found the gap you created in the fence so that you could get on to my land. It's been mended and reinforced.'

'Send me the bill. I'll pay it instantly.'

'There are some things you *can't* repair with money,' said Freed, sharply. 'One of them is my wife's low opinion of you and the other is my loss of confidence in you as the person best qualified to replace your father in the House.'

'Don't say that!'

'Oliver Trant would never descend to antics in the way you did.'

'I've *got* to secure that nomination, Cecil.'

'How do you intend to go about it – by turning up at people's front doors and threatening violence if they don't vote for you?'

Swarbrick's head dropped to his chest. The assertiveness he'd shown since returning to Norwich had seeped away in its entirety. What remained was a pathetic need for forgiveness. Freed was in no mood to provide it. Walking across to his visitor, he stood over him.

'Your father would have been revolted by what you did last night,' he said with disgust. 'He and I had to withstand many stormy meetings together, but it never made him reach for the bottle. Dignity was his watchword. Whatever the circumstances, dignity had to be preserved.'

Swarbrick looked up. 'You don't need to tell me that.'

'Somebody has to, Andrew. The simple truth is that you're not and can never be a second Jarvis Swarbrick. I think you should abandon all hope of a parliamentary career.'

'No!' exclaimed the other, rising to his feet. 'I refuse to do so.

The House of Commons is not full of saints, you know. My father told me that some members only go there to frequent the bars. All right,' he went on, 'I was in a deplorable state last night. I confess it. In my case, it was a rare lapse. For some MPs, drunkenness is a permanent condition.'

'I don't care about other constituencies,' said Freed, vehemently, 'but I do care about this one. On the basis of what I saw last night, it needs to be protected from you.'

'That's unfair!'

'Inspector Colbeck was right. You should, by rights, have been charged with assault and trespass. A night in a police cell should have been the least that you suffered.'

Swarbrick winced. He walked around the room as he tried to gather his thoughts. When he spoke, his voice was much firmer.

'Father was always very grateful towards you, Cecil.'

'He had good reason to be.'

'He said you were the only person he could confide in.'

'I know how to keep a secret, Andrew.'

'His death removes the need for them,' said Swarbrick, 'so please tell me this. Did he ever speak to you about my inheritance?'

'Yes, he did.'

'And was the house ever mentioned?' Freed looked away. 'Please, Cecil, I need to know. I was the intended recipient, wasn't I? He as good as told me that.'

'Then you don't need my confirmation.'

'Yes, I do. I need it very badly.'

Freed faced him again. 'Your father did plan to leave it to you. I was amazed to learn that he changed his mind because it was so unusual for him to do so. The last time we spoke about it,' he said, 'the terms of the will remained very much in your favour.'

'Thank you,' said the other, moving towards the door. 'That's all I want to know.'

'Where are you going?'

Swarbrick spun round, shoulders back and jaw thrust out. 'I'm going to fight for what is truly mine,' he said.

It was not until he headed back towards the railway station that Leeming sensed that somebody was tailing him. He paused from time to time to look at a shop window, using it as a mirror to see if there was anyone behind him. Even though nobody was ever there, his doubts were never allayed. Leeming did his best not to advertise his suspicion. If his shadow became aware that his presence had been discovered, he'd vanish into thin air. The sergeant therefore strolled along with a casual air before turning in through the main entrance to the station. When he went straight to the appropriate platform, he could almost feel the person closing in on him. Leeming had no idea who was there but he guessed why he was being followed.

He believed that he'd picked up the trail of the killer. That meant he was in possession of dangerous knowledge, something that would send everyone involved in the crime to the gallows. The person behind him, he believed, wanted to stop him passing on the information. Thinking that the man would do anything to silence him, Leeming braced himself for an attack as he mingled with the crowd on the platform. The train then approached, passengers surged forward and he suddenly felt heavy pressure on his back. Wheeling around at speed, he grabbed the person behind him in the firm conviction that he was holding a would-be assailant. Instead, he had his arms around a portly woman in her sixties. Her scream was deafening.

\* \* \*

Since he'd returned from his visit, Terence Wardlow had hardly spoken a word to his friend. He felt too embarrassed. His attempt to pass off Kitson as a retired stockbroker had not fooled Tallis for one second. He'd known from the moment he'd met him that Kitson was a doctor. Wardlow wished that he'd been more honest with his guest. Afternoon found them seated together in the garden. Tallis had deliberately chosen a bench that faced in the opposite direction to Canterbury.

With an effort, Wardlow finally mastered his discomfort.

'I owe you an apology, Edward,' he said.

'I don't think so.'

'Kitson was here under false pretences.'

'I, too, was guilty of pretence,' said Tallis. 'Kitson was pretending not to be the doctor he so obviously was and I pretended not to notice his brave attempt at deceiving me.'

Wardlow was shocked. 'You *knew* all the time?'

'Of course, I did.'

'But you asked me what he'd done for a living.'

'I was teasing you, Terence. I can detect a doctor at ten paces. It's a noble profession and I'd never say that about stockbroking.' They shared a laugh and the tension eased. 'Let's go back to the question I asked you earlier. What was Kitson's diagnosis?'

'He felt that you were fatigued and desperately in need of a holiday.'

'*Holiday*?' repeated Tallis. 'There's no such word in my lexicon.'

'Then there ought to be.'

'I only function properly when I'm at work.'

'Sadly, that's not true,' said Wardlow. 'Let me speak frankly.'

Tallis was waspish. 'I was hoping you'd get round to it in the end.'

'You've every right to criticise me, Edward. In my own defence, let me say that you don't make it easy for anyone to help you.'

'Self-reliance is one of my touchstones.'

'It's led, in your case, to a dangerous isolation.'

Wardlow spoke frankly. For the first time, he told him in detail about the incidents that had made Alan Hinton catch a train to Canterbury to plead for help on the superintendent's behalf. Had Tallis been allowed to carry on as he was, his condition would have deteriorated to the point where the commissioner would have had no alternative to dismissal.

Tallis was disturbed. 'Was I really *that* bad?'

'I've only seen glimpses of it. Constable Hinton saw far more examples of your – let's call it by its name – decline. You're patently not the man you were when you first came here last December. You were brimming with good health.'

'Yes, I was – in every way. I want to be like that again.'

'You *will* be, Edward.'

There was a noticeable lack of conviction in Wardlow's voice. Now that his ruse had been exposed, he was not sure how to proceed. The one thing he had to avoid was provoking his guest in any way. Tallis was unstable enough. He had to be handled with extreme care. Talk turned to the flower beds in the garden and Wardlow regretted that he was no longer able to take any part in tending them. Pointing to various flowers in turn, Tallis tried to identify them. More often than not, he failed. But at least they'd moved into neutral territory. Conversation became easier. Half an hour glided past effortlessly.

Tallis then stiffened. 'Where's Colbeck's report?' he demanded.

'You're not in the office now,' said Wardlow, gently.

'He knows that I like to keep informed of every development.'

'I'm sure that the inspector is working hard in Norwich.'

'Then why have I had no telegraph from him?'

'You're having a rest, Edward.'

'I never rest.'

'Try to forget Scotland Yard completely.'

'Don't be ridiculous, man. It's where I work and where I'm entitled to the respect due to my rank. Colbeck is at fault and needs admonishing.' He snapped his fingers as if dealing with a servant. 'Find me the time of the next train to Norwich. I must go there immediately.'

Wardlow didn't move. Alarmed by the suddenness of the radical change in his friend's behaviour, he had no idea what to do. The man who'd been calmly discussing the flower beds only a minute ago was now wild-eyed and agitated. If he continued to have such lightning alterations of mood, Wardlow knew that he wouldn't be able to keep him there indefinitely. He had neither the resources nor the training to look after him. One of London's finest detectives would have to be confined to an asylum.

'When was this?' asked Colbeck.

'Earlier today,' said Jellings. 'Mr Trant came into the police station to find out if there'd been any developments.'

'Why didn't he ask me?'

'I think he felt that he'd get more luck here, Inspector. Trant has a lot of status in this city. We all look up to him whereas you don't have any need to do so. He couldn't apply any pressure to you.'

'I'd never allow anybody to do that,' said Colbeck, evenly. 'Why didn't you tell him that we were still in the early stages?'

'He wanted chapter and verse regarding our progress.'

'Did you give it to him?'

277

'I had to tell him *something* to get rid of him, sir.'

'That's all right, Jellings. I don't blame you.'

They were in the inspector's office and Oliver Trant had suddenly come to Colbeck's attention once more. He was struck by the urgency with which Trant had sought information and could see why Jellings had been forced into releasing more of it than he'd wanted.

'Have you ever had any trouble from him?' asked Colbeck.

'He does like us to tug our forelocks to him and know our places,' said Jellings with slight bitterness, 'but that's true of all the members of that particular breed.'

'Was it true of Jarvis Swarbrick?'

'To tell you the truth, he was the worst of them.'

'That doesn't accord with what Mr Freed told me about him.'

'He was never on the receiving end,' said Jellings, 'whereas I was. However,' he added, 'I'm speaking out of turn. I'm sorry.'

'No, no, please go on.'

'I don't wish to speak ill of the dead, sir.'

'But you may be holding back something that may be of use to me. That would be very regrettable.'

'What I could tell you is irrelevant to this investigation.'

'Nevertheless, I'd very much like to hear it. Anything about the murder victim, however trivial, is of interest to me. What we've been told is that Mr Swarbrick was a popular figure here. Do you agree?'

'Yes, I do. He was an impressive politician.'

'Was he equally impressive as a human being?'

Jellings was guarded. 'Like all of us, he had his failings.'

'But he was not like all of us, was he?' said Colbeck. 'He lived in a world of privilege. It's something that you and I can only see from the outside. Jarvis Swarbrick was a patrician. He enjoyed wealth, position and power. And he had a beautiful wife at his side.'

'That wasn't always the case, Inspector.'

'I thought that Mrs Swarbrick supported him to the full.'

'Only when he wanted her to be there,' said Jellings. Conscious that he'd said too much, he tried to back away. 'Anyway, that's all in the past. Nothing can be served by digging it up again.'

'If it's something that helps me to understand Mr Swarbrick better, then it needs digging up.'

'It's . . . best forgotten, sir.'

'Keep talking,' said Colbeck, watching him intently. 'Is this to do with that world of privilege he inhabited?'

'Yes, it was.'

'What happened?'

Jellings shuffled his feet and looked uneasy. Having got himself into an awkward situation, he tried to talk his way out of it but Colbeck refused to let him do so. In the end, Jellings capitulated.

'It was a couple of years ago.'

'I'm listening.'

'Late one night, I led a raid on some premises in the more affluent part of the city. We'd received reports that gentlemen were seen late at night visiting the house.'

'I can guess who one of those gentlemen must have been.'

'What could we do? Had we released his name, Swarbrick would have denied it and I would've been stripped of my rank. You can't fight privilege. It always wins. He got away with it.'

'This was when he was married to his second wife.'

'Yes, it was. I felt sorry for her. Why ever did he do it?' asked Jellings. 'He had *everything*.'

279

Colbeck remembered something Andrew Swarbrick had told him.
'I wonder . . .'

Extricating himself from an awkward situation took Victor
Leeming so much time that he missed the train altogether. It pulled
out while he was still apologising to the woman, assuring her
scandalised husband that he had not been deliberately molesting
her and trying to ignore the hostile stares of the passengers all
around him. When the train was in motion, the stationmaster
came over and threatened to call the police. Leeming took out his
warrant card and waved it under the man's nose.

'As you can see, I'm employed by the Metropolitan Police Force.'

'That card could be a forgery,' said the stationmaster.

Leeming was irate. 'Do I *look* like a criminal?'

'Frankly, sir, you do.'

'I'm a detective assigned to a murder case. You must have heard
about Mr Swarbrick, shot dead in a train at Norwich Station. I
came to Yarmouth as part of our investigation.'

'What made you think you were licensed to grab an innocent
lady in that way?'

'I thought she was the person dogging my footsteps.'

'This sounds very fishy to me, sir.'

'It's the truth,' said Leeming.

'You'll have to be detained until we can sort this out.'

'There's a very easy way to do that. You have a telegraph
station here. Why not send a message to Inspector Colbeck in
Norwich, asking for confirmation that I'm working on the case
with him?'

The stationmaster was dubious. 'I might do that, I suppose.'

'He'll speak up for me.'

'I'll get one of the railway policemen to take charge of you while I'm away.'

Leeming was incensed. 'You don't need to do that, man!'

'It's to prevent you running away, sir.'

'Why would I do that? I'm here to catch a train to Norwich. If it hadn't been for an unfortunate mistake, I'd be on my way there now.'

'The lady made a complaint and so did her husband.'

'I apologised to them time and again.'

'You had no right to molest her.'

'It was an accident,' said Leeming, trying hard to bank down his frustration. 'Now please go and send that telegraph. When it finally reaches Inspector Colbeck, he'll explain who I am and what I'm doing here. Off you go,' he added. 'I give you my word that I won't move from this spot or,' he couldn't resist adding, 'take liberties with another female passenger.'

The stationmaster eyed him shrewdly. After a few minutes of cogitation, he accepted Leeming's explanation and realised that he could assist a murder investigation. It gave him a sense of importance.

'The next train is in fifty minutes, Sergeant Leeming,' he said. 'I'm sorry for the misunderstanding.'

The moment his shift finished, Alan Hinton took a cab to Westminster and called at the Colbeck residence. To his delight, Lydia was still there. She explained the predicament that Madeleine was in and he agreed to make enquiries immediately. First, however, he had questions to put.

'Did the gentleman know who your husband is, Mrs Colbeck?'

'No,' replied Madeleine.

'Did he ask where he might be?'

'As a matter of fact, he did. I said that he was away on business.'

'Solving a murder is hardly just business,' observed Lydia. 'On reflection, it might have been better if you'd told him the truth.'

'I explained it to you before,' said Madeleine. 'Where my work is concerned, Robert insists on staying out of sight. He feels that I should be seen as an independent artist rather than someone's wife.'

'Might I see the letters he wrote to you, please?' asked Hinton.

'Yes, of course. I'll get them.'

When Madeleine left the room, the mood changed instantly. Lydia and Hinton smiled at each other and let their feelings show. She thanked him for responding so quickly to her summons.

'Mr Fairbank may, of course, be quite innocuous,' she said.

'He may indeed, Lydia.'

'In some ways, that will be a disappointment.'

'Yes, it will,' he agreed. 'It will rob me of an excuse to see you.'

'You don't need excuses, Alan.'

They gazed fondly at each other for some time. The sound of approaching footsteps made them move apart. Madeleine came in and handed the two letters to Hinton. The first one she'd received gave him some indication of Fairbank's character and showed a genuine appreciation of her work as an artist. The second letter made his eyes pop.

'Two hundred pounds!' he exclaimed.

'It's far too much,' said Madeleine, modestly.

'It depends what you have to do to get it,' warned Lydia. 'I think that he gave himself away by his second visit here.'

'You're right to be concerned,' decided Hinton, handing the

letters back. 'On the other hand, the gentleman deserves the benefit of the doubt, so let's not rush to judgement. If you're going to work for him, you need to know as much as you can about this person. I'll get over there now.'

'Thank you,' said Madeleine. 'It's very kind of you.'

'The inspector would want me to do everything I can to help.'

'Is there any news about Superintendent Tallis?'

'Unhappily, there isn't,' said Hinton, sadly. 'I can only hope that Captain Wardlow is looking after him. It's not a job that I'd care to do.'

When Tallis retired to his room that afternoon, Wardlow assumed that he'd gone off for a nap. Hours then passed, and he began to wonder what his guest was doing. Creeping upstairs, he tapped lightly on Tallis's door and waited. There was no response. When he knocked for the second time, he called out his friend's name, but it was in vain. Wardlow was gripped by the sudden fear that he wasn't there any longer and had slipped out of the house without anyone noticing. Grabbing the handle of the door, he opened it wide and looked into the room. Surprisingly, Tallis was still inside it but he was sublimely unaware that he had a visitor. Kneeling beside the bed, hands closed in prayer, he was sending up silent pleas to heaven. It was an affecting sight and made Wardlow feel guilty for bursting in. Mouthing an apology, he went out again and closed the door gently behind him.

'What happened?' asked Colbeck.

'I felt someone pressing up against me,' explained Leeming, 'so I turned round to grab him. It was a natural reaction, sir.'

'Go on.'

'Instead of catching the man I was after, I had my arms around a fat lady who screeched so loudly that everyone was looking at me as if I was trying to molest her.'

He went on to describe the incident and its consequences in full. Though he was very sympathetic, Colbeck couldn't help laughing and that only added to Leeming's distress. It took several minutes to placate him. The sergeant had taken a cab from Norwich Station to the cottage where they were staying.

'Did the *Flying Fish* come back?' asked Colbeck.

'No, sir, they couldn't give me an exact time for its return. Steamships depart regularly from Yarmouth and their estimated times are fairly predictable. When a vessel is under sail, it's more difficult.'

'So what have you brought back – apart from the urge to tell me about your unintended embrace with a corpulent woman?'

'It's not funny, sir,' protested Leeming.

'I'm sorry, Victor. I shouldn't poke fun.'

'That man was following me. I swear it.'

'And did he get on to the second train after you did?'

'No, he didn't. He'd disappeared before it arrived. My guess is that he got on the earlier train that I should have caught.'

'That means he was heading back to Norwich. Did you have the feeling that he was waiting for you when you got to the station?' Leeming shook his head. 'Let's forget about him for the time being. Tell me why you were so keen to report to me?'

'I think I made a discovery, sir.' Moving to the table, Leeming opened the atlas at the requisite page and stood back. 'What do you notice?'

'I can see that the atlas is on its last legs. It's falling to pieces.'

'Look at Yarmouth. Can you see how far it is to Cherbourg?'

'Yes,' said Colbeck, studying the map, 'it's quite a way and could well be a tricky voyage. They'd have to sail through the Strait of Dover.'

'What else do you notice?'

Colbeck pored over the atlas for a few minutes, letting his eye trace the likely course of the journey between Yarmouth and the Normandy peninsula. His gaze then drifted back out to sea and he jabbed a finger at a group of islands.

'This is what you mean, isn't it?'

'Yes, sir, and it's the reason I went straight back to the harbour. I asked them if the *Flying Fish* would sail back by the same route and they told me it would call in at Jersey first.' Leeming grinned. 'Can you see the way my mind was working?'

'I can indeed, Victor, and I congratulate you. We thought that John Gorey was a false name and now we know why he chose it. The answer is right here,' said Colbeck, tapping the map. 'Gorey is a town in Jersey. The killer was going home.'

# CHAPTER NINETEEN

It was late afternoon when Caleb Andrews called on his daughter and he was puzzled. As soon as he was admitted to the house, he went straight into the drawing room to join Madeleine.

'I've just seen Constable Hinton getting into a cab with Lydia.'

'That's right, Father. They left a few moments ago.'

'Did they come here *together*?'

'No,' replied Madeleine, 'it was just a coincidence that Lydia happened to be here when Alan Hinton came to tell me about the superintendent.'

'Have they put him in a straitjacket yet?'

'Father!'

'Well, it's obvious he's out of his mind.'

'It isn't obvious at all,' she said, 'and it's wrong of you to make such a comment when you've never even seen the man. Superintendent Tallis has been under immense strain, that's all. He needs a rest.'

'It's all right for someone like him,' complained Andrews. 'When I was an engine driver, I was always under strain. I was out in all weathers and working long, hard, punishing hours. If anybody needed a rest it was me, but did they let me have it?'

'You can have all the rest you want now, Father.'

'No, I can't, Maddy. I get bored.'

She laughed. 'There's no pleasing you, is there?'

'Yes, there is. Just let me see my lovely granddaughter.'

'She'll be down again very soon.'

'Good,' said Andrews, contentedly. 'So, what did Hinton tell you?'

'He said that the superintendent was being looked after by his good friend, Captain Wardlow. Robert met him in Canterbury and thought he was the best person to turn to in the emergency. Alan Hinton doesn't envy him,' said Madeleine. 'The captain has got a very difficult job.'

'Tallis should be forced to retire.'

'That would be a heavy blow to his pride.'

'It's high time he stepped aside for Robert.'

'There's no vacancy. Tallis will be back somehow. I feel it.'

'Is that what Hinton told you?'

'It's what he's hoping.'

Andrews chuckled. 'I'd say he's got more important hopes to worry about,' he said. 'You should have seen the grin on his face as he helped Lydia into the cab.'

'They're good friends.'

'Where were they going?'

'I've no idea,' said Madeleine, coolly. 'Would you like some tea?'

'No, but I tell you what I *would* like, Maddy. I know that you don't want me to talk about him, but you did say that we were friends again.'

'We're father and daughter. That's an even stronger bond.'

'Then just answer a simple question.'

'What is it?' she asked, warily.

He beamed. 'How much is Mr Fairbank offering to pay you?'

Now that they felt they had a vital piece of evidence, they put it to the test. As befitted a former barrister, Colbeck acted as devil's advocate.

'How do we know that Gorey sailed on to Jersey?'

'I feel it in my bones, sir.'

'We need stronger proof than that, Victor.'

'They told me that the *Flying Fish* is the only vessel in Yarmouth that calls in at Jersey on its return voyage. If the killer wanted to go there, he'd have to be on board when it put to sea.'

'But we can't be sure that he *did* want to go there.'

'Mrs Swarbrick came from Jersey originally. That has to be important. I believe the killer was hired by someone in her past, someone perhaps who was upset when she married Swarbrick.'

'What if his name really *is* John Gorey?'

'Then he'd be the only villain I know who tells the truth. He used the false name in order to cover his tracks.'

The questions kept coming and Leeming answered every one of them with confidence. In the end, Colbeck gave up.

'You did well, Victor.'

'It was that moment in the bookshop,' said the other. 'Unlike you, I don't get sudden revelations that open a door on a case. But

I did get one today. I don't think it was pure chance that I picked up that atlas. I was *meant* to see it.'

'You spotted the town of Gorey far sooner than I did.'

'We'll have to go there at once.'

'Someone has to stay here, I'm afraid, and that will be me.'

Leeming was worried. 'I'll be on my own?'

'I have to continue the investigation here,' explained Colbeck. 'Meanwhile, you'll sneak off, but nobody must know where you've gone. The killer had help from someone at the railway station. If the accomplice knows that you've gone to Jersey, he'll realise why.'

'Aren't you even going to tell Mr Freed?'

'He's the last person in whom I'll confide.'

'I'd have thought you could trust him, sir.'

'I can't trust his wife, Victor. Mrs Freed is an intelligent woman and she'd sense right away that her husband was keeping a secret from her. Somehow she'd wheedle it out of him. And the moment that *she* is aware of our movements . . .'

'She's bound to tell Mrs Swarbrick. But wait a moment,' said Leeming, scratching his head, 'shouldn't we be asking Mrs Swarbrick if she knows anyone from Gorey?'

'I'd rather keep her in the dark,' said Colbeck.

'She lived in Jersey, sir. I'll be a complete stranger there.'

'It's a small island, Victor. You'll soon find your way around.'

'I have so little information to go on, sir.'

'Start at the harbour. Find out how many passengers disembarked from the *Flying Fish*. Contact the police. They'll know the local villains. There can't be many capable of doing what this man did.'

'I'd still like some help from Mrs Swarbrick.'

'She's in no position to give it,' said Colbeck. 'I've seen the state she's in. She's still very delicate. Her stepson's unwelcome visit last night certainly won't have improved her health.'

'It's just as well we turned up when we did.'

'As for the killer, you have to remember that Mrs Swarbrick was face-to-face with him, albeit briefly. She saw his face clearly yet didn't recognise him. What I can do,' he said, 'is to give you the address in St Helier where Mrs Swarbrick's brother lives. I made a point of asking Mr Freed for it when he talked about Mrs Swarbrick's former life in the Channel Islands. Freed wrote to tell him what had happened to his sister. He's probably on his way here now, but there'll be other family members still at the house.'

'That will be helpful, sir. I need all the assistance I can get.' Leeming gritted his teeth. 'I can't say I'm looking forward to it. Do I have to sail from Yarmouth?'

'No, Victor, it would entail unnecessary delay. You'll go by train to Portsmouth and sail by steamship. It will be much faster.'

'I feel so . . . unprepared.'

'I have every faith in you, Victor.'

'Is there nothing else you can say?'

'Yes, there is,' said Colbeck. 'Bon voyage!'

Andrew Swarbrick's urge to see his father's will was greater than ever. Because of his aggressive behaviour towards Neville Gilby, the solicitor had refused to let him see the document until there was a formal reading of it. Swarbrick spent that afternoon making an even more exhaustive search of his father's study, but his efforts were wasted. He came to the conclusion that it was no longer in the house but must be kept in the apartment that his father routinely used in London. Getting his hands on the document was vital. If he was to contest the will, he must be familiar with every word in it. He could then take legal advice. Having made the decision to return to London, he was about to leave the study when there was a tap on the door and the housekeeper entered. She bobbed.

'There's a gentleman to see Mrs Swarbrick,' she said.

'You know full well that she's not here.'

'I told him that, sir, but he's asked to speak to you.'

'What's his name?'

'Michael Hern.'

Swarbrick scowled. It was Grace's brother.

They had the pleasure of sharing the same cab because the address that Alan Hinton had been given was on the way to Lydia's house. They were able to enjoy warm proximity for once. When they reached Belgravia, the driver brought the cab to a halt and Hinton alighted, collecting a dazzling smile of farewell from Lydia as he did so. He waved the cab off, then began work. Finding the address he wanted, he went across the road to the house directly opposite. The properties were uniformly large, stylish and in an excellent state of repair. Compared to them, his lodging was cramped, mean and uncomfortable. He had to fight off the mixture of resentment and intimidation he often felt when confronted with evidence of wealth. It suddenly occurred to him that he could have asked Lydia Quayle to stay with him. In such surroundings, she'd have been completely at ease. Moreover, she would have been delighted to be involved, if only fleetingly, in detective work. Hinton scolded himself for not suggesting that they worked together, albeit illicitly.

He used the knocker and stood waiting. When the door opened, a pretty young maidservant came into view.

'Can I help you, sir?'

'I hope so,' said Hinton. 'I'm looking for someone who lives at this end of the road, but I don't have the number. The name is Fairbank. Does that name mean anything to you?'

'I'm afraid not.'

'How long have you been here?'

'I've been here long enough to know some of our neighbours,' she said, 'and there's no Fairbank among them.'

'Oh, I see.'

'But that doesn't mean the person you're after doesn't live here somewhere. These houses have six bedrooms. You might have people with three or four different names under one roof.'

'Thank you for your help.'

As he turned away, the girl closed the door behind. Hinton realised that it was not going to be as easy as he'd imagined. He was not daunted. Doing a favour for Madeleine Colbeck meant that he got closer to Lydia and he'd do anything to achieve that. It was time to knock on more doors.


As he drove the trap towards the station, Colbeck was able to give Leeming some final instructions. Knowing that the sergeant would probably be approached by Horace Pryor, he told him to say that he was returning to Scotland Yard to deliver a report. The same information could be used to parry Duff. Since his companion clearly had misgivings, Colbeck told him to see the trip as an adventure which would, hopefully, end with the arrest of the killer. Bolstered by that thought, Leeming began to look forward to his assignment.

'What will you be doing, sir?'

'Oh, I'll have my hands full talking to everyone who might have something useful to say – Andrew Swarbrick, for instance.'

'You've already spoken to him, sir.'

'His mood has changed now that he realises that his father gave preference to his wife in his will. I'd like to probe him about his dislike of his stepmother. It seems to be quite out of proportion.'

'From what I saw of him, he's just a nasty, spiteful man.'

'He's a prickly individual, I agree,' said Colbeck, 'but I suspect he'll be more amenable after last night's display of bad temper. If he wants to win votes in this city, he'll have to learn to be nice to people.'

Michael Hern was a tall, well-built, elegant man in his late forties with a face that was striking rather than handsome. When they'd first met, he and Swarbrick had disliked each other on sight. The hostility remained. Swarbrick didn't offer a handshake and Hern would not, in any case, have accepted it.

'Your sister is staying with Mr and Mrs Freed,' said Swarbrick.

'Why is she there?'

'It was her decision.'

'This is her home. Why couldn't Mrs Freed move in here to be with Grace?'

'Ask her.'

'I think she left here because of you,' said Hern, accusingly. 'When my sister offered the hand of friendship, all you did was to turn your back on her. Grace deserved better than that, Swarbrick.'

'That's a matter of opinion.'

'I already know yours. I can still remember the way you looked down your nose at us when you first met our family. Well, you won't do that to Grace while I'm around.'

Swarbrick bridled. 'Are you threatening me?'

'I'm just giving you fair warning,' said Hern, coldly. His tone softened. 'I'm sorry about your father's death. He was a decent man in every way. I liked him. What have the police been doing? Have they made an arrest yet?'

'No, they haven't, and they don't look likely to, if you ask me. The famous Inspector Colbeck is running around in circles without getting anywhere. He's floundering.'

'Things may be different now that I'm here.'

'Really?'

'I haven't just come to console my sister,' said Hern, resolutely. 'I want to catch the killer and strangle him with my bare hands.'

Hinton was mystified. After knocking on four doors, he still hadn't found anyone familiar with the name of Fairbank. Born and brought up in a quiet backstreet, he'd known the names of every person in the houses around him. It was a community where secrecy was at a premium. Everyone knew what everyone else did. No barriers existed. He was now in an area of Belgravia where most residents didn't even seem to be on speaking terms with their neighbours. In answer to his question, all he got were blank faces. As a last resort, he went to the house next to the address he'd been given and rang the bell. A manservant opened the door and raised a polite eyebrow.

'Hello,' said Hinton, 'I wonder if you could help me?'

'What is it you want, sir?'

'Does Mr Fairbank live here?'

'No, sir, this is the Edbrooke residence.'

'What about next door?' he asked, pointing. 'Is that where Mr Fairbank lives?'

'Oh, I don't think so. In fact, I don't think there are any gentlemen there. I haven't seen one, anyway.'

'So who does own the house?'

'It's a group of women, sir. They're a colony of artists.'

Colbeck stayed on the platform until the train pulled out with Leeming aboard. He then headed for the exit. As he expected, Duff fell in beside him, his breath foul with tobacco.

'How long is the sergeant going to be away?' asked Duff.

'He'll be gone as long as is necessary.'

'That means you'll be a man light.'

'Are you volunteering to take his place?'

'I'm here if you need me, Inspector.'

'It's kind of you to offer,' said Colbeck, 'but I can manage.'

'Actually,' said Duff, stepping in front of him and forcing him to stop, 'I just wanted a word. It's true that I was dismissed from the Metropolitan Police Force but only because my sergeant took against me. I was in a public house late at night when I was still on duty. The licensee was a brute, sir. We all knew that he beat his wife. When I heard her screaming that night, I went in to rescue her.'

'That was very noble of you,' said Colbeck, not believing a word. 'Did you arrest the husband?'

'He'd fallen asleep in a drunken stupor.'

'Ah, I see, so you had to console his wife.'

'It's what any right-thinking man would've done, sir.'

'And the sergeant caught you at it, did he?'

'It was so unfair,' said Duff, bunching his fists. 'I was ready to give her husband a dose of his own medicine.'

'If the man had a history of battering his wife, you could have arrested him for assault. Battering him in turn would have solved nothing. For what it's worth,' said Colbeck, 'I believe what the records say about your police career.'

'But that gives a false impression of me.'

'It's in perfect accord with my own judgement.'

Easing Duff aside, he walked briskly away.

When he came into the room, Grace emitted a cry of joy, leapt up and ran into Hern's arms. All that Anthea Freed could do was to stand there and witness the tearful reunion. When Grace had stopped crying and Hern had stopped assuring her that everything would be all right, Anthea had an opportunity to give the visitor a proper welcome.

'May I offer you some refreshment, Mr Hern?' she asked.

'It's been a very long journey. I'd love a glass of whisky.'

Anthea was firm. 'We're teetotal in this house.'

'Oh, yes, I forgot. I do apologise. In that case, I'll have nothing.'

'I was hoping you'd come earlier, Michael,' said Grace.

'The moment I heard the news, I packed my bag and set out. It's so maddening to live that far away.' He hugged her again, then eased her back into her chair before turning to the other woman. 'I'm very sorry, Mrs Freed. I've worried myself sick about my sister. What I should have done was to thank you for everything you've done for Grace. It's a huge imposition on you.'

'I don't feel that,' said Anthea. 'Grace is a dear friend. I'm glad to have her where I can look after her. Leaving her alone at the house with Andrew would have been cruel.'

'I can well believe it. I called on him first just to let him know that I was here. He won't bother my sister any more.'

'I simply had to get out of there,' said Grace, 'but, we were in such a rush, I didn't have time to bring everything I needed and I'm too afraid to go back there.'

'It's quite safe now,' he told her. 'Andrew is going to London. You can go and get whatever you need, Grace.'

'Better still,' offered Anthea, 'you can make a list and I'll fetch everything for you.'

'I couldn't ask you to do that,' said Grace.

'We'll go together,' decided Hern. 'But, first of all, I want to hear what the police have been up to. Andrew mentioned a famous Inspector Colbeck. Who is he and what success has he had so far?'

It happened once again. When they went into the garden so that Tallis could smoke a cigar, he looked and sounded as if there was nothing wrong with him. There was no mention of his resort to prayer and he was patently unaware that Wardlow had entered his bedroom and seen him on his knees. He was pleasant and moderately cheerful.

'I've been thinking about that suggestion of yours, Terence.'

'Which one do you mean? I made several.'

'You thought we might pay a visit to the barracks.'

'Oh, yes,' said Wardlow. 'When you stayed here last, you were forced to miss the regimental dinner. As you were the guest of honour, it was particularly galling.'

'I was presented with my award in a private ceremony.'

'It wasn't the same, Edward.'

'I know,' said the other, sombrely. He forced a smile. 'They did invite me to return at any time.'

'Then we'll go tomorrow. Will that suit you?'

'Yes, please. I miss the sight of army uniforms.'

'I still have my old dress uniform,' said Wardlow with a chuckle. 'It's upstairs in a wardrobe, smelling of mothballs.'

'It was so kind of you to invite me here, Terence. I've really started to enjoy this break from work.'

'That's good.'

'You were right. I pushed myself far too hard.'

'You did, Edward.'

'My life was nothing but a treadmill.'

'You deserve to get off it for a while.'

Tallis pulled on his cigar then exhaled a cloud of smoke. They strolled around the lawn and reminisced about their army days. Coming to an abrupt halt, Tallis turned to his friend.

'You will tell me, won't you?' he implored. 'If I behave badly, you must rebuke me, Terence.'

'You've been a trifle erratic, that's all.'

'I'd hate to upset your wife.'

'It hasn't happened so far.'

'That's a relief. Help me to make sure that it never happens. My mind plays all kinds of tricks on me, but I feel so much better now. That's largely thanks to you and Mrs Wardlow.' He pulled on his cigar again then waved a hand to dispel the smoke as he exhaled it. 'Retirement has a lot of virtues. Perhaps it's something I should consider.'

Colbeck was on his way to visit Cecil Freed when he saw the jaunty figure of Oliver Trant coming towards him. They exchanged greetings.

'I hear that Sergeant Leeming was heroic last night,' said Trant. 'He overpowered Andrew Swarbrick who was trying to force his way into a certain person's house.'

'Is that what Mr Freed told you?'

'Oh, no, he's far too discreet. I got the information elsewhere.'

'May one ask from whom?'

Trant smirked. 'That's a secret, Inspector.'

'I should imagine that you were delighted to hear something about Mr Swarbrick that's to his disadvantage.'

'I wish I'd been there to witness the event.'

'It's water under the bridge now, Mr Trant.'

'I'll keep a bucket of that water,' said the other. 'It may come in useful if Andrew and I compete to replace his father in Parliament.' He glanced towards the building behind him. 'If you're going to see Cecil, you must have news about the investigation. Am I correct?'

'That's confidential information, sir,' said Colbeck.

Walking past Trant, he went into the building to be shown immediately into Freed's office.

'I've got some news for you, Inspector,' said Freed. 'My wife sent word that Grace's brother has arrived at last from Jersey.'

'That's good to hear. I look forward to meeting him.'

'Michael Hern is an interesting man. You may find him a little forthright at first, but he improves on acquaintance.'

'What does he do for a living?'

'He's not exactly an estate agent but is involved in all manner of property deals. On the one occasion when Jarvis visited the island, he stayed with Hern and his family at their wonderful house by the sea. It had its own jetty. Jarvis was very impressed.'

'I'm surprised that Mr Swarbrick found the time for a holiday. You told me that he was dedicated to his political career.'

'He and Grace were only in Jersey for a few days. The moment they got back, Jarvis went off to a series of meetings in London. He was very much an absent husband, I'm afraid.'

'His wife seems to have coped with that,' said Colbeck. 'By the way, I just bumped into Mr Trant.'

'Yes, he came to solicit my support once again.'

'Your vote would go to Mr Swarbrick, surely?'

'It ought to – if only out of loyalty to his father. But last night's episode has made me question Andrew's fitness for the office. I told him so to his face.'

'Politicians are not known for their sobriety.'

'Unlike my wife, I don't censure a man if he has a drink now and again. But I abhor any kind of violence – especially on my doorstep.'

'Mr Trant somehow got to hear about the fracas.'

'How did he manage that?'

'You might ask that question of your servants, sir.'

'I most certainly will,' vowed Freed.

'I just came to tell you that we're making slow but steady progress. Sergeant Leeming has gone back to London to deliver a report and to request some additional help.'

'Don't you have enough police at your disposal?'

'They don't have the skills of a detective,' said Colbeck. 'That's not a criticism. Their prime function is to uphold the law and protect the public. They've had no experience of dealing with a murder.'

'None of us has, Inspector.'

'The perpetrator may have fled but his accomplice is still here. In fact, there may be more than one. When the sergeant was in Yarmouth earlier today, he had a distinct feeling that he was being followed.'

'It could have been a pickpocket. They're always mingling with the crowds because people tend to be off guard when they're on holiday.'

'Pickpockets choose their targets carefully, sir. They'd never go after someone as sturdy as Sergeant Leeming. He's far too alert and, as you saw, he can handle himself well in a brawl.'

'So, who was this person following him?'

'He never found out,' said Colbeck, 'but I believe that it could be someone connected to the murder. If so, it's a good sign. It means that he's worried by the amount of progress we've made. Now that the sergeant is no longer here to be followed, I'm hoping that he'll switch his attention to me.'

'Is that wise?' asked Freed in alarm.

'I think so.'

'You could be in danger.'

Colbeck smiled. 'I've been in danger from the moment I joined the police force,' he said, airily. 'I've learnt to live harmoniously with it.'


Bartram Duff was late leaving the station because some cattle broke out of a stock wagon and he had to help to round them up. Once they were safely restored to the wagon, he made his way to a pub in one of the less salubrious parts of the city. His friend was seated in a corner. Duff went swiftly across to him.

'Well,' he asked, 'what did you find out in Yarmouth?'


Alan Hinton was bewildered by his discovery. Though he was tempted to pass on the information to Madeleine, he saw an opportunity to see Lydia Quayle once again. He'd been to her house before and knew that it was only ten minutes away by cab. On the way there, he speculated on the reason why Lionel Fairbank had told what turned out to be a blatant lie. When he reached Lydia's house, she was surprised yet delighted to see him, sensing that he had some important news. He told her who lived at the address and her jaw dropped open in astonishment.

'It's a colony of female *artists*?'

'There are such things. Madeleine is one of them.'

'But Mr Fairbank said that his son lived there.'

'Nobody had ever heard that name.'

'But that's definitely where he was staying,' said Lydia. 'We know that he was honest about that because Madeleine's letter reached him at that address.'

'It could have been passed on to him by one of the occupants.'

'How many of them are there?'

'I've no idea. I didn't want to knock on the door in case Fairbank really *was* there. If he's as intelligent as Madeleine said, he might have guessed that he was being spied on and taken offence.'

'You did the right thing, Alan.'

'Perhaps Mrs Colbeck should think again about working for him,' he suggested. 'Nobody can trust a man who told such a barefaced lie.'

'What do you think we should do?'

'We need to gather more evidence before we tell Madeleine. I'll be at Scotland Yard all day tomorrow, so you'll have to take over.'

Lydia grinned. 'That sounds exciting!'

'I think you should go to the gallery that sells her paintings. If there's anything of Madeleine's on display, show an interest and ask if he has work by any other female artist.'

'Should I mention Mr Fairbank?'

'No,' he cautioned. 'Keep his name out of it. When you've got some details from the owner, you can go to Madeleine and tell her what we've found out between us.'

'That's a brilliant idea, Alan!'

'It's what Inspector Colbeck would have done.'

'Oh, I think he'd have been more suspicious of Mr Fairbank at the very start. We can't blame Madeleine. She was flattered by the praise he heaped on her. In her eyes, the commission was a bona fide offer.'

'It may still turn out that way,' he said. 'We mustn't condemn him out of hand. There may be a straightforward explanation for what I discovered, and we'll both be left red-faced for jumping to a conclusion before we weighed up the evidence properly.'

'That's true,' she said.

'Anyway, I must thank you for involving me in this little mystery. It's really intrigued me.'

'You were the obvious person, Alan. Oh,' she went on, 'this commission has meant so much to Madeleine. I'd hate to disappoint her. I do hope I'll be able to tell her some *good* news tomorrow.'

When he got to the house, Grace Swarbrick and her brother had already returned. They told Colbeck that they'd been to retrieve some clothing and other items from Grace's bedroom.

'It was wonderful to be able to walk so freely around my own house again,' she said. 'As you know, when Andrew was there, I hid upstairs.'

'He had no right to make you do that,' said Hern, 'especially, as it now transpires, the house has been bequeathed to you.'

'I didn't expect that, Michael, and I'm not sure I want it.'

'Would you rather it went to that reptilian stepson of yours?'

'I'd just prefer that there were no family rows,' said Grace. 'At a time like this, it's improper as well as lowering.'

The three of them were seated in the drawing room. Colbeck's first impressions of the brother were favourable. He found him frank, direct and astute. Colbeck particularly liked the man's deep, rich voice.

'I'm sorry that you had to be dragged back here like this, Mr Hern.'

'It's my own fault, Inspector,' said the other. 'One of the penalties of living in the Channel Islands is that you're rather cut off. And, of course, we're far closer to France than we are to the British mainland.'

'The French have been pointing that out for a very long time.'

'That battle is finally resolved,' said Hern. 'We're firmly in British hands now. But you didn't come to hear about Jersey. Tell me about the investigation. Mrs Freed gave me some information, but I suspect that there's a lot more I need to hear.'

'Some of it may be a little disturbing for you, Mrs Swarbrick,' said Colbeck, considerately. 'If you wish, we could adjourn to another room.'

'I'm not that frail, Inspector,' she said. 'I feel well enough to hear the truth now. Please go on.'

Choosing his words with care, Colbeck gave them a concise but fairly comprehensive account of what he'd done so far. The one thing he omitted was any mention of his belief that the killer might have returned to Jersey. Hern interrupted with an occasional question but otherwise sat there with his brow furrowed. Grace winced at some of the details. As soon as Colbeck finished, Hern announced his decision.

'I'll work with you, Inspector.'

'There's no need for you to do that, sir.'

'*I* feel the need. Jarvis was my brother-in-law, after all. I'm not going to sit on the sidelines while you do all the work. From what you've just told us, it's clear that the killer had one or more confederates. They either work for the railway or have done so in the past and therefore know how everything operates.'

'All members of staff have been questioned, Mr Hern.'

'Have any suspects emerged?'

'As a matter of fact, they have.'

'Then let me have a word with them,' said Hern, tapping his chest. 'I can be very persuasive.'

'That's not the answer. Resort to violent interrogation and we'd frighten the culprits away.'

'I demand to be involved.'

'I'm in charge of this investigation,' said Colbeck with a note of authority, 'and I'll submit to nobody's demands. Be aware of that, sir.'

'Michael doesn't mean to interfere,' said Grace, apologetically. 'He'd simply like to help.'

'He'd do that best by looking after you, Mrs Swarbrick. But let me ask you a question,' he continued. 'When you were still recovering from the initial jolt, I didn't feel able to touch on your private life before you met your second husband.'

'What do you wish to know?'

'Well, an attractive woman like you must have had admirers.'

'My sister was a real beauty in her younger days,' said Hern with a smile. 'She had many admirers. When she moved to England after Roland's death, two of her suitors followed her. They were wounded to the quick when she met and married Jarvis Swarbrick.'

'I'd like to have their names, if you please, sir.'

'You can forget one of them, Inspector. He went off to America.'

'What about the other one?'

'Oh, I daresay that he's still carrying a candle for Grace.'

'That's a ridiculous thing to say, Michael. He lost interest when I met someone else. Inspector Colbeck was right when he said that the explanation of Jarvis's murder is right here under our noses.'

'It has to be connected with the Eastern Counties Railway,' said Colbeck. 'That's why it happened in an ECR train. It was a symbolic act. Mr Swarbrick could have been murdered far more easily in any number of locations, but the branch line was chosen so that it was done in public view. Our search starts and ends right here.'

Victor Leeming was huddled on a seat as the steamship battled the choppy water. Within minutes, his stomach began to heave, his eyes clouded over and his head began to pound. He was in agony. Finding a killer was no longer his sole aim. First of all, he had to stay alive long enough to reach his destination.

# CHAPTER TWENTY

Grace Swarbrick's presence was an inhibiting factor. Colbeck had wanted to talk to her brother alone and speak more freely than he was able to with a grieving woman sitting opposite him in mourning attire. On his own, Colbeck felt, Michael Hern would have given him far more information about his sister. In particular, Colbeck would have liked to find out more about the suitors who'd pursued her when she moved to England from Jersey. It was clearly an episode in her past that she was keen to consign to obscurity. In marrying Swarbrick, she had – apart from occasional visits there – apparently renounced her birthplace. That was Colbeck's starting point.

'Tell me, Mr Hern,' he said, 'how did you feel when your

heard that your sister was about to marry a British politician?'

'I was shocked at first,' admitted Hern. 'I couldn't see how Grace could adapt to a life so different from the one she'd been leading in Jersey.'

'And yet Mrs Swarbrick appears to have done so.'

'It took a lot of effort,' she interjected, 'but I didn't mind. I loved my husband. Being with him was always a joy – unless we had to travel by train, that is.'

'We have no railways in Jersey,' said Hern. 'They're bound to come in time, I suppose. Returning to your original question, Inspector, let me say that I warmed to Jarvis eventually. At first he looked rather staid and could be quite pompous but, when you got to know him, you realised that he had a wicked sense of humour. The determining factor for me was that he adored my sister and promised to look after her.'

'And he kept that promise, Michael,' she said, quietly. 'I wanted for nothing.'

'Many wives in your position,' said Colbeck, 'would have been overwhelmed by the demands of their new life but, according to Mrs Freed, you settled into it with commendable speed.'

'My sister has always had great willpower,' said Hern, proudly.

'When did you first meet Andrew Swarbrick?'

'It was not until I paid a visit to London. Jarvis took me to the House of Commons, then we later met up with his son.' His face darkened. 'It was not a happy occasion. Andrew managed a surface politeness, but I could sense his rooted opposition to the notion of his father taking anyone from our family into his life.'

'Were you shocked when he refused to attend the wedding?'

'No, Inspector, I was heartily relieved.'

'How often have you met him?'

'Three or four times in total – and that was more than enough.'

'Was he so objectionable?'

'He was loathsome. We invited him and his wife to come to St Helier, but he snubbed us as if we were creatures from a lower order of Creation.'

'Let's not talk about Andrew,' pleaded Grace.

'We can't ignore him,' said her brother.

'I'm so afraid that he's going to do something dreadful.'

'He's already done that, Grace. He treated you abominably.'

'That's why I don't wish to discuss him.'

'But I'm sure that Inspector Colbeck does.'

'Well,' she said, getting up, 'since he has to be part of this conversation, if you'll both excuse me, I'll leave you alone to talk about Andrew as long as you wish.'

Colbeck rose from his seat and opened the door for her to leave, closing it behind her. When he turned to face Hern, he felt able to speak more freely and probe more deeply.

'Why did your sister decide to leave Jersey in the first place?'

'That's a long story, Inspector . . .'

Over dinner that evening, Tallis made more of an effort to talk to his hostess, even rising to a few clumsy but well-meant compliments. Wardlow was pleased to see how much more relaxed he was now. It was a marked improvement on his earlier discomfort in female company. When they adjourned to the drawing room after a meal, Wardlow reached for the brandy decanter.

'Not for me, thank you,' said Tallis.

'I've never known you refuse a drink, Edward.'

'The glass of wine I had at dinner was enough. I don't wish to

311

be rude but, to tell you the truth, I'd like to have an early night for once. Would you mind terribly if I just . . . slip away?'

'It's very early.'

'Yes, I know.'

'Are you unwell?' asked Wardlow with concern.

'It's more a case of fatigue.'

'Did you get much sleep last night?'

'Not really – it was rather intermittent.'

'Brandy usually does the trick for me. I nod off instantly.'

'Then I'll leave you to attack the decanter. Goodnight, Terence.'

'Did you want a call for breakfast tomorrow?'

'No,' said Tallis. 'I'd appreciate a lie-in.'

'We didn't get many opportunities to do that in the army,' said Wardlow with a chuckle.

He opened the door for his friend to leave, then watched him going up the staircase. Tallis had completely lost the spring in his step. Moving slowly, he was using the banister to haul himself up the steps. Wardlow closed the door, lowered himself gingerly into his armchair and poured himself a ruminative glass of brandy. There was cause for anxiety and reassurance. Having taken an afternoon nap, Tallis was now going to bed hours earlier than usual. It worried Wardlow. Against that could be set the fact that he'd been calm, controlled and pleasant throughout the rest of the day. His readiness to speak at length with his hostess was a welcome sign in a man who normally avoided talking to women.

Then there was Tallis's assiduous bout of prayer earlier in the day. It had startled Wardlow. He had never thought of his friend as a religious man. During their time in India, when the chaplain had been unavailable, Tallis had led his men in a service from time to time, but it tended to be rather perfunctory. Of his Christian values, there could be no doubt, but he had never been passionate about his beliefs. Finding him on his knees in prayer had been both surprising and, in an odd way, rather unsettling. Wardlow couldn't decide if Tallis was seeking help or forgiveness.

It was not long before the glass was empty. As he poured himself a second brandy, Wardlow came to a decision. It was time to consult Dr Kitson once again.

After an hour of feeling sorry for himself, Victor Leeming experienced a small miracle. The swell eased, the howling wind died down and the roar of the ship's engines became less intrusive. While he felt that he'd never enjoy sailing, he began to feel it less of a trial by ordeal and more of an irksome duty. His queasiness vanished and his headache slowly faded away. It was even possible to have a conversation with one of the ship's officers who'd offered him a nip of brandy. Hearing that the man lived in Jersey, he was quick to use him as a source of information.

'Do they have a police force there?' he asked.

'They have one of sorts, sir,' said the man. 'Thanks to an Act passed by the States of Jersey, it came into being just over seven years ago. In fact, my brother is one of the first ten paid policemen on the island.'

'What's his name?'

'Peter Voisin.'

'That's a French name.'

'Most of them have French names. They had to be able to speak French and English fluently before they could be appointed.'

'Where are their headquarters?'

The officer laughed. 'That's too grand a name for the place they use in St Helier. Peter, my brother, used to be a carpenter but thought he could earn more money as a policeman.'

'How much are they paid?'

'They get eighteen shillings a week.'

'What do they have to do to earn it?' asked Leeming.

'They patrol the streets between the hours of 6 p.m. and 2 a.m. They're a night watch or *garde de nuit*.'

The officer went on to describe the duties of the paid police and told Leeming that they were answerable to the Constable of St Helier who, in turn, needed the sanction of the Bailiff in order to suspend any of the men. Leeming was staggered to hear that law and order in the island's capital was in the hands of such a small band of policemen when it had a population in excess of twenty-five thousand.

'What about a town like Gorey?' he asked.

'They don't have paid policemen there.'

'How is crime controlled?'

'People look out for each other,' said the officer. 'For the most part, it's only a question of petty crime. Rural areas refused to accept paid officers. They either rely on the local constable or police themselves by word of mouth.'

'Is it really as primitive as that?'

'It seems to work, sir.'

Leeming was dismayed. He'd hoped for an organised constabulary covering the whole island, but it had yet to come into being. Instead, therefore, any assistance he got could only come from a group of policemen who sounded as if they were essentially nightwatchmen. A task that had already seemed daunting now took on the character of an impossible dream. Leeming was in pursuit of an armed man who had already killed one victim and it looked as if he'd have to search for him alone. His stomach began to heave all over again.

Two long uninterrupted hours gave Colbeck the opportunity to fill in the many gaps relating to Grace Swarbrick's former life. Her brother had explained how, when she met Jarvis Swarbrick, she'd gone back on her vow never to remarry. Though it had seemed like a case of the attraction of opposites, Michael Hern pointed out that the couple had far more in common than was initially thought. Once having wed, they grew even closer and became more dependent on each other. From her letters, Hern said, he could see that his sister had found real happiness again.

'When she first met your sister,' recalled Colbeck, 'Mrs Freed was struck by her extraordinary poise.'

'Grace has always had that, Inspector.'

'How would she respond to an emergency?'

'She'd do so much more calmly than I would,' said Hern with a grin. 'Somehow my sister always maintained her composure. It took the murder of her husband to make her lose it.'

'What does the future hold for her, would you say?'

'It's too early to predict.'

'She's talked of returning to Jersey.'

'There's unfinished business here first.'

Before Colbeck could ask another question, Cecil Freed came into the room and exchanged greetings with them. He gave Hern a cordial welcome and pressed him to stay with them there as long as he wished.

'By rights,' said Hern, 'my sister and I should both be at the other house. It is, I understand, bequeathed to her. In my view, we shouldn't let Andrew stay there at all, but Grace doesn't want any confrontation with him. I'm hoping to talk her around.'

Colbeck had the feeling that Hern would succeed. He was an intelligent, highly articulate man and his sister had always consulted him when about to take a major decision in her life. Having met Hern only a few times before, Freed wanted to catch up on his news. Happy to leave them alone, Colbeck excused himself.

'It was good to meet you, Inspector,' said Hern.

'The feeling is mutual, sir,' said Colbeck. 'Thank you for answering my questions so frankly. Our discussion was very fruitful.'

'There'll be lots more discussions with me from now on.'

'Why is that?'

'It's because I intend to work alongside you.'

'That won't be possible, I'm afraid,' said Colbeck, stoutly. 'It's kind of you to offer your help, but I have to decline it.'


Victor Leeming had quailed when told that they'd be sailing through the night. He couldn't understand how the captain could plot a course in the darkness. His fears were not allayed by the passenger who chose to flop down into the chair beside him. He was a middle-aged man, returning to Jersey after visiting his son who was at school in Winchester. A merchant by profession, he sailed to and from England on a regular basis and was accustomed to sea travel. Leeming envied him. While the sergeant still felt ill, his companion was glowing with health.

'Is it always this bad?' asked Leeming.

'It can get far worse, believe me,' said the man. 'This has been a relatively easy voyage so far. We just have to hope for fine weather when we catch sight of Jersey.'

'I don't follow.'

'The captain and his crew have to take account of rocks, reefs, tides and currents. They can all be fatal. There have been shipwrecks galore. Then there's the problem of actually getting ashore.'

'What do you mean?'

'The harbour facilities at St Helier are far from ideal. The English and French Harbours are situated around La Folie. The jetties there are inaccessible at low tide so passengers have to be ferried by tenders to the landing stage at La Collette. If you think this is uncomfortable,' said the man, chortling, 'wait until you're bobbing about on the waves in a small boat. That will test your nerves.'

'I don't have any left,' said Leeming, gloomily. 'How do we get into St Helier itself?'

'There'll be carriages waiting for us.'

'That's a relief.'

'Where are you going?'

'First of all, I have to call at an address in St Helier.'

'It's a pretty town,' said the other, 'and the people are very friendly as a rule. How much French do you speak?'

'None at all,' admitted Leeming.

'That's a pity.'

'Why?'

'Most of the place names are in French.'

Leeming gulped. His mission was hopeless.


Lydia Quayle was so eager to begin her work that she arrived at the Red Gallery before it was even opened, forcing her to walk around the block a few times before the premises were unlocked. After giving the proprietor time to settle in, she went over to the window and studied the paintings on show. There was nothing about any of them to suggest that they were the work of female artists. When she got inside, however, she spotted a print of a railway scene and recognised the distinctive hand of Madeleine Colbeck. She was still examining it when Francis Sinclair walked over to her. He, too, scrutinised the print.

'You'd never believe that it was painted by a woman, would you?'

'Really?' said Lydia, feigning surprise.

'It's hardly the kind of subject matter that would appeal to the average woman. This artist is the exception to the rule. Her father was an engine driver and she had an urge to paint railway scenes.'

'It's very realistic. You can almost smell that cloud of smoke.'

'Does that mean you're interested in buying it?'

'I wouldn't go that far,' said Lydia, 'not least because I can't see it fitting in with paintings I already have on my walls. But I like it.' She turned to him. 'How rare are female artists?'

'Oh, they're not as rare as you might imagine. Including the work of this artist, I sell paintings by five or six women. One of them is a talented portrait artist and another specialises in landscapes.'

'I'd be interested to see some of them.'

'Then you'll have to come into the storeroom. Space is limited out here,' he said with a broad gesture, 'so I have to be very selective.'

'Is it easy to sell the work of the other women?'

'In some cases, it's very easy; in others, alas, the paintings take longer to find an admirer. But I have one customer who has a preference for the work of female artists.'

'That's unusual, isn't it?'

'This gentleman is very unusual,' he confided. 'Follow me.'

As soon as he'd finished his breakfast in the cottage, Colbeck drove to the railway station to read the telegraph sent from Scotland Yard. He composed his reply and had it despatched there and then.

When he came out on to the platform, he was ambushed by Pryor.

'Good morning, Inspector,' said the railway policeman.

'Good morning.'

'I was wondering when Sergeant Leeming will return?'

'He'll be back before too long.'

'Will that be this morning, this afternoon or this evening?'

'Who can tell?'

'Don't you *know* where he is, sir?'

'As a matter of fact,' said Colbeck, 'I don't.'

'But he's supposed to be assisting you.'

'There's more than one way of doing that, Pryor.'

'What does that mean?'

'Work it out for yourself.'

'All I want to know is where he went,' complained Pryor.

But he was talking to thin air. Colbeck was already striding quickly away without even a backward glance. In his frustration, Pryor spat on to the platform. Duff came out of the shadows.

'I've warned you about doing that,' he scolded.

'I'm sorry, Bart.'

'What did he tell you?'

'Nothing.'

'Did you ask where the sergeant was?'

'Yes,' said Pryor. 'He told me that he didn't know.'

Duff looked angrily after the retreating figure of Colbeck.

Since he'd be warned that Tallis might have a lie-in that morning, Wardlow was not disturbed by his friend's failure to come down for breakfast. As time went by, however, he did slowly begin to worry. It was all of fourteen hours since his guest had gone to bed. Could he possibly still be asleep after that length of time? His anxiety intensified. On his arrival in Canterbury, the superintendent had drawn back in fear at the sight of the cathedral. Because of the memories it revived, it was a source of terror for him. Wardlow began to wonder if Tallis was not simply slumbering in his bed. What if he'd taken impulsive action to rid himself of the terror? Was it possible that he might *never* wake up?

In spite of the pain from his arthritis, Wardlow went upstairs as fast as he could. Casting decorum aside, he flung open the door of the guest bedroom and stepped inside. It was empty. Tallis had gone.

Madeleine had been waiting some time for her friend to arrive and was delighted when she heard Lydia being admitted to the house. The next moment they were locked in a warm hug. Lydia explained where she'd been.

'You went to the art gallery?' asked Madeleine in surprise.

'I was the first customer through the door,' said Lydia. 'Not that I really was a customer, of course, but I pretended to be one.'

'What did Mr Sinclair say?'

'He was very complimentary about you.'

'What about other women artists?'

'Oh, there are a handful of them, apparently. You're not the only one with an urge to paint, though your subject matter sets you apart from the others.'

'That's hardly surprising.'

'Mr Sinclair sells work by some of the other women. He showed me some examples of their work. It has real promise.'

'Did he mention Mr Fairbank?'

'He referred to him but not by name.'

'What did he say?'

'He told me about a customer with a marked preference for paintings by female artists. That corresponds with what Alan Hinton found out. Some of those women live together in that colony he discovered. It's clear proof that Mr Fairbank sponsors them in some way.'

'Why?'

'You'll have to ask him.'

'I'm not sure that I want to,' said Madeleine. 'I'm beginning to wish that I'd never met Mr Fairbank. Underneath that charm, there's something about him that disturbs me.'

Getting ashore in Jersey was an exercise in slow torture. Seated in the tender with the other passengers, Leeming was soaked by salt water and tossed about in all directions. His one advantage over the others was that he wasn't impeded by a large amount of luggage. He could keep both hands firmly on the edge of the boat instead of holding down a trunk to prevent it being catapulted into the sea. When he was finally on dry land again, his legs were like rubber.

The first thing he did was to find a port official who spoke good

English. He was in luck. The man remembered the recent arrival from Cherbourg of the *Flying Fish*, bound for Yarmouth. Only six people had disembarked. Two of them were women. Of the four men, three were middle-aged. The youngest of the quartet, Leeming was told, was a surly young man with a black beard. It was a good start. Leeming's hopes revived.

When he'd recovered from the shock of Tallis's disappearance, Wardlow had been able to take comfort from the fact that his guest had left all his belongings there. It might indicate that he was not running away and intended to return. Having ordered that the horse be harnessed, Wardlow drove off towards Canterbury in the dog cart, convinced that was the way Tallis must have gone. As the horse trotted briskly along, he was high enough on the driving seat to see over the tops of the hedges and could scan the fields on both sides. Hampered by carts and other traffic on the way, it took him the best part of twenty minutes to reach the city. He went straight to the police station to raise the alarm.

The duty sergeant wrote down the details then looked up at him.

'Edward Tallis?' he said. 'That name is familiar.'

'He was kidnapped just before Christmas,' explained Wardlow. 'Your men joined in the manhunt.'

'Oh, so you've lost him again, have you, sir?'

'He left the house during the night of his own accord.'

'Losing him once was bad enough,' said the other. 'Letting him escape for the second time was even worse. If you get him back again, I suggest you put a ball and chain around his ankle.'

Wardlow growled, 'We can do without your pitiable attempt at humour, Sergeant,' he said. 'I want your men out there looking for him.'

'Do you know where he might be, sir?'

'No, I don't. What I tell you is that he's on foot and needs to be found quickly. It may be a question of life and death.'

Leaving the station, Colbeck tried an experiment. In the hope that he might attract attention, he ignored the trap and instead walked. Within minutes, he knew that he was being followed. Someone had been lurking in readiness and trailed him from a safe distance. Walking along, Colbeck gave no indication that he knew he was being shadowed. At one point, he went into a newsagent's shop to buy a newspaper. When he came out again, he felt that the man was still there, albeit invisible. It was not long before he left the road and turned into a lane, walking to the end before swinging right. He immediately sought a hiding place. Tucked away in a doorway, he waited patiently. Minutes ticked by. He then heard footsteps.

Someone was approaching stealthily. Colbeck was ready for him. The moment he caught sight of the man, he jumped out, grabbed him by the shoulders and threw him against a wall. It took all the breath out of his stalker. Though the man tried to escape, he was up against a far stronger opponent. Turning him round swiftly, Colbeck tugged back his arms and pulled the handcuffs from his pocket before clipping them on to his prisoner's wrists. Colbeck spun him around again and pushed him hard against the wall again to stifle his protests. He found himself looking at a rather nondescript individual in his forties.

'Who are you?' demanded Colbeck.

'I've done nothing wrong,' bleated the other.

'You followed my colleague to Yarmouth and today you kept watch on me. If you won't give me your name, I'll find it for myself.'

Ignoring the man's indignant yell, he searched his pockets and found his wallet. Inside was a card with a name and address printed on it in bold letters. But it was something else that interested Colbeck.

'Ah,' he said with a note of irony, 'so you're a private detective, are you? Well now, Jack Noonan – if that really *is* your name – what are you up to?'

'I'm trying to solve a murder, that's all.'

'Do you have any training as a detective?'

'Well, no, to be honest,' conceded the other, 'but I know how to gather information. We were slowly building up a picture.'

'*We*?' repeated Colbeck. 'Who's your partner?'

'It doesn't matter.'

'Oh, yes it does. You had someone helping you, didn't you, and I have a very strong feeling that his name was Sergeant Duff.' Noonan shook his head. 'No wonder he was so keen to be part of the investigation and keep abreast of any developments.'

'The reward money was very tempting, sir.'

'So you decided to get it by any means at your disposal.'

'No, sir, I swear it. I told Bart that we had to play fair.'

'Is that how you describe following the two detectives who were summoned to solve this crime? Do you really think that stealing what we found by dint of hard work was an example of fair play?'

'We know things about this city that you don't,' said the other with a touch of aggression. 'Bart works for the ECR and nothing escapes his eyes. Also, he knew Mr Swarbrick well whereas you've never set eyes on him. We had lots of advantages over you.'

'I've heard enough,' said Colbeck, taking him by the scruff of the neck. 'If you want to see how a real detective operates, you can come with me to the police station and wait in a cell until I drag Sergeant Duff there to join you.' Noonan began to yelp and plead. 'It's no good begging for mercy now. You and Duff only hampered our investigation. Your chances of getting that reward money have just vanished for good.'

The address he'd been given was near St Brelade's Bay at the western end of the island. Having hired a driver, Leeming was able to forget about the horrors of the voyage and enjoy the scenic beauty of the coast road. Warmed by the sun and with the rhythmical sound of the waves in his ears, he felt that he'd stumbled upon an island paradise. Wherever he looked, there was something to delight his eye. When he reached the house, he gaped in amazement. Perched on a rock above the bay, it was an arresting sight, a dazzling white castle with an imposing tower rising above the crenellation topping the walls. Stone steps had been hacked from the rock and curved down to the jetty where a boat was moored. The Hern family evidently lived in great style.

Leeming was relieved. He would be making contact with people who knew the island intimately and whose advice would save him a great deal of time. There was also the promise of refreshment. Leaving the carriage, he walked to the front door and rang the bell. It was opened by a manservant. Leeming smiled at him.

'I'd like to speak to a member of the Hern family,' he said.

'Nobody of that name lives here, sir.'

'Are you quite sure?'

'Yes, I work for Monsieur Fauvel.'

'But I was told that this was the right address.'

'Leave this to me,' said a voice with a heavy French accent.

The servant disappeared and was replaced by a tall, dark, lean man in impeccable attire. He looked Leeming up and down suspiciously.

'Who are you and what do you want?'

'My name is Sergeant Leeming,' said the other, 'and I'm a detective in the Metropolitan Police Force back in England. I'm in pursuit of a man wanted for a murder in Norwich. I was told that this was the house owned by Michael Hern.'

'Nobody *owns* it. We rented it for six months from an agency. My name is Gaston Fauvel. I have never heard of this man you talk about.'

'There must be some mistake.'

'You are the one making it, Sergeant.'

'But I was told that Mr Hern and his family lived here. That's why a letter was sent to this address to break the news to him that his brother-in-law had been killed.'

'Ah,' said the other, 'now I see. You are right, Sergeant. A letter did come a few days ago. I can't remember the name on it. One of the servants took it to the agency. Other people have rented this place before us. I think maybe that the letter was for one of them.'

Leeming shuddered. He felt that he'd been completely cut adrift. Patently, he was working in good faith on false information. Counting on cooperation from the Hern family, he was hit by the frightening thought that they might not actually exist.

Madeleine Colbeck and Lydia Quayle were chatting in the living room when they caught sight of a cab drawing up outside the house. A passenger alighted from the vehicle and paid the fare. It was only when he turned around that they realised who it was. Lionel Fairbank had returned yet again. Both of them got immediately to their feet.

'Have him sent on his way,' advised Lydia.

'Oh, no, I intend to speak to him.'

'But you told me that you were going to refuse his commission.'

'And I will,' promised Madeleine. 'But I'd like the satisfaction of telling him why. Nothing will rob me of that.'

They waited until he was let into the house and shown into the room. When he saw the two of them standing side by side, he smiled.

'Ah!' he cried. 'A welcoming committee – how touching!'

'You are not welcome here, Mr Fairbank,' said Madeleine, sharply, 'and I propose to tell you why.'

He was taken aback. 'What is going on? I only came to make a second appeal to you to accompany me to Windsor so that you can make some preliminary sketches.'

'I have no intention of working for you, Mr Fairbank.'

'Is it a question of money?' he asked. 'If that's the problem, I'd be happy to increase your fee.'

'The money is irrelevant,' said Madeleine. 'When I told you that my husband was away on business, you seemed pleased. What I didn't tell you was that he's a detective inspector in the Metropolitan Police, presently leading an investigation into a murder in East Anglia.' His face clouded. 'Were he here, our relationship would never have got this far. He'd have seen through you at once.'

'What on earth are you talking about?'

'Miss Quayle will explain.'

'The last time you visited this house,' said Lydia, taking her cue, 'Mrs Colbeck was troubled by your manner. She was worried about your motives in offering to commission her.'

'She's a fine artist. Why shouldn't I commission her?'

'Because of her disquiet, we asked a friend to find out a little more about you. A police officer went to the house in Belgravia that you claimed belonged to your son.'

'It's true. He does own it.'

'Then why does one of the neighbours say that the only occupants of the property are a group of women artists?'

Fairbank's voice hardened. 'What are you getting at?'

'You've been lying to Mrs Colbeck.'

'You tried to employ me under false pretences,' said Madeleine. 'Miss Quayle called at the Red Gallery this morning and asked how many paintings by female artists are sold there. Mr Sinclair told her that one customer seemed to have a preference for them. That person was you, Mr Fairbank.'

'This is intolerable,' said the old man, testily. 'Sinclair had no right to discuss me or my tastes. I won't go near his gallery again.'

'Who are those women of yours?' demanded Lydia.

'I'm a patron of the arts,' he declared, 'and I have the good fortune to possess sufficient wealth to sponsor the work of talented artists.'

'But why are they always women?' asked Madeleine.

'I happen to like female company. Is that a crime?'

'I'll leave it to my husband to decide that.'

'There's no need to do that, Mrs Colbeck. If you have any doubts about me, let me take you to that house right now so that you can meet the occupants. They are not as fortunate as you. Without my help, they'd never have been able to become painters.'

'How many of them are there?' asked Lydia.

'You're welcome to see for yourself, Miss Quayle.'

'I'm not sure that I'd care to.'

'Good heavens!' he exclaimed. 'You behave as if you think I'm keeping a harem in that house. If the idea were not so ludicrous, I'd find it quite insulting.'

'You deliberately deceived me, Mr Fairbank,' said Madeleine, eyes blazing, 'and I'll never forgive you for that. You may actually help some other artists, but I don't like the way you go about it.'

'That's a shame. I'd have felt honoured to have that painting of yours hanging in my house.'

'It won't happen now. I'd rather work for customers who are completely honest with me – and you were not. My husband will be in touch with you.'

'I look forward to meeting him,' said Fairbank, smiling. 'He's married to a very special woman. Good day to you both!'

He went off smartly into the hall and was let out of the house.


Sergeant Duff was strutting along the platform when he felt a heavy hand descend on his shoulder. Brushing it away, he spun round but his anger melted into surprise when he saw Colbeck standing there.

'Can I do anything for you, Inspector?' he asked.

'Yes, you can accompany me to the police station. You'll meet an old friend of yours there – Jack Noonan. I took exception to the fact that he followed me today in the same way that he followed Sergeant Leeming.'

'I've never heard of a Jack Noonan.'

'He employed you to feed information to him.'

'That's nonsense.'

'No, it isn't,' said Colbeck. 'The pair of you set your sights on that reward money and decided to get it by fair means or foul. You were very cunning, weren't you? To make sure you knew how the investigation was going, you bribed the man responsible for sending and receiving any telegraphs. By that means, you had confidential information and passed it on to Noonan.'

'I deny it.'

'He doesn't and neither does the man who's just been sacked from the telegraph station. He admitted that he was in your pay.'

'It's a lie.'

'Incidentally,' said Colbeck, 'I have to pass on the bad news that you will be dismissed from your post as well.'

'I did nothing wrong!'

'You did everything wrong, Duff. I'll explain why when I drive you to the police station. Come on,' said Colbeck, taking him by the arm. 'Let's not keep Jack Noonan waiting. You and he will have a lot to talk about.'


As they walked through the cathedral cloisters, Dr Kitson had to slow down to keep pace with his hobbling friend. Wardlow had called on him, explained the situation and told him that he believed he might know where Tallis had gone. Kitson had been sceptical. When they reached their destination, his doubts had been justified.

'Why should he come here, Terence?' he asked.

'It was just an idea.'

'But you told me that he was scared when he saw the cathedral again. It's the last place he'd want to visit.'

'You may be right, Donald.'

They were standing in the tunnel that connected the cloisters with King's College, the school through which Tallis had been hustled away by his kidnappers. Nobody else was about.

'I just had this feeling he'd be here somehow,' said Wardlow, voice filled with despair.

'Where are the police searching for him?'

'They're combing the whole city.'

'Why don't we leave it to them?'

'I must do *something*, Donald. I feel so guilty. If I'd spotted the signs, I could have stopped him leaving. The next time I see Edward,' he said, worriedly, 'they'll probably be dragging his body from the river.'

'Oh, I don't think there's any risk of suicide,' said Kitson. 'If there had been, why walk all the way to Canterbury? You still have your old army revolver and you showed me some other weaponry once. If he was bent on taking his own life, the means were under your roof.'

'That's true,' said Wardlow, slightly cheered. 'But the fact is that he sneaked away in the night. Where the devil is he?'

Edward Tallis trudged across the field. Tired and confused, he was driven on by an impulse he could neither understand nor resist. When he paused for a rest, he could hear the bells of the distant cathedral floating on the air. It was a hot day and he was already feeling uncomfortable. Removing his hat, he took out a handkerchief to wipe away the sweat trickling down his forehead. After allowing himself a brief respite, he put on the hat again and set off, each step a conscious effort. Punctilious about his appearance, he nevertheless took no notice of the dirt on his shoes and bottoms of his trousers. Whatever was guiding his footsteps made him blind to the consequences of going over rough ground in his best attire. He had been on the move for hours now. Tallis knew that it was only a matter of time before complete exhaustion set in.

Victor Leeming was fast approaching desperation. He felt that he'd been deliberately led astray by someone with malign intent.

On the return journey to St Helier, he did not admire the scenery. He was too busy trying to work out what to do next. At the back of his mind was the thought that, in order to get back home, he would have to endure another terrifying voyage. He'd never felt so alone in his life.

When he reached the island capital, it took him the best part of an hour to find the estate agency that owned the property overlooking St Brelade's Bay. Tucked away in a side street, it occupied the ground floor of a quaint terraced house. Though Jersey had nothing on the scale of Yarmouth's holiday traffic, it was starting to attract more and more people there. Gregory Milner was one of the people employed to find accommodation for them. He was a sleek man in his thirties with a permanent smile painted on his face. Leeming suspected that he was French and was relieved to hear an English voice coming out of his mouth.

'Good day to you, sir. How may we help you?'

'I've just come from that castle in St Brelade's Bay.'

'Ah, yes,' said the other, 'it is not available, I'm afraid. The Fauvel family have taken it for six months.'

'I don't want to stay there. I simply want details of people who were there three or four years ago.'

'That was before my time, I'm afraid.'

'You must have records, surely?'

Milner frowned. 'I can't let a complete stranger look at them, sir.'

When Leeming explained who he was and why he was there, the man looked at him with more respect. Since he'd only been with the company a couple of years, he had no memory of renting out the castle to a Michael Hern. The name did, however, ring a bell. He reached under the counter to bring out a letter.

'This was handed to me a day or so ago,' he said. 'It's addressed to Michael Hern and I agreed to hold on to it for a while before destroying it.'

'Let me open it,' said Leeming.

'I'm not sure that I should do that. It's private correspondence.'

'Mr Hern will be in England by now. He's the brother-in-law of the murder victim and has gone to console his sister. Hand it over, please.'

Milner did so reluctantly, and Leeming opened it. Written by Cecil Freed, it told of the murder of Jarvis Swarbrick. It ended with a plea to Michael Hern to sail to England at once to be with his sister. Leeming was bewildered.

'Yet he never got this letter,' he said to himself. 'How could he go to England when he had no idea that he was needed there?'

As he read the letter again, an idea began to form in his mind.

'Let me see your record book,' he said.


When Colbeck returned to the house, he was told that Hern was in the garden with his sister. He came upon them in an arbour. Hern had an arm around his sister. When he saw Colbeck, he rose to his feet.

'I've been looking for you, Inspector,' he said, showing his annoyance. 'Where have you been hiding?'

'I was called away, sir. I had information that one of our suspects had been behaving strangely. As a result of questioning him, I made an arrest. He's now in a cell at the police station.'

'You arrested him?' said Hern, worriedly. 'Who is the man?'

'His name is Bartram Duff, a sergeant with the railway police.'

Hern inflated his chest. 'Let *me* have a word with him.'

'There's no need for violence, sir.'

'It will save someone the cost of an execution.'

'I'm not absolutely sure of his guilt, Mr Hern. That's to say, we don't have the cast-iron proof we'd need in court. I just wanted to let you know as a courtesy what was happening.'

'Thank you very much,' said Grace.

'How are you feeling today, Mrs Swarbrick?'

'I'm much the same, I'm afraid.'

'Grace has been cooped up indoors ever since it happened,' said Hern. 'That's unhealthy. I brought her out here to put some fresh air in her lungs.'

'You did the right thing, sir,' said Colbeck. 'Anyway, now that you know what I've been up to, I'll leave you alone.'

'But I want to come with you, Inspector.'

'That's out of the question, sir. Please don't pester me again.'

'Stay here, Michael,' said his sister. 'There's nothing you can do.'

'I'd be an extra pair of hands,' he told her.

'Yes,' said Colbeck, 'but my fear is that you'd use those hands on the prisoner. I'd hate to have to arrest you for assault. Your sister needs you. Leave the investigation to me. That's an order.'

Grace touched her brother's arm. 'The inspector is right, Michael.'

'Heed your sister's advice, Mr Hern.'

'Very well,' said the other, resignedly, 'but I want to hear about any major development. I have a personal stake in this case, Inspector. You don't.'

'Oh, yes, I do,' said Colbeck, forcefully. 'A murder investigation is always a personal matter to me. That's why I never let anyone get in my way when I'm looking for a killer.'

Walking across the lawn, Colbeck disappeared around the bushes.

Notwithstanding the fact that he thought it a waste of time, Dr Kitson agreed to accompany his friend as he drove into the countryside. Wardlow kept the horse going at a steady canter even though the frequent bumps and swerves made him wince with pain.

'This could be another wild goose chase,' warned Kitson.

'Please humour me.'

'If the man was too scared to go to the cathedral, he's even less likely to visit the place where he was actually imprisoned. Superintendent Tallis would dread going anywhere near it.'

'I'm not so convinced of that,' said Wardlow.

'Well, I am, Terence. What would he gain by revisiting what was, in effect, a torture chamber? It must hold appalling memories for him.'

'That's *exactly* why he might be there, Donald.'

They carried on until they caught sight of a straggle of farm buildings that had fallen into disuse. Even from a distance, they could see the holes in some of the roofs and the decayed wood in the walls and doors. Remote and deserted, the place had an unfriendly air about it.

'Do you know where exactly he was held?' asked Kitson.

'Yes, I came here once on my own. I was interested to see where Edward had suffered so much.'

'Would you have dared to bring him here?'

'Oh, no,' said Wardlow. 'I'd never have suggested it.'

Kitson was complacent. 'I rest my case.'

'I just have this feeling, Donald.'

'Is it the same one you had about that tunnel by the cloisters?'

'Don't mock me.'

'I'm just trying to be realistic. I've dealt with patients who've undergone ordeals. To a man, they've avoided the places and the situations that brought them such misery. Why should your friend be any different?'

'I can't answer that,' confessed Wardlow.

When he reached the buildings, he brought the horse to a halt then got out of the dog cart with some difficulty. Kitson surveyed the abandoned stables and barns with distaste.

'Which one was it?' he asked.

'Follow me.'

Wardlow stumbled over the uneven ground until he came to a building with a broken window. When he gazed through it, he let out a cry of alarm, a hand to his heart. Hanging from a beam was a noose.

What struck Leeming as he walked to the heart of St Helier was the strange absence of police uniforms. There was no sense of the city being under supervision. Having started his career as a uniformed constable in London, he knew that officers were walking their beats in twos day and night. A police presence, he'd always been told, was a visible deterrent to crime. Looming up in front of him was the Newgate Street Prison, named after the notorious Newgate Prison in London. Architecturally, the two were very different. Had he been able to peer over the high perimeter walls, he'd have seen the attractive granite facade of the main block, complete with a series of exquisite arches that gave the structure an almost palatial look to it.

Leeming went up to the main gate and rang the bell.

Fearing the worst, Wardlow and Kitson went into the building. The sight that met their gaze was shocking. Seated on the floor among the sodden remains of some straw was Edward Tallis. He'd removed his top hat, coat and shoes. Because he'd also taken out his cufflinks, his cuffs were hanging loose. The extraordinary thing was that he didn't seem to be in any pain. If anything, he was remarkably serene. Lost in thought, he didn't see them until Wardlow spoke to him.

'What's going on, Edward?' asked his friend.

Tallis sat up. 'Oh, hello, Terence,' he said before noticing his other visitor. 'It's nice to see you again, Dr Kitson.'

'I had such a fright when I saw that noose through the window. I was afraid that you were going to hang yourself.'

'No, I'd never do that. When I got here, I noticed that length of rope. It had been used to tie me up. I made the noose and dangled it from a beam so that I could contemplate it.'

'Why did you do that?' asked Kitson.

'I wondered if it would have been a kinder sentence.'

'I don't understand.'

'The two men who abducted me were sentenced to transportation to Australia. For the rest of their miserable lives they'll be in hell. How much quicker their deaths would have been at the end of a rope. They did plan to kill me, after all. Fifty years ago, they'd have been sentenced to hang for kidnap and attempted murder. Given the choice,' Tallis went on, 'they might well have chosen the noose.'

'But what brought you here, Edward?' said Wardlow, 'and why are you dressed like that?'

'This was how they tied me up, you see.' He held up his wrists. 'Worst of all, they took my cufflinks with the regimental crest on them. That angered me more than anything.'

'Were you trying to . . . recreate what happened?'

'Yes, Terence, I wanted to stand up to that horrendous experience again and look it in the eyes without flinching. I wanted to see and smell the sheer desolation of this place.' A

337

radiant smile spread across his face. 'I feel so happy now. I've won my private battle.'

'Let me help you up,' said Kitson, taking his arm.

'It's all right. I can get up on my own without any effort.' He scrambled to his feet. 'It's all in the past now. I'm free at last.'

'At least, let me help you on with your coat.'

'You're forgetting something, Dr Kitson,' said Tallis, taking something from his pocket and opening his palm to display them. 'I have to put in my cufflinks first.'

Admitted to the governor's office, Leeming at last felt that he was getting somewhere. Jonas Yarrow was an angular man of middle years with side whiskers that curled down his face to meet under his chin. Having been in the prison service for many years, he gave the impression that nothing could ever surprise him. When Leeming explained why he was there, the governor listened with increasing interest. He soon came to admire his unexpected visitor.

'You made a good decision, Sergeant.'

'The man I'm after is a killer,' said Leeming. 'I can't believe that a murder would be his first crime. The chances are that he'll have had convictions for earlier offences and may well have ended up in here.'

'That sounds more than likely but, if it does prove to be the case, then we failed in our purpose. This is a mixed prison,' said Yarrow. 'Our aim is to discharge a male or female prisoner who has become a better human being because of his or her stay here.'

'It's an ambitious target, sir.'

'They're here for improvement as well as punishment.'

'I don't think you would have improved this man,' said Leeming. 'He was cold, calculated and quite ruthless.'

'Tell me again what you know about him, Sergeant.'

'He's a young man with a dark beard and we think he must be an expert horseman.'

'You've just described a lot of people on this island. Beards are popular and those people who own a horse can ride it well. Are you sure there isn't something else, some crucial detail that will set him apart?'

Leeming was dubious. 'Not really, Governor . . .'

'It's an article of faith with me that I know every prisoner here by name, but I can't really identify the man you want on the strength of such flimsy evidence.'

'The name he was using was John Gorey. Is that any help to you?' Yarrow shook his head. 'Ah, there is one thing I forgot,' said Leeming, snapping his fingers. 'He's a sort of perfectionist. He rehearsed the crime very carefully before he committed it. Inspector Colbeck found the exact place where he'd practised.'

'Then maybe I *can* help you, after all.'

'Do you recognise him, sir?'

'I might do,' said the other. 'The man I have in mind is David Le Brun. He lives on a farm near Gorey. He spent time in here for a robbery. What upset him most was that he wasn't able to take part in the annual point-to-point. Do you ride, Sergeant?'

'Not if I can help it, sir.'

'Le Brun did. He won the point-to-point three times in a row. I must confess that I once bet on him and went home with a profit.'

'What makes you think he may be John Gorey?'

'It was your description of his careful rehearsals. An expert horseman who knows the value of practising something time and

339

again until there's no room for error – it has to be David le Brun. He lives on a farm, but he has another string to his bow.'

'What is it?' asked Leeming.

'He's an actor who occasionally belongs to the company at our Theatre Royal.'

Michael Hern walked quickly through the streets until he came to a row of small, half-timbered Tudor cottages. The whole lot of them were at peculiar angles so that they looked like drunken revellers staggering home after a night of abandon. Hern went to the house at the far end and knocked on the door. It was opened by Horace Pryor. Delighted to see his visitor, he let him into the house immediately. The transaction took less than a minute. When it was over, Hern opened the front door and put his head out to check that nobody was about. He then glided back down the street and rejoined the main road where his cab was still waiting for him. As he was driven away, Hern felt a sense of achievement. He had orchestrated a perfect murder. Wallowing in self-congratulation, he failed to notice that he'd been followed by Robert Colbeck.

One mystery was solved. Leeming had wondered how Hern could respond to the news of the murder when he didn't read the letter that told him of it. Written testimony of the crime was unnecessary. As soon as he saw David Le Brun – alias John Gorey – arriving on the island, Hern had sailed off to England. He'd had visible proof that Jarvis Swarbrick was dead. It had all become clear to Leeming. Once he'd been able to link the killer with Michael Hern, he realised that they'd been confederates.

His visit to the island's prison had been a brainwave. It

changed everything. Instead of feeling alone and befuddled, Leeming was now on the road to Gorey in a carriage with three policemen in support. The odds were at last in his favour. When they got close to the farm where the killer lived, Leeming ordered the driver to stop. He then told the three policemen to creep up on the farm from different directions, cutting off any avenues of escape. Having given them plenty of time to get into position, he sat back in the carriage and let the driver take him down the track towards the farm.

A young man with a dark beard was schooling a horse in the paddock, sending it round in circles at the end of a long lead rein and cracking a whip from time to time. Leeming reasoned that it had to be the man he was after. When the carriage rolled to a halt in front of the farmhouse, he got out and strolled nonchalantly across to the paddock. The man came over to him. Square-shouldered and muscular, he had a face of almost endearing ugliness. He spoke with faultless English.

'Did you want something, sir?' he asked.

'I did, as a matter of fact. May I ask your name?'

'I'm David Le Brun.'

'Then I've got the wrong person,' said Leeming. 'The man I'm after is John Gorey. I've come all the way from Norwich to see him.'

'Who are you?' demanded the other, fists clenching.

'I'm a policeman, sir, and so are they.'

Leeming pointed his finger and the killer looked behind him. Three men were coming resolutely towards him from different directions. He was surrounded.

'You're mistaken,' he asserted. 'I've never even been to England.'

'Yes, you have. Michael Hern sent you there to murder someone.'

'I don't know anyone of that name.'

'What about Jonas Yarrow? Do you know him? He would have sent his regards but he feels too let down by you. The governor had wanted to discharge you from prison with a clear sense of right and wrong. Obviously, he failed to do so.'

'Yarrow was an idiot,' snarled the other.

'Don't be so unkind to him. Mr Yarrow was an admirer of yours. He was hoping to bet on you again in the annual point-to-point but your racing days are over, aren't they? The governor will have to put his trust in another rider.'

Le Brun looked over his shoulder again. The other policemen were closing in on him. His only option was flight. Running to the fence, he put a hand on it and vaulted nimbly over it. He then used the whip to drive Leeming backwards. After hurling the whip at him, Le Brun went haring off in the direction of the stables. Leeming yelled to the policemen to hurry up and they broke into a trot. Holding his hat in place, he ran towards the stables. His quarry had already disappeared inside. As he got close, Leeming slowed down and approached cautiously. Le Brun was desperate and would be prepared to kill his way out. The other policemen were still some way away. If someone was going to stop the fugitive, it had to be Leeming.

Twenty yards from the stables, he was suddenly thrown on to the defensive. Having no time to saddle a horse, Le Brun had slipped a bridle over one animal and was riding him bareback. He came out of the stables with a hay fork in his hand and every intention of using it on Leeming. With a horse and two vicious prongs heading straight at him, the sergeant wanted to jump out of the way but he couldn't let the killer escape without at least trying to stop him. He therefore relied on instinct. Whisking off his hat, he waved it madly in the horse's face and shouted at the top of his voice. The animal neighed loudly and reared up on its hind legs.

With no saddle to help him, even an accomplished rider like Le Brun could not stay on the horse. He was thrown backwards, landing on the ground with such a thud that the hay fork was knocked from his hand. The frightened horse immediately bolted. Leeming kicked the weapon out of the killer's reach then dived on top of him. There was a fierce struggle on the ground. Le Brun squirmed wildly but, no matter what he did, he couldn't dislodge Leeming. As they traded punches, the sergeant struck the more telling blows and his adversary's strength was gradually sapped. When the man made one last effort to escape, Leeming used a head butt to stun him. He then hit him with another relay of punches. By the time that the other policemen came panting up, Le Brun was almost senseless. Covered in dust, Leeming got to his feet and looked down at the killer with contempt.

'He's all yours,' he gasped.

After reaching the siding, Colbeck waited for a quarter of an hour before a train thundered past. It was as he thought. Confident that the noise of the train would have masked the sound of a shot, he walked over to the first-class compartment used beforehand by the killer. He opened the door and hauled himself up into it. A diligent search of the upholstery behind one seat soon yielded the treasure that he sought. Colbeck had four separate bullets in his hand. They'd been embedded in the upholstery during rehearsals.

When he set off to start his shift, Horace Pryor found it hard to keep the smile off his face. The reward he'd been given earlier was more than he'd earn in five years and all he'd had to do was to arrange for a friend to switch the points when nobody was looking. He'd wept no tears for Jarvis Swarbrick. In his eyes, the man was a rich, arrogant, detestable politician who treated people like Pryor as if they weren't so much as dirt. His smile lasted as far as the railway station. The moment he appeared, Pryor was confronted by Jellings and two policemen.

'Hello, Horry,' said the inspector. 'We'd like a word with you.'

Pryor's face flushed. 'I've done nothing.'

'You had a visitor earlier on, didn't you?'

'No, I didn't.'

'Inspector Colbeck thinks otherwise – and so do we.'

Pryor was still protesting loudly as they hustled him away.


The warm weather had brought them all into the garden. Cecil and Anthea Freed were seated on the terrace with Grace Swarbrick and her brother. The women enjoyed the cover of a sunshade while the man wore hats to shield them from the glare of the sun. Talk had turned to the question of the future.

'I want Grace to come back to Jersey,' said Hern, 'so that we can look after her properly.'

'It's too early to make that decision, Michael,' she said. 'I want to take things one step at a time. The inquest is tomorrow. Let me get that ordeal out of the way first.'

'Your home is here in Norwich,' Anthea pointed out. 'You'll inherit a beautiful house and we'd love you to stay.'

'We would, indeed,' said Freed. 'I know that Andrew is going to contest the will, but his father's wishes will be upheld. There may be some unpleasantness involved but that shouldn't trouble you.'

'It might be more sensible to sell the property,' said Hern, 'and return to the place where you were born. Norwich holds so many bad memories for you, Grace.'

'It holds many good memories as well,' said Anthea, stoutly.

'That's true,' agreed Grace. 'I feel that I belong here.'

'Forgive this interruption,' said Colbeck, coming into view from behind a yew hedge nearby. 'I couldn't help overhearing what you just said, Mrs Swarbrick. It's just as well that you feel at home here because the law will insist that you remain.'

'What do you mean?' demanded Hern.

'Don't worry, sir. You'll be required to stay with her.'

'My sister is in mourning for her husband. Barging in here like this is unforgivable.'

'Let's be honest, sir,' said Colbeck, 'Mrs Swarbrick is not your sister. The last time I was in this garden, I saw the two of you alone and there was an intimacy between you that helped me to understand what's been going on.' He looked from Anthea to Freed. 'It's my painful duty to tell you that you, and everybody else in Mrs Swarbrick's social circle, have been grievously misled.'

'That's slander!' howled Hern, rising angrily to his feet.

'Do you deny that, when you left here, you went straight to the home of Horace Pryor to pay him for his part in the plot?' Hern blanched. 'He is presently in police custody. I'm confident that the same can be said of the man who shot Mr Swarbrick dead. He came to this country under the false name of John Gorey then fled back to Jersey.'

'This is nonsense,' said Hern, scornfully.

'Sergeant Leeming has gone to the island to arrest the man. My job is to arrest the people who employed him.' Colbeck signalled with his hand and two uniformed policemen came out from behind the hedge. 'I brought these gentlemen to assist me.'

Freed was outraged. 'What, in the name of God, is going on?'

'You and Mrs Freed have been victims of a grotesque confidence trick, sir. Mrs Swarbrick used her charms to entice Mr Swarbrick when he was at his most vulnerable in the wake of his wife's death. As he learnt to his cost,' Colbeck went on, 'the marriage was a charade. The new Mrs Swarbrick had no intention of being a real wife to him. She pleaded ill health to avoid sharing a bedroom with him.'

Anthea was aghast. 'Is this true, Grace?'

'Of course, it isn't,' said the other.

'Mrs Swarbrick is not in mourning,' said Colbeck. 'She and Mr Hern have been congratulating themselves on their success in fooling everyone. I don't think you realise what an extraordinary woman you befriended, Mrs Freed. She was fearless. The murder was not only meticulously rehearsed by the killer with the help of a disused carriage, his victim's wife was also involved. She agreed to sit in the compartment so that the pistol could be fired close to her. Only a professional actress would play the part to the hilt like that.'

'This is sheer lunacy!' yelled Hern.

'Did you hear that?' asked Colbeck. 'It's the voice of a trained actor. When I first met Mr Hern, I was impressed with the way that he spoke. He and Mrs Swarbrick gave us a beguiling performance.'

'This is monstrous,' said Anthea, trembling with anger. 'You betrayed us, Grace. I can't believe we were so gullible.'

'Nor me,' said her husband. 'We owe you our thanks, Inspector. We'd never have suspected that we were dealing with confidence tricksters. But the real victim was Jarvis Swarbrick.'

Grace laughed harshly. 'He was the biggest fool of you all.'

'Don't say anything,' warned Hern.

'It's too late, Michael. The inspector knows.'

'I do,' said Colbeck. 'When I said that you'd be remaining in Norwich, I meant that you'll be condemned to death here. There'll be no return to Jersey for either of you. The last audience you'll entertain is the one that comes to watch your executions.'

After the excitement of the arrest, Leeming was brought to a dead halt. Before he could take the prisoner back to England, legalities had to be observed. It meant that he had to stay on the island. David Le Brun, meanwhile, was able to renew his acquaintance with the governor when he spent the night at Newgate Street Prison. Leeming had no qualms about the return journey. He'd been promised the assistance of two policemen to guard the prisoner during the voyage, and he was told to expect a report of his bravery when he opened the newspaper on the following day. He would arrive back in Norwich as a hero.

Having left the whole city bemused by the turn of events, Colbeck caught the train back to London, delivered his report to the acting superintendent then went home to his wife and daughter. He was pleased to find Lydia there and interested to hear that she and Constable Hinton had taken part in the investigation of Lionel Fairbank.

'Alan Hinton is very modest,' said Colbeck. 'He made no mention of that when I spoke to him at Scotland Yard. What he did pass on was good news about Edward Tallis. The superintendent is now on the road to recovery. He's on extended leave and will not return to work until he feels that he's fit enough to discharge his duties.'

'That's very heartening,' said Lydia.

'He sent you his regards, by the way.'

She was astonished. 'Superintendent Tallis?'

'No – Constable Hinton.'

'Thank you, Robert.'

'Alan is the person you need to thank,' said Madeleine. 'But my husband has kept us in suspense for long enough already. I want to know *everything* about the case.'

'You'll have to settle for the salient facts, my love.'

'What are they, Robert?'

He gave them a concise account of the investigation, leaving out a great amount of peripheral detail. Colbeck pointed out the irony in the fact that it was Andrew Swarbrick who instinctively distrusted his stepmother.

'Had his father listened to him,' he said, 'there would have been no second marriage. The son was right about that woman all along. When Mr Swarbrick visited what he thought was her family home in Jersey, it was filled with members of Michael Hern's theatre company, all playing their assigned parts. And the house wasn't owned by Hern at all. He'd rented it in order to impress Mr Swarbrick.'

'What about her first husband?' asked Lydia.

'He didn't exist,' replied Colbeck. 'Strictly speaking, he *did* exist but he was never married to her. Roland Coutanche was simply a name she picked off a gravestone. When she took Swarbrick to see it, he was convinced she'd told him the truth.'

'It sounds as if she'd never do that.'

'Why did Mr Swarbrick have to be murdered?' asked Madeleine.

'He'd served his purpose,' replied Colbeck. 'The point at which he became disposable was when he changed his will and made her the chief benefactor. My guess is that, in exchange, she promised

348

to behave like a real wife to him instead of occupying a separate bedroom. Before she needed to do that, he was murdered.'

'She was just as evil as her brother.'

'Michael Hern was her lover. That's why she never gave herself to another man. The moment Mr Swarbrick married her, he signed his own death warrant.'

EDWARD MARSTON has written well over a hundred books, including some non-fiction. He is best known for his hugely successful Railway Detective series and he also writes the Bow Street Rivals series featuring twin detectives set during the Regency, as well as the Home Front Detective series.

*edwardmarston.com*